Haterz

James Goss

SOLARIS

CHAPTER ONE
THE QUEEN OF LULZ

THERE'S SOMETHING WRONG with the internet. If you think about it for a second, you'll see I'm right.

I mean, I'm not saying the internet made me kill Danielle, but it certainly helped.

I didn't set out to murder her that evening. Actually, I just wanted to meet up with her for a drink. But she kept on dodging my emails about it. Then I saw on Facebook she was going to an event. So I decided to pop along.

Of course, it was the kind of thing that only Danielle would go to, in the kind of bar that only Danielle would go to. When I got there, the place was heaving with Danielles.

You know more Danielles than you need to. I hope you're not one. They're the people you avoid in the office, who you grudgingly put a pound in the birthday envelope for. You don't hate them, not as such; you just can't quite see the point in them. But that's fine—you nod to them in the lift and have nothing much to do with them.

Only Danielle was going out with my best friend Guy. They met at an exercise class and for some reason... oh, I know you can't control who your friends go out with, but it would be nice to be able to have a say. Just once in life. Just one vote that declares, 'You May No Longer Share A Duvet With This Person.' I think it would be good for everybody. It would keep us all on our toes.

* * *

I REMEMBER THE first time I met Danielle. It was a miserable evening at the cinema. Guy had been so keen for me to meet her. "She's really interesting." So interesting that she talked through the trailers, kept checking her phone, licked popcorn off her fingers then dived back into the bag, and would occasionally say "I don't get it" very loudly.

She can't last, I thought, I hoped. I mean, I knew Guy. He'd see reason. I didn't say anything to him, but, as I left, I gave her a look. When I was young I used to love it that Paddington Bear gave people Very Hard Stares. I thought that was great and I assumed that all old people were somehow related to him because they did it. I decided that I would do it too and spent ages copying my gran. Because Very Hard Stares would make people behave nicely towards me. When I was a child, I knew nothing about people. I still don't.

My very hard stare at Danielle made no difference to her. On the way home, Guy texted to say, 'She loved you!!' I knew she didn't. 'Great!' I texted back.

But, you know, it was okay. She wasn't actually, actively evil, and if I saw Guy a bit less and didn't go on holiday with him any more, then I'd have to endure her less than ten times a year, maybe. That would be fine. Bearable.

Only... only Danielle made the internet hell. A daily hell.

IT ALL STARTED when she sent me a friend request on Facebook. I tried to ignore it for a day. But it hovered, sometimes on the left of the screen, sometimes on the right, like a sinister game of Pong, until I knew I couldn't put it off any longer. Any more and it would be beyond the bounds of 'not really been checking this weekend.' So I gave in and clicked 'Accept.'

Instantly she posted 'FINALLY! :)' on my wall.

And then she broke the internet. For someone who was all over it, she certainly didn't understand it. No matter how I tried to hide her, somehow she always came back. Like nettles or Freddy Krueger.

However I fiddled with Facebook, there she was, all over my feed, a sticky sweet rash, liking photos of babies, uploading blurred photos of her toes or breakfast, constantly posting statuses from meaningless places (who checks-in to Wetherspoons?). It was a constant stream of noise. And, if I ever doubted she loved Guy, Facebook made me absolutely certain. She posted selfies with him all the time, she posted pictures of him asleep, even one of him in the shower ('hes gonna kil me lol!'). A decade or so ago, a bedroom wall plastered with obsessive photos of someone was the sign that you were a psychopathic stalker and a bunny boiler. But this was seemingly how Danielle thought girlfriends should behave.

In return Guy posted a few sheepish pictures of her (a handful of carefully Instagrammed shots). Never enough ('u took loadsmore!! where r they???eh lol'). Woe betide Guy if he went away somewhere without her. The day of departure was marked with an epic wail of 'Where are my dragons?' proportions. Then, after somehow getting through 'a night without my GooGoo :(:(' there'd be the bitter recriminations should he dare to mention a meal or post a picture—'how dare you be having fun without MEE?!?' was a genuine, actual, real and literal post. I know this because I took a screengrab of it. I don't know why, but I kept a folder about Danielle on my notebook. Okay. Typing that I just realised how weird that sounds. But do bear in mind—I did end up killing her.

MY FOLDER CONTAINED all her worst crimes—the way she just didn't get jokes, clicked 'Like' on bogus campaigns to get free iPhones and cardiograms, was always passing on unhelpful borderline-racist warnings about 'funny bearded men saying you shouldn't go near town on weds.' She never used the possessive apostrophe. It was so neglected by her I wanted to give it a hug.

And then there was Father's Day. Strange how Facebook has turned a fairly small annual event into a vast national holiday. But Danielle had to own that too. It was the day when underneath everyone's statuses she posted, 'So pleased you had a great day with youre dad on fathers day—cant help thinking of my own dad. rip pop. Xxxx.'

My own father died a few years ago. It still hurts. If I'm feeling
low I just try and avoid Facebook on Father's Day. It's one of
those things that's just not for me any more. I've accepted—
looking at Facebook on that day's not going to do me much
good. But Danielle didn't see it that way. She saw it as a great
opportunity to piss on everyone's chips from a great height.

IS THIS RINGING any sort of bell with you? I hope it is. You know
someone like Danielle, don't you? And don't you sometimes
think, *Wouldn't it be great if I could do something about them?*
  Well, I did. This is my story.

IT'S WORTH REPEATING: I didn't set out to the bar that night to kill
her. I just wanted a chat.
  I will admit, thoughts of murder did enter my head as soon as
I walked into the bar. But that was just the idle urge to massacre
that anyone feels on the Northern Line. I mean, you walk into
a wine bar full of people in identical long red wigs and how else
are you going to react?
  As I stepped in, someone took a tenner off me and handed
me a long red wig. "It's the Red-Headed League," he explained.
I love Sherlock Holmes. But I'm not sure... I'm not sure how
he'd have felt about one of his stories becoming an excuse for a
PR networking evening sponsored by Sodobus. I think the joke
was that everyone had to look alike, so you'd have to search to
find your friends, and in the process make new ones. Brilliant for
people who like networking. But it did make finding Danielle
difficult.
  Everyone looked alike—even the men looked equally ridiculous,
clustered around each other, hootingly selfying their delight at
how funny they all looked. Why, I thought, as I pushed through
a throng of them, would you want any of these people to be your
friends?
  Someone tapped me on the shoulder. I turned, expecting it to
be Danielle. Instead it was Amber. It took me a second to get
that. I'd met her at a couple of parties. I'd bumped into her with

some friends at the cinema. Every time that... slight... pause. Why couldn't I remember her name? Even hidden under a big red wig she was pretty stunning. She had a huge laugh and dark skin and always looked as though she was having a good time... and the best I could manage was a "Hey!" while my brain tried out names. Yes. You are right to want to kick me.

"Amber!" she offered. She smiled as she said it. Maybe it wasn't just me. Maybe she spent her entire life reminding people who she was. Maybe she made a joke of it. Maybe.

"How are you, David?" She used my name. Reminding me that at least she remembered. I smiled and small talked at her. Annoyingly, I could see Danielle now. Or someone who looked like her. I tried to keep my eyes on Amber. But they kept hovering above her head and a little to the right. I felt bad about that. I rather liked Amber. And she was telling me about her new project. It sounded kind of interesting. For a moment I was struck by the irony—I was actually networking at a networking evening.

"What are you doing here?" I heard myself asking her.

"Oh, you know," she sipped her drink. Half a glass of wine down and her soft accent became just a tiny bit Scottish. "Came here with my friend Michelle." She nodded to a pretty woman with cold eyes stood behind her. I almost lost the name under the blart of Mumford & Sons.

We made the awkward small talk that people do in a loud bar. Michelle, with cold disinterest, headed for the loo. Which left Amber to ask me why I was there.

"Oddly, I'm here to..." I managed four words and then stopped. My brain couldn't quite come up with a decent lie. Nor would it let me tell the truth. It fumbled around and I heard myself saying a really long *errrrrr*. Then my tongue worked again: "Really just checking in with a friend's girlfriend. Picking something up." That didn't sound so bad. And, if Amber wondered why you'd pay a tenner and slap a wig on just to pick a package up, she didn't quibble. She just nodded and smiled and we talked for a bit more. Or rather, I tried to carry on the conversation. Suddenly I didn't really want to go and have an awkward chat with Danielle. I didn't want to stand around with these braying idiots. I just wanted to get a bit drunk on nasty wine with Amber.

"Hey, you should go, get on. Don't waste your evening with these losers," Amber said, patting my arm. "I'd better get back to my friend Michelle."

"Sure," I said. "It's been nice catching up with you. Hope to bump into you again soon." The short stilted sentences sounded leaden as they fell out of my mouth.

"Yeah." Amber had clearly been as entranced by them as I was. She'd shifted her feet and her eyes a thousand miles away. She was already on the move.

"See you around." As I said it, I knew next time I saw her, I'd have forgotten her name again. This was going to turn out to be very far from the truth.

Amber turned and walked away into the crowd, her head just another red wig bobbing in a sea of red wigs.

I turned back. Danielle had gone. I cursed, but felt an enormous wash of relief. If I couldn't find Danielle, I could go back and find Amber. Buy her a drink. Have a laugh...

"Hey, trouble!"

Danielle was suddenly standing in front of me. Smiling. "I thought I saw you here," she said, "What a surprise!" She was all smiles. The giant fright wig actually suited her. She still somehow looked kind of hot in it. Yeah, Danielle was kind of hot. Emphasis on *kind of*. Not stunning, but pretty enough to get away with lots of stuff. She seemed confident. Her hair was hair that had always had friends. Her smile was the smile that knew that people would always talk to its owner, and would always forgive her.

In an odd move that was a bit like a bear hug, she was around me and grinning. There was a flash. She'd taken our photo. She was uploading it.

"Fark," she sighed, shaking her phone. "No signal in here."

"Oh," I said. "Pity." I did not say: "Why not wait an hour and do it at home? Or not?"

"What are you doing here, champ?" she asked me, punching me on the shoulder. "This place is mental, isn't it?"

Well, that was a word for it. I muttered something about catching up with an old work colleague. She nodded. I noticed her eyes were weaving, her attention darting somewhere beyond my left ear. Clearly she didn't really care. So I wheeled out my secret weapon.

"Listen," I said, "I'm so glad I've bumped into you. I really want to apologise."

THE THING IS, I did owe her an apology. A month ago, I'd tried hiding her completely on Facebook. I'd won about a week's blissful silence and the joyous ignorance of not knowing how she was doing on Candy Crush. And then, all of a sudden, it had gone wrong. I'd been busted, simply because she was arranging a surprise party for Guy and I'd neither noticed nor responded.

She'd sent me a message. Or rather, she'd popped a note on my wall about it. I'd apologized at the time, blaming Facebook's security settings (Danielle was a great believer that Facebook was Up To Something Fishy with her data; sometimes the high priestess thought herself enslaved to a devious god).

I repeated my apology. But added in a bit more truth. "I was just trying to... er... well, one thing, to make sure I was only getting the best updates from you. Truthfully, I was feeling a bit swamped."

Danielle barked. "Oh, gawd, tell me about it! Don't you hate those people? There's a guy I went to school with who posts every single thing *Daily Mash* does."

I smiled, connecting with her. You'll have guessed by now—I don't quite relate to people easily. But this was finally common ground. Maybe we could—

"I hate those fake news sites," she continued. "It's so easy to get taken in by them."

Oh.

WE TALKED FOR a bit. In that Danielle told me about her day at work (it was, since you ask, worse than being down a coal mine). And then, and I don't know how, I genuinely don't, we got onto the subject of foreigners.

Now, my mother is racist. Unintentionally and constantly, in the way that slightly batty old ladies are. Last time I went home to see her she was busy telling the pharmacist that, "You are such a jolly little man. But then all you people are quite smiley, aren't you?"

I think it's moving to the countryside that's done that to Mum. Suddenly, away from the bright multicultural lights of Wolverhampton, she can't help noticing and pointing out that people are from abroad. In the same way that she can't pass a nice tree without remarking on it.

It doesn't help that some nutter in her tiny town pushes leaflets through the letterbox saying that immigration is swamping Britain. My mother glances at them as she lights the fire with them, and occasionally repeats bits of them as fact. Well, not fact. Gossip. As in, "I heard that there's two hundred and fifty thousand Romanians on their way over here right now. Which is funny when you think about it. Italy's so nice this time of year."

If my mother's racism was unconscious, Danielle's was quite the reverse. Remember how a few years ago, people would say, "Call me a racist, but..."? Then that became, "I'm not being racist, but..."? And now we have, "I'm not being funny, but..."

Danielle was like that. Her day had been made worse by the *Big Issue* seller at the Tube. "I'm not being funny, but she was wearing a hijab, right. So, you know, it makes you think doesn't it, there's something wrong when they're even stealing jobs from the homeless."

I blinked a little. It's odd, when someone says something racist, you don't say "That's racist" and punch them. You don't even say, "Sorry, but that could have sounded a tiny bit racist." Instead, weirdly, you just kind of find yourself bleating something that sounds like it's come from a badly-written charity press release.

"Actually, something something even if they recently came over something something unable to access benefits therefore something something helping hand something."

It didn't matter what I said, really. Danielle waved her hand. "Yeah, that's as maybe. But I think it's funny, that's all I'm saying."

She didn't think it funny. Have you ever stopped and looked at who a friend follows on Twitter? For instance, that matey guy who, it turns out, follows a surprising number of topless men and a club night called Rough Bear City?

Or, in Danielle's case, she followed a surprising number of Union Jacks and Britain First. Previously, you had to wonder

what an average Britain First supporter looked like. Thanks to
Twitter, we have the answer. They seem to be a lot of quite glum
looking people posing in front of flags. I guess they're unhappy
because the country is so full of Foreigns, Fundamentals and
Islams.

It's funny what autocorrect tells you about yourself. I remember
feeling a bit surprised the day my phone went for 'fuck' not
'dual.' Oh dear, I thought, perhaps I should swear less in texts. I
wonder if your average racist has that moment of self-realisation
when their phone picks 'scum' over 'science.'

They do use 'scum' a lot. They're also very good at the indirect
threat. Don't say, 'We're going to kill u, scum.' Do say, 'Will u be
laughing scum when sharia law beheads u? Haha.'

I said some of this to Danielle. Actually, I didn't get to say much
of it at all. I got as far as mentioning that some of the people
she follows are maybe, a bit, fascisty UKIP, and she just gave
me a look. "Have you been stalking me? You're weird, David,"
she said, biting the rim of her glass. "Has anyone ever told you
you've way too much time on your hands?" Then she laughed.

DANIELLE GULPED DOWN another glass of white. I don't really drink
that much, and sometimes I'll be out, surrounded by a group
of people, all laughing and talking loudly over each other, and
I'll think, *I'm happiest going home and getting on with a bit
of work.* I don't think I'm better than them (well, maybe I do a
bit), but when you're fairly sober it's suddenly quite hard to fit
in with people who aren't. Remember those Fisher-Price Activity
Centres— the ones where you had to tap plastic blocks into
differently shaped plastic holes with a plastic hammer? That,
really. Suddenly, I'm surrounded by a lot of drunk people loudly
hammering themselves and there's nowhere really for me to fit in.

She held up her glass to the light, and it shone around the
lipstick prints, the lees of wine dribbling from the edges in
vampire kisses. I looked at her instead.

As I've said, Danielle's good looks weren't beautiful, but they
were stunning. When the British Empire acquired the largest
diamond in the world, Prince Albert is said to have looked at

the Koh-i-Noor diamond and immediately sent it away to be cut, chiselled, trimmed and polished. He just wasn't happy with it, and he kept on being not happy with it until forty per cent of it had been chipped away. Danielle's face was angular, pushed-back and hard-edged. Natural points had been polished into facets—cheekbones, nose, eyebrows, ears and eyes.

Remember video games ten years ago? When they'd got the motion of people right but were still trying to work out how to render them realistically? Lara Croft would turn around to you, halfway through her grail quest, and her face would be a mass of polygons? Like Prince Albert had been at her natural beauty with an angle grinder, polishing and trimming and hardening every facet.

Danielle had that same quality to her face. Every potential smoothness had been flattened, matted and simplified. Don't get me wrong here. She wore a lot of make-up, but it didn't look like it was there at all. It simply looked like someone had selected a triangle between cheek, lip and jaw and pressed 'Fill.'

The Guy I knew, the Guy I'd shared a damp, mousy house with in the second year, he was impatient. If you spent too long on the loo reading *Q* magazine there'd be a hammering on the door. So I tried to imagine the patience he'd have had to develop to put up with Danielle. Either that or she woke up at 5am. But that didn't work either. She'd be at the gym first thing. So did that mean that she put the make-up on after...?

"DAVID?"

"Oh, sorry. Miles away."

"Thought so. You looked like you were about to lick me, mate. You okay?"

I winced, just a little. There was something about the way she used words like *mate*.

"Yes, sorry, miles away," I repeated.

"What's the malarkey?"

"Oh, you know, work..."

"Nightmare." Danielle grimaced. She had her phone in one hand, pressing the keys on it over and over. She thumped it down on the table again. "What a mental idea, picking a venue with no signal. What is the point? What *is* the point?"

She looked at me over her wine, her smile bent around by the glass. "Do you... you don't fancy me, do you? A little?"

"I..."

"It's just that you keep looking at me. You do!" She laughed. "That is hashtag hashtag!"

I know what you're thinking. *Hashtag hashtag.* That's the moment when you decided to kill her.

BUT IT WASN'T. It was the next drink.

I'd got her a drink just for a moment's grace. I'd stood at the bar, feeling jostled and helpless, picking away at some bar snacks, strands of other people's nylon red hair in my face. My own hair was itching under my wig, I felt hot and out of place. The drinks were expensive. I thought about paying with my card, but I could just get a wine and a soda water and change from a tenner. That's a thing, right there. If I hadn't got that extra £10 out when passing Boots, then I probably wouldn't have killed Danielle. I would have known that there was a card receipt, nestling in a stack behind the bar. I'd have remembered and thought twice.

I brought the glasses back over, rubbing salty snack debris from my fingertips.

"Imagine you having a crush on me—just wait till I tell Guy!"

"Well, please don't," I pleaded. It was useless to say "I don't fancy you" or anything like that. In truth, Guy would probably laugh it off. I'd stood at the bar, surrounded by loud people, enjoying the silence, trying to work out if I did, in any way, find Danielle attractive. Is that why I found her so annoying? The problem was, I kept getting words back like 'pretty' and 'striking.' Each one rang false. Like I was being polite.

It must be terrible to have worked so hard to be beautiful and to find that people just think you're kind of sort of hot.

That was it. I'd realised it as I'd tucked into the free snacks at the bar. I felt sorry for Danielle. All that loudness, all that look-at-me. Inside, somewhere deep inside, was someone who wanted to be told that it was all okay.

And that's when I knew why she loved Guy. Because Guy was reassuring, and comforting, and kind, and never failed to tell her how good she looked. Whenever she posted a picture, he'd comment below. Danielle wanted reassurance, and she had that with Guy, broadband and on-demand. And now, stuck in a bar without any mobile signal, she was floundering. No Guy to gossip with, no you-go-girl from friends. At a networking event where, thinking about it, she wasn't even networking, she was just sat in a corner, getting drunk with the boyfriend's best friend she didn't really care for, because there was no-one else here to talk to.

I was sat there, opposite Danielle, and I finally knew her and understood her. I only found her kind of hot. But I did kind of like her. Hashtag hashtag and all.

"What are you doing?"

I was rubbing my fingers again.

"Oh..." I rubbed up the dirt from between two fingers into a thin, tiny green worm. "There were rice crackers at the bar. I love those... but the coating. I wish I knew what the coating was. It's like Northern Line snot, really, isn't it? I guess it's wasabi and seaweed..."

Danielle wasn't interested. She was pushing the wine glass back at me, revolted.

"Rice crackers?"

I nodded. She just stared at me, bafflingly furious. The music was blaring, someone was singing, the bar was hot and loud and she was just across from me, so angry.

"You stupid shit," she screamed at me.

"What?"

"I'm allergic to peanuts," she yelled.

Well, I knew that. Everyone knew about Danielle's allergy. There'd been a bowl of peanuts at the bar I'd quite fancied the look of, but I'd avoided those. I just helped myself to the bowl of slightly less exciting rice crackers. And I'd scrupulously avoided the peanutty ones. The ones with the flavour.

I tried explaining this to her, sensibly and rationally, but she was having none of it. She was just screaming words at me, fingers snapping. I tried saying how I'd just gone for dull crackers, and not the nice nuts, and how, surely, if they were wrapped in a shell, then that was like they were sealed and...

Yes, okay, I had been babbling at her. I think saying "nice nuts" may have been the giveaway.

She was staring at the little dirt worms I'd scraped from my fingers. They lay on the table and she looked like she was trying to edge away from them with disgust.

"How could you be so thoughtless?" she screamed. I believed I'd just demonstrated that I'd been quite thoughtful. But no. Noise and words. I'd touched something that had been made in a factory that contained nuts. I'd not thought about it. I could have killed her.

The words went on and on. It was like a wall. When you see on the news five protesters with guitars and a party streamer facing up against armed guards with bulldozers and tear gas? That kind of onslaught.

I realised that what had excited Danielle so much was that she'd realised she had an advantage. She'd spotted a flaw and she was slicing through it. Diamond-cutting.

"What were you thinking?" She pushed the glass further away from her, nudging it with the tip of her phone. Shove. Shove. Shove. "I can't drink this! You've touched it, you've touched it with your hands!" She was screaming at me with fury. Loud enough, her voice raised, her fingers snapping, just enough to ensure that she was getting attention over the mingling, the conversation, the spontaneous karaoke and the Coldplay. Danielle was it.

"You knew, you knew I'm allergic and you still touched peanuts—you stupid freak!" She tried to make the last word hang there, but, let's be frank, any sentence that contains 'peanuts' in the middle of it, the concentration is going to hang there a little, isn't it? It's such a silly little word. It's hard to get around.

She fished out wet wipes and started scrubbing at her hands with them. A scouring like Lady Macbeth until the air reeked of clean baby-bum. "I'm really sorry. I was so thoughtless," I stood up. "I'll get you another drink."

She flung a wet wipe at me like a gauntlet. "Wash your hands first," she hissed. "They're disgusting."

＊   ＊   ＊

NOW, WHEN PEOPLE talk about getting angry, they talk about the red mist. Their jaw sets. There's a singing in their ears as though someone has twanged a wire and it's all happening and they're not in control and it's a rush of marvellous wonder. Somewhere lost in there, there's a regrettable action. Something wrong. But for that moment, when their system is full of amazing chemicals, they are off and away doing something splendid.

I'm not like that. I walked to the bar. I bought Danielle another drink. I decided to kill her.

IT JUST HAPPENED along the way. I don't want you to think that I'm a psychopath. To be honest, I don't know what the word means. I've not looked it up on Wikipedia. That'd be like using the internet to self-diagnose. I just knew, as I walked to the bar, that the easiest way out of this situation had presented itself. It didn't even seem like murder. Just the easiest thing to do.

IT WAS ALL really simple. Danielle's shouting match had attracted a little attention, but not much. Someone looked at me sympathetically as I walked to the bar, and I made a little 'it's just her' grimace. If anyone would remember the conversation, they'd remember her mention of a nut allergy. It was as easy as that. They wouldn't remember me. Hardly anyone ever did.

And how would they describe me? Oh yes. A man in a long, cheap, red wig.

I went to the bar. I waited for someone to serve me. I ordered a cocktail. As I waited to be served, I took a handful of peanuts. And, while the cocktail was poured, I ground that handful of peanuts in my palm. I couldn't say I powdered them, but I crushed them. Tiny little chips that slid neatly into the glass as I walked back with it. Then I cleaned my hands with the wet wipe.

＊   ＊   ＊

I SAT DOWN opposite Danielle. She was still steaming with triumph. I knew what she was going to do. I knew that as soon as she left the bar and went home, she would do several things.

She would tell Guy that I had tried to come on to her.

She would put up a post on my Facebook wall, probably with a lot of lols and exclamation marks about bumping into me and how I'd accidentally tried to poison her. 'Som ppl are so SAD!!! Lol.' Yes. That is how it would begin.

It would all be so very difficult.

This, this was easier.

SHE SAT, SUCKING her cocktail through a straw like it was a kid's milkshake. In between slurps she smiled at me, a nasty little smile. You could see inside her head, like it was as clear and brilliant as the Koh-i-Noor. Her thoughts were that she'd be nice as pie to me now, finish her drink, leave and then unleash hell. She was smirking at the simple cunning of the idea. It delighted her. It shone. And all the time, she sucked and sucked away.

I had a qualm, then. A little worry that she'd get down to the bottom of the glass and there would be, among the little melting diamonds of ice, the shards and chips of nut. She'd see and she'd know. Was that an actual crime? It probably was.

But she talked about holidays and hotel bookings and cheap flight operators. And I smiled and said how nice, and what a bargain and aren't they criminals.

And while all this happened, the level got lower and lower, the sickly orange syrup pulling itself down and away from the ice and up into her straw. My guilt revealing itself slurp by slurp.

Then her straw rattled and Danielle coughed.

"Bit of ice... sucked it up... swallowed." She worked her teeth, crunching away. And coughed again.

"Are you okay?" I asked her. I don't think, I really don't think there was hope, or triumph in my voice. I've often been told that my voice is too flat. I grew up near Wolverhampton, and while I don't have that accent, I've somehow got no accent or intonation at all. When I was at school, someone used to call me Speak-Your-Weight. I wonder if they still have those machines now? Or is the idea of having your weight read out in public the modern equivalent of being thrown in the stocks?

"I feel sick," groaned Danielle. "I'll go to the loo..."

"No," I offered. "I'll help you."

I was firm. I was helpful. I gathered up her handbag, and her jacket. I left the glass behind. It gnawed at me as I led her through the crowd. Would anyone notice? I tried to work out. There was maybe a three per cent chance that someone would notice ground peanuts at the bottom of her glass. If I didn't draw attention to her. And, if they did notice peanuts, and there was no connection, they'd just assume someone had dropped them in, bored like they were tearing up a beer-mat or folding cigarette packet cellophane into shapes. You wouldn't see it and think that I had tried to kill her. Would you?

But still, my guilt hung there. A worry as I led Danielle to the loo. She was coughing, and her hands were clawing at the air. I was careful to make sure she didn't make contact with the flesh of my arms under my shirt—I realised then, coldly and clearly, that I did not want her to have any of my skin under her fingernails.

There was a queue outside the ladies. The disabled loo was locked. Danielle shook her head at going to the gents. Well, who wouldn't? So I led her out on to the fire escape. As I pushed the door bar, someone looked at me and asked me if I needed help.

"She's had a bit too much," I said, "You know... breath of fresh air."

After the fire door banged shut behind us, I wondered who had asked that question. Would they recognise me?

The sharpness of the night hit us. Danielle turned to look at me, her face twisting in pain and bewilderment. "Breath of fresh air," I said again. She tried out words, but just gasped. She was grabbing at her own throat now, squeezing it as she coughed. Her face was red, red in the dark, showing through the layers of careful make-up in ugly blotches. She staggered against the metal fire escape, her feet drumming on a step.

"It's okay," I said, holding her, comforting. "I've got you."

She vomited. It wasn't much, but it hung in strings down between the metal steps like sticky stalactites.

Her shoes pattered against the stairs like rainfall and then stopped.

*   *   *

I HAD KILLED Danielle. Interesting.

The night was cold and quiet.

I stood there, collecting my thoughts.

It really was, genuinely, without the shadow of a lie, God's honest truth, the first time I had killed anyone. I'd thought about it at school. I think we all have.

But doing it for real had been so easy.

I felt a rush. I can admit that. I guess now came that sudden, unhelpful wash of chemicals. But I thought my way through them. It wasn't going to help me. I needed to be absolutely sure I was doing the right thing.

Did I need to go back into the bar? No. I had everything. If I tried to go back through the fire escape, maybe someone would ask me how Danielle was. Or remember me. Or something.

What about her drink? Leave it in the bar.

What about the red hair? Tricky. I would slip my wig off, and place it in a Boots carrier bag. But not now. Not just now. If there was CCTV covering the fire escape, then the wig would help to hide my features. There was a risk, sure, that it would attract attention. But I'd stride it out.

I stepped around Danielle's body. If anyone stopped me now, I could say I was going for help. If anyone stopped me now, and if anyone knew about the peanuts, I could swear it was a stupid, drunk practical joke gone wrong.

I was going for help. I was going for help.

I repeated that as I walked up the metal stairs from the basement club. I pushed open the tiny gate at the top. I didn't touch the ironwork with my fingers. I just nudged against it with my sleeve, like I was opening a toilet door and feeling fussy.

And then I was up and out into the street. Walking purposefully.

I was going for help, I was going for help.

I was going home.

I POPPED THE wig in a bag. I got off the tube a stop early. On the way, I passed a charity clothing bank and slipped it in there.

There were a lot of students in the area. Lot of fancy dress. Lot of charity shops. Someone would soon be wearing... well, not quite a murder weapon, but still... something.

I walked back into my flat. I fed the cat.

I still felt calm.

I felt very calm.

I put the kettle on. As it boiled, I wondered about a drink. There was some kind of fun rum from a party in a cupboard. Maybe I'd have that. I poured it into a glass. I sipped it. Not quite right.

Then I smiled and dropped some ice into it. And then, as the finishing touch, a peanut.

I sipped it and laughed.

It felt good.

I thought about tomorrow. About how Danielle would no longer be on Facebook. I had made the internet a better place. I really had.

I may have killed her, but I had made the world a better place.

I SAT DOWN in front of my notebook, ready to see if there was anything on iPlayer. An old *Top Gear*, or *Buzzcocks*. Something simple and cheering. My mind kept pulling back into itself, telling itself how pleased it was with itself.

Idly, I checked Gmail. There was a message from an account I didn't recognise. I wonder how my life would have changed if the spam filter had picked it up? The message was just a link to a site. I knew better than to click the link. But hey, live a little.

The page it took me to had just one line on it. Small. Dull. Times New Roman.

We know what you've done. Killer.

INTERLUDE
WHEN CATS STOPPED
BEING FUNNY

THIS IS A picture of a cat.

IT IS BECAUSE I like cats. A long time ago, when the internet was invented, it was a military operation. Nuclear war would have been run through the internet. Now the internet is mostly porn, shopping and cats.

And cats are best of all. Once, when I was having a bad day at work, I looked at all the pictures of cats on Flickr. This was a few years ago and it was still possible to look at *all* of the pictures of cats on Flickr on a dull day. Before the cats took over. Before the cats took charge.

Don't get me wrong here. I'm not saying that somewhere there's a darkened room where the internet is controlled from a comfy chair by a cat. Running things. Although, sometimes, when the world is bad, I like to think that. It would be better than the truth.

It's just that I like cats. The cat has had two greatest hits. In Ancient Egypt they were worshipped as gods. Then came a few millennia where they didn't quite fit in, and were frequently burned. Then along came the internet and the cats came into power again. You can't move for cats on the internet.

This annoys dog owners. Every now and then someone will try and make the internet happen for dogs. Pictures of Pugs looking miserable in hats will appear. But Pugs in hats are not a thing. So they go away.

Cats remain. Somehow, whatever you throw at them, cats survive.

A few years ago, the lolcat was invented. There is almost entirely no point in me explaining the lolcat to you like it's 2007. A lolcat is a picture of a cat with a misspelt caption. The joke lies somewhere along the lines of 'if cats could almost spell, and were a little evil, and a little more intelligent, this is what they would be like.' Cunning and haphazard.

For a long while, the cat joke worked. The site was an enormous success, fuelled by people coming to stare at a cat doing a thing. Then the site changed. People started making their own lolcats. These started being posted on the site. For a while it was a glorious, churning tide of endless pictures of cats doing a thing with a hilarious caption.

But the problem was...

The problem was that we've all stood next to someone at a gig saying, "They're not as good as they were in the early days." We've all been that person. For me it was trying to tell my friends at school about this amazing new, obscure, arty and independent (I had just discovered independent films) sitcom they'd started running late at night on Channel 4. It was, I said, like Steven Soderbergh or Jim Jarmusch if they did a sitcom about people living in New York. I told them the title. They nodded. They hadn't heard of it. The sitcom was called *Friends*.

I stopped watching *Friends* a couple of years later. I don't know why. Perhaps it was because I could never get a Rachel cut. That's a glib answer. I just simply couldn't stand that my beautiful secret thing was now the most famous sitcom in the world, and it knew it was and it felt the pressure, the terrible pressure of having to be the funniest sitcom in the world. I couldn't forgive it for not being unpopular.

Lolcats was the *Friends* of the internet. Suddenly, everywhere. Suddenly golden and wonderful. And then the wrong kind of people started watching. The kind of people who buy pink kitten plates. Who buy calendars with soft focus cats shot through a sock like they're Joan Collins. Only they're cats. They don't need vaseline on the lens. Because they're cats. They don't have wrinkles. They're cats.

The rest of us, we carried on laughing at the clever, snarky meme about cunning evil cats who couldn't write. But you'd notice the comments. 'Aww cute!' 'LOL.' 'CUTE x100000!!!' 'sooo hugzy.' 'kitty.' The people writing the comments were less clever than the cat.

Here's where lolcats broke. Because the way the site worked was that you took a picture of a cat, you slapped a caption on it and you sent it in. It sat in a slush pile of cats. And, if the people looking at the site went through the slush pile and liked it enough, it was promoted to the front page.

In the early days, it worked like a charm. Some genuine genius found a picture of a cat sleeping purposefully on a television and called it 'MONORAIL CAT.' Someone else decided that a cat peering down from a loft door was 'CEILING CAT.'

Smart.

Funny.

Lol.

But the pictures that were now coming in were just pictures of cute cats with captions saying how cute they were. Or CUTEZ. Or ADORABLEZ. Or, worst of all, 'purrfect.' I'm sure these came in in the early days. But they didn't get voted up. Because the people looking at the site were, by and large, people who got the joke.

The Turkish phrase for 'foreigners' translates as 'Those Outside The Tent.' But those outside the tent had pulled open the flaps and crowded in. Grinning inanely.

For now a comedy site was being driven by people who didn't quite get the joke. And weren't funny.

Friends was once the best programme on television. For a time, lolcats was the best thing on the internet. Then things changed. Other people got involved. People not like us.

If you want to know how far things have gone, there's now a payday loans company called Lolcat Loanz. Oh, yes. They're on the list.

The difference between lolcats and *Friends* is that it's easy for us not to take the blame for *Friends*. All we did was watch it. We didn't write the jokes. It's not our fault (although it is) that it somehow wasn't as funny anymore. We can blame the network.

You cannot blame the internet for lolcats stopping being funny. You can only blame the people. The people who crowded into the tent and didn't understand.

CHAPTER TWO
THE CHARITY MUGGER

I SAT UP long and late that night.

I looked at a lot of cats.

I'd killed someone—and I felt fine about it. Right up to the point that I got an email saying that someone knew I'd done it. We none of us ever grow up, really. We're all still somewhere between twelve and fourteen. Some of us are more broken by the world, some of us less. But the big, key, important point is that we all of us like doing bad things so long as we can get away with them.

For a glorious moment, I thought that I had. Killing is the one big thing that should be so difficult and so bad and so wrong. It should have been harder than it was.

If killing Danielle had been easy, then getting away with it should have been just as easy. Especially because, and don't get me wrong, I was cleverer than she was.

But by the time I'd got home, got home and poured myself a congratulatory drink, someone had already got in touch to tell me I'd done it. Not even Hercule Poirot was that fast. The internet already knew I'd done it. Maybe yeah, somewhere, a cat in a dark room had nodded to itself as it had written that message. Maybe.

I stared at that message. I wondered about it.

I did not reply to it.

One lesson in life I've learned is that, if you don't like the look of an email, don't reply to it. A colleague sends you an email that makes you angry? Just ignore it. A Facebook status makes you boil with rage? Ignore it. An online column makes you shake at its wrongness?

One golden rule in the world: Never Hit 'Reply.'

A MESSAGE TURNS up accusing you of murder?

Well obviously. I mean what reply could I send? I couldn't say 'Guilty' or 'Not Guilty.' Or anything much of anything. I could just stare at it.

So I did.

For a while. Then I went and looked at pictures of cats. Not on Flickr this time. All over the place. And videos. Videos of cats falling over. Or riding on robot hoovers. Or skateboards. Or hiding in boxes. Or just videos of cats sleeping. Untroubled.

Or just pictures of cats sleeping. Untroubled. Hunting dreams.

Then I'd look again at the email.

Then I'd look at some more cats.

I LOOKED AGAIN at my inbox. Another email had arrived from the same sender. This time a link to an eCard.

'Don't worry,' the caption said. 'We want to know what you'll do next.'

The eCard was a picture of a cat.

I STARED AT the notebook screen calmly and quietly. Which is how it ended up at the other end of the room, sliding down the wall.

I got up off the sofa, breathing heavily, my legs shaking. I made my way over to the notebook. My flat's not a large one, but it took a long time. I flopped down onto the ground by the computer, praying it wasn't damaged. After all, if it was damaged... well, if I threw it away, wouldn't someone look at it? And, if I took it in for repair... wouldn't someone wonder why? I mean, there was no guarantee that that email would be sat open on the desktop. But then, I'm fairly sure that no celebrity keeps their kiddie porn open on their hard drives either, and yet that never seems to go well for them.

My head whirled. Hard drives aren't unlike record pla[...] really—just a big disc of data spinning round and round being read by a needle. And, inside my head, my disc was spinning but the needle just wasn't connecting.

I lay on the floor. The floor was dirty. I could see dust bunnies gathered under the DVD shelves. I could see grit. I could even see, horridly, peanut shells. That must have been from... when had I last eaten monkey nuts? Last Christmas? Would I ever earn enough to afford a cleaner? If I went to an internet café, could I log on to my Gmail and delete the email? Were there such things as internet cafés any more, or would I have to travel back to 2002?

I eased the notebook open. It flickered back into life, suggested restarting in Safe Mode and then announced that Windows would be installing 128 important updates. Its way of punishing me.

The needle bounced along the disc and connected. My phone! Of course. There was Gmail on my phone. I picked my phone up. As I did so, a text arrived.

'THAT WAS STUPID'

I stared at the number. Unrecognised.

I'D NEVER EVER felt sick with panic before. But now, everything... everything was empty. It wasn't just my brain that was spinning. Everything was out of control. Nothing made sense.

I pecked at the phone. I started a reply.

'Who are'

Then stopped. Deleted it.

'What do you want?'

No. I started a third time.

'Fuck off.'

I nearly sent it. Instead I put the phone down and scrabbled under the cabinet, fishing out the empty monkey nut shells, one by one, and stared at them.

Rational thought just didn't come.

The police weren't this good. No one was this good. No one could know.

Unless Danielle wasn't dead.

That was the only explanation. But it didn't work. I could imagine her sitting in a cab, smiling as she sent a text. But not this... Why would she do this? It just didn't make sense.

Her phone. There was a picture of us on her phone. What had happened to her phone?

I stared at my mobile, and my horrified reflection stared back.

And then my phone started to ring.

Unknown number.

I held it in my hand, feeling it jump each time it rang.

I waited for it to stop. But it didn't stop.

I ANSWERED THE phone.

"What do you want?" I yelled. My voice sounded strangled. Panicked. Guilty.

"David, David, sorry it's so late. It's me, oh, God, it's me..." cried a voice at the other end. More panicked and alarmed than me. It was Guy.

My best friend Guy. Had Danielle told him?

"It's Danielle. It's Danielle..." He broke off. There was an odd sound. Like a gasp, but lower down in the throat. "She's been in an accident. I'm, I'm on my way to the hospital. It's bad. Sorry for ringing you so late, but oh, my god."

"That's... that's okay." I heard my voice. Calm. Clear. Very, very strange. Like a swim in a cold pool. "It's fine. Would you like me to come over?"

"No. I'm not at my flat. I'm at Danielle's." Hence the unrecognised number. Right. "I'm off out. I'll... I'll call you from the hospital."

"I'll come. I'll come. It's fine, I'll come. I'll put some clothes on and come." Again, an odd tone.

"No, no it's fine... well, look, could you? If you could... Maybe. I just need someone. It's St Stephen's. I'm going with the police."

"The police? What? How bad is she?"

"Er... yeah." A terrible pause. "I really need a friend. If I'm not disturbing you."

"Don't be daft. I'll get a minicab."

"Thanks, mate. I can't go through this alone. You're one in a million." Guy tried a laugh, but it was just that same odd gasp. Oh. He was crying.

I ended the call. The police had come for Guy. Did he know she was dead? Still, no-one had called me. That was fine. The police didn't know I'd done it.

I pulled my trousers on.

My phone beeped. An email. Linking to an eCard.

'BE OUTSIDE LEICESTER SQ MCDONALDS IN HALF AN HOUR.'

What to do, what to do? The needle in my brain bumped uselessly across the surface of my mind.

So. I DIDN'T go to the hospital that night. I'd promised, but I didn't go. Which meant that Guy wasn't speaking to me.

Instead I went and stood outside Leicester Square McDonalds. Which, at 2am on a Wednesday, is a weird place to be. It was cold, and my jacket couldn't keep the wind out. A nightbus roared past, its side advertising careers with Sodobus in neon. A few people wandered in and out of the cafe. Men wandered past, shouting in Eastern European into their phones.

I waited. I was frightened and bored. Like waiting for a date.

A car pulled up. An oldish women with tight silver hair got out of it. She marched up to me. I looked at her, questioningly. She stood, appraising me coldly, waiting for me to say something— maybe to ask her for directions. Then she shrugged and walked away into the restaurant.

Clearly, it wasn't her. Well, I didn't think it could be.

I waited a bit longer.

Normally, you'd text the person you were waiting for. But I didn't dare. Not in this case.

I waited half an hour, then I went home.

THE NEXT MORNING, I sent Guy an apologetic email, explaining that I'd fallen asleep. This was after he didn't answer the phone.

It was a long time before he answered the email. 'I needed you. She's dead.'

Well, this was horrid.

I couldn't tell him the truth. I couldn't tell him any of the truth. I couldn't say, 'Well, yes, I killed her. Oops.' I couldn't even tell him that, half an hour after I got home, there was another message: 'MADE YOU LOOK.'

I did not reply to the message. I said plenty to it out loud.

I WAITED FOR the police to come and knock on my door. They didn't. No one came and knocked on my door. I thought about skipping work. But then realised that would look suspicious, so I went even though I pretty much zombied my way through it. I thought I'd never sleep again, but the night after I killed Danielle, I got home and fell straight asleep. I'd just about taken my shoes off.

I did not dream about Danielle. That came later. Dreams where I stood over her while she looked up at me with her eyes wide, as she choked and choked. Over and over.

There was an inquest. It was ruled to be an accident caused by an allergic reaction. That was it. No mention of her phone. Why? Why was that? Someone had it. With a photo of me and Danielle on it. I just prayed someone had stolen it.

As Guy wasn't speaking to me, I wasn't invited to the funeral. I wouldn't have gone anyway. I'm not sure I could have spent two hours not looking at her parents.

But, at least, the funeral was over. And the mysterious eCards had stopped.

I figured that would be it. I don't know why I thought that, but I really did.

THEN I GOT an email from Guy. The preview began, 'Dear Friend,' so I opened it, thinking it would be an olive branch. That we could get back to where we were.

Instead, it was a round robin:

Dear Friend,

As you probably know, my beloved fiancee Danielle [what? They were engaged?] died last month. She was my angel.

She didn't deserve to die—and certainly not from accidentally eating a peanut. The whole thing would be funny, if it weren't for the fact that I've now lost the love of my life and my best friend.

Yes, this is a begging email. I'm going to be running a marathon for Danielle and to raise awareness of allergies. My life is over. I don't want other people's to be ruined too.

Here's the JustGiving link. If you ever met Danielle, you'll know she was really difficult to buy presents for. But just this once, I'm hoping you'll find it easy. #DoingItForDanielle

Best wishes,

Guy

I read it a few times. He made Danielle sound so nice.

Right there and then, I almost emailed him and told him everything. But that didn't seem such a clever idea. At all or ever. Plus, by the third time I was reading it, I was laughing. Laughing at how wrong he'd got her. She was a warped fascist with appalling punctuation. Sure, thinking about it a bit, she didn't deserve to die... well, not exactly. But I'd had my reasons for what I'd done.

I told myself that over and over. When I stood in the shower. When I boiled the kettle. When I stood waiting for the Metropolitan Line. She deserved it.

I'd made the internet a better place. Because I'd got rid of Danielle.

ONLY, I HADN'T.

Guy's email was just the start of it. Suddenly Danielle was everywhere. He wasn't the only person running the marathon for her. Lots of our mutual friends were. They started up a Facebook group. They changed their avatars to pictures of Danielle, which meant that I was now seeing her dead smiling face everywhere. She was out clubbing, she was crawling home late, she was uploading pictures of her breakfast, she was watching *Britain's Got Talent* and she was taking a quiz to find out which member of One Direction she was.

It was as though Danielle was still alive. But everywhere. I couldn't forget her. She was all over Facebook and Twitter. (Not Google+ though. No-one's on there. Not even ghosts.)

I WONDERED IF this was my divine punishment. The internet was going to be #DoingItForDanielle all the time and forever.

There was something. In among the marathons, the raising awareness march and the charity collection of Danielle's favourite nut-free cupcake recipes (oh, yes, I was right to kill her). It took me a while, but I noticed it. I was helped. I got one further eCard.

> These shoes are about to run #26Miles #DoingItForDaniele.
> Lucky shoes.

ONE OF DANIELLE'S friends was particularly everywhere. No matter how I tried to ignore him. I wasn't even friends with him, but I knew everything that he was doing.

There was no shutting up Edward ('Call Me Fast Eddy') Atkinson. His profile picture was of him hugging Danielle. He was walking from London to her hometown (#WalkForDaniele, #DoingItForDaniele #FastEddy). He would regularly post pictures of her, or memories of golden times they shared together.

And people would retweet them, or share them on their Facebook wall. So that Fast Eddy would creep into my feed.

That's one of the odd things about the internet. When it started out there was an amazing amount of information and it was difficult to find. Then we got Google. But for some reason, people think we need leading to stuff.

We don't. For the first time in mankind's history, we have a vast amount of data out there which is ours for the taking. And the more we go and look for it in our own way, the less its wants us to. Facebook's constantly throwing itself in front of us going, 'Don't do that—see this!' Worse is 'The One Trick That Mums

Know To Cure Belly Flab.' Those adverts now actually jiggle. They're refusing to take the hint that we just don't want to know. We've not clicked. We are not going to click. But maybe, one day, we will.

FAST EDDY WAS one busy charity bunny. Not only was he off running a third marathon for Danielle, he was constantly tweeting about his training schedule ('18 miles today. Need chocolate SOOO BAD. But no. #DoingItForDaniele'), and he was always begging celebrities for retweets ('Running for Danielle, tragedy death tht can be avoided, any chance of a cheeky RT? #DoingItForDaniele'). And people did. And people retweeted those retweets. And all of them linked to Fast Eddy's JustGiving page. He fucked me off.

All of my resentment, self-hatred and fear about Danielle was crystallised in this one man. Who would not, *could* not, shut up. He was just there.

True, he looked nice enough. In all the selfies he posted of himself, running around, or dousing himself with ice. He was always smiling, his little eager-to-please chipmunk face covered in just enough stubble to not quite be a beard. His cheeks were ruddy (from all the running in the rain) and he just looked nice and normal and desperate to be liked.

Late one drunken night (oh, yeah, I was drinking a lot these days #DoingItForDanielle), I clicked through to his JustGiving page. I don't know why. Maybe to give him some money. Or to torture myself reading some of the messages from donors. Just... life, really. The kind of late night link trawling that happens when you're drunk but you don't want to go to bed.

I sat on the sofa. My vodka-tonic was too strong. But I didn't care. I stared at Fast Eddy's profile, at his training blog. At his sheer, clear goodness. He was everything I wasn't. He was taller than me. He glowed with charity. I'd never done anything that good. I'd never...

Then I noticed something. In the small print. Way beneath the list of '57 Things I Bet You Never Knew Had Nuts In Them.' The charity name was slightly different from the fund that Guy and

Danielle's family had set up for her. He'd mistyped 'Danielle' as 'Daniele.' Just one 'l.' Odd how good your proof-reading can be at the wrong time. It annoyed me. But then, anyone can make a mistake.

I carried on surfing through his previous campaigns. He'd misspelt her name again. And again. Not all the time. But how curious.

Maybe he'd just pasted the wrong block of text over. Or autocorrect.

I did a drunken Google, pecking the keys with awful caution. 'Doing It For Daniele' brought up a link on a different donations site. This one gave bank details of the account. Same sort code as Guy's. Different account number.

Odd. I went to the main Doing It For Danielle page. It didn't list full accounts, but there was a reasonable stream of donations coming in. I wondered if Eddy had transferred his across. But none of the figures matched. He'd raised £2,700 last marathon. No sign of that. Or the £1,450 from his first marathon. I carried on. It was boring cross-referencing and I wouldn't have bothered if I hadn't been pretty smashed. He had moved some money across—£200 from a fun run here and £75 from a sponsored walk.

But, adding it all up, doing drunk maths, there was about £10,000 missing.

Fast Eddy was a fraud.

I googled Edward Atkinson. Then I tried a few variations.

And bingo. A 'Ted Atkinson' had once worked as a Systems Analyst at Sodobus before being convicted of running a fake charity calendar door-knocking scam. Thank God for local newspapers online. There was even a photo of Fast Eddy before he became fast—long hair, clean-shaven, same eager face. Next to a jiggling advert for That 1 Weird Tip That Only Moms Know.

I leaned back and stared at the screen.

I wondered about emailing Guy to tell him. My eyes fluttered closed. I was finally falling asleep. I stood up, went to pee and then staggered to bed. I lay there, thinking about it.

The mystery eCard had said, 'We want to see what you do next.'

And now I knew what I wanted to do next.

* * *

THE THING I'VE not told you until now (because you'd have stopped reading and backed hurriedly away) is what I do for a living. I'm a chugger.

Yes, that's me. I stand on busy streets, just waiting to ruin your lunch hour. I have a clipboard and a big smile and I just need a moment to talk to you about cancer/kittens/children. My really big hope is that you won't punch me or spit at me or just shoulder through me. My hope is that you'll listen, listen longer than "Not today, thank you," listen to me long enough to fill in a form with your bank details on it, agreeing to give a large amount of money to cancer/kittens/children.

You assume I'm working for cancer, or kittens, or children's charities. But I'm not, not directly. I'm working for a man who owns a lot of race cars. So many race cars he's had a basement garage put under his basement garage in Notting Hill. Charities don't hire chuggers directly—they hire Mr Racing Car. The cancer, the kittens, and the children pay his firm to hire us to stand out in the rain for minimum wage (any more would be taking from charity, wouldn't it?). We bring in subscriptions to the charities, and every month a tenner leaves your bank account and goes to the kittens, the cancer and the children. Of course, this is where Big Maths comes in.

You sign up through us, and on average it'll take three years of your subscription for the charity to pay back Mr Racing Car's finder's fee. The typical lifespan of your direct debit before you go "aw, fuckit" and cancel? Three years and two months.

In other words, you've paid £380. Mr Racing Car gets £360. The charity gets just £20.

Big Maths is the game the charities play. Because, while the average subscription is going to be just over three years, there are going to be a few outliers. People who discover they really like giving a tenner a month to kittens/cancer/children. And keep on doing so. And among those, there's going to be at least one who leaves their house to children/kittens/cancer. Quite a lot of people who sign up are little old ladies. We love the sexy young people, they tick all sorts of good demographic boxes. But we're also very grateful to the little old ladies. Thanks to demographics, we know they're more likely to live alone, and be grateful to stop and chat. They're also sentimental, so they're more likely to suddenly care about whatever we're selling. And they're statistically less likely to cancel their direct debits and more likely to leave us their house. So God bless little old ladies.

So, thanks to Big Maths, it's all worthwhile, and Mr Racing Car can sleep at night. He knows he's made the world a better place (sort of) and can enjoy his sweet dream about which of his cars he's not going to drive tomorrow because actually he lost his licence when he ran over a little old lady.

But anyway, enough about Big Maths and Mr Racing Car. The point is, he gave me a job.

HAVE YOU EVER wondered why all us charity muggers are so smiling and so friendly? Because we're pretending. We don't really feel like that. We're not really happy to see you. We don't much care whether you give us money or not. And we don't give a stuff about kittens or cancer or children. Some of us do, when we start, but you see, it's kittens on Monday, cancer on Tuesday, children on Wednesday. A different coloured tabard, a different cause that's close to our heart. They all blur into one. We go out there and we're just playing a part. We've even got lines. Which we're really good at learning.

Because we're all actors. In the olden golden days, actors between jobs would wait tables, or sit at home collecting the dole and working on their one-person show. Now waiting jobs are hard to find, and we're all signed up to temping agencies, sorting the post of the people who last week paid £50 to see us sing and dance and shout.

But actors make very good chuggers. We're mostly young, we're mostly pretty, we're really good at pretending to care, and we love a tough crowd.

IT'S WORTH BEARING in mind that all this was accidentally the perfect training for being a serial killer.

- I'm really good at playing a part. Tick.
- I'm really really good at not being noticed. People actively look away from me as soon as they see me. Just a glance— nice looking guy, good hair, nice teeth, uh-oh tabard. Then they do everything in their power not to notice me. Tick.
- And, finally, I am supremely qualified in that I know a lot about people. And I really hate them all. Tick. Tick. Tick.

You're all awful. You may think you're not, but you are. I despise the ones who push past me. And I despise the ones who stop and talk to me. One lot are rude and the other lot are idiots. If you really cared about cancer, children or kittens you'd be giving directly to them already. And you wouldn't suddenly do so because someone stops you on a street corner. And you'd have researched charitable giving and carefully picked which charity to put your cash into, choosing one that spends the most of its money on the actual cause, rather than on paying Mr Racing Car's Chugging Firm. There we go. You've just fallen for a scam, one shouted at you by someone who last week was pretending very hard to be a Gentleman of Verona. But also, in a way, thank you for falling for the scam. Because it means I'm good at being an actor. You idiot.

THIS ALSO MADE me excellently qualified at seeing right through Fast Eddy. I could see a fellow scammer. He was making money out of my killing. It was *my* murder. So I'd teach him a lesson. The slight problem was working out what to do next.

But what about the mysterious eCard sender? They'd tipped me off to Fast Eddy—did they want me to kill him? Who or what were they? Was it someone who'd seen me in the pub, or a Vast Syndicate Of Conspiracy to deal with? I mean, did I need to ask their permission in order to kill someone? Or could I just do what I liked? They could, in theory, expose me at any moment. I didn't like that very much, but then again, Mr Racing Car wasn't particularly lovely to work for. So I was just swapping one dose of fear for another.

I texted the mystery number.

Nothing happened.

And then, a day or so later, I received an anonymous invitation to join MySpace. I laughed a lot at that. The internet is littered with abandoned social networks, places that once flourished and thrived where people shared their entire lives and told flirty lies to their Not Girlfriends. I'd had an account on MySpace long ago, but I'd forgotten what it was. And so, blissfully, had my notebook.

I signed up, applauding the logic of this. A lot of dead communities were switched off (Menshn, for instance). Actually the howling tundra of Google+ would have been brilliant, but sadly Google had allowed the NSA to snoop on it. This wasn't good. Whereas MySpace was still active, if totally forgotten about.

I imagined that, as soon as I signed up, a bell went off in a long-undusted office and someone, walking past down a corridor wondered idly what that noise was. Maybe they even told Tom. You remember Tom? The one default MySpace friend everyone had, the one half-turning and smiling at you in the act of going somewhere better.

Soon I was able to communicate with the person who held my life in their hands:

> DUSTER: Hi.
> ME: Who are you? And what do you want with me?
> DUSTER: We're friendly. And we wish to stay that way.
> ME: Not. At. All. Creepy.
> DUSTER: **Would you prefer if I used Comic Sans?**
> ME: No. That's worse.
> DUSTER: Fair enough. The thing is, we know what you're doing.
> ME: What's that?
> DUSTER: Let's just say that you are an enterprising individual. And we're supportive of that enterprise.
> ME: But who are you?
> DUSTER: We're everywhere. And we wish to act as your sponsor. To fund you in continuing your work.
> ME: I'm sorry? I have no plans to continue my work.

DUSTER: Really? FastEddy
ME: *... is typing a response ...*
ME: *... is typing a response ...*
DUSTER: Are you still there?
DUSTER: Are you still there?
ME: *... is typing a response ...*
DUSTER: Are you still there?
DUSTER: Are you still there?
ME: Yes. [I'd tried typing several witty, pithy and righteous responses. But "yes" was the best I could come up with.]
DUSTER: We don't want to frighten you away. We just want you to know that we are everywhere. We know everything about you. And we want to encourage you in your plans.
ME: Look. I don't have any plans.
DUSTER: Make some. If it helps, we may have some suggestions for you.
ME: Seriously. Can't believe we're talking about this. I don't want your help!
DUSTER: Fair enough. But we're sending you the details of a bank account we have set up. To assist you. Purely should you need it. We wouldn't want to force you to do anything. But you have real talent. And we feel that talent should be recognised and encouraged.
ME: Thanks. But I don't need your help.
DUSTER: We'll see. Good luck with FastEddy
DUSTER has left the conversation.

I SAT STARING at MySpace. I had two friends. One was SmileyTomWhoCreatedMySpaceThenSoldItTheFirstChance HeGotWhichIsWhyHeIsSmiling. The other was Duster. I needed to make some new friends, so I quickly liked a few bands who seemed struggling and someone who really loved the colour yellow back in 2007.

Out of curiosity, I looked up Duster's friends. Duster was a fan of internet pioneer Henry Jarman, the music of teen sensation Harry Paperboy, an ebook publisher, and a comedy show on E4.

Edward Atkinson @FastEddy · 8m
I'll be doing #MuddyHell eeep! I'll be #DoingItForDaniele
Here's my justgiving, so just give you lovely fools

WHAT WAS MUDDY Hell? I'll let their homepage explain:

MUDDY HELL
The Ultimate Dirty Workout

Have you got what it takes to be one of the 10 per cent?
That's right, only 10 per cent make it to the end of our
gruelling half-marathon charity challenge. Designed by
ex-SAS soldiers as revenge, this is purely hell on earth.
We've seen squaddies cry. And you know what we did
then? We laughed and turned the ice hose on those
squaddies.
This ain't no fun run.
Burn your pussy pilates mat, fuck your free weights and
come join our fitness revolution.
We promise you tough love and a happy finish.
But no hugs. Cos you'll smell disgusting.

SIGN UP TODAY.
**When it comes to slinging mud,
we say bring it on!**

FAST EDDY HAD made my life easy for me. His hobby involved
nearly killing himself in order to scam money out of people. He
may have been a thief, but he certainly worked hard for it. He'd
signed up for the Muddy Hell challenge. It featured a whole host
of 'fun things' that were basically a collection of small suicide
attempts. There was crawling through a tunnel filled with water,
there was jumping into a mud bath, and then there were the
electric fences. It wasn't so much murder as nudging him a tiny
bit further into the next life.

The challenge was to make sure that this didn't turn into a
massacre. Without boring you about the detail, I had to work out

how to make the fun run specifically lethal so that it just killed
Fast Eddy and not every stupid lunatic in lycra who'd signed up
for it. It would perhaps have been easier to run him over on one
of his practice jogs, but that was:

a) Too easy (well, actually, I can't drive).
b) In danger of making him a figure of sympathy.

I needed Fast Eddy out of the way and in a way that exposed
him for the fraud he was.
I had to come up with a way that didn't involve running thirteen
miles through mud.

TURNED OUT, MUDDY Hell needed volunteer Mud Marshalls,
whose job it was to stand along the course, looking after the
various obstacles and challenges and manning the hoses. They
really needed marshalls as these were unpaid positions, normally
taken by friends of those competing. And I was Fast Eddy's
friend. He just didn't know it.

Come the day, I didn't even need to bother with a disguise. It
was raining, bitterly raining, and we were all issued with cagoules
with hoods that condomed our faces. I stood by my little patch of
course and waited.

The runners were sent off in little groups. I'd finally found
a use for RunKeeper. I could use all the data from Fast Eddy's
endless feed of practice runs and last week's obstacle course
try-outs—called the 'Dry Run' because they'd not created the
mud or baited any of the traps. I could make a reasonable
guess of how long it would take Eddy to get round the course.
I was helped by the groups themselves being staggered, with
runners being set off at one-minute intervals. I should have
a clear field. And the rain itself meant that there should few
spectators. People pretend interest in their friends running
through fields. They may even turn up to support them. But
not if it's chucking it down—then cars tend to break down, or
the kids play up, or alarms get slept through. You know the
drill. It's far easier to just like the photos when they turn up

on Facebook. And they will. Admit it, you've done it yourself plenty of times.

I stood by the course and I waited. Despite the waterproofs, I was soaked through. Twitter told me that Fast Eddy had just posted 'and were off!!!' so I calculated how long I had to wait and how bad the resulting head cold would be.

My first runner came past. This meant there would be five minutes until Fast Eddy.

"Excuse me?"

I turned. There were two hikers there.

"Has Eddy been through?" One of them waved a flag.

Oh, God. Spectators.

I thought quickly. "Er... which one is he?"

"He's wearing a t-shirt with Fast Eddy on. He's doing it for a friend of ours. Sandwich?"

They produced a tupperware box of sandwiches. I guess that would be what you'd expect from the Venn diagram overlap of 'Friends of Danielle' and 'People Who Would Turn Up In This Weather.' I had to move them on and quickly.

"I'm Brian," said one of them, inevitably.

"I'm Suze," said the other. Christ, why do all the dull people have to introduce themselves to everyone?

"Pretty amazing, isn't it?" said Brian. He was wearing a bandana.

"I wish I was doing this," said Suze. The henna was running in her hair.

They both nodded and vowed to do it soon. They never would.

They stood and watched, the damp air filling just a little with the pot pourri of cheese and pickle.

"Fast Eddy's brilliant, isn't he?" said Brian.

"We follow everything he does on Twitter. Do you?"

I shrugged and checked my watch. He was due here in two minutes.

"Hey," I said tapping the canister that fuelled the ice-water hose. "Can you give me a hand here? The pressure's a bit low, and we don't want your friend to miss his dose of cold water."

"No, we wouldn't want that," they both agreed, doing the odd little laugh of people who feel they should find something funny but don't. I asked if they wouldn't mind changing the cylinder for me while I ran a safety check on the mud jump. In reality, they were becoming unwitting accessories to murder, because the hose was no longer quite what it appeared to be.

"Lovely," I said. "I'll just go and check the jump. Health and safety. You know." I rolled my eyes. They rolled their eyes.

While Brian and Suze busied themselves with the cylinder, I ran over to the vault. It was, in reality, a fairly simple wooden gymnasium horse. But I'd used it to alter the course slightly. People were supposed to round the corner into the copse, be doused with the ice hose, dodge under the mild electric fence, and then onto the vaulting horse, trying to jump from it to the rope swing over a mud pit and down.

I'd simply moved the vaulting horse, concealing the mud pit. There were so many of these on the course that no-one would notice this one missing.

I checked the supporters, in case they were looking. They weren't, so I pushed the horse quickly back into its proper position, calling out to the supporters "Fresh mud!" They looked up just as I finished. "All good!" I said.

"Looks great from here!" they enthused.

Thumbs up all round.

Fast Eddy approached at a ragged stagger. He already looked a mess.

"Give him hell," I said to Brian and Suze.

"Woo hooo!" Brian and Suze called out to him, and turned the hose on him. The pressure was a little higher than he was expecting. He looked dazed. He probably also wasn't expecting the fast-setting concrete. Well, I'm lying. It was mostly a liquid called QuickSet I'd got from a hardware store. Like gravy granules, it would turn a soup into a stew in seconds and make the mud pit very hard to get out of.

Eddy staggered under the high pressure, falling against the electric fence rather than crawling under it. Brian and Suze howled with laughter, and, bless him, Fast Eddy tried to laugh back, his face gurning with the strain. It wasn't that bad—the voltage was reasonably low. Perhaps a little higher than on all the other fences on the course, but not too bad.

Leg spasming slightly, Eddy dragged himself up onto the vaulting horse. The QuickSet was already making his clothes stiffer than a teenage boy's pyjamas. The extra weight was dragging him back, but he made it up onto the top of the horse, wobbling a bit. He fist pumped the air. "*King of the World!*" he roared.

Brian and Suze clapped. Brian wolf-whistled. He was the type.

Eddy sized up the rope and threw himself into the air. He caught it, which was brilliant. I'd concealed another electric cable inside it, with a rather stronger current running through it. He yelped and fell into the mud pit. And vanished.

I had (and believe me, this took time) dug the pit a bit deeper than it was supposed to be. A foot deeper.

FastEddy surfaced to the cheers of Brian and Suze. They were taking pictures. Bugger me, they were taking pictures.

"My legs!" screamed Fast Eddy.

"Oh, it's cramp, probably."

"No it's not," Eddy wailed. "They're not working! Help me!" His arms thrashed weakly about and his head slid under the surface.

Supporters: These Are Your Rules
DO NOT shout namby-pamby encouragement
(ie "You can do it, mate!")
DO shout "Try harder, you Muddy Funster"
or "Go ahead and drown, weakling"
NO HELPING. NEVER ANY HELPING.

A THICK, TREACLY bubble broke the surface.

Brian and Suze, unbelievably and wonderfully, asked me to take a picture of them next to the mud pit. They positioned themselves, and I took the shot when Eddy's head bobbed up again. I'd actually framed it quite nicely. They posted it immediately.

"Help me! For God's sake help me!" Eddy cried.

Brian and Suze looked at each other, concerned for a moment.

"Try harder..." Brian started a little self-consciously, but then found himself. "You Muddy Funster!"

"Go ahead and drown!" bellowed Suze, a little fiercely.

They both laughed, and checked their phones to see how many likes their selfie had.

Eddy gave a screeching howl and tried to lift an arm out of the mud. Brian and Suze faltered in their chanting, wondering if something was wrong.

"Something may be wrong," I suggested. Brian and Suze nodded, reassured that someone else had said it, and carried on chanting. Eddy, standing on tiptoe, just about kept his head up, but he was grunting with the effort. The muscles in his legs were failing. He was trying to say something, but mud was coming out of his mouth in big, thick gobbets.

"I'll go and get an official," I volunteered.

Brian and Suze looked quite pleased about this, and their chanting grew in volume, almost drowning out Eddy's frantic bellows. Brian and Suze weren't worried. They knew an official was on the way to assess the situation.

I ran off into the woods, stopping after ten yards. I paused only to reach up to the rope, and tug out the concealed cable. I then watched Brian and Suze.

Pleased that Officialdom was being informed and that Help was on its way, they were doing what any other concerned bystander would do. They were filming Fast Eddy's struggles and imminent rescue, mugging away at the camera with thumbs-up and everything, all the time keeping up the chants of "Try harder, you Muddy Funster" and "Go ahead and drown!"

From where I stood, I couldn't quite see his head go under for the last time, but that was alright. I'd see it later on YouTube.

GOD BLESS BRIAN and Suze. They'd uploaded the video without thinking what it was. The spectacle of a charity fun runner being chanted to his death by his friends was a massive hit. The *Daily Mail* screengrabbed and analysed almost every frame like it was the Zapruder footage, but then again, the *Daily Mail* do this with a video of a kitten sleeping.

No one noticed or even thought about me. Muddy Hell came in for a lot of flack for torturing their contestants to death. Jackie Aspley wrote a column titled 'Who are the sick people who sign up for these Nazi death camps?' which got charity fun runners and a fair few World War II historians enraged. Brian and Suze ('Are these the nastiest people in Britain?') were hounded, a little unfairly, I thought.

No one even thought about me. I think I was mentioned in an early report in *The Independent*, which claimed that the 'Death Pit' was only manned by 'an unpaid volunteer who was unable to find someone to bring help.' The Death Pit soon became 'A Plague Pit' after chemical analysis. The QuickSet did show up, but the press were more interested in the sexier ingredients I'd added. The night before the race I'd gone round all the mud pits adding pigswill and cow manure. The organisers of Muddy Hell claimed, quite rightly, to have no knowledge of this. No one believed them, and they soon found themselves fighting lawsuits from former contestants who weren't happy that they'd signed 'I don't care, Break Me' contracts.

Fast Eddy, annoyingly, emerged from all this as a martyr. That was the one thing I'd got wrong. Well, until someone spoke to Guy, to ask him what he thought about the person who'd raised nearly ten grand for his dead girlfriend. Bless Guy, he said, "Who? I've never heard of him." There was a small exposé of Eddy's financial shenanigans, but it wasn't very thorough. Everyone was a bit too transfixed at the sight of the man drowning slowly in mud.

I'd finally got something done. My first planned murder. I'd done good.

I'd watch that video, late at night, and think, *I did that.*

CHAPTER THREE
GIRLS, GUNS AND GAMES

I DIDN'T KILL Guy's next girlfriend. Actually, I rather liked her. I really liked her. The problem was it was Amber Dass, the girl I'd met in the bar the night I'd killed Danielle. I'd always hoped to bump into her again, and when I did, she was going out with Guy.

And she was great. So great I had no problems remembering her name this time. Her family were rich Malaysian lawyers. You'd imagine this would mean she was confidently petite, graceful in a gown that flowed in straight lines, with a smile as delicately balanced as the rest of her. Actually, Amber was a shambles. Confident, yes, but the Cinderella of Stoke Newington constantly looked as though she'd just got out of bed to sign for a delivery, and yet was still ridiculously hot. She was always wearing yesterday's t-shirt, which raised the question of when she ever got around to changing it. She drank like a fish, she sometimes dyed her hair, played in a band and was amazing at video games.

Guy was in love with her from about three seconds after he met her. "Can you believe this girl?" he hooted. "She's just such fun."

"Yeah," I said. I was pleased we were talking again (Amber's idea). I was pleased he'd moved on. I just... well, why did it have to be with her? All of a sudden, I was having no trouble remembering her name.

Amber made Guy so happy. Almost without trying. Which was a complete contrast to Saint Danielle, who had made him miserable by either clinging to him or belittling him. Danielle had constantly told Guy what he couldn't do, but Amber was delighted by what he could.

"He is an *amazing* cook," she told me one evening, which was a bit of a bombshell. She caught my glance before I could hide it. "Augh! I know what you're thinking. Malaysian girl, brilliant cook. But I'm not a walking takeaway. I can turn on the rice cooker and that's about it. At home we had people to do that. No, seriously. Staff."

That was Amber's issue. She just couldn't help reminding you about her family life back home. It sounded pressured. "Such a big house! So many Aunts! All of them with a different lecture about eligible young accountants or the even more eternal torments of pincers in hell. You should come out and visit. Dad loves to have the driver take visitors through the slums. Just to show what it's really like. I'm not sure what they think when a limo comes crawling through their shanty town with tourists taking pictures. But la! Anyway, all that family pressure's eased off now that my three lovely brothers have got married to rich girls. That's the line taken care of, and so I'm free to come to London and get a little job and stay out of the way." She rolled her eyes. She'd tried working for a proper global firm, hated it, and was now someone's PA. She just liked the irony ("I'm someone's staff!"). "It's handy for them, me being in London. It means I've always got a cousin somewhere in my flat. But that's okay. So long as they don't ask too many questions or finish off my scotch."

It was one of those evenings—Guy had got in from work shattered, found the energy from somewhere to cook dinner, and had then fallen asleep on the couch. So it was just Amber and me, talking over his snores. I liked it when this happened.

Yes, I can see what you're thinking. But she was so bloody cool. I couldn't help having a tiny crush on her. More than a tiny crush on her.

The thing was, not everyone loved Amber. Guy hadn't changed his Facebook relationship status, but she had started appearing in pictures. And madly, people started to object to this:

Didn't take you long to move on lol.
  2 hours · Like
NO RESPECT :(:(:(1 hour · Like
Mail order? 52 mins · Like
She's Not even cold. 46 mins · Like
Disappointed. 15 mins · Like
Looks foreign. 8 mins · Like

Little snide comments from friends of Danielle's who were Facebook friends with Guy, and seemingly unable to cope with the idea of him moving on, of being happy. He did what he did when Danielle was alive, and knuckled down to ignoring it all very hard, like a well-trained old hound who didn't put up a fuss when someone kicked it.

One evening it all got a bit much for him. I don't like drinks after work—I'd far rather rush home, have some food—but Guy had asked. He looked a mess, his hair all-over-the-place and his eyes baggy. "People are mental," he said, taking a drink of what was clearly not his first pint. "Mental. Right. I mean, I get that not everyone is going to be thrilled that I've got a new girlfriend. And I can see that, yeah, a few people might have a pop at me on my wall... but this is..." He pushed his hand through his hair, found a tangle, and tugged away at it repeatedly. "Right. So some people I don't even know have got an opinion about it all. That's fine. Wrong, but fine. That's what the web's for—having the wrong opinion. Say what they like behind my back. 'S fine. But they're yack yacking about Danielle turning in her grave, and me dancing on it and so on... and someone tags me in the post. So I log on, and I just have to read it. And every time that updates, I get more of it. And they've tagged Danielle as well. So it appears on her wall... I mean... why would you even do that?" He shrugged. "I've kept my privacy settings open, you know... after she... er... anyway. The point is, you know, I'm now having to lock my profile down. And I'm even getting flack for that. Mental. Just 'cause of Danielle."

"Sorry," I said. "I'm really sorry."

"Why?" he shrugged. "It's not as though you've done anything."

For a moment, I felt really guilty. I probably shouldn't have killed his girlfriend. Then again, I hadn't actually planned to. And he was waaay better off with Amber. For an insane moment, I nearly told him what I'd done. That I'd killed Danielle, and you know, also the idiot fundraiser. But that was all. Just the two. And they'd made his life much better.

We sat there, looking at each other across our drinks, utterly at peace in Lloyd's No1's. If there was ever a moment to tell your oldest friend you'd slaughtered his girlfriend and it had all worked out for the best, this was it. And I did. I very nearly told him.

But I didn't. I doubt he'd actually have thanked me. He should have done, but he wouldn't.

"Anyway," Guy said. "Just getting if off my chest. And telling you. In case you see anything. Just don't tell me. Okay? I'm really better off not knowing. Really."

I nodded. That's me told.

"Right then." Guy drained his pint. "Another?" He sauntered off to the bar. Well, sort of sauntered. Little bit of a drunken lurch. But he seemed more his normal self. And at least we'd had the worst of it.

We were wrong.

AMBER POINTED AT the screen.

"I can't ignore that, can I?" For once, she looked helpless. Utterly so. I mean, she must have been, to ask me for help.

"What do you want me to do about it?" I asked.

She glanced up then, sharply. "Nothing," she said quickly. "I mean, there's nothing you *can* do, Dave. There's nothing anyone can do. And anyway..."

I finished the sentence for her. "...it's not like people like me ever solve anything."

"No." Amber was quiet, not looking at me. "That's not what I meant at all."

EVERY TIME SHE logged into a multiplayer game, it happened. A team assembled: 'TEAM DIE PAKI WHORE.' And they blasted

Amber's character to pieces. And as she went down they shouted at her. The kind of stupid threats we used to do in improv sessions at drama school ("Now then, guys, imagine you're football hooligans on your way home from a match, yes?"). Only these people were shouting these threats without any sense of middle-class guilt or any hang-ups. They just wanted Amber Dass dead.

I WAS GENUINELY angry. My instinct was to find these people, go round to their homes and...

I went home and slept on it. In the morning, hungover and reeling from the smell as I doled food out for the cat, I slowly realised that my first instinct was the right one.

Sticks and stones may break my bones, but words can never hurt me.

I'd always thought that was wrong and stupid. Time to prove it.

I TRIED TALKING about it with Duster on MySpace:

> DUSTER: Leave it.
> ME: But... this is wrong. It's unprovoked violence against women.
> DUSTER: Woah!
> ME: Surely that's wrong.
> DUSTER: Says the man who bumped off a woman for annoying him in a bar.
> ME: That was... different. Wasn't it?
> DUSTER: Wasn't that the tiniest bit sexist?
> ME: Then, surely, if I go after some men, that'll even up the score?
> *DUSTER has left the conversation.*

FIRST OFF, I thought about taking revenge on everyone who'd had a go at Amber. But that was an idiotic plan. The first thing they'd look at is what everyone had in common.

So I did a little bit of research. And hooray, these people did this kind of thing a lot. There wasn't a shortage of this kind of stuff. On Twitter, on Facebook, on Xbox. Often with a background of a football team's colours. Basically, it seemed as though, if you were a woman daring to use any form of social media, it was inevitable that, at some point, you would be called a slut, a bitch, or a whore.

Rape also became boring. The abuse was really dull. I could compose it for you like it was a choose-you-own-adventure game or scrabble or bingo:

> Hey [Bitch/Slut/Whore], [STFU/get back in the kitchen/ fuck off back to Candy Crush/die] before I [rape/kill/rape and then kill/fuck you up/bomb u] you [stupid/fat/ugly/ cunty/bitch] [whore/slut/bitch/cunt]. [Get a boyfriend/Play Farmville/Seriously, die].

Given this matrix, it was possible to allocate scores. Maximum points went to 'cunty cunty bitch cunt,' but really, there was rarely the opportunity to impose such a rigid structure on the sentences. It really all boiled down to:

> "Hey Woman. I don't like you. Cos. Signed, Man."

A really weird Venn diagram overlap emerged where sometimes these same people who liked games (especially the ones with strong female characters with big tits who also shot guns nicely) also loathed women who played the games, were on quite a lot of dating sites (with the same username, rookie move), and also used Twitter to express their terror at what it would be like when 'the Islams ruled Britain/America.' (Presumably meaning that they didn't care for what would happen when a severe form of Sharia Law was imposed which would severely curtail the rights of women to have jobs, vote, or have big tits, short skirts and wield guns. Kapow. #Irony.)

So, basically: I like girls, I hate women, I loathe foreigns.

*　　*　　*

WHAT WAS SO curious about the expression of all this was that, when challenged upon it, the reaction was, essentially, to talk about the internet as a boys' club. When asked why women were abused when playing games, one commentator genuinely told a news site: "It's like going to a strip club as a female and getting upset that the chicks are all naked. This is just guys being stupid guys." He was referring to a specific incident. A group of gamers were playing a game on a streamed TV show sponsored by Sodobus. The host (a man, obvs) constantly belittled the only female player, and then instructed everyone to sniff her. He also physically sniffed her. She'd been playing well up to that point, but shaken, her game play deteriorated. As the other players rounded on her, the host shouted "Rape her! Rape that bitch!" In public. In front of a live audience. When asked about it afterwards, he'd shrugged it off. "Sexual harassment is part of the culture."

In other words, and I'm really sorry to be so boring about this: games are for boys, and girls should run off back to the kitchen if they don't like them. Which was odd, because nowadays a lot of gamers are female. They're not doing it to pretend to be blokey, or to learn how to run a farm. They're doing it because they like them.

Which a lot of men seemed to find baffling and unfair. Things were so much easier when the ladies weren't around. Like with GamerGate, which may have been about ethics in games journalism, or it may have been about female games writers getting death threats which they then took way too seriously. Which raises the question, how seriously should you take a death threat?

Hmm. Food for thought.

YEAH. ALL THE internet proves is that we find it terribly hard being nice to each other and it isn't helped by people who love wilfully misinterpreting what people say to prove they're racist, fascist, sexist or just plain nasty. Treading a safe path through the minefield of Twitter was all so complicated that killing people seemed relatively easy by comparison.

So, I decided I was just going to stick with straight men who hated straight women as my next target, as an excuse for taking revenge on the people who didn't much like Amber.

I TRIED TO pick just five tweets to take revenge on. And couldn't. In the end I built a random sampler (in a spreadsheet, get me; next I'd be doing PowerPoint decks), and from that was able to construct five generic tweets.

My guiding principle in all this was pleasingly Old Testament. Do As You Would Be Done By.

Tweet One:

Stupid bitch, I'll kill your dog.

"Goodbye, Fido," I said, looking into its soft wet eyes.

Tweet Two:

YOURE HOUSE IS GOING TO BOMBED AT 8.14pm TONITE.

Boom! Went a not-terribly nice upstairs flat in Reading.

Tweet Three:

SUTPID BITCH ILL RAPE U WITH A BROKEN BOTTLE.

Red or white? I think, on balance, red.

Actually, I'll stop there. Because this wasn't me. I'm sorry to disappoint you, but I couldn't do it. Not like this. I'd combed through several thousand tweets. So much anger and hatred; they surely deserved a lesson. But you know what? No. It was actually pretty difficult. And it wasn't as simple as I'd just made out.

I'LL START AGAIN. Perhaps a bit more truthfully.

The easy bit was finding where they lived. We love to tell people everything. If your Twitter username is pretty much your name with a number on the end of it, if your profile says "Swindon and Proud of It" and you've posted a photo of your car in your drive by the street sign then thank you. Breaking into your house is going to be a bit harder, but you're dealing with a failed actor who has been in a lot of *Crimewatch* reconstructions.

The bomb was the easy one. It's easy to blow up a house. I'd even checked to make sure the guy was out, and luckily picked a time when downstairs were too. I felt sorry for them, but I'd done what I could. I hadn't actually built a proper bomb—I'd simply jiggered around with the gas hob.

I'd had a quick look round the flat while I did it. It was kind of similar to the others I'd looked at. This belonged to @HAND_SOLO84. His name was Derek. Everything about the flat said Derek. There was a squishy black leather sofa too large for the living room. Behind it was a bookcase containing 5 books and a lot of DVDs. The only neatness in the entire flat was in the ordering of the DVDs, done perfectly alphabetically, by box set, by season, and by slightly disappointing spin-off movie. The bathroom contained a lot of man wash and shed pubic hair. The bedroom was a tableaux of t-shirts steadily crawling from the carpet into a double bed that smelt of digestives.

And the kitchen... well, blowing it up was the kindest thing to happen to it.

There were a few photos of Derek in Ikea frames in the hall. He was wearing XL black t-shirts. His skin was bad. His hair needed a wash. There was one of him on a beach with girls—slim, happy girls. They were standing around him smiling and he was holding up his gut. He was grinning about his belly, making a laugh out of it, but that grin never got above his lips. And yet he'd printed out the picture and framed it. Just to prove that Derek could have a laugh at himself. Good for Derek.

I sauntered away from the house, pulling my brand new 'Yes I commit crime' hoodie up. The good thing about the area was that it had no CCTV.

It did, annoyingly, have a Neighbourhood Watch.

"Excuse me, can I help you?"

Really, no, my mind was on a kitchen currently filling with gas. I made to push past, tapping my headphones, but the man was insistent.

He was a little rat of a man. People who care so much about everyone else's business often have none of their own. He was sneering at me with a nasty look of triumph, as though he knew I was a bad 'un.

"I don't know you."

"Well, I don't know you either," I replied. I kept my voice flat. I didn't want to be recognised by it.

"Funny," he sneered. "What are you doing here?"

"Walking."

"Where?"

"From A to B."

"I see? Really?" There was a look of triumph. "Why?"

I did an elaborate mime of taking my headphones off and pausing my iPhone. "I am sorry," I said, "I was just pausing *The Archers*. Yes?"

He looked at me, reconsidering. No-one had ever committed a crime listening to *The Archers*. *The Archers* itself was crime enough.

"Look," I said, same flat vowels. "Are you lost? Would you like directions?"

It worked. He was wrong footed. "No," he snapped nastily.

And all the while the gas hob hissed.

"I see," I said. "It's just you stopped me and I thought..."

"No," he replied, "I wanted to know what you were doing."

"Getting to my bus."

"Which number is that?"

"None of your business," I replied, not being a great expert on the buses of Reading.

"I'll call the police!" he yelled. "We've enough of your sort around here."

"Foreigners?" I asked, putting on a slight accent.

"Yes!" he glowed with triumph. "We don't want you lot around here."

"Because...?"

"Of crime. Everyone knows that it's the foreigners who..."

"Good night," I said and walked away. He stood there, yelling "Stop, thief!" at me. I kept on sauntering casually away. He was the sort of person who, a few hundred years ago, would happily burn old women on the village green. As it was, he just had to settle for terrorising the people of his cul-de-sac.

It was an enormous satisfaction to me when I later saw him yelling on the news. He lived in the flat downstairs from Derek. The whole building was already in flames by the time my bus passed it. It was the No. 13 back to the station, since you ask.

KILLING THE DOG was more problematic. I've never liked dogs. Just, you know, can't see the point of them. They say extroverts like dogs, which is a bit like saying yappy people like yappy things.

There's no profound science lurking in this.

Anyway, I tracked down the guy who'd threatened to kill Amber's dog. She didn't own a dog, but he did. Lots of pictures of it on his timeline. The flat was nearly identical to Derek's. These men really were identical—nasty sofa, nasty bed linen, horrifying kitchen, the 'Keep Calm And Carry On' poster, the hard drive soaked in porn. The differences were minor—whether they had *Star Trek* on DVD or Blu-ray, whether original series or *Deep Space Nine*. Which *Alien* boxset they owned.

The only real difference was that this flat smelled of dog. The poor thing was clearly desperate for a walk. It looked at me eagerly. It's always baffled me that nasty people can own nice pets. You'd assume the pets could tell, but, rather like Tory wivess, they're capable of being very loyal to the most horrific people.

The dog had growled suspiciously at me when I'd first come in, but had then settled down in a wary 'shall I eat you or will we play a game?' routine.

"Sorry, Fido," I said. "I've actually come to call on you because your owner is an asshat."

The dog just carried on looking at me wetly as I pulled out the knife.

I looked at the knife. The dog looked at the knife. Shiny.

It knew I wouldn't do it. I just couldn't. The poor thing was so utterly innocent and just seemed bored. Plan 1 was to knife it. Plan 2 was to feed it some poisoned kidneys.

I tipped some blood from the bag of kidneys onto the dirty cream carpet, and then took the dog for a walk.

We reached a park, and I patted the dog fondly. "Right then, go find someone better," I said. It looked at me with complete trust. I threw it a stick and it bounded off to fetch it. I was gone before it got back.

I figured it would maybe find its way home, or find a good owner. I'd leave it at that.

THE BEER BOTTLE was the worst thing. As in, genuinely, everyone involved in this is coming out badly. It went horribly wrong.

Breaking into Antony Gillingham's house was easy enough. The door was really well oiled, and he'd not bothered locking the front door of his flat before going to bed. (A surprisingly large number of people do this. Because they're morons, or because they figure the statistical danger of a stranger wandering in with bad intentions and a beer bottle is quite small.)

Inside, I couldn't get over the absurd feeling that I was being watched.

Antony's bedroom was at least a bit nicer and tidier than the others. Well, initially. I'd picked a time when he was fast asleep, as this would make my life easier. He was spread across his duvet, snoring in the dim emerald glow of a paused game. He was wearing tracksuit bottoms and a stained football shirt. I was able to roll him over without him waking up.

I even strapped him down to the bed without too much trouble.

Then I tried waking him up. This took a while. He was a really heavy sleeper, his breaths the proper *Tom and Jerry* cartoon snores of the overweight. I can assure you right now I wasn't at all turned on. The whole thing was repellant.

I placed tape over his mouth, and then pinched his cheeks, the ones on his face. He stared up at me, at first lazily and then with a look of dawning horror. I'd never heard someone scream "What the fuck? Who the fuck are you?" through masking tape before, but I understood him perfectly.

"Good evening, Antony Gillingham," I said. I was going for Welsh this time. One great thing about drama school—I can do a Welsh accent pretty well. And fight with a sword. There's more call for the former than the latter. "Antony Gillingham, on the twenty-third of last month, at eleven fifty-eight pm, you tweeted the following, and I quote." I unfolded a small sheet of paper and declaimed, "SUTPID BITCH ILL RAPE U WITH A BROKEN BOTTLE." Agree?"

He shook his head. I nodded.

"I'm afraid you did. And don't say your account was hacked. Only sutpid people say that." I tutted. "Now then, Antony Gillingham, it wasn't a very nice thing to say, was it? To a lady? Or to anyone."

He just stared at me. I think he was dribbling a little.

"They say that feminism means the death of courtesy, Antony Gillingham. But I don't agree with that. Previously, men just held doors open for women. But now I think, we should hold doors open for everyone. Talking of which..."

I pulled down the back of his trackies, and then I showed him the bottle.

He screamed.

YOU KNOW AN earworm will start up in your head and will just loop and loop. I stood there holding a beer bottle, in a stale sweaty bedroom, its owner turkey-trussed, and a string quartet started up in my head. Not a great classical work, just some background noodling from a car advert or something. Over and over.

It wouldn't go away. Absurd. I turned the beer bottle around and around in my hand. I don't even like beer, but I'd had to buy a pack of six. The other five were sat in my fridge. I guess the safest thing would be to drink them, but I didn't really feel like it tonight. The label told me how the hops had been cultivated, fermented and then carefully bottled, all the flavour sealed in the thousand kilometres it had come from the brewery. The label advised me the correct temperature to store it and the slightly different temperature at which to drink it. This one wasn't chilled. It would never be drunk.

The string quartet yammered on in my head. They say the best way to get rid of an earworm is to sing something out loud, the first thing that comes to mind.

Absurdly, it was 'Reach,' by S Club 7. You know, "Reach for the stars..." Or was it 'sky'? Oh, yeah, 'sky,' because the next line rhymed with 'mountain high.' I sang it out loud, and then remembered the other person in the room.

Staring at me in utter terror. As I sang a song, skipping over the words I didn't remember. Oddly, he didn't find it absurd. He seemed completely terrified.

I leaned over him. "Antony Gillingham," I whispered, enjoying the power I had. "Do you fancy a beer?"

He screamed again and then wet the bed, which was gross.

I shook my head at him, tutting, every inch my third form geography teacher. "Sticks and stones, Antony Gillingham. They're bad. But words can come back to hurt you too. I have one bit of good news for you. I am not going to break the bottle. I'm not as bad as you are. But you're still going to learn your lesson."

I reached down, plunging the beer bottle into him.

"You—are—going—to—learn—to—be—nice."

Only, it didn't go in. Probably due to terror, Antony Gillingham was tighter than a miser's purse. And the screwtop was... catching.

I was clearly causing him a huge amount of pain, but getting nowhere.

"Let me do that," said a voice.

This time I screamed. The stupid, yelping fear anyone gives when they're startled.

She stepped forward from the shadows. She was wearing one of those painter's outfits with a built-in hood—like a serial killer's onesie, only painted black. It was drawn over her face. The only thing I could tell about her was her voice. Which was Scottish. And her figure under the overalls seemed... well, not waif-like. The overalls did nothing for her. I don't know. My mind was racing in all sorts of ways.

Who the hell was she?

What the fuck was she doing there?

Was there an innocent way to explain my actions?

Christ, I must look utterly absurd.

What the hell?

Climb every mountain high.

There's a line here.

And then your dreams will all come trooooo.

That's really not right. I'm going to have to listen to this on Spotify when I get home.

Was she a policewoman?

Wait, what the hell had she said?

"Who are you?" I asked.

She shrugged. "Better at this than you?" Again, that Scotch burr. Not the soft purr of Edinburgh, but something rougher and more practical. Aldi Scotch.

She flowed forward and took the bottle from my gloved hands. She pushed me aside. Not roughly, but not gently. With enough force to achieve what she wanted.

Which was exactly what she used on Antony Gillingham.

He made a lot of noise. Even through the duct tape.

I'D SPENT A lot of time thinking about this. A model once made a carefully-chance remark about her famous ex-boyfriend in an interview. "Yeah, he used to love it when I shoved a vodka bottle up him."

I kept thinking about this while watching Antony Gillingham struggle. Because, when the model said that, what had she meant? Was it one of those novelty bottles, shaped like a tower in St Peter's Square? Had she kept the screwcap on—I mean, surely that would chafe? But she couldn't have taken the screwcap off, because then there'd be some kind of terrible vacuum, wouldn't there? Or had she—oh, God—meant the thick end of the bottle? I mean, that was less problematic but also hideous.

A lot more thought had gone into the sodomising of Antony Gillingham than he'd put into his tweet.

I stood and watched the girl go to work on him, feeling absurdly left out, as when your mum takes over when you're trying to cook.

After the initial horror subsided, there remained awkward questions—like who the hell was she, and how much longer was this going to go on for? At what point did this just become absurd?

Antony Gillingham wasn't helping out, his screams alternating with a weird noise. A strange buzzing. I realised the duct tape had turned into a paper-comb-type instrument, buzzing as he twisted and somehow breathed.

I was hoping he'd just pass out and then I could ask her some questions. I never got to ask her those questions.

Instead, something terrible happened. A noise, far inside Antony Gillingham. And then a terrible spurting and a screeching that no tape could mask.

The woman swore. "Fuck, the bottle's broken." And then she punched me.

I ran then. I ran from that final Derek of a flat, out into the empty road, and then I threw up. And then I ran further into the night.

IT RAINED THAT night. I couldn't sleep, so it was some comfort to me. The cat, sensing I was still awake, jumped onto the bed, but I didn't stroke her. I didn't deserve it. Instead, I just lay there, curled up in a ball, trying not to think about Antony Gillingham, about that woman, about those terrible sounds.

Instead, I fretted about the vomit. I'd not had anything very interesting for my last meal. A value tin of spaghetti hoops, deposited on the pavement like a spew of worms. But there'd be DNA all over them, wouldn't there? Ludicrous way to be caught. I knew that, as a welcome home present, housebreakers used to take a dump on people's carpets until that turned out to be a great way of catching them. But would the stomach acid and bile break down the DNA? How many steps had I been from the house? Far enough away for it to be written off? Or would someone curious...

I heard the rain against the window, and smiled, reaching down to stroke the cat. The hoops would wash away, writhing in the gutter. Maybe.

I still felt bad about myself. Watching that mysterious black-clad figure, going about my work with cold efficiency. Ruthless enthusiasm. Skill. It kind of put me to shame, but also put the wind up me. An expression I am suddenly never using again. Who the hell was she?

At my gym there are two mirrors. One by the shower, one in the changing room. They're like good cop and bad cop. Somehow, the changing room mirror makes you look thin in the right places and bulky where it would help. But the bad cop mirror, as you pass it, catches everything in the wrong light, the bits of you that sag even though you didn't know you had them, the wrinkles on your elbows that have no reason to be there, the bulging belly that tells you that you need to cut back on something.

That woman was like the gym mirrors. She showed me what I should look like, but also how flabby and ugly I really was.

What the fuck was I doing? What had I become?

THEY SAY THAT a criminal returns to the scene of the crime. The police catch a fair number simply by watching the crowds, or even scanning through the vox-pop interviews with friends and neighbours on the news. Is there a figure who's always there, shiftily at the back of the crowd, or slightly too far forward, on every channel saying the victim was "an angel"? Too shifty, or too keen to speak.

So far, I'd managed not to return to the scene of the crime, but this time I couldn't resist it. I was helped by it being on several bus routes. So I could simply sit up the top of a double decker and cruise past. The police surely couldn't be pointing a camera at a bus full of people, who would rubberneck at a slow moped, let alone some crime scene tape.

The bus took a frustratingly long time, even for a bus. It bumped and banged through housing estates and past abandoned arcades and lonely scrubland parks. Finally it turned a corner.

Interesting.

There were police there, but hardly a huge number. Not vast amounts of fluttering blue tape. I almost felt disappointed. I thought about getting off the bus, trying to find out why. But sanity prevailed.

I FOUND OUT what had happened later, thanks to the internet.

Antony hadn't died. The bottle hadn't shattered inside him. Instead the screwtop had twisted off, and the bottle had been launched from his colon with the velocity of a rocket. I realised then that the Lady Ninja hadn't punched me. It had been the bottle. I'd spent a long time in the bathroom, staring at my forehead in the mirror. There was a small bruise. There were no—abrasions. That was the word they used on *CSI*. Was my skin crusted around the best-before-date along with bits of Antony? It didn't seem so.

Antony had been released by neighbours alerted by the screams. At first they'd not taken his story seriously, had assumed it was the elaborate sort of nonsense people make up when they trip out of the shower and fall on the vacuum cleaner. But they realised there was something worse here, from the sheer mess on the bed and the presence of someone else. Someone who'd tied him up.

Antony's description of this someone was bizarre. I've a slight build. And, if I was hoping for a better description of the mystery woman, I was sorely disappointed. Instead, conflated through panic, he claimed to have been attacked by one large man in black with the build of a bouncer. The only thing he'd got right was the Scotch accent.

He claimed complete ignorance, and, at first the police were baffled. But it didn't take them long to go through his Twitter account. And once they'd found the tweet, along with his following of several rather extreme political parties and a football club whose supporters were quite angry, a picture of Antony Gillingham emerged that was less than sympathetic. You could sense the mild distaste in the police reports, the slightly loaded pause after 'Clearly,' in 'Clearly, a horrible thing has happened to this man...'

Someone bright on BuzzFeed connected the various attacks. Or, rather, they noticed someone using a hashtag for it. #TrollTwatter.

So, that was me. As a kid, I'd always wondered what my superhero name would be. And there we go. TrollTwatter. With a hashtag in front of it. Because these days there's always a hashtag.

But the thing was, it wasn't me. Initially, it wasn't me because there was the mysterious woman. And then it really wasn't me, because #TrollTwatter became a craze. People were hunting down aggressive tweeters and lamping them. Suddenly, saying that a celebrity was so ugly they needed a baseball bat makeover wasn't a harmless bit of fun, but quite likely to find you in a bloody alley behind the Student Union. Some people even filmed the attacks.

I had tried to stamp out aggressive language, and instead I'd created a wave of violence. If I'd been worried that someone would trace it back to me, no one did.

AMBER WASN'T IMPRESSED at all the violence that she had no idea was being done in her name.

"Fucking idiots," she told me one night. "This is no way to solve things." And it wasn't. It was kind of inevitable that another of the people saying awful things to Amber was going to get attacked. And, naturally the victim posted a photo of her bruised face on Amber's wall sneering 'You happy now bitch?' The victim got a lot of sympathy. Amber got even more abuse.

I'd not really helped.

But then, it turned out, it wasn't my idea at all. Turned out that BuzzFeed found a student rugby player from Inverness who claimed to have invented TrollTwatting down the bar after his girlfriend got slagged off. He gave them an apologetic interview, saying it had all got out of hand and that it should stop now. The police interviewed him, as he matched Antony Gillingham's description of his attacker to a tee. They realised it wasn't him, and then they released him with a caution over the original assault after the victim said, "Fair does, I did deserve it." Both of them shook hands on *The One Show* and talked about the phenomenon and how it should stop. Which actually drove it to greater heights for a bit.

Someone got killed in Bali. I watched that news footage over and over again. It was a young girl who'd sent angry drunk tweets to her ex's new girlfriend. It was getting badly out of hand.

And then it all died down. Having claimed its scalp, the news speculated frantically on whether there would be more deaths, and then, realising that was going to be it, moved on, slightly disappointed, to talking about something else.

*   *   *

DURING THIS PERIOD, I kept logging onto MySpace. But there were no messages. No chats.

I started the morning after the attack on Gillingham had gone so wrong.

> ME: Was that you last night?
> ME: Who was that?
> ME: Do you know who was there last night?
> ME: Seriously, you've got to know what was going on?
> ME: Did they work for you?
> ME: Are you covering up for them?
> ME: Come on. Answer me.
> ME: Hello?
> ME: Hello?
> ME: Hello?
> ME: Give me an answer. What the fuck's going on?
> DUSTER: ... *is typing a response* ...
> DUSTER: ... *is typing a response* ...
> DUSTER: ... *is typing a response* ...
> *DUSTER has left the conversation.*

CHAPTER FOUR
KILLING HARRY PAPERBOY

So, WHO WAS I working for? The problem with working for a secret conspiracy is that it's very hard for them not to seem simultaneously terribly sinister and utter bullshit. Suddenly cast out by them into the utter darkness, I questioned whether there even was such a thing. Had I simply imagined them? Had I become so paranoid as a result of killing Danielle that I'd invented a secret underground bunker stuffed full of sinister cats who were ordering me to kill?

Well, look, it did seem more likely than that an esoteric order would pick an unemployed actor to become an assassin. Yet, there was the money. That secret bank account... unless (and I did check) it was just an old credit card I'd forgotten about, one with a really high limit. I was really suspicious about the money. When you're used to working for minimum wage, being suddenly handed a fat wodge of free money makes you suddenly reticent. I felt like, if I hadn't had to stand out in the rain for hours, then I hadn't really earned it. So I was surprisingly reluctant to spend it.

I'd printed screenshots of my chats on MySpace with 'Duster' at the time. Just to prove they existed. Then I realised that that seemed ludicrously incriminating. I parcelled them up in a lever arch file and buried them. There's an outdoor gym which the council had lavished funds on. No-one ever went there. Even the local drugs dealers seemed embarrassed by it, so I figured my box file would be safe in a flowerbed there. I decided I was going to get good about security. I still had access to the KillFund, so I figured I'd use it to hire some offsite storage space. Turned out, hiring a storage unit was harder than getting through airport security with fireworks taped to your t-shirt. The sheer amount of ID, the copious volumes of shifty evasion, the raised eyebrows when I asked if I could pay in cash... all guaranteed that I ran out into the street, expecting to be shot by the Met at any moment, and vowing to never go back.

Recycling bins proved to be a good temporary solution. Our area requires us to file our rubbish like we're competing in the OCD Olympics. Woe betide you if you put a can in with the glass. The bin would be left untouched. I picked an empty recycling bin on a nearby estate, and built a false top layer in which tetrapak mingled with wine bottles and plastic bags. Underneath that was a box (from Ikea, since you ask) which contained a wiped notebook I'd decided was too hot to continue using and a discarded phone. I considered chucking both in the Thames, but I'd read a George Monbiot column where he'd complained that this practice was starting to poison the fish. I was unsure about whether or not he was joking, so tried to find a better solution. A couple of weeks went by, and the bin remained ignored. In the end, I got chatting to someone down the pub who had a shed for his motorbike. For the odd tenner he was happy to let me keep a box there.

Meanwhile, I got on with mulling over who the conspiracy were. They'd mastered the sinister silence, I'd give them that. Not a word. Not even incriminating documents sent through the post. Just silence. I wondered if they were the Government, the *Daily Mail,* or someone really bored at BuzzFeed. What were their motives? Clearly they didn't trust me—or else, why would they send a properly-trained, ruthless, faceless assassin to shadow me and step in when the going got tough? Or was it that they were helping me out—like a driving instructor, or on *Blue Peter* when they said "You might want to ask a grown-up to help you"? Was that it? Had they put someone in to help me if I got out of my depth, while I got used to killing?

Oddly, I was more-or-less fine with the actual killing. A few bad dreams, but nothing compared to those when I was in a low-budget horror film stumbling around the Brecon Beacons on a hot day wearing real offal as zombie make-up. I guess that's where being an actor helped. You've done so many awful and unlikely things in order to pay the rent that assassination just seems like a tough temping job. True, I'd chickened out of a few bits and bobs in the last assignment, but that was just me finding my limits. And luckily, as I said, Ninja.

My efforts to find out who the conspiracy were got me nowhere. I tried searching 'Duster' to see if the username had any links anywhere. I went to the public library and did a few Googles on worrying phrases like 'lethal secret internet conspiracy' but ended up watching an awful YouTube video in which a chain-smoking Canadian explained how Amnesty International and Greenpeace had formed a cabal who were behind most acts of terrorism. Seriously, guys, why can't you just accept that some people are just awful? I had, and I was doing something about it.

With no-one to check in with, life got back to normal, which felt strange. Evenings with Amber and Guy. Work. I toyed with doing a couple of freelance assignments off-the-grid, but firstly, when had I become the kind of person who said 'off-the-grid'? And secondly, I hadn't found anyone annoying enough online to want to harm. Especially when the whole #TrollTwatting thing had made me a bit cautious about the consequences of my actions.

So anyway, a couple of weeks passed. I didn't kill anyone. No-one tried to arrest me. I acquired some space in a shed and annoyed the local dustmen. And, one thing I did manage. Failing anything else, I gave the conspiracy a name—the Killuminati.

SUDDENLY, DUSTER'S SILENCE ended. Whoever was behind it—the government, a syndicate, or simply U2—had assigned me a target.

You all know who I mean when I say 'Harry Paperboy,' don't you? The aspic-faced teen singing sensation behind 'Hey Gurl,' 'Sweetheart Dreamdays,' 'Sundae Kisses' and other inanities you only ever hear coming out of mobile phones on buses.

Teenaged girls *loved* Harry. Like really, really loved him.

*   *   *

DUSTER HAD SENT me a Twitter profile for @PaperGurlRME. And the message, 'End her.'

OKAY, COUPLE OF problems. Firstly PaperGurlRME's name was Jeannette Turlingham III (which meant that there were two people before her who had thought that name was okay). And secondly, Jeannette was fourteen.

What could possibly make the Killumanti think that I would kill a fourteen-year-old?

THEN I READ her tweets:

To a famous actress who said she didn't fancy Harry Paperboy: 'ru a lesbain or ru 2 old? Die dyke.'

To a reviewer who didn't like Harry's latest single: 'shut ur mouth fag.'

To a gossip columnist talking about Harry's behaviour: 'bitch ur not harry's mother. Stfu.'

To a twenty-five-year-old dancer seen out with Harry: 'ur 101 back off he's 19.'

Again: 'ur 1 ugly cow.'

And: 'get the fuck away from my babe whorecow.'

And to a dad who hadn't enjoyed the concert his daughters had dragged him to: 'Sick peedo works at @DinksToys BOYCOT. #byebyejob.'

BASICALLY, JEANNETTE WAS like the sinister henchman to Harry Paperboy's dictator. Whenever someone criticised Harry, Jeannette would unleash the dogs of war. Specifically an army of several hundred thousand tweeters. Say @victim posted 'Harry sucks' and Jeannette's PaperGurlArmy would bombard the offending account with block capital hatred, death threats and abuse before declaring them Nazis who hate free speech. But that was just the start. They would spread out like a biblical plague, bombarding @victim's followers and the people who @victim followed with abuse. They would go further. They would find out who @victim worked for and deluge their official Twitter account. Basically, a single derogatory comment by someone could see them lose their friends and their job.

NICE WORK, JEANNETTE Turlingham III. But I wasn't going to kill you. You're still a child. I'm not going to start killing children. I did stupid horrid stuff when I was fourteen. I think everyone did. The problem is that when I was a teenager we did all the stupid stuff in comparative privacy. Without Facebook or Twitter, the worst we could do was blog about how our life sucked, or email some friends. We'd still write our poetry in notebooks (the old paper ones, I mean). The poetry would be about how lonely and isolated and messed up we felt. But now, the Jeannettes of this world got to be messed up and isolated and lonely in front of an audience of hundreds of thousands. And instead of just staring at a poster on a wall, they could track their idol's every move, shout directly at them for attention, and terrorise people on their behalf.

I'd like to imagine that, in a few years' time, Jeannette (now happily married and with a less crazy surname) would check back through Facebook and think, *Oh, God. I did that? Thank fuck I had that tattoo removed,* before hurrying off to do the school run.

It seemed as insane to assassinate Jeanette for her schoolgirl crush as it did to hunt me down and kill me for a poem I'd once written about Snow ('Hail, winter's shivery blanket...'). But, for the moment, Jeanette was a problem. And one I couldn't kill. Also, she lived in Arizona.

I WAS STILL getting used to having a KillFund. The idea seemed so utterly insane that I carried on going to work. Standing still in the rain waving at strangers became even more pointless. But it was also a cover. If I ever became a suspect, it would seem suspicious if I suddenly stopped doing my ludicrous job. So that was the reason I carried on chugging.

I did think about going out to Arizona to get to know Jeanette. But the logistics utterly defeated me. For a start, I would need to book a plane, which would mean using my passport. I could, I supposed, fake one, but the cost of doing this would pretty much have drained my KillFund. Just to go and not kill a teenager. I looked into it all, though. Obviously, I used the local library's internet access. I didn't want 'Buy a fake passport' and 'Death penalty for accidental child murder in Arizona' to show up in my Google cache. I also, it has to be said, spent a lot of time looking at pictures of teenage girls.

I didn't want that at home. Jeanette and her friends shared *everything* and didn't appear to have heard of Facebook privacy settings (while at the same time 'LEAVE ME ALONE' was one of their favourite sayings). I could look at Jeanette cleaning her teeth (she had braces), watch videos of her doing cheerleading, and see her singing along to Harry's songs in six-second chunks.

It was all weird. Weird as in, 'Why the hell would I want to experience any of this?'

Don't get me wrong. I'm not a paedophile. Looking at all those pictures of teenage girls proved it. Oh, crap, that sentence was all wrong. But why would you be a paedophile? Quite apart from it being inherently horrid, children are pretty unhygienic, you'd be bound to catch a cold. Also, children are appallingly selfish, so they'd be terrible lovers. I'm trying to see a single positive side to paedophilia, and I'm really drawing a complete blank.

Still, I had spent a lot of time looking at pictures of teenage girls. Thankfully using the computer at the library. A glance into its history revealed all of humanity's despair and that quite a lot of people can't spell 'porn.' Plus that someone had tried to find out how to make a bomb. That caused me to glance around the library nervously before I remembered that I'd actually killed people. So no moral high ground there.

MY FIRST GOAL was to make contact with Jeanette. I figured I would build up an identity for myself as a PaperGurl. So I set up a blog and posted lots and lots of reviews of everything he'd done. I carefully backdated the posts, and included lots of YouTube appearances on chat shows. It counted as handy research. I really began to feel I knew a lot about Harry Paperboy. I posted links to all the gossip sites, and joined in the mockery at the reporting. Of course it wasn't Harry, but someone *else* at that party, who spat at the child from the Make-A-Wish Foundation who wanted an autograph. He never urinated through the windows of parked cars. And he would never, ever get Mexican caterers fired for being Mexican. And all those rumours about a sex tape were just unfounded—although I would totally LOOOOVE to see it as I bet he looks awesome in it—LOL ;)

I really enjoyed putting together the blog and thought it was all fine. I was hoping it would get Jeanette's attention.

It did. But in the wrong way.

I suddenly woke up to find the blog flooded with comments. Screaming comments. Outraged comments. They were calling me a hater. I was puzzled—but, wading through the barrage, I realised that in one or two of my reviews, in an attempt to appear honest, I'd said I 'didn't much care for' a track. Just one track. On each album. I think that's fair enough.

'CALL YOUSELF A PAPERGURL???!? DIE' summed up most of the comments. But there were masses of them. And a similar flood to the Twitter feed I'd built for the blog.

In other news, that day Jeanette had tweeted Harry that 'Failed Math Test. FML. Send me smoochies.' No smoochies had been forthcoming, so maybe Jeanette had had a pretty bad day and was taking it out on me. Coincidentally, that same day, Harry had failed a meth test. But his PaperGurls were silent about that.

My blog project was basically a heap of smoking ruins. Jeanette was certainly thorough. Could I use the burning embers as an excuse to apologise to her and make-up? I doubted it. She seemed pretty final about these things, picking up and then discarding BFFs for minor differences of opinion, or for the heresy of preferring One Direction to Harry. Or claiming to have seen said sex tape ('YOU LIAR. SHOW ME OR IT'S NOT TRUE. OH GOD HARRY WOULD NEVER HARRY SO MANY FEELS').

So I came up with another plan. I 'reached out' to her pretending to be a PR from Harry's record label. I was pretty pleased with a lot of the phrases I used. Basically I said that I worked for the label, really appreciated all her support, and wondered if we could work together to come up with any campaigns she could promote. Innocuous. I didn't suggest she meet him, but I figured she would read it and be thrilled.

No such luck.

Jeanette's reply, which I won't transcribe, went on for a lot of screens. A rough translation would be:

> Dear Sir
> Thank you for your recent communication. Sadly, I must decline your kind offer. As you did not use the codeword set by Harry's management with me, I can only conclude that your offer is bogus and your intentions unfriendly. Furthermore, your IP address does not match the expected range for the offices of Harry's record company. In short, you sir, are a loser, a hater and a paedophile.
> Your humble servant,
> Ms. Jeanette Turlingham III
>
> PS: Die.

I glanced over the email, interested to see that she'd told me that she had an existing relationship of some kind with Harry's people. Also, she was smart. Good. I could work with smart.

I HASTILY DISCONNECTED my real self from any connection with the email address Jeanette had just replied to and threw away the notebook. Now I had a KillFund, I could afford to buy new ones. A touch sadly, I hung the meticulously crafted PR man's online identity out to dry and let it be savaged by Jeanette's pack of wolves. I watched as the various firms my fictitious PR agent had claimed to work for all winked out one by one, their servers taken down by Jeanette's legions, their social media bombarded by messages. Even the servers of a charity subsidiary of Sodobus.

Dragged puzzled and blinking into the spotlight, each company hastily denied ever having employed me. The question of who I was, and what exactly I had done to upset Harry Paperboy's fans, puzzled the internet for a few moments. There was even a *Slate* article.

I TOOK A quick step to the side. I'd been going after Harry's fans. What if I went for Harry himself?

ACTUALLY, IT TURNED out to be really easy. What you have to remember is that I wasn't up against a rabid army of hyper-smart fans. I was up against a canny (yet fundamentally stupid) popstar. Also, I had quite a bit of cash on me. And he was coming to England soon.

JEANETTE'S PAPERGURL ARMY helped me find out which hotel he was staying at. As soon as the news was announced they'd worked it out 'Oh, it'll be the Waverley again, I bet!!!', 'See you outside the Wave posing with George the Doorman yeah??? <3 George!!!'

How to get to him? Annoyingly, it would have been so easy if Harry had been gay. Book a room, log on to Grindr, and wait. Until about 2am, probably, for a profile to match up with. Right age and height but no picture. And then, bingo.

But no. He wasn't gay and neither was I. So.

The next vice was easier. Drugs are great. Thanks to Harry's range of DUIs, I even knew what drugs he was partial to. I could use the KillFund to get some and then... then what? I couldn't stand outside his hotel with a placard advertising free drugs for Harry. Nor could I establish myself as a top drugs dealer. Anyway, he wouldn't come to me. He'd send a minion. He wasn't that stupid, otherwise some tabloid would have snapped him doing coke off the back of his iPhone already.

No. I messaged Nuala, one of my fellow actor/chuggers:

> Do you, by any chance,
> know any drugs dealers?

WTF?

Just, you remember that show you were in, in that
theatre opposite the Waverley?

The musical about Jane Eyre?

Christ yes. Why?

Who dealt the drugs? It's just, I've a friend who's
working there and...

This friend wouldn't be a chugger
would they?

NOT ME. NOT ME. But yes. A chugger with a habit.
He's loaded. He really is just chugging cos he likes
charity.

And coke?

Organic, responsibly-sourced coke with an amusing
slogan on the wrap.

I'll put him in touch with Jaramy.

DRUGS DEALERS AREN'T fun people. Nor do all of them go around
with scary dogs and the sharper bits of their kitchen. The ones
I've met are about as far away from those people in those films
about Troubled Estates as you can get. But there's one thing
they've all got in common—they really hate people. The only
guys I know who hate people more are waiters.

Jaramy was a waiter *and* a drugs dealer. A tiny, neat Frenchman,
he kept on the waitering (at a really posh restaurant) in order to
put him in touch with clients. He was forever being beckoned
over quietly, and softly being asked if he knew anyone. And
he so often did. He would even, smilingly, offer to take care of
the deal itself as "drugs dealers are all so terrible, aren't they,
monsieur?"

Models, Russian businessmen, and bankers—all of them
found themselves coming to Jaramy's restaurant for the spendy
wine and the quite excellent drugs.

I got a couple of shifts at the restaurant washing dishes. It's
a great way to watch people, but it ruins your hands. I saw
Jaramy at work. He was actually a great waiter and a brilliant
drugs dealer. I joined him for a cigarette break or two outside.
And, once we had bonded, I brought up the subject.

"No," he shut it down immediately. "I never deal to staff here. And never on the premises."

"That's fine," I reassured him. "It's more that I would like you to give someone some drugs."

"What?"

"I'm a reporter," I told him. He groaned. "And I'd like you to give a celebrity some drugs. There's nothing wrong with the stuff. They've just got a tracer in them—a marker which means we can find him with the drugs inside him. Just tipping us off to his location. He'll never know you were involved."

"No, thanks," said Jaramy. "I don't like my clients, but I do like having them. I'm respectable."

"I'm a reporter," I repeated and handed him over a wodge of photos I'd taken, showing him handing over drugs to a variety of interesting names.

"Oh," sighed Jaramy appreciatively. "Good blackmail."

"I thought so."

IN THE END it didn't cost that much money. I had the pictures. I also told him who the victim was and he laughed. "I hate that little shit," he sighed. "He's a very rude customer."

Rude to a drug dealer?

"No, rude to waiters. He was once smoking in the restaurant, and my friend Paula asked him not to. He smiled, apologised ever so nicely, and then stubbed the cigarette out on her hand."

I boggled.

Jaramy shrugged. "She got some money out of it. No one saw because he always dines in those clam-shell booths. That's kind of why they're there."

He was disappointed when I gave him the drugs. "Where the hell did you get these from?" he asked. Brixton Market actually, behind a vegan falafel stall. "These are awful. Seriously, man, I have my pride to consider." This was a worry—there were ingredients in these drugs which were important, I started to explain. I had done my research carefully and...

Jaramy sighed. "Listen, don't give me any of that genetic marker bullshit. You've put laxatives in here. I can tell. It's fine and fairly normal. But the drugs you've cut them with are pretty pound shop."

Trust me, when a Frenchman says 'pretty pound shop' it's kind of sexy.

"Tell me what you're up to."

I started to explain what I was doing, but I chose the wrong words. "I was looking on Google and—"

Jaramy did a lot of laughing then. "Seriously, what kind of shit have you been reading?"

I told him I had actually been reading about shit. Specifically, I had noted all of the prescription drugs that Harry was taking, as listed on his various charge sheets. Then looked up all the side-effects. And one of the three antidepressants reacted badly, prodigiously, with laxatives. I knew that drugs were frequently cut with laxatives, but I needed there to be a lot in order to cause the right reaction.

Jaramy seemed a bit more impressed by that. "Fine," he said, "I'll cut the drugs. The things I do for you, eh?"

He then went back to serving people food that they could take pictures of, and I went back to washing the leftovers off the plates.

JARAMY HELPED ME get a job at the hotel as a night cleaner. It was through the same service company who provided washers-up to Jaramy's restaurant, so it actually wasn't that hard, but he acted as though he was pulling a massive favour. The trick, of course, was to be on the list for at least a week before and after Harry was supplied with drugs. So that I didn't come under suspicion. Whenever anything like this happens, the casuals rota at a hotel was bound to scatter—they knew the police would be coming, and anyone with even a spent conviction, let alone a dodgy immigration status, would run for the hills, thus attracting plenty of police attention. But, if I just remained where I was, changing towels and wiping down tables, then all would be fine.

Not, of course, that there would be any police attention, because this was all going to work out fine. But, you know, just in case it all went wrong.

The great news was that, according to a budget I did on the back of an envelope, I was saving loads of money on this project. I could have flown to Arizona, at a cost of thousands. Instead, I was actually doing shifts at three different jobs—admittedly all of them minimum wage, but there we go. I was down £50 on drugs mixed with laxative, but Jaramy reckoned he could palm them off on someone ("I have a client I want to get rid of," he said with a shrug).

The week passed in the way that these things do. Night cleaning in a hotel, actually utterly exhausting. Most new jobs are tiring, but this is *advanced tidying* at a time when your body is screaming, 'Let me go to bed, please.' Plus, the kind of cleaning you get to do at night is grim. A lot of toilets, vomit in the corridors, cleaning the steps, scrubbing out the hotel restaurant, then, if there was spare time, trying to polish the brassware of the hotel doorstep. Plus there was a mountain of sheets back from the laundry that needed pressing, but no-one really seemed that bothered by all that.

I had to grab all the shifts they offered me, in case that was the night that Harry's people placed the call. I had to stay alert, which was proving tricky. When I'd finally slump home the cat would want to play with me, and I'd have to placate it for a bit before grabbing a couple of hours' sleep before staggering out to chug. This all felt bloody grim.

Finally, just as I was dealing with a dead rat in the basement, my disposable phone bleeped. 'Deal's done.' We were on.

I SPENT THE next few hours nervously trying to do everything casually. I think I looked like a disaster, but then again, no one was looking at me. I steered clear of CCTV as much as possible, just to practice. I'd spent most of the last week learning where the cameras were in the hotel, and had worked out ways through the building without showing up at all, and also ways of ducking in and out of vision so that, if someone were checking the logs, I'd be accounted for without arousing suspicion.

The only problem was that no one had yet summoned a cleaner. There was an outside chance that they'd just do a runner and leave the company to pick up the bill. But I was hoping the results would be so explosive that they'd need a cleaner immediately.

Jeez, how long can it take a pop star to take some drugs?

The call came at 2am. Actually, that made sense. He'd had the supplies laid in for when he got back from some club or other.

I hurried up to the floor he was on. There's a wing of the Waverley that is 'discreet.' It's a little L-shape on one floor. There's one way in, half-a-dozen rooms for entourage, a nice suite at the end and no cameras. I trundled through, making sure I was seen on a camera, and tapped at the suite door I'd been summoned to.

A groan answered, "Door's open." I walked into the suite. It was in darkness apart from a slit of light from under the bathroom door. The smell was fairly incredible. You could chew it. But you wouldn't want to.

When I was a child we'd had a puppy. It's why I hated dogs. It had started on the diarrhoea in the car back from the kennel. It had continued, spraying the kitchen in a fine cloacal mist until Dad banished it to the garden while he phoned the vet. The vet said the dog just needed to calm down. It lived in a shed for a fortnight. After which, Dad burned the shed rather than attempting to clean it.

This £3,000-a-night suite looked like that shed. An interesting thing I'd learned about hotel rooms is that they're like prison cells, branches of McDonald's and pub carpets. There's almost nothing you can do to them that can't be reasonably quickly hosed down. It's why they always look immaculate. The cleaners work hard, but their lives are made easier.

But this... this was something else. The sofa was leather. That I could clean. But the carpet—I made a valiant attempt at it, but someone had been running around. Probably howling as their insides escaped. At a guess, the carpet would need replacing. I got to work on the walls, listening to the moans of bewildered self-pity from the bathroom.

Once I'd made a decent attempt at the carpet, I tapped on the bathroom door. "Are you okay in there, sir?"

There was a long silence, and then a surprisingly deep voice said, "...yeah..."

"I can call a doctor."

"No... no doctors."

"Then do you want me to come in and try and help? Don't worry, sir, there's nothing I've not seen before."

"...no."

"Sure?"

I could hear a ragged breath. Then, "...actually..." and the door clicked open.

I opened the door and stared.

Somehow, I'd got this very wrong. Instead of the third most famous nineteen-year-old on the planet, I was staring at a giant black security guard, sat on a toilet, pants around his ankles, head in his hand, staring at me with the bleakest of misery.

He was also pointing a Taser at me.

"Be very careful, sunshine," he said, "I've had a really bad night."

THAT COULD HAVE got nasty quite quickly. He stood up, filling the room. He was weaving around a little, his gait not helped by the boxer shorts clinging to his shins.

"Hi," I said, sounding terrified. "Room service?"

"The hell you are," he said. He reached for the light switch. Disaster. He'd be able to recognise me. This would be a huge mistake. I tried to stop him. The Taser went off, hitting the lightswitch with a bang.

The guy fell backwards, hitting his head solidly on the tiles. He slid to the ground, snoring, his massive frame knocked out by an electric shock.

I BACKED OUT into the hall and suddenly realised I wasn't alone.

There was a small red glow coming from the living room. A lit cigarette.

"You've done a pretty good job in here," drawled a voice. "Though I don't think we can save the carpet."

I wish I could say I froze in fear or something clever like that. Instead I'd already let out a shriek that a six-year-old girl would tut at.

Sat on the freshly-cleaned sofa smoking a cigarette and wearing a bathrobe was Harry Paperboy.

"Ted's an idiot," he said, "He should know better than to have called a cleaner. I always take care of my mess."

That sounded sinister. But Harry shrugged. "Momma was a cleaner at my school. Taught me everything she knew. Life was kind of hell growing up, but there was something kind of reassuring about cleaning up their shit. Whatever they said, whatever they did, their shit still stank." He pointed to the chair opposite. "Hey, man, sit down. If you're not too filthy."

"I wouldn't mind washing my hands," I heard myself saying.

"Suit yourself," he drawled and carried on smoking. Insanely, in a room full of drugs and diahorrea, with an unconscious security guard in the bathroom, the thing that most appalled me was that he was smoking indoors. I washed my hands, running the tap, checking for any breaks in the skin. Any DNA.

Then I sat down opposite Harry Paperboy.

"So anyway," he said. "True fact: I'm a good cleaner. Mom taught me well. She would still be cleaning that school if I hadn't bought her a huge house to clean. Anyway, if I make a mess I clean it up myself. Less chance of any one with a camera—hey, have you got a phone on you?"

I shook my head and he smiled wider.

"Course you have, give it here." He patted me down and took my phone from me. I wondered if he'd be able to unlock it, see any messages or—oh. He stamped it underfoot and then handed it back to me along with a hundred-dollar bill. "Sorry. Can't take any chances. Everyone's got a camera, everywhere, and *maan* would I just like to get wasted not in a hotel room. Do you know, if I'm out in a club and I get so smashed I'm gonna puke, I either have to somehow get back to the fricking hotel, or throw up with three Teds stood outside the washroom. I meet a girl, and most of the time I can't stop thinking, *Will she take photos of this? Is that all the reason why she's doing it? For the hashtag?* Most of the time, you know, that's fine—she's hot so whatever, and I can't even jerk off without shutting the curtains and never to TV porn. In case someone at the hotel knows. So yeah, if there's a girl and she wants to whatever then sure. Just getting Ted to search her on the way in to the room and take her phone and stuff... it's kinda bad when you're in the moment. 'Hey, come back to my room, I'll fix you a drink and we can get nasty, but first Ted here's going to take your handbag and pat you down, oh, baby.'"

He lit another cigarette and, absurdly, I found myself liking him a little.

"Know what, I haven't banged a chick who doesn't know who I am for two years now. Which is—you know... My age, you're supposed to walk into a bar, find a girl, spend some time on it. You know, either you luck out, or you end up with her friend, or you go home to jerk alone. But the point is, you have to *try*. It's like these hotels. First few of them, Mom was like 'Don't get fat, kid, not with all that food.' But there's so much of it. It never stops. Not like in a proper restaurant, where you place your order and you wait for it. It's all there. In big steaming trays. Even room service in these joints—I send down, it comes up, I send down, more comes up. And none of it tastes of anything 'cause you've not had to wait for it. I've not been hungry for two whole years."

He smiled.

"Fuck me, I'm fucked up." He sighed. "Talking to a cleaner. I don't even know if you speak English. Do you?"

"Yes," I managed a reasonably thick Somewhere-Eastern-Europe accent. It suddenly struck me that he was very, very drunk.

"Yeah." He confirmed my supposition: "I'm steamed. My trainer is going to kill me tomorrow. Still, that's tomorrow. Now, can I fix you a drink?"

I demurred. He shook his head.

"Thing is, you know, we've bonded. Or rather, you and me, we're sharing a secret. You know, knowledge is power or somesuch. Basically, I know you. You're a good guy. You won't go to the papers or the cops or anything. No. But everyone I meet's a good guy. And they all go to the papers. So, here's what we're going to do," and he giggled. For a moment he was the seventeen-year-old he'd never got to be, drunkenly playing truth-or-dare and trying to French kiss through a girl's braces. In a weird parallel world, give it a few years, bump into each other at uni, and he and Jeanette Turlingham III would have made quite a good couple. Smart and cunning.

He flipped open an old-fashioned CD of one of his albums, pulling out a little bag of powder. He sprinkled two lines of it on top of the CD case.

"This, my man, is our bond. We do these drugs together. I've got something over you, you've got something over me. You can tell your friends you did drugs with Harry Paperboy. Some day. But not today. Or next week. Or anytime soon, really. Because I can end your job here."

I could have stood up then. Stood up and walked out and been on my way. Only suddenly there was, in his hands, a Taser.

"Ted always lets me have a spare," he grinned. It wasn't nice. I felt like an ant staring up at a boy with a kettle. "Come on, man. Have some. It's good shit."

It was good shit. I knew that. I'd had it manufactured to precisely that specification.

"Don't worry about Ted," he said. "Never could keep his hands off my stuff. And can't take it. Just can't. Tomorrow, he won't remember a fucking thing. Except that he's a loser. But you aren't, are you, Polski? You're a winner and you'll have a line and you'll love it." Then that grin. The grin of someone who hasn't been told 'no' in a very long time.

How fast would it work? How off my face would I be? And how long did I have before the side-effects kicked in? I tried mentally calculating this. Didn't have a clue.

"First you, then me," he laughed. "Last time this happened, poor guy caught me banging some fan. *Never* do the hardcore fans, by the way. Not that you'll ever need to, but my holy god, you've barely stuck it in them and it's all, 'Let's talk about us.' Us? Sheesh." He pulled back his teeth and made a weird smacking sound. "Come on, take the stuff."

I snorted the drugs. My head did not fall off.

Then Harry did a line. He leaned back. "Man," he beamed, like he was graciously acknowledging some applause at the O2. "I have done so much of this shit tonight."

That was when I knew I was in with a chance.

We sat there for a couple of minutes, nodding to each other like old friends smelling each other's farts. Then Harry's little baby face crumpled. "Oh, boy," he winced, "Gotta go use the bathroom."

I worried I'd hit him too hard on the head when he came out of the loo. I was starting to feel over-confident but also stupid-paranoid. Not the best conditions for getting away with a kidnapping. But it had, pretty much, worked like a charm. Harry Paperboy fitted perfectly in my cleaner's trolley, his body just a little childlike, swaddled in towels. I wheeled him down the corridor, and then, just to the right hand side of the lobby, away from the gaze of the camera, and down towards the service lift, the one that didn't have a camera in it. And then away we went, out into the night. Although, and this really started to nag at me, the thing was, I really needed the bathroom.

THE NINJA MET me in the basement.

"How did you know to find me here?" I asked her.

She just nodded her balaclava'd head. She didn't offer to help me drag Harry out of the van. She just watched.

"Are you checking up on me?"

She didn't answer.

"Then what?"

She considered her reply. "Well, I guess I'm here to make sure you don't chicken out."

TRANSCRIPT

Hey everyone, this is Harry.

So yeah. I have been kidnapped and strapped to a chair. I'm being held—*shiiiit. Fuck, man, fuck Jesus fuck.* Okay. I'll stick to the script. I promise. *Promise. Just don't do that again.*

I am being held here to teach all of you, my fans, a lesson.

My captor wants you to know that he actually rather likes me, the sick fuck *fuccccck! Man! Man! Please! Okay! Sorry.*

[some gasping, indistinct]

He likes me. He wants me to survive this. And with your help, we can do this.

He wants you to learn how to be nice. Okay. That's how we're going to get through this. He will hold me in this place for one hour. That's all. If, at the end of that hour, all goes as well as my captor hopes, I will be allowed to go free. It's that simple.

There's only one condition. For that one hour, my captor would like you to be nice. Okay. He's kidnapped me because he's noticed a lot of hatred among you. He says (and I don't believe it *fuck but seriously stop that shit*) that you're kind of mean. You love me, but it's a bit aggressive. Full on, you know? And he just wants you all to play nice for an hour. No shouting. No hate campaigns. No death threats. That's all he wants. Okay?

Thing is—as you may have gathered—wait, you put that in? You mean bastard—I'm tied to an electric chair. Every time you tweet something mean or nasty, I'll get a shock. Not a big one. But you know—it'll hurt. So let's not do that. For one hour, okay, play nice, yeah? Do it for me.

And now—oh, God—the power's going live. Okay. I love you, Mom.

I'D PLANNED THIS carefully. I'd really thought it through. I was hoping to fail. I'd worked through a few possibilities—I'd meticulously selected the hashtags I was going to use. Screams of rage, they'd fall by the wayside. But anything with his name in it was reasonably fair game. I'd run a few sample tests. I'd even anticipated any attempt to game this, by people wanting to electrocute Harry. I'd set up a Twitter account that followed just a few hundred accounts. Jeanette Turlingham's army. The resulting feed fed into the power to Harry's chair.

The Ninja helped me checked the wiring. It turned out she was really good at this kind of thing. Me, I was basically running it off YouTube tutorials. Oh, yes, you can learn how to build an electric chair on the internet. You might boggle at that, but, as Henry Jarman said, "All Knowledge Good."

We stood back and surveyed our handiwork. It would do.

I explained the plan to Harry. He stared at us in horror.

"My friend and I will be here," I said to him, absurdly trying to sound reassuring. "With the two of us, it'll be okay."

His eyes went wide at that. I think he didn't believe us. But I'd done the calculations carefully. I stepped to one side, and the Ninja nodded to me curtly. She stepped up to the controls.

"There's a big lever?" she said in that disbelieving Scots burr. "Of course. Idiot like you would put in a big lever."

She yanked it.

I figured it would be a bit choppy for the first few minutes, and then probably okay for the rest of the hour. Nervous, but okay. With a bit of luck and allowing for the different time zones we were operating in, I may even have picked a time when most of them would be asleep, or heading for bed.

It turns out, I had got Harry's fans wrong.

It took him ten seconds to die.

FUCK U. #FreeHarry.
NO HARRY NO. I'LL FUCK YOU UP #FreeHarry.
DIE FAG. #FreeHarry.

I WATCHED IT happen. I made it happen. But really, honestly, believe me, I didn't kill him. They did. I'd thought it through, I'd installed limiters, I'd done everything. But I'd underestimated the power of their hatred.

THE THING IS, the thing I'd hoped for was that this would teach everyone a lesson. And yes, there were a lot of long think pieces on news blogs that took that viewpoint. You know the kind of articles—the ones written by people who own Moleskine notebooks and like their articles spread over five pages?

The problem is, the tabloids didn't see it that way. They had footage of the planet's most famous teenager exploding. It was a good story, whatever way they went with it. They didn't, however, go the way of accusing his fans of killing him. Teenage girls make bad tabloid murderers. Instead they zeroed in on the 'sick psychopath' who tortured Harry to death. But I didn't do a thing; they did. The people who loved him the most.

You want to know about the girls themselves, don't you? They're the guilty ones in this, not me. But they didn't see themselves as guilty. They saw this as something that had been done to Harry, but not by them. For a long while, they saw it as a publicity stunt. Even when his body was found by the police, they didn't believe it. Then the conspiracy theories started, with the guilt landing anywhere but near them. The thing I had forgotten was that, for teenagers even more than adults, nothing is ever their fault. There are several stages of grieving. Well, the PaperGurl Army had anger and denial, then some more anger and denial. Then came the sense of loss. They had had something beautiful, and it had been taken away from them. So out came the floods of grieving. 'SO MUCH HURTS. SO MANY FEELS. CRYING SO MUCH I CAN'T EVEN.' Sad face sad face sad face sad face. And oh, God, the deviantART portraits. It was like the Pope's funeral in pastels.

Somewhere in the middle of all this wailing, the infighting began. As each scrambled to prove that they, and only they, were grieving *more* than anyone else, the counter-accusations began, that you weren't grieving enough, because you weren't a true fan. Which is when the hashtag #HarryKiller emerged. Jeanette invented it. She decided who it was, which of them amongst the group had killed Harry. Like the Witchfinder General, she unearthed and named and shamed and executed the fans. Some fought back, some committed suicide.

Now, this is where the press got confused. No-one actually committed suicide. They simply closed their accounts. But in fandom, this was called 'suicide.' And treated as such. '47 angels in heaven now. 47 lives lost because of Harry.' Or, as Jeanette put it '47 #HarryKillers executed.' She emerged as the Queen of Blood and Hellfire. The inquisition became a pogrom. It raged online, a rage that was becoming incoherent and unfollowable.

I STOOD BACK from all this. Did I feel guilty? No, not for a second. I had allowed a terrible thing to happen. That much was true. But I hadn't had my finger on the button. Jeanette had.

I ran analyses. Or tried to. I wanted to find out who had spread the most hatred, had caused the most shocks, had actually been most responsible for the death of Harry Paperboy. Because it certainly wasn't me.

The results were inconclusive. I really wanted it to be Jeanette, but I wasn't sure. A news site that specialised in piechart politics did very much the same thing, and they said it was definitely Jeanette. I still wasn't sure. But it didn't matter. A website had said so, and since it was a news website, it was definitely true. And so, the real #HarryKiller was revealed. And the angry mob turned on their killer queen.

I FELT REALLY bad. Sometimes, I wondered if I was the only person actually mourning Harry. And then I remembered his mother and his three sisters, and I felt bad. He was just a kid. But I wasn't responsible for his death. I don't kill children.

PERHAPS, OUT OF all of this, a lesson had been learned. Certainly, those nice people with their Moleskine notebooks wrote a lot of articles saying that it had. But no one could agree about what had been learned. And the PaperGurl Army simply swamped the comments page on each article angrily saying how wrong it was in block capitals. Which the sites themselves didn't mind as traffic went through the roof, so they commissioned even more think pieces on the subject and basked in the ad revenue.

In the end, the only thing that stopped it, seriously, was the announcement of new tour dates by One Direction. Suddenly, a lot of teenage girls took off their black armbands and started buying tickets. A month later, Harry Paperboy was all but forgotten. And if you're reading this and wondering who One Direction are, then that kind of proves my point.

CHAPTER FIVE
THE DEATH OF MR CUDDLEZ

"I DON'T SUPPOSE there's any chance I can get the rice cooker back?"

Jay put down his cup and wiped a finger round the froth before answering me. "I'm sorry?" he drawled. But then, Jay drawls everything, like he's voicing Mr Sleepy Sloth in a kids' cartoon. Which is ridiculous, because Jay is huge.

By which I do not mean fat, obese or stocky. But huge. Like the progeny of an American Footballer and an SUV. At first glance you'd assume Jay's wearing one of those novelty superhero fancy dress outfits. Then you realise—no, he really is built like that. And squeezed behind a tiny table at Costa, licking coco foam off his finger and trying to hide a broken heart.

He looked at me. He has blue-green eyes that don't blink much. I wish I had eyes like that. At university they meant he never went home alone. "Let me just check. I tell you I'm getting a divorce and you tell me you want your wedding present back?"

"You've only been married six months," I pointed out. "And now you're single, you're not going to be using a rice cooker. 'Cause carbs."

Jay shrugged sadly. It looked like a momentary indecision by the Waitrose meat counter. "Fair enough," he sighed. "You know far too much about gays. Are you sure you don't help out when we're busy?"

Jay's always wanted me to be gay. At uni this would involve him buying me shots and then throwing me on his Jedi bedspread. But it never really went anywhere. The handy thing about being a lightweight was that I could always run off to throw up when he started striding around his room in a pair of shorts trying to belch seductively.

But that was all long ago. A few months ago, Jay had got married to Vladimir, clearly The Love Of His Life. Jay was a corporate lawyer for Sodobus, Vlad was an imports manager. He was as tall as Jay, but broom-thin. You could just about imagine them taking up the right amount of space in a double bed. But I'd rather not, as it's always weird thinking about your friends' sex lives. I've made my peace with it. I imagine they had a wild fortnight and then settle down to cream teas and long country walks. (Out of interest, does anyone actually really like long country walks? I mean everyone says they do, but in practice they're an awful thing.)

Anyway, Jay had just told me that he and Vladimir were splitting up.

"Okay," I said, "We'll leave the rice cooker to one side for a bit. Why are you splitting up?"

Which was when Jay told me about Romeo.

Here's me & my teddy #ToplessSelfie.
#hungoverRomeoSelfie.
Any #BigSmoke friendz with a spare floor I can crash on next week? #Auditions.
Who wantz to buy me a holiday? I fancy New York!
Here's my new #tattoo design. Any1 want to pay for it?
#Poor Student.
Romeo is lonelio. Need cuddlez.
BRING ME HUGZ AND BACON.
Hey @JayMonstah, you guys look amazing!

ROMEO WAS, IT turned out, a drama student in Wolverhampton. A shuddering glance at his Twitter feed told you that he spent a lot of time on Twitter, posting topless photos of himself and his teddybear, and asking people to give him hugs, bacon, cuddles, work, money and attention.

"How do you know him?" I asked Jay.

Jay gave me another of his miserable mixed-grill shrugs. "I don't. Well, I didn't... but you see..."

IT HAD ALL started when he and Vladimir got back from one of their holidays. They'd posted a lot of pictures (I hate friends like that, but then, I never really go on holiday, so I guess I may as well see what a beach looks like). But Jay and Vladimir had filled Twitter with the two of them, on beaches, in treehouses, surfing, drinking cocktails. The two of them looked perfectly happy.

Barely had they climbed on the Heathrow Express home than they'd got the following comment from Romeo. 'Hey guys! Next time, hide me in yr luggagez! #RomeoNeedsAHoliday.'

This had been repeated a few times. Then Romeo had uploaded a couple of pictures where he'd photoshopped himself into their holiday photos. 'This is what I'd be like. I take up NO SPACE, REALLY!!!'

"DIDN'T YOU FIND that creepy?" I asked Jay.

He looked at me blankly for a moment. "Look, it's easy to say that kind of thing after the event. Hindsight's a great thing," he paused. "If you're a smug arsehole."

"Oh-kay, but still..."

"To be honest, it was a bit sweet. And silly. You know, naff. And the attention was kind of nice. When you get married... I mean, when you get gay married, you kind of feel as though the world stops looking at you. But Romeo'd be there. You know, noticing everything we did, and commenting, and popping up and being nice. And then, when he had an audition in London, we offered him the sofa."

"You offered?"

"Well, he sort of invited himself, but we agreed. And he came round with a bottle of wine and he was very polite and so earnest and..." Jay petered out awkwardly rubbing his hair. "I mean...

the thing is, Vlad and I didn't have an open relationship at all. Or anything like that, in any way. But, you know, he'd come round, he was so young and naïve and sweet and we'd drunk the wine and, while he excused himself to go to the bathroom—"

"He excused himself?"

"Yeah! As in stuck up his hand like he was five and asked for permission," Jay smiled, almost fondly. "Anyway, my point is, we decided to be all thrillingly modern and offer him a throup-on."

"Is that what I think it is?"

Jay nodded. "And it was lovely. I mean, you know, as I said, once you get married, you kind of think... well, it's lovely to be wanted by someone else."

WHAT FOLLOWED WAS, in hindsight, predictable, and reached its peak in a weekend away at Alton Towers. "The wildest rides were not the roller coasters," said Jay. "If you see what I mean. Huh, huh, huh." One weakness about Jay. On the rare occasions he made jokes, he underlined them in highlighter pen. As if that made them funnier. Huh, huh and huh—three barks from a bored and distant dog.

For a while it had been clearly brilliant. Both Jay and Vlad had sort-of known they were being used and paying for endless meals and rounds of drinks and little gifts, but it was all "sweet," insisted Jay. And yes, sometimes, he and Romeo would hook up when Vlad wasn't about, but that just made it feel furtive, and kind of even more fun. Until the inevitable time when Jay came home from a cancelled gym class to find Vlad and Romeo in bed.

Turns out, they'd both been carrying on with him behind each other's backs.

"ODD REALLY," SAID Jay. "I wonder what would have happened if I'd just shrugged and laughed"—huh, huh and indeed huh—"and climbed into bed with them. Instead... I don't know. I suddenly went all Enid Blyton. Is that right?" No. "I started shouting. And Vlad started shouting. I don't know what caused it all. But I felt—stop me if I'm being crazy—weirdly as though I was being wound up to it. And Romeo, he just sat there, while we fought and screamed about him. He looked... pleased."

The row had been furious. Furious in a neighbours-knocking-on-the-walls way. (This was an interesting thing to learn. In London, if people hear screaming next door, they do not call the police. They bang on the wall with a broom. Something that would, I'm sure, help me at some point).

> DUSTER: What's up? You've been quiet.
> ME: So. I may have a new target.

I COULD SENSE that this was an Assignment. Neither Jay nor Vlad were exactly heroes here, but they were definitely victims. But what had Romeo got out of this?

The great thing about social media is that it is all about *now*. Where are you now? What are you eating now? Who are you with now? People rarely travel back through their timelines unless they are hungover or getting a divorce. As much as we dedicate ourselves to recording the moment, we forget that we also annotating the past. And it's quite easy for a stranger to work through that.

Romeo was a gift. He had no sense of privacy. His Facebook account was wide open—he thought it wasn't, but his pictures were all public, and they told quite the story. His little face scrunched up on countless Megabus journeys off to see 'The Boyz.' The names of the boyz would change. I found Vlad and Jay quickly enough, but going back through was Peter and Juan, Stevie and Ryan, Bill and Ted, Bill and Ben, Simon and Garfunkel, oh, I'm making them up now, but you get the picture—a long list of couples. And it was easy enough to find out about what had happened to them. There was a litter of heartbreak and changed relationship statuses.

A typical pattern of Twitter would start with Romeo being:

> @victim1—hey, in townsies tonight! You around for a quick natter? #RomeoLonelio.
> @victim2—here's me having a brilliant time with @victim1.

Thanks for lending him. Your so lucky.
Megabus megaexcited seeing @victim1 and
@victim2 #cocktails.
Three tired fellas lolz.
HazTheSadz, back to real life #Wolverhampton. Thx @
victim1 @victim2.
Hey @victim1 @victim2 how dare you go on holiday without
me!?? :)
Comparing tanlines with @victim1 @victim2.
Duvet hogging with @victim1 @victim2.
Sorry @victim1, used all of yr moisturiser.
@victim2 said it wld be ok!!
@victim1 where are you? Out with @victim2 :(
#drinkies with @victim1 while @victim2 works to pay for
#drinkies.
Must get job in the big smoke so I can spend more time with
@victim2 @victim1.

And on it went. Fucksake, he was only twenty-three, and he'd gone through the coupled gays of London like nits through a primary school. Romeo had to be stopped.

I HAD TO build a honey trap. I had never done this before. Sketching it out idly, I got:

1. be gay
2. invent perfect boyfriend
3. laugh about our wonderful lives on Twitter
4. get Romeo's attention with some foreign travel and a whiff of money
5. and then...
6. something.
7. I mean, not kill him. Really, that's not the answer to everything.

First, where to get a boyfriend? I needed to do this quickly. Tricky. As far as I could tell, it took real gays weeks and sometimes months to do it, and they needed to have a lot of sex. I needed to get a boyfriend fast, and without the sex.

I stuck my toe in the water and joined a gay dating site, and targeted the profiles which said, 'I'm not looking for sex.' They sent me pictures of their genitals, so I figured I'd misunderstood something. Also, I'd been hasty here. The problem with getting a 'real' boyfriend is that they were real, therefore they'd become aware of Romeo, and so a little suspicious if he suddenly vanished. Especially when I vanished at about the same time. Not that I was definitely planning on killing him, but, you know, if it became absolutely necessary then I was setting myself up with an extra complication here. So.

I then thought about hiring a male escort. I figured it would be a relief for them, just to pop round for the odd drink and a chat and no actual sex. But they turned out to be horrifically expensive. And there was also the danger that they'd wonder why I was insisting on taking so many photographs of us together. Aside from the paper trail of bank details and transactions, if they ever actually met Romeo they'd fall foul of his divide-and-conquer routine—he'd be bound to try and see them without me and then it would either all come out, or I'd get a huge bill the next day for services repeatedly rendered.

So, I turned to the giant banks of online stock photographs trying to find happy gay couples, one of whom looked a little like me. The problem was, no-one looks like stock photo models. Once I'd spent a fortune on plastic surgery and special Hollywood teeth, I'd then have to explain why me and Geraldo spent our entire time high-fiving each other on beaches at sunset. Or, on the rare occasions that we had rows, we'd do it in our immaculately tidy kitchen and get someone to take photographs. Also, stock photo models only ever wear their jumpers tied round their neck, like they're advertising the 1980s or something. And I'd either have to buy the pictures or explain away all those watermarks.

With stock photos out, I was starting to feel a little desperate. And then, thank the gods, I stumbled across #TeamGeeks. A whole tribe of gays who spend all of their time saying, 'I am such a geek.' They take so many pictures of themselves, reading comic books, drinking posh coffee, walking someone else's Pug, all the while pulling 'Quizzical Face.' Quizzical Face is best described as half 'look at little me' and half 'I'm having a stroke.' So I suppose 'look at little me having a stroke.' That sounds smutty. I'll start again. If you want to try it for yourself, hold up a coffee mug as though you've never seen one before and then raise one eyebrow at an imaginary camera. There you go. That's 'look at little me having a coffee, don't mind if I do.' It works equally well with running marathons, hot air ballooning, open sandwiches, going on a rollercoaster or taking the Northern Line.

The fantastic thing about Quizzical Face is that everyone doing it looks a little bit alike.

The other great thing about #TeamGeek is that they all have beards. All I had to do was get a tufty beard. Pull Quizzical Face. Buy the cheapest web designer glasses Specsavers offered. And I could pretend to be one.

Oh, and buy a *Star Trek* uniform. The ultimate #TeamGeek achievement appeared to be getting a fairly identical boyfriend, dressing up in *Star Trek* uniforms and pulling quizzical faces together. Like you were a mirror image of yourself all grown up telling yourself that your lonely childhood was all okay now.

Brilliant. I could steal a whole wodge of photos, and no-one could tell. Even better, it's fairly easy to photoshop yourself in a *Star Trek* uniform and stick yourself into a picture. Or, if you're feeling lazy, just paste your head over someone else's in a *Star Trek* uniform. See also, onesies. Because yes, #TeamGeek wear a lot of onesies, still. It's like they've signed an unholy pact with Primark to keep the fashion going.

While I grew my beard, I assembled my fake identity. I would be Markus, because I'd always fancied that as a name. My boyfriend would be Trent. He would be an online interface designer. I would be a digital strategy manager. No one really knows what either of these jobs is, but it involves buying things from Apple geniuses and drinking a lot of coffee. We'd met on *Guardian Soulmates*—or in the column thing that they still run which is mostly about quite nice women in their early twenties meeting awful men who work in Shouting and have a thoroughly miserable time. (She: "I would quite like to meet him again, I think. Perhaps." He: "She didn't shout enough.") I mocked up a column for Markus and Trent. We'd met, had quite a 7 out of 10 time, but bonded over the bad service from the wine waiter, and revealed that we each thought the other was 'a nice kisser.' A snap of the article was my first Tweet as Markus. Trent was all 'omg you haven't posted that LOL' and things went from there. Over time Trent got a bit less like a cheerleader as I got the hang of the two of them.

Trent's online interface job sent him away a lot on work, as he had to fly to foreign countries to find clever ways of making big firms' websites load even more slowly. This left me with quite a lot of lonely nights in, pining for Trent while reading *X-Men* in a Mothra onesie.

But still, we went on a lot of holidays together (just the odd photo of us together, and then a lot of stolen instagrams of other peoples' meals). Trent and Markus soon emerged as quite happy, really. I liked their life. The good thing was that they were so typically #TeamGeek even their identikit apartment proved no problem to fake up. I found a pretty generic 'white walls and wooden floor boards' place for hire on Airbnb near Shoreditch. Some rich businessman from the UAE had bought it for his daughter, but she'd shacked up with a bicycle repairman in Hackney and did quite nicely from letting it out at a bargain rate.

Everything was all set. The trap was baited and oozing with honey. The difficulty was no bite so far. The waiting was the difficult bit. I'd look at Romeo's profile, waiting for him to notice us. But he didn't. I'd stand out in the rain, chugging slowly away at the day job, and wondering how Markus and Trent were getting on. How were the complicated navbar problems in Berlin going? How was Markus coping with the adserver implementation phased roll-out? It all seemed pretty important as I waved my clipboard around in the hail and tried to make passing strangers care.

I moved my chugging to near Old Street Roundabout, as if being ignored by the massed ranks of #TeamGeek would tell me more about them. It didn't, really. None of them wore their *Star Trek* uniforms to work, and all of them were too busy with their headphones to bother talking to me, let alone signing up for relieving kittens from floods or curing cancer of the drought.

I got home exhausted one day, soaked through to the skin and so miserable my teeth ached. My feet were beaten up in the way that only feet that have trudged around in JD Sports' cheapest trainers can feel. I felt broke and a failure. It was, I decided, time for Markus and Trent to go on holiday. Without touching the KillFund, I couldn't afford it; but they could.

I went back through my archive and found some pretty good photos of a couple of men with beards who'd been on a pilgrimage to the original *Star Wars* sets in the Tunisian desert, pulling faces next to mouldering fibre glass. I borrowed a few of those, stuck in some others from Tumblr of the same location, and did a pretty rough photoshop mock-up of myself in a Storm Trooper costume tagged 'Looking for the right droids #StarWars #Holiday.'

Then I spent two hours trying to work out if I could afford to go camping somewhere at the weekend without drowning and then went to bed.

When I woke up the next morning, I'd hit pay dirt. A message from Romeo: '@MarkyMarkuz @TrentSwish #Hot guyz SO JEALOUS! I needz a holiday!'

I felt my heart beat just a tiny bit quickly as I wrote a reply from Trent: 'Lol.' Trent played things safely. Markus favourited the reply. Because Markus favourited everything that Trent did.

And then another tweet from Romeo: 'Promise me next time you'll sneak me on the plane? I'm really small and good company!'

#TrapSprung

FROM THERE ON it was actually quite easy. Romeo mentioned that he was going to be in town for an audition next week and that he'd love to meet us for gin and tea. Trent apologised, explaining that he had to user test some White Space in Hamburg, but that Markus needed the company.

"THERE'S A BUS," he explained. "It didn't take long."

And here we were. Meeting in a bus station, standing by a pillar just out of reach of the CCTV, with me wearing Bland Hoodie

#3. I actually felt nervous, which was insane. Romeo was tiny. Practically hand luggage. For some reason he told me that he'd managed to squeeze himself into the overhead storage on a train recently. And, naturally, taken some really bad pictures of the event. Romeo documented his life in constant photographs, but never had anyone else to take them for him.

He brought his camera up. "I want to take a picture with you," he said, his voice a little bit of a whine.

"It's fine," I said firmly, taking the camera from him. "I'll do it." A picture of us together could be fatal. So I took the photo of him, casually thumbing the flash off. (Why do people leave the flash on? Are they all idiots?) He smiled and grinned, then grinned and smiled. He seemed to be hovering on the balls of his trainers.

"How was your journey?" I asked. It seemed like reasonable small talk.

He retched dramatically. "Having to read play texts. We're having to do really old stuff this term."

"Shakespeare?"

"No!" He looked cross. "I'm studying *English* Drama. No, this is Ayckbourn. Old shit like that."

"Ah," I said. It seemed the easiest thing. As the conversation was boring, he immediately forgot all about it.

"Where's Trent?" he asked excitedly. "Hamburg?"

"Yeah," I said.

"You must be lonely," he said.

And that was it.

I WAS OUT with Romeo one evening. I bumped into Amber and Guy. Guy seemed oblivious of my body language. "Long time no see" and all that.

Amber—well, she was different. She looked at me, an eyebrow raised, a little surprised. If she'd said anything, it would have been "So...?"

I didn't say anything really. I mumbled as the bar around us got hot.

"Your friends are nice," said Romeo.

＊　＊　＊

ANYWAY. IT WAS Tuesday morning and I was supposed to be killing Romeo today. But first I really wanted a lie-in. A clown car running over a one-man-band. That's the sound Romeo made moving around my flat.

At first the hangover didn't seem so bad. A paracetamol would have cleared it. If only I could be bothered to reach over and get one. But my head rattled away, and it annoyed me. Just a little. Not enough to wake up. Not enough to yell at him to shut the hell up. I drifted in and out of sleep. Yes, in a bit I'd wake up and kill him.

He came in, and tried to ask me something, but I pretended to be asleep. He pottered away and I slept on for a bit.

The door opened again and he came bounding in, leaping onto the bed with an excitement that nearly killed me right then. Then he kissed my forehead, and waved something under my nose.

"Darling," he said. "This time I have brought you bacon."

And he had. He'd managed to make me a bacon sandwich. Bless him.

It was the most lovely, heartwarming thing. So heartwarming I didn't even think of the mess he'd have made of the kitchen for a whole minute. I ate the sandwich and decided not to kill him today.

It was the hangover. That was the reason. Not the sandwich. I had no feelings for him one way or the other. I had decided he had to die. I'd made up my mind. It was important to get rid of him before I became attached to him, just another of his victims. Would I leave Trent for him? Probably. But maybe he'd already talked about it with Trent. That was how he worked. He collected couples. Romeo had no interest in men. As soon as I told him I was leaving Trent for him, it'd be over. I'd have lost my charm—wouldn't I? I guess I could talk it through with him, but I knew how he worked, and anyway, it was easier to kill him. Much easier.

Jeez, how long did it take paracetamol to work? Should I take some more? Or aspirin? I was a mess and I couldn't think straight and he was sitting there watching me eat my bacon sandwich like he was a puppy dog. Yeah. I wouldn't kill him today.

"I like this place," he said. "The kitchen at the other place is so empty. This is homelier. I love your cat."

Then I realised what was wrong. The reason I really couldn't kill him. This was my flat. My real flat. Not the fantasy flat that Markus shared with Trent. But my own home. I'd been an absolute idiot. I guessed I must have got completely hammered last night and got us a taxi here on autopilot. Because, obviously, that's what trained killers do. They get minicabs (which have cameras) from nightclubs (which have cameras) and casually blow up their carefully-constructed false identity.

Because I was an idiot.

"Yeah..." I said slowly. "Do you like it? The other place is Trent's."

He nodded, accepting it without question. "Two flats? You guys must have so much money."

Ah, yes. Money. That's what it always came back to. "You should rent the other place out—" A tiny, calculating pause. "I mean, you know, if I got a job in London, perhaps you could let it to me. Or... you know, I could stay here. After all, your cat must get lonely. She likes me." He beamed, happily. "It's a shame to have a place going to waste. That's all. How much is this place?" He smiled wider.

I ducked that one off. My aching head was considering his plan, completely forgetting for the moment that I did not, in fact, have two flats. The Shoreditch flat came from the KillFund, and I used almost every penny of my own money to rent this place. This was not good.

Romeo needed distracting, quickly. So I had some sex with him. I was actually getting quite used to it. Enjoying it, almost. I mean, you know, these things aren't easy to talk about. (Don't you hate it when your friends start talking about their sex lives? I do consider us friends.) But sex came in handy with Romeo. You know how you can distract a dog by throwing a stick? That, really. And he was very good at it. I guess he had to be. It's how he worked. It was so easy to forget during it that all the while, simple, stupid, loveable Romeo was calculating away. Working things to his best advantage with his natural dull cunning. I was using sex to distract him, he was using sex to make me think he liked me. Neither of us was having sex because we wanted to.

So it was kind of funny that we were having so much of it.

"I AM TOTALLY stealing your cat. She's gorgeous." Romeo was just wearing a towel and a pair of Primark socks. And my cat was all over him. For some reason I found this worrying. I know that, on a purely rational level, cats don't really like you, or have any affection for you. They're just cats. They see you as a source of food and warmth that has to be slightly protected. I was used to my cat being surly. It suited me.

When I first started chugging, I kind of hoped the cat would come along. We could be the Street Cat Bob of chuggers. But it didn't happen. The first morning I strapped on my tabard and headed meaningfully to the door, the cat narrowed its eyes and trotted off to the far corner under the bed reserved for imminent vet visits.

But here she was, a purring heap of fur wrapped around Romeo. I definitely couldn't kill him today. He was, after all, covered in cat hair. Would I really want to be the first killer to be tracked down by cat hair? No one wants that as a first on their LinkedIn profile.

"You're lucky," I said to him.

"How?"

"Oh, you just are," I said. I ruffled his hair, and Romeo purred. "Come on. Enjoy being alive. I'll take you out for second breakfast."

> Hey @TrentSwish wish you were comic-book shopping with me and markus. WANTS!!!
> Here's the BEST CAT EVER. AND ME!!!
> Behold my breakfast. It is MIGHTY.

FOR SOME REASON, the fiction was all getting a little complicated to maintain. Part of it was just the grinding certainty of work. I still had a job (of sorts). I still had to pound the streets being totally ignored by everyone so that my boss's boss's boss could buy another race car plus cure cancer. I was slogging away at the minimum wage and yet having to pretend very hard to Romeo that I was a successful digital strategy manager. I'd made the job title up, which hadn't seemed a problem when I'd thought of it, but it was getting more complicated as he started asking me casual questions about work. What the hell did I do all day? I didn't have a foggy clue.

Could I really justify dipping into the KillFund in order to keep taking him out for meals and buying him comic books? I mean, that was a bit against the spirit of the thing. Also, always having to pay cash for everything and make sure he took no pictures of me.

The easiest thing, I decided, was to not kill him. Just tell him some sort of truth and then get on with it. I mean, there was a way through this. Perhaps I could tell him that I'd invented Trent and a job to... to make him like me? Wait, that was utterly nuts.

But then, if I told him, and he was fine with it, what would that make him?

My boyfriend?

> DUSTER: How is the latest assignment going?
> ME: ... *is typing a response* ...

HE CAME UP on the Friday night so I could take him clubbing. He assured me it would be a cheap night out for both of us. Which was fine, but it never seemed to be his round and he always wanted expensive doubles and this was nice as it meant my urge to kill him was rising again. Each drink here cost more than an hour of chugging. That helped ease my conscience. But, of course, I couldn't kill him here. The whole club was soaked in CCTV. I amazed myself that I actually clocked these things now. Like a spy. Or someone really shifty.

That was bad. I was changing. But clearly not that much, in that I was out dancing with my victim. Rather than fitting his body parts into bin liners and popping them in the 'Food Waste' recycling bins.

Anyway, Romeo became suddenly excited. He started waving, and then hugged me. I worried he was about to ask me for a cocktail. Instead he pressed himself really close to me in a hug that reeked of Jean Paul Gaultier (I knew this 'cause he never went anywhere without it). "Thank you," he said. "I'm having such a wonderful time with you."

Then he took a picture of us together on his phone. In the picture he's smiling. And I'm looking startled. And there's someone behind us in the photo. Someone who has no reason to be there. Someone who... someone who is the reason for Romeo grabbing me.

But I don't know that yet.

"I love you," whispers Romeo.

"Oh," I say. I'm not sure which is more troubling—that he's just taken my photo or said that he loves me. Hmm.

Then he turns around, pantomiming surprise and grabs a complete stranger by the hand.

"Trent!" he says.

Standing there is my completely imaginary boyfriend.

I WANTED TO go home. This is pretty much my default setting when I'm out. Age is odd, really. In my twenties, you could stick me in a loud, crowded bar and I'd love it. You could make me queue for an hour in the rain outside a nightclub and then cram me into a corner with other people's elbows and I'd still dance happily away and tell you I'd had a brilliant time. Not anymore.

I was suddenly all too aware of myself. I was in a large concrete bunker in Vauxhall. Lights were going off all over the place without illuminating anyone's faces, there was noise everywhere and a smell of amyl nitrate, Lynx and drains.

I was suddenly all at sea. All these people. All these bloody people. And for some reason, some God-alone-knows-why reason, I was trying to tell them how to live their lives when I couldn't even look them in the eye or talk to them. Because I was lost and alone and broken and... Romeo was standing there on my left. Smiling.

Trent was standing opposite us. Not smiling.

And I wondered what the hell was going on.

Because Trent wasn't real. I'd made up Trent. But here he was. Or rather, I realised, the man whose pictures I had stolen to make Trent.

He was here, of course he was, because he was real and real people went out and got shitfaced on a Friday night. Small world, funny old world. But completely possible. The thing was, he was here. And he had no idea who I was, who Romeo was, or that his name was even Trent.

Ooh, nightmare.

Not-Trent is being held by Romeo's hand. Not-Trent looks perplexed. The window until someone says something else is closing. What to do? My first impulse was to brazen it out. "That's not Trent. It just looks like him." This seemed easy enough. But there was something else. Nagging away in my head. Something I needed to pay attention to, or I'd miss. Life doesn't have Sherlock-vision. The best you can hope for is a flash of inspiration on the night bus on the way home.

Instead, I stole a trick from my old team leader, Alison. She used it to terrorise new recruits. Especially ones who weren't that good at English.

"I beg your pardon?" I said. "Could you repeat that?"

It worked. Not-Trent leant forward, puzzled. "Sorry?"

"I didn't catch that," I repeated.

Not-Trent frowned. "I didn't say anything."

"Oh, fine," I replied, dismissively. About three seconds had passed. But it was enough.

Let me tell you what I'd learned. For a start, Not-Trent was off his face. You could tell from the way that he'd not disengaged his arm from Romeo's grab. And his eyes. And his gentle swaying. His frown was that of a smashed man trying to concentrate very hard on things which demanded his attention. He'd wear it later having a last piss before using it again to try and work out the number of the night bus he'd caught home a hundred times before.

I'd also learned something about Romeo. He'd kissed me in front of Not-Trent, thinking it was Trent. He'd wanted us to be seen by Trent. If he hadn't engineered the situation, he'd seen it arising and was making the most out of it. But I didn't have the first clue what he was making. So...

"This is Romeo," I said to Not-Trent.

Not-Trent, a bit dazed, said, "Yeah. Hi." Romeo said hello back, and then gave Not-Trent a hug. The hug lingered a bit. I wasn't surprised by this. Also, mercifully, neither was Not-Trent. He beamed a mooncalf beam. As far as he was concerned, a tiny randy gay had just come on to him in a club. Result.

"Not in Frankfurt, then?" I said, my voice low.

"What?" Not-Trent hadn't heard, but it was the right reply.

"Thought not! I can't talk to you now!" I said.

"Oh, Okay..." Not-Trent tried to care. But he was very out of it and Romeo was rubbing his arm.

"I'm going home. Stay if you want, Romeo," I said, and turned on my heel.

I'd built a rough binary logic-gate flowchart for this with two outcomes. Get me. Using some incoherent phrases, I'd hopefully left Not-Trent mildly baffled and given Romeo the impression we'd had a huge row and I was storming off. What happened next would be interesting.

If Romeo followed me, then it would be fine. I could tell him that Trent and I had split up. I could even use Romeo as a reason. He'd probably like that.

If Romeo didn't follow me, he'd clearly be going home with Trent. At some point he'd realise that Trent was Not-Trent. Maybe he'd assume it was a case of mistaken identity or something, but it didn't matter. I would never see him again.

Only... well, I knew it would be a relief, but I didn't really want him to go home with Trent.

I paused briefly in my storming out and then went.

LUCKILY IT TAKES a while to storm out of a nightclub. More of a slowly drifting cloud. Nightclubs really are just long queues with short breaks for dancing. I collected my coat with a rictus smile, and made my way up some stairs, past a crowd of people wanting to get in and a woman with a clipboard who may have been working for a cab firm or may just have been a passing woman with a clipboard. I nodded past and then was out into London, making my way up a pissy alley to the giant desolate roundabout of Vauxhall.

I could, I thought, get a bus and be home in an hour.

I really wasn't thinking straight. I got on and paid for my ticket with the *wrong* Oyster Card. I keep two, you see. The easiest way to get around London without being clocked is to dig your own tunnel. Walking is possibly the second least traceable. Even Taxis have cameras in them. My main Oyster Card, the one I use when I'm not saving the world, is linked to my bank account. It automatically tops itself up and has a lovely long list of all of my journeys similarly linked to my bank account.

My other Oyster Card does none of these things. I top it up with cash at a machine at a different tube station every time. It's just a series of anonymous journeys that builds up over a week or so, and then I throw it away and get another one, or ditch it with just enough credit for someone to pick it up and take it on some completely random journeys.

But I'd just used the wrong card. It was turning into a bit of a wrong night, really. It showed that I was off my guard. I'd not even bothered booking 'Markus and Trent's flat.' If Romeo had come back, he'd have come back to mine. I'd even got bacon in for breakfast.

I climbed the how-drunk-are-you stairs to the upper deck of the bus, pulling my hood up over my face and sitting away from the camera through habit. I needed to think. I felt a complete failure and I needed to think my way up from it. It had gone wrong. Somehow, like a pill you swallow the wrong-way round, I'd hunted down Romeo, I'd built a trap for him. And then I'd moved into it myself. And I didn't know what to do next.

In theory it was all fine. He was, even now, trotting off with Not-Trent to Not-Trent's real and amazing apartment and having real and amazing sex and that should, in theory, be fine. But, if that was the case, why did I feel so screwed up about it?

My phone bleeped. It was a text from Romeo.

You guys had a row, yeah?

Yeah

Want a hug? :(

I stared at the text. I knew that wherever he was, he'd see the '...' of consideration appear on his iPhone as I started typing my reply. I didn't know what to say. In the end I went for, 'Why?'

Because I'm downstairs on the bus. Hug.

ROMEO CAME TROTTING up the stairs, wearing his normal puppyish look. I felt genuinely relieved to see him. He hugged me, and for once his regional gay cologne was as comforting as the vinegar tang of a Fish & Chip shop.

The hug also gave me a moment to work out what we'd said.

"Sorry," I said. "We had a massive row. He met someone in Frankfurt. Sort of. You know..."

Again he stared at me with those eyes. "Is it serious?"

"Yes."

"And are we?"

He didn't blink. And I didn't know what to say. Not at first. Then I smiled.

"Want to come on holiday?"

LOOK, THIS ISN'T a cop-out. And please don't slam the book down in disgust. Especially not if it's a Kindle. They're fragile. Look, Romeo wasn't evil. Not like most of the people I've been talking about. He genuinely meant well, sort of, drawing close to people like moths to a flame. Or, to go back to the Fish & Chip shop analogy, like flies to those little blue buzzing boxes. The same as when the cat climbs on me when I'm running a temperature. It may feel like real concern, but also, you're simply an amazing and irresistible source of heat.

He just wanted what we all want, to be liked.

"Why do you seek out couples?" I asked him.

"What?"

"Oh." Waterloo rattled past. "I looked into your Twitter history. You know. You spend a lot of time making friends with couples. Is it because they're stable—you know, you figured that if they're going out with each other then they're at least sane?"

Romeo considered this, or maybe he was just looking at the London Eye. "Well, perhaps," he said at last. "It's more that every couple, every couple I've ever met is secretly very unhappy. They're clinging to each other because they each feel very insecure. And so, if you show them a little bit of affection... well, they're all broken. And they like the attention."

"Oh."

The bus moved on, crossing the bridge that no one can quite remember the name of.

"I mean, look at you and Trent. You both claim to be so happy. But I've fucked both of you."

I HAD NO idea where the bus was going now. He can't possibly have... I mean... I ran Trent's Twitter account. I'd not been checking it every day, obviously. For one thing, he was supposedly in Frankfurt, and it didn't do to be updating from Tottenham Court Road by accident. So, he couldn't possibly have been tweeting him. Could he...?

Romeo was looking at me, and still smiling that little empty smile of his. "He didn't answer the messages. Not like you did. I found out where he worked. From the photos it was fairly easy—the Sodobus building was in the background. And, after I'd seen you, I'd always leave at lunchtime and stand around the plaza outside the office. Waiting for him. I saw him on the second go. I don't think he recognised me. Not at first. But he noticed me. People do. I'm pretty. And he definitely looked back the next time I saw him. So I went over and smiled and we went for a coffee. It wasn't serious, I could tell that. He gave me a made-up name, even lied about his job. But it didn't matter. Because, as soon as he took me for coffee, I had him." Romeo leant forward, his smile stupidly big and bold, like an angry email. "He took me back to his office, and signed me in as a guest with a trembling hand. Then he took me to the disabled loo and we shagged." Romeo licked his lips. He got his phone out. "I've photos on my phone. The angle's a bit funny, and I couldn't turn the flash off, but hey..."

I glanced at the images, and felt furious for all the wrong reasons.

I handed him back the phone without even noticing what he did with it. The sudden flare told me that he'd just taken a selfie of the two of us. Me looking horrified. Him pulling Quizzical Face. Still with the flash on—he was such a dreadful photographer.

"I always do that," he laughed. "I've a gallery of them."

What was odd about his laugh was that it wasn't evil. No-one has an evil laugh. It wasn't even malicious. It was simple delight.

He held up the picture of the two of us together. Him looking like a triumphant Bell's Palsy sufferer, and me, lost and confused and, although he wouldn't notice it, admiring.

Romeo had done very well.

MY NEXT MOVE was interesting.

If I was going to kill him, I couldn't act immediately. There was now CCTV of the two of us together on a bus. Screenshots would appear all over the Metro of his mysterious last journey. So it couldn't happen now. The phone was an issue, though.

Devices sync. As soon as he plugged it into his laptop a copy of the photo of the two of us together would appear on it, and probably on Dropbox and in the cloud, and maybe even Facebook—what if he kept a private rogue's gallery on Tumblr? The phone would have to go immediately. Or rather, it would have to leave his possession immediately. That was easy enough. He was looking out at the South Bank, after all, his phone poking out of his pocket.

I could send a tweet from Trent's account to his—'Hey! Did you find your phone?'

Then the next day, his phone would spend an hour or so with me on the Circle Line, shunting back and forth until the battery ran down. If he had an iPhone tracker installed, it would seem as though he'd dropped it on the Tube. While underground I would wipe it. Then I'd surface. A surprisingly quick way to get rid of it was through a charity scheme to send old phones to the third world. That amused me. Kids in a village in Ghana taking selfies. With the flash on.

In the meantime Romeo would apparently get a replacement phone, pestering people on Facebook with, 'Hey, got a new phone, send me your numbers!' He'd done this twice since I'd known him, which meant he'd never got the hang of syncing contacts, which was a good thing. He'd get through the next few days with the replacement phone, excitedly talking about the new model he was going to get, and getting increasingly cross with the couriers from the delivery firm. With any luck, he'd even post exactly when he was going to be waiting in his flat for them. A nice long window—say 8am till 1pm. When he'd be home. Alone in Wolverhampton. We'd both come so far from there.

Travelling down to see him would be easy. I'd get the bus and pay in cash. If anyone noticed me popping in and out of the building, I'd take care to look incredibly generic. Just another internet hookup. While on the bus, I'd use their wifi to add a single word to the Wikipedia entry for his performing arts course. That would be very, very important. As would be announcing on Twitter that Trent and Markus were going to spend some time away with each other ("healing"). Before protecting their accounts. Then they'd vanish.

Perhaps the police would identify Not-Trent. He'd then have to explain why he had a fake account with a fake name. The more he protested his innocence, the guiltier he'd look. That was good.

I could see it all in my mind. So very clearly. The thoughts felt sharp, like I was sat in a cold bath. It was all so easy. And there was something else in the water. Romeo had been sleeping around. It made me feel jealous. But just the fact that it made me feel anything made me admire him even more. He'd got to me.

No, it was interesting. Late night London crawled past as we slouched up Tottenham Court Road. There was rain outside and someone downstairs on the bus was hammering the window and yelling "Barry" over and over again. I glanced around the top deck of the bus. Sat at the back, wrapped up in a hood, staring at me, was the figure of the Ninja. How had I not noticed her before? She nodded to me. I nodded back and turned away, shivering.

Romeo was talking. "Basically, it feels like I own you. And that's nice, isn't it? I wonder if McDonald's is open. Romeo Hungry. I could do with a burger. If you can lend me the money?"

At McDonald's they have a shovel for fries. Someone must have sat down and invented it. There must have been a meeting where the ongoing issue of moving chips from pan to box was raised and various solutions were suggested. And someone—let's call her Helena—came up with the suggestion of a metal cone. At first, everyone found reasons not to do it, but someone there—perhaps Ronald McDonald himself—squeezed his nose and said, "Let's give it a whirl." And thus was Helena's unique chip shovel created. I mention this only because I can't make up my mind. I'm trying to decide whether or not to kill someone and I'm weighing up all the factors. I watch Romeo tip back his head and empty the box of fries into his gullet in a smooth move. Yes, he is definitely my chip shovel situation. Do I do something about him, or do I just let him go?

Let him go. That suddenly made me sad. Letting go would mean not waking up with him again. Even though I'd simply been having sex with him because I had to, I knew that I would miss it. Which in turn meant a whole lot more thinking to do. Even more chips to cram into a neat cardboard box.

I was aware of a figure watching us from across the street. It wore a hoodie and kept to the darkness. Was it the Ninja? Was she watching to see what I would do? To see if I chickened out?

Romeo was talking again. He belched up some coke, swirled the ice around in the bucket and then dropped it onto Oxford Street. Irritated, I wanted to pick it up. But I didn't. Justifying it to myself, I'd say that I was worried about leaving my fingerprints on anything he touched. But I think I just didn't want to be seen as being prissy. He looked at me, his lips glistening with coke and salt and ketchup. Should I take him home? I thought. Would he want to come? Should I risk us being seen? There would be DNA. Lots of DNA, hopefully.

And then, suddenly, he made my life so much easier. He belched again and grinned. "Ever had sex in an alley?"

AFTERWARDS, AS WE were walking back towards Oxford Street, he turned to me. "I don't know what to do with the two of you," he said.

Neither do I, I thought. I hadn't decided. He was already patting his pockets, idly wondering where his phone was. Ah well, it would probably turn up.

He turned away into the sludgy dawn, heading towards a bus that would take him the long way home. He smiled at me. I smiled at him.

Should I kill him? Would I kill him? Could I?

"Hey," I called after him, my voice cracked with surprising nerves. I felt like I was asking him on a date. Which I was. I guess.

"Yeah?" He smiled. I noticed for the first time how narrow his eyes were.

"Would you like to come on holiday with me?"

"Will you hide me in your luggage?" He laughed, a delighted little laugh.

I hugged him. No, I wouldn't kill him.

Body-In-The-Bag Student
Death Mystery

INVESTIGATORS ARE STILL trying to solve the cause of death Romeo Flexeder, 23. The student was found in a bag in his flat in Wolverhampton last week. While there are no suspicious circumstances or any evidence that anyone else was in the flat, police are still baffled as to how he sealed himself in the large holdall. Or, indeed the exact cause of death. Officers are trying to trace his movements over the last few days, and are appealing for any witnesses to come forward.

Wolverhampton Post

Cat Hair Clue In Bag Death Mystery

A SINGLE STRAND of cat hair found on the clothing of Romeo Flexeder may hold the clue to his death, a police source has claimed. "Of course, it may have come from a cat he stroked on the way home. But it could hold the vital clue to how the student ended up dead in a holdall." The problem currently facing officers is tackling the task of identifying the cat hair. "It is a problem which would be made a lot easier by investment in the £200million Sodobus DNA cross-matching programme currently being considered by the several forces across the country," a Police spokeman told us.

Wolverhampton Post

Wolverhampton School Of Performing Arts: Difference between revisions

Line 24:

The course offers tuition in the classics of performance, speech and drama, with extensive vocal and movement coaching. Optional modules include sword-fighting, modern dance, ballet and stage magic.

Latest Revision (edit) (undo)

Line 24:

The course offers tuition in the classics of performance, speech and drama, with extensive vocal and movement coaching. Optional modules include sword-fighting, modern dance, ballet, **escapology** and stage magic.

BAG DEATH RULED "TRAGIC ACCIDENT"

Wolverhampton Post

CHAPTER SIX
THE NEXT MRS HITLER

YOU'D HAVE TO BE DESPERATE TO KILL THESE PEOPLE

*Has **Jackie Aspley** uncovered a serial killer
who may just be a mercy killer?*

OH, THIS BAR is awful. As I look around it, at the walls trying
too hard to please, at the dark wood that went out with the
Tea Party and the desperate-to-be-noticed subtle lighting, my
heart breaks. What a terrible place, and what an awful place
to die. I wouldn't be seen dead here, but that's exactly what
happened to marketing manager Danielle Audley.

Audley? Even her surname sounds ordinary, doesn't it?
Well, she was here having a perfectly ordinary night out in this
perfectly ordinary bar in a perfectly ordinary bit of London with
her perfectly ordinary friends... and then she died. It is about
the only extraordinary thing she ever managed. Poor cow.

I order a glass of white wine from the bar, and it's enough
to make you weep. I imagine that this was her last drink and I
shudder in sympathy with her dying thoughts. They say your
whole life flashes before your eyes in your last moment. (Ye
gods! I'll have to think about my marriage again. So many
traumae.) I am trying to imagine Danielle's flashback. Like
a tiresome *Big Brother* best bits package where they've

forgotten to include any best bits and it's all tragic Primark bargains and Müller corners. She must have died feeling so disappointed.

But at least she didn't have to drink any more of this terrible wine.

Someone killed Danielle. Well, that's what I think. And a few of her friends think so. And they're ordinary people. Ordinary people don't have conspiracy theories. I've just had to sit through two hours with her parents. They cried a lot on their DFS sofa. They must miss her. She must have meant something to them, even though she managed to do so little with her life.

Perhaps, like Philip Glass, she'd have been a late developer. As any cabbie will tell you, he was a taxi driver until the age of 43 when he suddenly discovered that if you took all the tunes out of music, what you had left was plinkety-plonk and a fortune. I asked Danielle's father if she played any musical instruments, and he just shrugged sadly. Ah well, she may have one day. There would have been time.

It's Danielle's ex-boyfriend who believes she was killed. I say ex—he only left her because she herself left this mortal coil. Everything about her suggests that she's not the sort of woman to leave a man. Especially not a nice normal man. Like Guy, who is so very normal and so very grieving. He's run charity marathons for her.

Initially, the coroner reported her death as a tragic accident. Like many spoiled children of the 80s, she had a peanut allergy. One that, science has shown, she could easily have overcome if she'd only shown a little effort. But, like learning the recorder, she just didn't put the time in, and then, one evening, she ate a peanut in this bar and died.

People always call this kind of death a tragedy. But it isn't. *King Lear* is a tragedy. My last marriage is a tragedy (one of epic proportions that could only be sung by fat Germans for nine hours). But Danielle Audley? Not really. She just died.

The bar owners protest that they are careful to ensure no cross-contamination of their drinks (God knows, their wine is contaminated enough already). This backs up Guy's theory that his girlfriend's death, at least, has something interesting about it. There is CCTV in the bar which shows her talking to a stranger—but this may just have been a friend. A witness has also reported seeing someone help her to the toilets. But no-one has come forward. That, at least, is a mystery.

And there are other mysteries. Other similar deaths happening to ordinary people. Everything about them seems to make sense. And yet, as with ley-lines and the Kennedy assassination, something is clinging to them, as sticky as the surface of this table in this sad little bar. Perhaps someone is killing these pointless people.

Has being dull and tawdry become a crime? If so, then we could wipe out a lot of people in this country (including, thank God, my ex-husband). I could put together a fairly good list for someone to have a crack at. Mostly the people who will, with a grinding of the single gear they have in their heads, lurch forward to comment beneath this article. Go on, do it. You're just putting yourself on a list. A list of the drab who, just perhaps, deserve to die.

Jackie Aspley, The Daily Post

I'D ALREADY READ the article, but I wasn't surprised when I received a message on MySpace alerting me to it.

The mysterious Duster was worried.

So, of all the people to join the dots, it was Jackie 'Hitler' Aspley who was the first person to suspect that it wasn't a series of accidents and suicides, but actual murders. Everyone knows about Jackie Aspley. No one likes her. No one feels sorry for her—apart from her ex-husband, who once said, "I kind of pity her" before bursting into laughter on *The One Show* after the people of the village she'd decamped to burnt her in an effigy made out of cow dung on Bonfire Night.

The odd thing about Jackie is that, for someone who manipulates the internet, she doesn't really use it. She proudly writes that she has an ancient laptop that's in black and white and still uses a dial-up modem. She once tried to look at the newspaper website that publishes her articles (alongside long lens pictures of topless teenagers and thought pieces about why women over forty have fat thighs). And yet, for someone who isn't on Twitter and never uses a website, she's single-handedly responsible for making the internet a worse place.

About two or three times a week she writes a column. It's always deliberately-provocative linkbait. Jackie Aspley has a genius for rambling insensitivity. Within moments of going live, each piece is being blarted out across the world:

> Jackie Aspley latest! I CAN'T EVEN. Someone please kill her. Or me, I don't care #EyesBleeding.
> Hate linking to this stuff, but LOOK at what she's done #TrollQueen.
> Well said, our Jackie! Sometimes she's a lone voice of reason #HasToBeSaid.

Unrepentant (unless she could get a column out of it); clearly troubled (no-one could forget her article on how Princess Diana deserved to die based solely on the scatter cushions she would now buy)—the shameless inventor of wasp nest soup.

True to form, her latest column was now pinging into my inbox. Amber's message was typical. ('My god have you seen this? Guy MUST NEVER SEE IT. I'll tell him not to look.')

Jackie Aspley. Such an obvious target. I sat back in my chair. I was winded, excited, scared and just a little bit hungry.

When I went into the kitchen I went in there an angry man. I felt personally attacked by Jackie, I felt defensive of my friends, and I felt scared. The cat weaved its way around my legs, making another first stab at an invisible wicker basket that it never got around to progressing with. I just stood there. The quote 'Someone please kill her' flashed through my mind like a challenge. It would be so easy. It would be what she deserved. What she needed. I would be doing a public service.

But in the time it took the kettle to boil, I'd calmed down. Actually, no, that's not true. But I had a plan.

* * *

THEY HATE ANIMALS IN THE COUNTRY
Jackie Aspley on our countryside's
hate-hate relationship with pets

IF YOU WANT to see animal cruelty, you won't find it on YouTube, you'll find it in the Home Counties. It's the bit of England that protests so loudly about how much it loves animals. It calls dogs 'man's best friend,' it makes much of the sheep dotted around the rolling hills, and it gives prizes to inbred girls for combing the hair of ponies.

But the countryside's cruelty to animals really is unspeakable. Look at badgers. Everyone here behaves like they'd gleefully whack one on the head with a spade if only 'they' weren't looking. Ever since the government admitted they'd made a statistical error and that badgers didn't actually spread TB I have been loudly telling people I meet on the street about it. "Well, I dare say," they'll bleat at me like the sheep they enjoy slaughtering for Sunday roasts, "But all the same, there's something about badgers, isn't there?"

"NONSENSE," I will shout at them. "Badgers. Do. Not. Spread. Plague." And then, if the village shop photocopier is working (they tell me it's quite often broken when I go in at the moment) I will press a photocopy of the article that proves it into their hands, and wish them a curt good morning. "Good morning, badger killer!" I will declaim.

Of course, naturally, this forthright approach hasn't won me any more friends. Someone left a dead badger on my drive the other day. I don't know where they'd found it from, but I was needless to say horrified and hugged it to me, crying for two hours before I remembered to feed the chickens. Naturally, I phoned the police and demanded something be done, but they simply offered to help me pop it in a bin bag. I told them I was the victim of assault, that this creature had been murdered because of me and almost begged them to arrest me as an accessory before the fact. Instead they insisted with clop-headed mendacity that the poor thing had been run over while crossing the road and had just died there. What are the chances of that happening? I demanded.

All they could do was shrug and tell me, "This is the countryside. It happens all the time."

I felt sick. Vindicated, but sick. This is the countryside, where creatures come to die. All the time.

At least in Oriental countries they're honest about it—if it moves and isn't necessarily granny, then kill it and eat it and make some shoes out of the leftovers. It explains why their children are so bright—not a shred of conscience and no time wasted lying to themselves and others. At least they're honest. They hate animals but love to devour them.

We just hate animals. When I went into the local pet sanctuary to adopt another cat I was ACTUALLY derided for it. "Hello! Not you again," they said as a greeting. "Not after another one?"

"I only have 12 cats," I told them. "That's not many. And I assure you that they possess more love, affection and humanity than any of you."

With a resigned shrug they gestured me towards the cruel cages they keep the cats in, like they're battery hens that refuse to lay eggs. So many adorable fuzz babies, all staring at me hoping for a happy home. How could I refuse?

Since my vile ex-husband left me, collecting cats has become something of a hobby. At first, I got cats because they reminded me of him (fat, lazy and greedy) but then I started to see the true love that these adorable things possessed.

I stood there at the so-called sanctuary, for a moment possessed by the urge to fling open all their cages and cry, "Be free! Be free!" But I restrained myself and said aloud, "One can't have too many cats, you know."

Amazingly, the other person in there, (even more amazingly A Man), agreed. He nodded his head. I'm not used to a man agreeing with me, but there we go. Miracles can happen.

"How many cats do you have?" he asked.

"Twelve," I told him.

"And where do you live? How much land to you have?"

I told him about the four boggy acres and the miserable scrub of woodland nearby.

"Perfect," he said, taking me seriously. The last person to take me seriously was my divorce lawyer. "Cats require at the minimum ten cubic metres of space and are more than capable of sharing territory on a rota basis caused by a variation in their sleeping cycles and their territorial roaming patterns. You can get plenty more. If you so wish."

"Are you here to get a cat?"

He looked troubled. For a moment I thought he was going to cry. "It's Scuffles..." He halted. "She's in for a check-up, and she's an old girl and I'm worried, so I took just a moment to... you know..." He patted a cage, which mewed. "Just to see that life goes on." He then turned around and looked me in the eye. "You understand, don't you?"

"Yes," I assured him and immediately vowed to throw up breakfast. I didn't want to be too fat for this man. I had finally met someone in this God-forsaken county who understands animals (or, at least, has a fraction of the sympathy for them that I do).

Idiotically, I invited him around for dinner there and then (I wouldn't eat it of course, but I'd like to watch him). And he accepted. I may have left the animal sanctuary without another fuzz baby today, but I have found something almost as useful. A friend. One who understands how vile the people of the countryside are about animals.

And don't get me started on how they treat their dogs.

Jackie Aspley, The Daily Post

YOU SEE, I had decided on a new approach. Jackie Aspley was a woman who thrived on death threats. "If people hate me, then I know I'm popular," she'd once told an increasingly despairing interviewer. So, I used the KillFund to hire a tiny cottage on the outskirts of the village and hung around the local shop and the cat sanctuary. And, soon enough, bingo.

DUSTER: What the hell are you doing?
ME: Having dinner with her, actually.

*　　*　　*

Dinner at Jackie's was a very odd occurrence. She had a beautiful recently-converted barn that shone with money and cat hair. There were cats on the stainless steel worktops, on every club chair and snuggled among the ancient wooden beams. All of them watching me territorially. The only place lacking a cat was the cat basket.

Jackie herself stood at a brushed metal hob that cost more than my annual income, trying desperately to heat some kind of stew. It was a large pot into which she was sweeping things from cupboards while swearing. Frequently she'd pour some wine— either into the pot or into herself. She was stirring the stew like a cake mix, her jewellery jangling as she worked. Perspiration was on her forehead, making its way around her make-up.

"I would come over and give you a hug, but I daren't leave this in case it sets," she called. "Stroke a cat, would you? It's like a hug."

I sat down on a sofa in between two purring things which eyed me resentfully. One hissed. "Oh, don't mind the fluffballs!" she called. "Want some wine?" She made to pour me a glass, but the bottle was empty. She blinked at it in surprise, then shoved it into recycling.

We made odd small talk ("Wonder what happened to Harry Paperboy?" "Do you think Sodobus are taking over the country?" and, oddly, women's football) and then she served the food.

It was basically porridge into which an Ocado delivery had fallen. But it was very nice. I ate two bowls, while Jackie poked away at her tiny portion on a tiny plate with a child's fork. At regular intervals she'd drown it with heaps of leaves which she'd munch away at. She was working very hard at creating the impression of eating without actually eating. I started to feel absurdly self-conscious, especially as she started asking me questions. Despite all the appearance of chaos, Jackie was a highly trained journalist and experienced celebrity interviewer. People opened up to her. Worse than that, people had a terrible habit of saying to her, "Now, you won't print this bit, will you, but...?" before telling her some awful personal secret. Jackie would nod solemnly, and then print it anyway.

"So, tell me about yourself…"

I trotted out my careful little story. My name was Richard. I'd just split up with a long-term girlfriend and was 'finding myself' in the country. Luckily, the whole idea sounded so ludicrous to her that she started barking her own opinions at me immediately. "The only thing you'll find here is a lot of Edwardian bigotry. Even the plumbing's inbred." She slumped forward, helping herself to another glass of wine. "God, I hate it here. Hate it. I turned up at the shop the other day and they wouldn't serve me."

"Oh, why not?"

"They were closed," Jackie screwed up her face. "Seriously. Like at five o'clock on the dot. They stay open later in Wales." She drank some more of the expensive Norwegian sparkling water she'd put on the table and then slugged back another glass of wine. "I was banging on the door demanding they let me in. 'I am not one of your nineteen-fifties housewives!' I screamed at them, but they wouldn't let me in. I could see them inside, tutting at me. So now I get everything delivered by a van. And they all *hate* me for it. I don't know what I've done wrong."

"Perhaps…" I began, but noticed her eyes had thinned warningly.

"Do go on," she said, her voice flat. I noticed the cat which had been rubbing against my leg beating a hasty retreat.

"Well," I pressed on. "The country isn't like London. It's not even like Primrose Hill. They're different here. You know, perhaps if you don't treat everyone like they're a Starbucks barista, it might work better."

"I see," she said. She clearly didn't. "It's like being surrounded by a load of stupid interns you can't fire. At least when I worked on a magazine they'd burst into tears when I was frightful, but they don't do that here. They're so hard to read. And they're so placidly friendly. What's all that ridiculous nodding about? You know, you can't walk past one in the street without a nod. If I did that in Piccadilly I'd be locked up. There's a column in that, I'm sure of it."

"Oh," I said. Clearly she'd never read a self-help book. "Have you ever read Desmond Morris?"

"*Catwatching.*"

"Ah. Well, it's a bit like... well, you know how cats show other cats that they are not a threat when they meet them? I think that's what the Country Hello is. We simply meet strangers and nod to them to reassure them that we're not a threat and we don't view them as a threat. It's an empty road and there could be highwaymen about. And we don't do it in town because the streets are always full. Unless it's three am and you're on an empty road in which case you may well nod at people to show that you're friendly. If you're not running the other way."

There was silence, apart from a distant purring. I braced myself for an outburst. As far as I could tell, she had drunk nearly two bottles of wine on a stomach lined only with rocket. She seemed fine, but could turn at any moment.

"That... is... fascinating..." she said eventually. "Brilliant. I am so doing a column on that. Tomorrow. I am going to walk the shitty little lanes nodding at people and see what happens. Wonderful." She stood up with a scrape of chair. "And now I'm going to make you pudding."

"You're having some?"

She narrowed her eyes. "No, of course not, and it's rude of you to even ask."

She doled out the desert, cutting me a huge slice of cheesecake out of a box, a full quarter-of-an-hour, and then giving herself the smallest tick. She took half of it on a teaspoon and pronounced it delicious. Personally, I found it hard going. To her it was delicious because it was forbidden food. To me it just tasted like over-sugared supermarket cheesecake. But we both stared at each other, smiling and pretending that this was a perfect dessert.

"Do you ever eat?" I asked her.

"Of course I eat. I just don't *eat* eat." Her voice was bored. "Years ago, I decided that food bored me. I was eating most of my meals wrong—a bowl of porridge while drying my hair in the morning, queuing for frozen sushi from outside the office and then cramming a sandwich into my mouth while running to get to the theatre in the rain. And I just thought to myself, *Why do you do this? Why do you spend all of your time memorising the calorie content of these things, none of which have any flavour? It's no fun, so why not just stop eating?* So I did."

Actually, this seemed straightforward enough to me. Like giving up jogging or Mandarin classes. Only...

"Well, of course, I still have to eat something, but I know when I absolutely have to. I love everything about food but the eating of it. And it means that here I am in my late forties and I have a better figure than when I was half my age. It's what"—her eyes glinted with triumph—"makes those biddies in the village resent me so much. There they are in their big floral print behinds and Matalan gilets, and here I am, a size ten head-to-toe in McQueen. Even the wellies. It works for me, and who are you to judge?"

I wondered if she realised how ironic that motto was.

WHY DO POSH RESTAURANTS
HATE THIN PEOPLE?

Jackie Aspley is victimized on an evening out.

DON'T BE A mum with a pram in a coffee shop, and don't be a thin person in a nice restaurant. The one place where not being obese is obscene is in our modern halls of fine dining, where a lack of appetite is treated as a personal affront.

I had gone out to have a nice evening. I went on an actual date (his name's Richard and he's very nice for a bumpkin). While I would have been perfectly happy with a glass of wine in the local pub (well, not the most local pub, as they water their wine down), Richard insisted on taking me to a local fine dining experience. You know the place—a thatched old inn with swans by the riverbank outside and a vacuum of bare walls and bare tables inside. I signed up for the degustation menu, figuring it would be a bit like sitting down at a party with canapes, but no such luck. They just kept bringing me food. And I kept on sending it back. I ate a little of all of it, but not since I saw the photos of my ex-husband's stag-do in Blackpool have I seen such excess. All the food was lovely, don't get me wrong, but it just didn't stop.

I had come to this restaurant to get to know Richard, but there just wasn't a chance with all the food and the puffs of vanilla kidney air, and all the questions about whether Madam was enjoying her food, perhaps Madam would like another slice of bread, would Madam like a little more water, let me light a bacon incense stick, was Madam really finished, and on and on it went. The idea of an intimate dinner for two had seemed perfect, but we may as well have been kissing in a crowded lift.

If I wished to have my every social move quietly judged by strangers, I would have gone round for tea at his relatives. Instead just endless judging from cheap foreign labour, and a quiet little sneer every time a course was picked up and taken away, simply because I hadn't cleared my plate.

Society expects women to be thin, and then gives us a hard time when we try our best to do it. Meanwhile, all Richard was doing was filling his face, with no regard for how little or how much I was eating. Instead he kept on asking me questions. Good job I wasn't eating much—I was singing for my supper!

Whenever I tried to ask him something, naturally, he was filling his face. Could I love a man who would probably be clinically obese fairly soon? I began to hate him (just a little). And this is no use, of course, as I know you'll want to hear everything about him.

For a start, not another foreigner. Not even a Belgian. Richard just seems to be normal. He doesn't have a job (but isn't claiming benefits), but he has a degree. When I ask him what's the worst thing his last girlfriend could have said about him he shrugs and mutters that he was perhaps a bit confining. I'd love that. Frankly, I'm in it for Mr Clingy. I wonder if I can get her number out of him? For enquiries over a girly chat. But he seems a bit shy of all that (FYI readers, I asked if he could be photographed on our date for this piece and he demurred). But don't worry, I'm sure he's an axe-wielding monster and I'll be filing pieces even as he's chopping off my limbs.

The thing is I was finding it very hard to get to know him with all the waiting that was going on in the restaurant. I felt like a zoo exhibit being stared at by polite penguins. I finally put my foot down and asked, pleasantly but firmly, for them to leave us alone. When I'd finished, they beat a retreat, but all had not gone down well with Richard. "Jackie, you really can't treat everyone like a Starbucks' barista," he said and left.

Thanks Restaurant. You owe me a boyfriend.

Jackie Aspley, The Daily Post

JACKIE PHONED TO apologise. Well, she phoned a lot over the next few days. Sometimes to apologise, sometimes to harangue me, and then to tell me she was leaving me alone, before immediately ringing me again. There were a lot of texts too, but autocorrect and wine got in the way of them making any sense.

The phone lurked on a table in the cottage. I'd turned it onto silent, but the cat would watch it buzz and jiggle periodically.

Interesting, I was in hiding from my quarry. You could argue I was being clever and playing the long game. But if so, what game was I playing? If I threw away the sim and abandoned the match, then I'd wasted money. I could, I supposed, just hang around here until the rent on the cottage was up, but then I'd be bound to bump into Jackie in the village shop. And then she'd start hunting me down and that would go terribly wrong.

Another text, and the phone edged its way a little closer along the coffee table.

Or I could stick to my original plan. And make her happy.

FINE I GIVE IN. JUST C M AGAIN. WHAT R YR DEMANDS????

My demands? Just 2 –
Sanity and courtesy.

BEING NICE

Jackie Aspley goes to finishing school

BEING NICE IS easy, everyone. Well, pretending to be is, at any rate. I've learned a few things from Richard in return for him agreeing to go on another date with me. The first is that we won't try a restaurant, we'll just go for a long country walk.

Since I live in the country and all my dating profiles ever have said I like long country walks, I figured I may as well go on one, and it might as well be with the man I am dating.

Truth to tell, it is cold and wet and when you do reach a view you're so out of breath you're kind of wishing it was a view of a packet of crisps and a sofa and not some dull old rolling hills. But there we are.

Richard is a proper gentleman of the old school. He's very dapper and he knows what to wear. Or, at least, more than I do. I turned up for my walk and he said, "Oh, you can't wear those." I've spent my entire life refusing to be told what to wear by a man, but in this case he was right. You cannot wear crocs on a long country walk. Or even a short one. He'd packed some spare wellies in the back of his car ("Just in case"), and even if they were a bit big, I like to think the extra effort in wobbling was like those walk-yourself-thin-trainers that gave me bunions. Anyway, so armed, we set off to go and embrace the countryside. Or, at least, as much of it as we could manage. It's strange to live in the countryside and go for a walk in it. Like a busman's holiday, really.

A lot of my London friends talk a lot about Slow Food (which sounds like an excuse for forgetting to turn the oven on till your guests arrive) but let me tell you about Slow Walking. It's about picking a spot in the countryside and heading towards it at a snail's pace. At first you resent how stubbornly it refuses to get any closer and then you welcome any marginal drawing nearer it makes as a huge leap-forward. You go from thinking, *that's a nice hill* to kind of hating it to developing a Stockholm Syndrome obsession with its beautiful curves in the hope that one day it'll turn up and let you go. And then, just as you've decided you've made heroic efforts at mounting the hill, and are doing pretty well actually, some blasted hill runner will come skipping past you like a smug mountain goat. This is, BTW, pretty much the story of my life.

Anyway, we finally reach the top of the hill and I feel pretty much like I did when I got divorced (wrung out, wearing horrid shoes, and not wanting the man standing next to me to see me cry). And then Richard claps his hands together and says,

"Shall we go for a bit of lunch?" And, as if by magic, a little fairytale pub appears.

It was all rather wonderful really—there was a roaring fire, a friendly dog, the smell of spilt bear, and a snug little table with a view down the hill. Richard pushed a ten-pound note into my hand. "Go up to the bar and order us a drink, would you?"

I knew right now that this was a test, and I viewed myself objectively. No table service. Fine. I could walk to the bar without tapping my coin on the counter, or waving the note around. I could do this.

"Hello," I said, smiling sweetly. "Lovely day. What kind of red wines do you have?"

The Ancient Personage behind the bar smiled a Santa Claus smile. "Well, they're all red," he said.

I risked darting a nervous glance back at Richard, but he gave me a tiny, encouraging nod.

"Then that will be fine," I told him. "And a beer."

"What kind of beer?" said the barman. Typical! The kind of pub where they don't care about wine but it's all kinds of beer named after things in Hogwarts. I damped down the urge to say something and simply pointed to a beer tap, figuring that if I wasn't allowed to complain, then neither was Richard. I handed over the money and (again since it wasn't mine) let the barman keep the change. I took the drinks and we sat down to enjoy them while looking out over the hill. My wine, I'll have you know, turned out to be a very lovely Italian Merlot.

MISSION ONE VERDICT: Success

Jackie Aspley, thedailypost.com

COMMENTS [most popular]:
Squidgee: 'What has happened to Our Jackie? #NoFunAnymore.'
Benifite: 'Why does no-one ever go to a Little Chef on a date? Too much real life!'
SanityClause: 'She'll screw it up. She always does.'
Read all 457 comments

*   *   *

IF YOU FOUND it hard making it through the article above, it really wasn't any easier actually dating Jackie. For one thing, she left out a few things—the muttered swearing when it rained, the complaints about the blister she got, and the rude things she kept saying about the barman just loud enough for him to hear. But, overall, you know, it was quite a successful date.

I'd made a list of things I had to work on with her. I wanted to make people like her. I wanted the village she lived in to like her. I wanted her to feel happy. Then, just kind of, I figured she might start to understand people.

DUSTER: Jackie Aspley update please?
ME: Wait and see.
DUSTER: You have not, we notice, killed her.
ME: It's all in hand. Trust me.

BEING HER BOYFRIEND was tricky. One thing was easy, though—we didn't have sex. Having had sex with Romeo, I figured it would be easy enough, but for some reason I really didn't much feel like it. Luckily, neither did Jackie. She just asked me to hold her and told me that was nice. One evening, when far too drunk, she told me that she'd never had proper sex. At uni, she'd kept on dating gay guys, then the people on the first newspaper she'd worked on were all awful, so she'd never done it until she'd met her husband, and he turned out to be so bad at it that it left her forever wretchedly disappointed.

"And," as she said, "I like you so much, I'm not sure I could face finding out that you were crap in bed too. So I'd like to postpone it as long as possible. Hope that's okay. You're being so nice about it."

I nodded, and added 'Give Jackie Orgasm' to my list. I looked at it and changed it to 'Give Jackie Orgasm?' Something she said nagged at me. Overall, though, it was quite cushy. I'd spend the nights hugging her, watching television, sleeping in the expensive bed with her, and then sneak home in the morning to feed the cat.

*   *   *

WHO ARE OUR ROMANIAN INVADERS?
Jackie Aspley befriends a Romanian Beggar

SUVENA USED TO be a dentist. Now she sits on a bench on Marble Arch in the rain. When it stops raining she ventures as near as she can to a 5 star hotel without getting arrested and begs for money.

"I tell my family back home I have got work at a dentist's," she tells me in flawless English. "They would be so sad if I told them the truth. They would order me home. But the problem is, I was promised work over here, and then the dental surgery who offered it me cancelled it after I arrived. They said the position was no longer available, but I think they didn't want to get the bad publicity your paper gives people who employ Romanians. So I must beg until I can get the air fare home. It is very cold."

I feel awful for her, and insist she takes my Hermes scarf. I assure her that she can eBay it for at least £200, but she tells me she does not even own a smartphone. She refuses to take my phone, partly because it seems to embarrass her, and partly because it seems to always be ringing with people wanting to shout at me. I have to take three calls during our interview.

"You make so many people so cross," she says with a laugh. "What do you do to them?"

"I don't know," I tell her.

"I used to be a dentist. And yet people like you less than me." She lays a hand on mine. "Poor you," she says, and I get the taxi back to the station thinking that things must be pretty bad if a homeless Romanian dentist pities me.

Jackie Aspley, thedailypost.com

COMMENTS [most popular]:
WinSomeArmy: 'These people are the vermin of Europe and you're sending this cow to give them hugs? Get over it!'
SanityClause: 'She's different now she's eating the happy sausage!!!

Read all 128 comments

* * *

HER NEXT ARTICLE went down even worse. The only thing you need to know about "Jackie Aspley' Search For The Perfect Teabag" is the dreaded phrase at the bottom. "There are no comments on this article."

JACKIE WAS IN a real mess. She sat in the village coffee shop and her hair looked matted together. She was wearing a designer dress that looked as though it had been slept in. She'd put on make-up, but it looked as though she'd turned her head to one side at the last moment. She kept smiling at me, and it took me a few seconds to realise she was trying not to cry.

I put my arm around her before I realised what I'd done.

It all came flooding out in words, so many words I didn't know what to do with them. "My editor took me out to lunch, which is normally when she tells me that I've *really* upset someone. And I was wondering what I could possibly have done... and then she told me that I'd upset no-one. And that that was the problem. No one cares about me any more."

She looked up, and before I'd even thought about it, I said, "But I care about you."

"Don't say that," she said, squeezing my hand. "My editor says it's all because of you. At first there was a proper spike in interest, but then when you turned out to be nice and normal and... and... good for me, then people started complaining."

Wait. People complained that someone was less broken?

"She showed me print outs of *horrible* things they said about you on the site. It's so lucky you refused to be in any pictures or let me use your last name, because you'd hate it all. You'd hate it all so much. And that's not the worst of it. My editor said that my articles since I've met you have become less good. No one looks at them. No one wants to advertise next to them."

The irony of all this floored me. I'd meant to make her a better person, but in doing so I'd made her less good. Although, thinking about this, I could have killed her, rather than her career. And that was worth it. She still had an amazing house and fields of animals. She had kept on telling me how much she hated being a journalist.

"This is good, isn't it? You said you wanted out. This is the chance."

"Yeah," she said, and her voice was small. I talked on about her running a food business, of creating jobs in the community, and she kept on agreeing in a smaller and smaller voice which eventually faded away entirely.

"What's wrong?"

She looked up, running fingertips around her eyes, drawing the make-up out in panda smudges.

"My editor has given me an ultimatum," she said. "I'm either to dump you or I'll be dumped from the paper."

This was my out. Amazing. But it felt like a hollow victory.

"What did you say?"

"I refused. She told me to think about it over the weekend. She's spiked my piece on cupcake recipes."

"Okay." I gave her a hug.

"Okay?" she said, her voice picking up again. "I've committed columnist harakiri for you and you just say okay?"

"I'm stunned, that's all I can say. The woman I first met would never..."

"Oh," Jackie laughed. "She was just as bat shit crazy. But now she's the same in a nicer way."

We hugged for a bit. She wasn't wearing perfume for the first time ever. She smelled really nice.

"We'll always have cats," I said.

"Yes," she said, rallying as she raised her cup. "Here's to cats."

I woke in the middle of the night to hear a noise that I thought was mice in the skirting board. My first thought was that the cats would be pleased. Then I worked out what it was.

I followed the tapping noise through to the living room. In front of the chilled embers of the fire, Jackie sat typing.

"I've come up with a third way," she said. "I've told them to print this and, if they don't like it, just to sack me. No redundo, nothing. Just get me out the door. But they won't. This is personal dynamite." She gave me a tiny little smile. "And, if it is a suicide note, then it's a brilliantly honest one. It explains everything about me. And every word of it's true."

She stood up and smiled.

"I'm going to make us a cup of tea and then come up to bed," said Jackie Aspley.

THE SHOCKING TRUTH OF
MY AWFUL FAILURE
Jackie Aspley gives a personal blast

I'VE SPENT MY life being criticised. I've always worried I'm too fat, too plain, too unattractive. I always watched my weight like a Tory minister watching foreign people. Fat was EVIL and mustn't be allowed to get under my skin.

All that changed when I became pregnant thanks to ex-husband. Finally, I knew that I could actually become the kind of woman who could get fat. Naturally, with all that came a whole load of worries—was I really the right person to bring another life into the world? Would it look at me, sack of mad neuroses that I was, and blame me for everything? Or would it somehow heal me?

When he told me I was pregnant, my GP urged me to "eat for two now." He'd always been worried about my bird-like appearance, but this was the chance to let rip.

At first my ex-husband was full of praise—for the first time in my life I had tits. Big boobies, knockout knockers. They started inflating almost at the moment of conception and just didn't stop. I loved them. I'd just sit around at home and play with them.

For a while my stomach stayed mercifully unchanged. I ate more but still went to the gym (just very gently). I missed drinking but the soup of hormones knocked me flatter than any red wine every night.

Then the morning sickness kicked in and I realised what an unfit mother I would be. I just couldn't cope with the morning sickness. All around me my friends were offering me joyously simple advice for dealing with it, every time with the added, "Of course, I got off scot-free, but poor you!"

It just wouldn't stop. It was like being on a constant hen-night on a cross-channel ferry. I was that little girl in *The Exorcist,* which also meant that my poor ex-husband no longer got his cherished jump start in the mornings. That was when he started staying out late in interns. It was grim.

And then, just when I thought it couldn't get any worse, I started to show.

I've been thin for so long I'd forgotten what fat felt like. At first it just looked like I'd eaten a heavy press launch lunch. But it didn't go away. The more I threw up, then impossibly the more it grew. I worried about what it was feeding off, as I certainly wasn't keeping down enough food to nourish it. Was my own baby eating me alive? Would it be born out of a pile of my own dust?

I struggled on. I'd turn up to work looking DREADFUL. My spending on fashion increased, which was ludicrous, as I could no longer guarantee to be able to amortise the cost of a dress across so many wears. Like a minor royal, I'd wear it a couple of times and then throw it to the back of the cupboard.

I tried wearing corsets a couple of times, but my GP was horrified, and I nearly died from the pain.

So Jackie Aspley carried on growing.

One day, my husband remarked, "You're fat."

I snapped back, "I'm pregnant," but he was unrepentant. "You're almost obscene. How much larger are you going to get?"

I really didn't know what to say to that. I was being fat-shamed by a man who nudged 18 stone and believed that two breakfasts were the right way to start the day. And he was calling me overweight. AND I WAS PREGNANT!!!

He also wasn't pleased that he had to make his own breakfasts. In the early days of our marriage, to assure us both that things were going okay, I played the homemaker and fried him sausage, eggs and bacon (my Muslim husband). Now I couldn't face the smell of raw meat, so he had to try and do it himself, which meant that he was in a foul mood and that the cleaner would later threaten to resign every time she ventured into the kitchen. Every single day. I ended up trying to wash the frying pan myself while dry-heaving.

Sex was also difficult. Like a child stuck on the first level of Pac-Man, despite being thoroughly bad at it, my husband kept on plugging away. He called having sex with pregnant me "mounting the insurmountable" or "Mohammed coming over the mountain," but we kept trying, even though I was sure it was hurting the baby as much as it was hurting me. Of course, I knew he had started having affairs by this point. He was always coming home late with some stupid excuse or other. In the early days he'd bring me back a nice little present (like a potted plant). As time wore on it became a pen he'd nicked from the office. I tried not to let it hurt me—my other friends had husbands who were delighted by their pregnancy. Baby-Nerds, we called them. But not my husband. He announced one night that he'd be thrilled so long as it was a boy. That was the sum total of his enthusiasm.

But I kept on—I'm sure many single mothers have had worse. I felt out of my depth, alone and afraid, but I also knew it was my job As A Woman to have a baby. To prove that I could get something right. At about that time I was sent out to do yet another piece on awful immigrants and was startled at their amazing fecundity. They seemed so good at it and relaxed by it. It was killing me and they just laughingly told each other jokes. I wonder if that planted a seed for some of the unkind things I said about them? Often we're mean about things we're jealous of. It's funny how it takes all of your life to learn how to be good at living it.

At 19 weeks, things got troubled. I'd just started working out whether or not to have cosmetic surgery at the same time as a caesarean. It was, I decided, going to be my big reward for all that morning sickness. But one morning, the sickness stopped. I felt such relief I cried. My husband came down to find that I'd cooked him breakfast again, and he patted me on the head. "At last," I told him. "It's going to be all right." When I went to pee later, there was blood everywhere. I screamed at him to phone an ambulance, but he pretended not to hear me. I had to crawl to my mobile, leaving a crimson smear across the cream carpet that never quite cleaned out. And they came, and they were nice, but tight-nice, forced smiles. They wouldn't quite answer any of my questions. When you're a journalist, that tells you that something is wrong. I knew long before they told me that my baby had stopped growing.

Jackie Aspley, thedailypost.com

COMMENTS [most popular]:
Naheed: 'Jackie, as your ex-husband I've long kept my peace. But this is it. You've gone too far. You had an abortion. I've got the paperwork to prove it. That's why we got divorced.'

Read all 1468 comments

CHAPTER SEVEN
IT TAKES A VILLAGE OF IDIOTS

THE INTERNET KNOWS everything. search.me had been set up to prove it. It was one of internet pioneer Henry Jarman's pet projects that he'd thrown himself into and then thrown himself out of five minutes later.

search.me was simple. 'Want advice? search.me.' That was the first slogan, and that's how it worked. You asked for advice, and the site gave it to you. Chat-app, forum, wiki, something in-between. From the early days here are the top threads:

- Should I adopt a cat?
- Is it worth repairing a toaster?
- What's the best way to order delivery pizza?
- What the flip is an HDMI cable?
- Do fake iPhone chargers work?
- My baby's not sleeping!!! HELP!!!

Men in sheds swapped tips with breast-feeding moms. Earnest Indian postgrads debated jam recipes with members of the NRA. In the early days, it was a success. An early review was: "Hillary Clinton once said it takes a village to bring up a kid, but when they've grown up, they'll need search.me." You know how it is. It burbled along.

Its first big hit was later described by Upworthy as, 'This lesbian teen threatens suicide. What happens next will choke you up.' A devout Muslim teenager in Afghanistan was outed at school as a lesbian. She ran home to kill herself before her family found out, pausing only to search.me. The site saved her life. Literally. At first it was a lesbian in Denmark, who, despite the piercings and the hair, turned out to also be Muslim, and then a whole flood of other people offering advice and heartfelt pleas. Then it was a worker at a local aid agency who had swiftly arranged a safe house for her. And then James Blunt posted a YouTube song (he later admitted, with admirable candour, he'd just got in absolutely off-his-tits and had no idea of what he'd done). But anyway, Aisha was soon safe and well and everyone felt good about themselves and could get on with talking about how good James Blunt looked playing the guitar in his pants. Even if his eyes were a little crazy and his t-shirt had half a kebab on it.

Those were the early days of search.me, when Henry Jarman was still talking it up. 'SIMPLE. THIS IS SAVING LIVES PPL' was one of his early statements about it.

But things shifted rapidly, especially as more people found out about it, and more journalists started to write about it ('Is search. me Google for the people?' was one pretty meaningless headline).

One problem is that there's actually a fairly finite number of common questions ('How do I poach an egg?'), but, as more people start using a service, those same questions will be asked over and over again, leading to a sense of entitled weariness from more established users ('Im closing this post as duplicate,' 'Pls see earlier thread on Eggs, Poaching,' 'HOW MANY TIMES? WERE NOT GOOGLE,' 'Why does idiots never bother searching first?' and 'Will you please change the sidebar text from "This question gets asked often" to "This question is asked often"?'). In fact, when setting up the site, Jarman had ensured that you'd have to be visiting really regularly to see the same questions, or actively searching for them. In other words, people were using the site to go and find things to be angry about.

The other drawback is that, while common questions were common, the uncommon ones really were out there. 'Best way to get child porn legally?' was actually quite uncommon, but it was the classic example used against the service. When he'd set up the search.me Henry Jarman had said "No question is off-limits" and "We've an answer for everything." When people started insisting he revise this, he dug his heels in, going in three easy stages from freedom of speech to censorship to 'THIS IS LIKE THE NAZIS BURNING BOOKS.' Underneath the CAPS LOCK he kind of had a point. He'd designed the site so that you'd only find information on child porn if you searched the site for it. Plus, he produced screenshots to show that, actually, you'd get pretty similar information to if you searched on Google. "Some things we're not the best place to look for stuff. Child porn's one of them," he admitted gleefully to journalists.

But that still didn't stop the finger-pointing. For a while it seemed as though a good way to fill in a dull afternoon at a newspaper was to unearth the more fringe questions on search. me. There was also a fair amount of deliberate trolling. Again, Jarman dismissed all this with lofty disdain. "Yeah, yeah, we've got recipes for cooking with faeces. But you have to go looking for them," he said, prompting a lot of people to go looking for them.

THEN CAME THE search.me suicide club. After the case of the noble Aisha, troubled teenagers flocked to search.me for help in their darkest hours. Bearing in mind what I've said about the community becoming intolerant of having the same questions asked over and over again, it was only a matter of time before some of the regulars became annoyed that the site which was predominantly for diets/recipes/work-out tips/porn/technical cables/cat care became swamped, in their eyes, with emoji-strewn posts from wretched goths. E.g.:

MY BOYFRIEND TOOK MY VIRGINITY, FILMED IT, SHARED IT, THEN DUMPED ME. I WANNA DIE :(

go on then
yeah. It'll show him
search.me/painless methods of suicide
search.me/music to kill yourself to
serach.me/eatshit & DIE!!! :):)

hey, you know that video will never go away, don't you, no
matter what you do, slut?
Good point RJ. That stuff sticks to the internet like shit.
YEAH. You'll always be TEEN WHORE.
Pray none from your school go to college with you, or it'll go
with you
Anyone posted it to your Facebook yet?
You Facebook friends with your mum? :)
32 paracetamol. And... GO!
Are you kidding? Paracetamol are IDIOTIC. Even this dumb
bitch wouldn't take them?

Paracetamol is a horrid way to kill yourself. You may wonder
why you don't see it used in suicide attempts more often in medical
shows. The reason is that, a few years back, quite a few shows
featured plotlines showing what an awful and horrendously slow
form of suicide it was, hoping to deter people. Instead, it saw
rates of attempted suicide by paracetamol *rise*.

If they can save you, there'll probably be terrible internal damage.
If they can't save you, it may take you days to die in agony.

And that's what happened to this teenager. Julie Dreyfuss,
barely fifteen. Lying in a hospital bed, sobbing as her body slowly
shut down, rejecting all the possible treatments, and screaming
in pain. And worse, with her iPad by her. Reading the search.me
forums reacting to the news of her attempt. And telling her she'd
made a stupid mistake. She answered a few.

Her parents, by the way, visited the hospital to drop off her
phone and charger. And then didn't come back.

By THIS POINT, Henry Jarman had sold the site and moved on, so
he felt fairly safe in condemning what had happened in CAPS
LOCK. He also issued an open letter to the people who were
running the site:

Hey Joel and Lucas,
   How are things? I imagine the last couple of days have
been pretty tough. My first piece of advice to you is to hang in

there—search.me is a thing of real value, and you guys have done a great job in building on my foundations to make it a really vibrant community.

The problem with any community is that there are bound to be a few village idiots. They shout loudly, but don't mean a thing. They're only harmful when they become policemen. I know you guys hate a back-seat driver, but if I can offer a bit of friendly advice, it seems as though the wrong people have now got too loud a voice. And, as I'm sure you'll agree, that's a bad thing.

When we started search.me, we could keep them under control. But it's a much bigger beast now, and our hydra has grown quite a lot of heads, and some of them are stupid. In the early days we always resisted calls to curtail the site's freedoms, but I think we can all agree that the tragic events of the last few days have shown us that there are some things that search.me shouldn't be offering advice on. I know there'll be some out there who cry foul, or censorship, but I really think we should redirect any queries about suicide to organisations like the Samaritans. They're experts. We're just mostly well-meaning people with opinions. And some village idiots who should feel ashamed of themselves.

I hope you won't take offence at the above. It really is meant kindly. I'll close by reminding you of one of the few bits of Latin everyone knows is, 'Who Watches The Watchers?'

Yours, Henry Jarman

ONE OF THE other bits of Latin everyone knows is 'et tu Brute?' Henry had neatly distanced himself from the site, offered advice he wouldn't have dreamed of following when he was in charge, and not used caps lock once. There were some people who reckoned he'd hired a pretty good PR. Which he could afford to do. He'd made quite a lot of money from a site famous for offering kids advice about suicide.

Joel and Lucas didn't take the advice. The wrote back the following open letter:

Hey Henry,
Why not just email us next time?
Love,
Joel & Lucas

They also issued a statement saying that they'd look into various measures, but also pointing out that, perhaps, the site wasn't the best place to go to for advice on suicide. The problem was, just as paracetamol inexplicably thrives on bad publicity, so too did search.me. Troubled teenagers flooded it.

As a columnist wrote, 'Suicide attempts are a call for help. Sadly, that call is now being answered by fools.' There were four deaths directly attributable to the site. There was also one case of animal cruelty after someone washed their puppy in bleach because someone on the site told them to.

For the lulz.

At about this point, a search.me user blogged about their experience of the site. 'Basically, everyone's getting the wrong end of the stick. Imagine Aslan, Batman and Gandalf all in a room with Stephen Hawking and Bill Gates and some brainy chick. That's what search.me is—you know, we're brain surgeons for the world. We could solve real problems. The thing is, people only really ask us for jam recipes.' Well, I was going to give them a real problem.

MY JOB WAS pretty simple. I had to teach search.me something it didn't know. The problem was, as Mrs Beeton would say, that first you had to catch your fuckwit.

This was easy. Of the people who'd goaded those kids to death there were at least six repeat offenders. All of them hid behind carefully constructed online personae, but—as with most people who were too clever for their own good—it was a fairly simple matter to track them down.

HotToddy84 pretty much selected himself. He posted on a variety of subjects, including vintage electronic keyboards and being an Englishman in Germany. Turns out, ToddyHot84 was the startlingly similar username of an eBayer in Cologne, who sold parts for electronic keyboards, and, weirdly, scented candles.

While search.me anonymises IP addresses, Wikipedia doesn't. The Moog9000 wikipedia page had quite a few amendments from a user called HatTip84. The IP address checked out to a small IT support consultancy in Cologne. Their website listed one of their staff as a former Sodobus systems analyst called Todd Halpern. In an attempt to give their website a wacky personality it said that the Number 1 single when he was born was 99 Red Balloons. That would be in February 1984.

Todd Halpern was my man.

I could have pursued the eBay route. If I bought something from him, the chances are he'd write the return address on the envelope or dispatch note. The problem was that this would establish a connection between us.

Instead, it was easy enough to browse through the list of his employer's clients and realise that they supplied on-site technical support for a Cologne temporary business-space company.

You're probably wondering, by the way, why I'd picked him. My other possible marks were in America, Australia or India. That was going to show up on my passport. However, it's a cinch to book the Eurostar, hop off at Brussels, and buy a train ticket to somewhere else in Europe without anyone having to know exactly where you are. Even buying the train ticket from Brussels to Cologne at the station in cash didn't raise an eyebrow—it's the kind of daft thing tourists do all the time. I spent some KillFund on a reasonably convincing fake passport from here on in. The kind of thing that was fine for fooling hotels and so on, but wouldn't stand a hope at Border Control.

Also using the KillFund, I then hired myself a business unit in the Cologne office space company Todd supplied IT Support for and set myself up. With a false name. It was pretty easy, really. The firm hired out offices for start-ups, but also had some space available for people who just wanted to have a meeting for an hour or two. They (brilliantly) were keen to look modern, so took payment through PayPal and Bitcoin. I made a research visit, and took a tour round with the building manager to pick out my office. Access to each floor was through a PIN number.

I scrambled to memorise them, and only afterwards realised the pin for Floor 5 was 7AE5, Floor 4 was 7AD4, for Floor 3 was 7AC3, and... well, you won't be surprised that I was able to get on to the completely empty seventh floor using the code 7AG7. The basement proved trickier, but, while 7AZ1 failed, 7AZB worked like a charm.

Both the basement and the seventh floor were possibilities. Both were mostly empty. I was tempted by the basement simply because I felt smug about having cracked the code. The problem was that it contained supplies for the coffee machines and a lot of cleaning products. People would come here. The seventh floor was only an issue if people were having a guided tour.

I spent some time establishing myself as a businessman who made frequent trips to Cologne, using it as a chance to get to really know the building. (Meanwhile, real me appeared to be going on quite a few thoroughly-Facebooked mini-breaks to Paris and Brussells. Was love in the air?) I'd often sit in my pretend office. I'd even have pretend meetings, by going down to the lobby expectantly, waiting until someone else came in for a meeting, and joining them in the lift. I'd make small talk in bad German with a reasonable French accent.

The seventh floor took a lot of exploring. The whole building had once belonged to a telecoms company who'd gone bust during the recession. The temporary office company was leasing the building from the receiver at a bargain rate, and, as they expanded, renovating each floor. The seventh floor hadn't been touched, and was littered with old office equipment, old slogans and signs, old décor. Behind a still-filthy kitchen was a glass box of a meeting room, complete with scuffed up scummy carpet. Some of the carpet tiles had been taken up on the rest of the floor, and teetering jenga towers of it were everywhere. It was simple enough to clad the glass box with it, forming a blacked-out, pretty soundproof and even mildly airtight container. I removed the carpet tiles from inside the box, exposing a concrete floor that was pretty unlike the neatly-laid laminate in the rest of the building. I figured Todd would suspect he was in the same building, but he wouldn't be sure.

In a storage cupboard at the back of the seventh floor was a computer so old, it was practically a museum-piece. Finger-stabs had erased the lettering from most of the keys, the processor was ancient, and the screen was a cathode ray box. I could have plugged it into the network here, but that might have given Todd a way out.

Instead I bought a portable wireless modem from a mobile phone shop. Todd's computer would be too antiquated for wireless, but that was fine. Electronics stores sell a method of routing wireless internet through the electricity cabling in houses where thick walls make the signal otherwise weak. I simply connected the PC that way.

Having set all this up, I then went back to England. It would soon be time for another mini-break.

THIS TIME, WHEN I booked a meeting room in the office in Cologne I set myself up with an entirely new identity. Not that it really mattered. Reception was pretty much automated, and I simply spent a little bit of time disguising myself. Whereas previously I'd looked like an identikit euro businessman with a completely forgettable suit, this time I spent a glorious hour or so making myself up as a travelling hipster. Possibly come over to talk about start-ups and synergies or something. It meant I could disguise myself a bit more, with a ratty ponytail poking out from under my beanie hat, and a fairly nice pair of sunglasses and slapped-on mutton chops disguising most of my face. If this sounded outlandish, bear in mind I'd been to Cologne a couple of times recently. People were at pains to look cool here, and I was actually a fairly close match for at least one other regular in the building. There was a chance that this would confuse people. Actually, I was pretty much counting on it.

"HI, IS THAT that Helpdesk?" I was at the limits of my A-Level German here.

"Yes, that is correct."

"I'm at the Cologne bZzOffice, and I am afraid I am having difficulty connecting some new equipment to the network here."

"No problem, we can probably talk you through that here."

"If it's all the same to you, can someone come out here and see to it? Someone who speaks English? I don't mind paying the call-out fee—this kit is very expensive, and I also want to make sure it's properly set up. That might be what's causing the problem."

"Okay, I can send Zara out to you this morning."

"I'm afraid I have a meeting this morning. Can she come in the afternoon?"

"No, if it's the afternoon, that'll be Todd."

"Okay, that's fine."

THE WEIRD THING was that when Todd Halpern turned up, I realised I'd accidentally come dressed as a clone of him. I'd researched everything about him, but had somehow subconsciously parked his appearance. I had a mental image of him (fat boiled potato in a stained t-shirt) and had completely failed to properly lodge that he was tall, thin, and hipsterish. With a ponytail.

Going up together in the lift, we made an idiotically remarkable image for the CCTV. I was trying to work out if our near-identical appearance was a good thing or a bad thing. The lift was very slow, and we were grinning at each other sheepishly. For a man who'd goaded four people to their deaths, Todd was in person rather shy.

"Hey," I said in my thick French accent.

"Hey," mumbled Todd.

I thanked him for coming, spoke English, and explained the problems, and took him over to my laptop in the meeting room I'd hired on the third floor. He nodded and sat down, working away at trying to get the laptop to recognise any of the devices I'd got. I'd deliberately disabled all of their drivers, so he was immediately engrossed. The idea would be that he'd stop thinking about me, but instead he kept shooting me sly glances.

After his fourth attempt to install the scanner, he turned. "Excuse me," he said, "but is this some kind of joke?"

I shook my head, and tried to look quizzically French. "I'm sorry?"

"It's just"—he gestured at me—"you look..."

"I know!" I beamed. "We are top fashion! High-five?"

He reluctantly high-fived me. Inwardly I was cursing. Why the hell hadn't I realised this was where I'd got my unusual beanie-hat and ponytail combo from? I must have seen a picture of him on an avatar at some point. I was trying to persuade him that this was all normal, and it was clear from the glances he was shooting me that he was far from at ease. Which was a problem, as I needed to sneak up on him, and I wasn't getting a chance. The longer this went on, the more chance he'd have to study me, the more to...

He was fiddling away at the scanner, and looking at me curiously.

"Excusez-moi," I said. "I must... the bathroom, yes?"

"Yeah, sure," he muttered, for once not looking in my direction. I headed over to the stairwell and slipped out to the bathroom. The advantage of this was that he was trapped—because this floor was tenanted, the PIN number was supplemented by a key card which made the building as hard to access as a Travelodge. He couldn't leave the office without a card. And I had plenty of time to change my disguise.

I hurried down to the basement in the lift, hopefully spreading some confusion as to who was leaving the building on the CCTV. I got out at the ground floor, then went down the stairs. I headed over to the supply room and helped myself to a cleaner's overall and slipped into an abandoned hoodie advertising a long-forgotten conference. It smelt mouldy, but helped with the disguise. I then called the lift and ascended, seemingly just another cleaner doing the rounds.

I got out at the third floor, but didn't go into my meeting room, instead circulating, going into other rooms and emptying bins, making myself known. No-one really noticed me. People try and ignore cleaners, especially when they're not the normal ones you've established a bit of a relationship with. It made it easy for me to flit from room to room, occasionally going past the meeting room where Todd was working.

My plan at this point was twofold. Ultimately, I had to get him up to the box I'd prepared on the seventh floor. But firstly, I had to establish myself as a cleaner. I went into an empty unit and turned on a vacuum cleaner. It was splendidly noisy, thanks to some gravel I'd thrown into it earlier. I then let myself into my own office and proceeded to do a reasonable job of cleaning it, without Todd paying me much attention. He barely glanced at me when I entered, and by the time I was emptying the bins was totally ignoring me.

It was all going brilliantly to plan.

"*Entschuldigung,*" he began in halting German. He was asking if he could borrow my key to go to the bathroom. He wasn't really looking at me, hadn't recognised me, just wanted a pee. I replied in reasonable German that I couldn't lend him a key, and he nodded, muttering something under his breath. I guess he really needed to go, which was a shame.

It was too good to last, of course. His eyes suddenly went wide and suspicious. "Hey—" he said, "Hang on, aren't you—?"

My spray bottle had done a pretty shoddy job of cleaning up spilt coffee. This was because it contained home-made chloroform (the results of a messy evening in the basement experimenting with bleach and duty free). Todd caught a blast of it full in the face and lunged at me.

He punched me twice. As I went down I suddenly remembered he'd contributed quite a lot of answers to search.me's martial arts forum. I'd made a huge mistake.

LYING ON THE floor, being kicked in the kidneys by my victim, I wondered how this was all working out for me. I blame the media. They make killing people look so easy. Let me assure you, it's really very hard. I wished I'd brought a Taser. Instead I had to wait until the diluted chloroform took effect. And that was a whole lot of kicks.

WHEN I WAS a kid, I loved shows like *The Crystal Maze* and *Knightmare*—you know, you go into a room, and you've got to complete a challenge against the clock in order to get out. Well, I guess you could say that I'd built my very own tribute to these games on the seventh floor.

Todd's prison was a trap. He needed to get out within a certain time before it turned deadly, but I'd carefully left him all the signposts to his escape.

At the risk of giving you spoilers, his room contained:

- Blacked-out walls (with instructions to escape written on them in UV ink).
- A UV pen-light taped to the back of the monitor.
- A door with the handle removed.
- A door handle stuck to the underside of the desk.
- A bucket. In case of toilet needs.
- An ancient PC with very limited internet access.
- An ancient webcam that would allow him to take pictures.
- Hidden in the browser's bookmarks instructions to allow him to escape.
- Hints written on the ceiling tiles.
- A small, but reasonably lethal bomb linked to a timer switch.
- Unlimited access to the people of search.me. *Want advice? Search.me.*

HotToddy84 [12.14AM]
Guys. This is serious. I've been kidnapped. Help.

> **ScarodPibs**
> Woah! WTF?

> **HotToddy84**
> I dunno. I've woken up in a dark room. There's no door.
> There's just an old PC, and the only site it'll link to is
> search.me

> **Diskloth**
> >Go west, young man.

> **LiloPadwa**
> LOL!!!!

YelloYelloYello
Use PC, get door, open wishing well, seek Gnome.

LiloPadwa
Sorry, I do not understand "Use PC".

Diskloth
Turn on the bloody light.

LiloPadwa
Sorry, I do not understand "bloody light".

HotToddy84
Fuck you all. This is SERIOUS.

LiloPadwa
Sorry, I do not understand "Fuck you all".

Isolder
(Screencapped for Quotefile) :):):)

HotToddy84
YOU CAN ALL PISS OFF RIGHT NOW. Idiots. I have been kidnapped, I am asking for help. Cockroaches.

LiloPadwa
oooooh, Get her.

HotToddy84
You. Are. Blocked.

LiloPadwa
Bit of a hasty move considering there are only 3 of us following this conversation. If you really are kidnapped and needing our help.

YelloYelloYello
I call HOAX.

Isolder
Seconded.

HotToddy84
Guys, seriously. NEED HELOP.

YelloYelloYello
*HELP.

Isolder
*ATTENTION.

LiloPadwa
"I don't begrudge him the oxygen of publicity.
It's the oxygen of oxygen I have a problem
with." Linda Smith.

HotToddy84
Get Fucked.

LiloPadwa
Sorry, I do not understand "Get Fucked."

Isolder
^ Amazing. YOLOL.

HotToddy84 [1.02AM]
Guys. This is serious. I've been kidnapped. Help. This is NOT
A HOAX. I have been knocked unconscious and have woken
up in a dark room. There is no door. There is no light. Just
this old PC that can only connect to search.me. I have no
mobile.
I need someone, anyone to CONTACT THE POLICE.
URGENTLY.

Pizander
"Dear Friend. This is serious. I've been kidnapped and
woken up locked in a room with no wallet. All have is an

old PC and the title deeds to this Nigerian Gold mine. I
need someone, anyone to SEND ME CA$H. URGENTLY."

BooBooBare
∧ PWNED

HotToddy84 [1.04AM]
Guys. This is serious. I've been kidnapped. Help. This is NOT
A HOAX. I have been knocked unconscious and have woken
up in a dark room. There is no door. There is no light. Just
this old PC that can only connect to search.me. I have no
mobile.
I need someone, anyone to CONTACT THE POLICE.
URGENTLY.

HotToddy84 [1.05AM]
Guys. This is serious. I've been kidnapped. Help. This is NOT
A HOAX. I have been knocked unconscious and have woken
up in a dark room. There is no door. There is no light. Just this
old PC that can only connect to search.me. I have no mobile.
I need someone, anyone to CONTACT THE POLICE.
URGENTLY.

HotToddy84 [1.06AM]
Guys. This is serious. I've been kidnapped. Help. This is NOT
A HOAX. I have been knocked unconscious and have woken
up in a dark room. There is no door. There is no light. Just
this old PC that can only connect to search.me. I have no
mobile.
I need someone, anyone to CONTACT THE POLICE.
URGENTLY.

Cantelooploop
∧ REPORTED AS SPAM.

HotToddy84 [1.07AM]
Look, I've found a webcam. This is a picture of me. I have
been kidnapped. I NEED HELP.

DogTurdian
Seriously, man, what resolution is that? Is that like 1Megapixel?

99RedBalloons
search.me/BuyingANewWebcamGuide.

FitsHerbertTightly
Oh, and now he's suddenly got a webcam #CriesWolf.

HotToddy84
So? I've got a webcam. What's the problem?

FitsHerbertTightly
Sorry bub, still calling this FAKEYHOXYFAKE

HotToddy84
Its spelled 'HOAX' asshat.

FitsHerbertTightly
What's an asshat?

99RedBalloons
www.google.co.uk+images=asshats.

DogTurdian
search.me/CanIWearAnAssHatToAscot.

BrianThePendant
*It's.

HotToddy84 [1.19AM]
Guys. This is serious. I've been kidnapped. Help. This is NOT A HOAX. I have been knocked unconscious and have woken up in a dark room. There is no door. There is no light. Just this old PC that can only connect to search.me. I have no mobile. I have taken the attached picture of me on the webcam to prove that this is legit.

I need someone, anyone to CONTACT THE POLICE.
URGENTLY.

PurposelessPorpoise
What make of webcam?

HotToddy84
GetFucked. Seriously.

PurposelessPorpoise
No. I am asking you seriously. I am trying to help u.

HotToddy84
I need you to call the police.

PurposelessPorpoise
Okay then Where are you?

HotToddy84
I DON'T KNOW.

PurposelessPorpoise
Fine. Then you may as well tell me what the
make of your webcam is.

HotToddy84 [1.25AM]
ANYONE. This is serious. I'VE BEEN KIDNAPPED. Help. This
is NOT A HOAX. I have been knocked unconscious and have
woken up in a dark room. There is no door. There is no light.
Just this old PC that can only connect to search.me. I have
no mobile.
I need someone, anyone to CONTACT THE POLICE.
URGENTLY.
I have no idea where I am. Three hours ago I was at
bZzOff in Filzengraben in Cologne, Germany. I have been
unconscious for at least 2 hours.
I have taken the attached picture of me on the webcam
to prove that this is legit. The webcam driver says it is a

PlayPlug rs259. It has a resolution of only 320x240px.
PLEASE. HELP ME.

PurposelessPorpoise
Cheers. Go to 'settings' on the Webcam Driver software.
Under the tab 'Flash' enable the box 'Flashlight Always
On.' There you go. Instant spotlight. Don't thank me.

HotToddy84
THANK YOU!!!!

PurposelessPorpoise
I said don't thank me.

TriaAnon
Can't see your IP address. Can you post it? We can
work out where you are from that?

HotToddy84
It says 0.0.0.0—guess routed through a proxy.

TriaAnon
Interesting. Possibly calls for a change in the
search.me terms of use to make location
mandatory.

88State
That wouldn't help here.

TriAnon
No, but may help in other cases.

88State
TOTALLY UNACCEPTABLE. Would
completely undermine user anonymity.

TriAnon
But May Help. That's all I'm trying to do.

88State
StateQuisling CyberPuppet.

HotToddy84 [1.41AM]
ANYONE. This is serious. I'VE BEEN KIDNAPPED. Help. This
is NOT A HOAX. I have been knocked unconscious and have
woken up in a dark room. There is no door. Just this old
PC that can only connect to search.me. I have no mobile.
The only light I have is on the spotlight on the PlayPlug259
Webcam. I need someone, anyone to CONTACT THE
POLICE. URGENTLY.
I have no idea where I am. Three hours ago I was at
bZzOff in Filzengraben in Cologne, Germany. I have been
unconscious for at least 2 hours. My IP address is routed
through a proxy.
PLEASE. HELP ME. PLEASE. HELP ME. FOR GOD'S SAKE
PLEASE. HELP ME.

> **HighHarry**
> Interesting. I had no idea the old PlayPlug259 had a
> spotlight feature. I must dig my old one out. Would you say
> it's as bright as the iPhone light? #AheadOfItsTime

HotToddy84 [1.47AM]
PLEASE. HELP ME. PLEASE. HELP ME. PLEASE. HELP
ME.PLEASE. HELP ME. PLEASE. HELP ME. PLEASE. HELP ME.
PLEASE. HELP ME. PLEASE. HELP ME. PLEASE. HELP ME.
ANYONE. This is serious. I'VE BEEN KIDNAPPED. Help. This
is NOT A HOAX. I have been knocked unconscious and have
woken up in a dark room. There is no door. Just this old
PC that can only connect to search.me. I have no mobile.
The only light I have is on the spotlight on the PlayPlug259
Webcam. I need someone, anyone to CONTACT THE
POLICE. URGENTLY.
I have no idea where I am. Three hours ago I was at
bZzOff in Filzengraben in Cologne, Germany. I have been
unconscious for at least 2 hours. My IP address is routed
through a proxy.

PLEASE. HELP ME. PLEASE. HELP ME. PLEASE. HELP
ME.
CALL THE POLICE.

HotToddy84 [1.49AM]
I am still kidnapped. I am in a dark room. There's no way
out. I don't know where I am. I can only use search.me on
this PC. I've no mobile. I may be at bZzOff in Filzengraben in
Cologne, Germany, but I have no proof of this.
PLEASE. HELP ME. PLEASE. HELP ME. PLEASE. HELP
ME. CALL THE POLICE. CALL THE POLICE. PLEASE.

   HotToddy84
   UPDATE: I've found a bomb.

      Ipecack
      Srsly????

       DudeClasm
       Too much.

      HotToddy84
      Here's a photo:

      Ipecack
      Amazing. I think there's a serious issue here.

     MotherBrown
     Yeah, from the looks of it, his browser's IE6.

Ipecack [1.53AM]
The user HotToddy84 uploaded the following picture at 1.49
this morning. At first sight it seems to show an explosive
device, but the central canister suggests that it is in fact a
chemical weapon of some sort. What do you guys think?

IservedAtThePleasure
Yeah. Looks viable.

7Erberus
Holy shit!!!

Laylala
Need context PDQ.

HotToddy84 [2.03AM]
I have been kidnapped and placed in a locked room with a suspected chemical weapon. It is counting down. I need urgent rescue.

QwerTea
Amazing, man. You are Schroedinger's Cat and I claim my 10 bucks.

Oooo36
Wow. Problem solved. NOTIFY THE CATS!!!

[I've not included the next 36 hilarious cat pictures and gifs posted in reply]

HotToddy84 [2.03AM]
I have been kidnapped and placed in a locked room with a suspected chemical weapon. It is counting down to go off at 3am. I am in Cologne, Germany. My last location was at bZzOff in Filzengraben in Cologne, Germany, but I have no proof that this is where I still am. Place call the police and emergency services and terrorist forces.

KnowHow
Seriously man, this is the internet. The secret services know already.

YesMan
Good point. Help is on the way.

HotToddy84
Have you called them?

HotToddy84 [2.07AM]
I HAVE BEEN KIDNAPPED AND PLACED IN A LOCKED
ROOM WITH A SUSPECTED CHEMICAL WEAPON.
IT IS COUNTING DOWN TO GO OFF AT 3AM. LAST
LOCATION BZZOFF IN FFILZENGRABEN IN COLOGNE,
GERMANY, BUT I HAVE NO PROOF OF THIS.
I NEED THE POLICE AND EMERGENCY SERVICES AND
TERRORIST FORCES ALERTING.

RutgrrrHowRU
Seriously man, caps lock off.

HotToddy84 [2.10AM]
I have been kidnapped and placed in a locked room with a
suspected chemical weapon. It is counting down to go off
at 3am. I think I am at bZzOff in Filzengraben in Cologne,
Germany, but I have no proof of this.
I need the police and emergency services and terrorist
forces alerting. Please. I am shitsacred.

My69
Shit sacred? What are you doing? Taking a crap in a
church?

HotToddy84 [2.10AM]
What are you people not getting? I am TRAPPED in
a room with A BOMB. I'm in COLOGNE, GERMANY.
This could be a TERRORIST ATTACK. I need rescuing,
the emergency services NEED to be informed. This is
SERIOUS.

Waltever
Genuinely interested, how are you certain you're in
Cologne now?

HotToddy84
I'm not, but it seems most likely.

Waltever
Okay. Please repost amended.

HotToddy84 [2.10AM]
What are you people not getting? I am TRAPPED in a room
with A BOMB. I'm probably in COLOGNE, GERMANY.
This could be a TERRORIST ATTACK. I need rescuing, the
emergency services NEED to be informed. This is SERIOUS.

DaveWave
Okay. I'm calling them now. Can you post your GPS
location?

HotToddy84
I don't have it. I think I am at bZzOff in Filzengraben in
Cologne, Germany. But I'm not certain.

Gertie
Oh, could be a trap. Like in *Batman Begins*.

Susanvoratrelundar
You mean The Dark Knight

Gertie
Oh yeah <3 <3 <3 that film. Heath RIP :(#Ledge

HotToddy84 [2.20AM]
Everyone on search.me.
I am TRAPPED in a room with A BOMB. I'm probably
in COLOGNE, GERMANY. This could be a TERRORIST
ATTACK. I need rescuing, the emergency services NEED to
be informed. This is SERIOUS.
I think I am at at bZzOff in Filzengraben in Cologne,
Germany. But I'm not certain. PLEASE INFORM POLICE OF
POSSIBLE TERRORIST ATTACK.

Xanvier
Sure thing man. I'm on this right now.

HotToddy84
Thanks! Thank you so much.

Xanvier
I've called the police and they're on their way to you.

HotToddy84
THANKS!!!

Xavier
Jokes.

HotToddy84
FUCK U YOU PIECE OF WORTHLESS SHIT.

HotToddy84 [2.25AM]
Everyone on search.me.
I am TRAPPED in a room with A BOMB set to go off at 3AM.
(pic attached)
I'm probably in COLOGNE, GERMANY. This could be a
TERRORIST ATTACK. I need rescuing, the emergency
services NEED to be informed.
This is SERIOUS. I am probably at bZzOff in Filzengraben in
Cologne, Germany. But I'm not certain.
PLEASE INFORM POLICE OF POSSIBLE TERRORIST ATTACK.
PLEASE INFORM POLICE OF POSSIBLE TERRORIST ATTACK.
PLEASE INFORM POLICE OF POSSIBLE TERRORIST ATTACK.

MotherBrown
Seriously, petal, turn down the spam. Some of us are
trying to talk about chutney recipes and you're just All Over
the feed.

Wander
Hi HotToddy84, I've looked at your picture of the bomb
and there's a really easy way   to disarm it. Please look at
this link to a video.

HotToddy84
Thanks.

Wander
Hahaah Rickrolled! :)

ExpletiveDeleted [2.32AM]
Hey Everyone!
I am COMPLETELY TRAPPED in a gingerbread house with A
CAKE set to go off at 3AM. (pic of cake attached).
I'm totally in THE 11-ACRE WOOD. This could be a
scheme by the Big Bad Wolf. Or a SHAMELESS PLEA FOR
ATTENTION. I need help. PWEASE WON'T SOMEONE
NOTICE ME. I've had to do a dump in a bag. I can upload a
picture of this with my crummy old webcam.
PLEASE INFORM THE CATS.
PLEASE INFORM THE CATS.
PLEASE INFORM THE CATS.

Bolshoe78
^ Brilliant. This is why I love search.me.

JannyAnn
I have told the cats. I have told the cats. I have told the
cats.

Billiant
Such bomb.
Many help.
Very cake.
So gingerbre3d.
Wow.

HotToddy84 [2.40AM]
Please guys. Stop this! Call the police!!!!

Frobo
Just kill yourself.

Riddler3

Listen – at the base of the device are two wires, yes? Just like in the movies.

HotToddy84

Yeah. What should I do?

Riddler3

What colours are they?

HotToddy84

Red and green.

Riddler3

Cut the red one.

Riddler3

No, wait the green one.

Riddler3

No, the red one!

Riddler3

Aw, shoot, just pull them both out and do the world a favour.

SensibarHashtag [2.43AM]

Not wanting to break into the lulz, but looking at that picture of the alleged chemical device and it does appear to be run from a fairly standard chipset. I'd suggest shorting across the 1st and 9th pins as a first move. What do you think?

Dooooogull

O rly? Cos looking at it, I'd argue that the pins are in reverse order. Without knowing more about the polarity, I'd suggest a tap test across pins 2, 4 and 6.

SensibarHashtag

I can't bring myself to agree. Short 1 and 9 and the timer will be disabled.

Dooooogull

How can you be so certain? The picture is too lo-res to be able to tell.

HotToddy84

Guys pls! I've got 15 minutes left. What should I do?

RimTimTim

It's okay—this vid shows the circuit board you need clearly. Take a look.

HotToddy84

Fucksake.

RimTimTim

HA HA RICKROLLD AGAIN LOSER.

StJohn

Not being funny, but the picture of that circuit board shows it to be of Chinese manufacture. Wonder what that means :)

Fiskali

Actually, looks more like a screengrab to me. It's very lo-res. Still calling this a hoax.

Dooooogull

It'd make sense if it was a screengrab. I'd say it's sourced from VCD-res at best and scaled to 320x240. There are clear artefacts that are a giveaway.

SanitySally

IIRC didn't HotToddy84 say that it was an old webcam, weren't they fairly lo-res? So may NOT be a screengrab.

PutItInPutin

Well, HotToddy84 claimed it was a PlayPlug259.
They're default resolution was 800x600 on
Windows95, not 320x240.

Fiskali

Nailed it. HOAX.

Dooooogull

Hoax.

MiskaGinTonic

Hoax.

LuvvinIT

Hoax.

SPACSLock

BUT there is also a 'lo-res' setting
at 320x240 for basic systems.
HotToddy84, can you confirm or deny
that that's the setting you're operating
at?

HotToddy84

SRSLY? For God's sake, call the
police. Please help me.

MiskaGinTonic

Hello, police? Yeah, I'd like to report
A HOAXER.

HotToddy84 [2.51AM]

Kate,

It's hard to type this, knowing that I may never see you again.
But I love you so much. Since I met you two years ago,
you've meant the world to me. I always thought I'd be in
love with people but that no-one would ever be in love with

me back. And I was fine with that. You know, I'd made my peace with the world. And then I met you, and I realised how wonderful it was to be loved. Simple as.

You've made me a better person. You've made me take risks. If it wasn't for you, I'd never have moved from Hull to Germany, got the amazing flat we've got, learned to cook, or tried skiing. You've made me do so much that I'd never have dreamed possible. If it wasn't for you I'd still be living in that damp and tiny box. It's been so wonderful, it really has, and I'm crying right now thinking that I can't say goodbye to you properly.

Sorry that I've got to type this somewhere where other people can see it. I didn't want to say goodbye to you ever, and NEVER like this. I'm so sorry. I love you.

Todd.

SensibarHashtag

Dear Kate

Thanks for all the sex and for not being too much of a whiny bitch. Can't believe I had to move to Germany just to get laid. Sorry I'm such a fucking loser.

Todd.

RimTimTim

^ AmaZing.

DawsonsCrack

If only they'd instituted the ability to RT posts in the last upgrade, we could infinityRT that.

LuvvinIT

Good call. I've opened a ChangeRequestPetition to make sure that add that. Direct link's here. Make sure you sign it if you've got a moment.

DawsonsCrack

Signed.

MiskaGinTonic
Signed.

SPACSlock
Signed.

AdmiralFapbar
Signed.

HotToddy84 [2.57AM]
You're all bastards. You know that? You could have saved me. You could have tried.

RimTimTim

[picture of a kitten in a field. EVERYTIME YOU MASTURBATE, GOD BLOWS UP HOTTODDY84]

HotToddy84 [2.59AM]
One minute left. Jesus, help me, I'm so scared.

Diablow
Hey everybody, shall we count down the number of fucks we give?

MiskaGinTonic
10

RimTimTim
9
Sweevil
8

Trisha10
7

HotToddy84
FUCK YOU ALL.

Kristol
6

DawsonsCrack
5

KatesAWhore
4

SPACSLock
3

AdmiralFapbar
2

LuvvinIT
1

SensibarHashtag
0

MiskaGinTonic
Happy New Year Everybody!

LuvvinIT
Boom, boom, boom, shake the room! Tick tick tick...

DawsonsCrack
BOOM!

Quargle
first.

AP MOBILE

Breaking (3.17amGMT) Cologne, Germany – reports of a small explosion in the city. Emergency services have confirmed they are responding to a small fire on the top floor of an office block. No reports of any casualties in the street. No confirmation of any terrorist involvement.

CHAPTER EIGHT
SHE WROTE MURDER

Vampantha @VampanthaWrites · 19m
To London for BAFTA meet and muchos-contractatas with
agent. Frantic call – can I meet a showrunner about pitching?
Seriously! #GoodTimes

Vampantha
28 mins · 🌐
is wondering if any of her WRITER friends are free
to do a local library visit next Wednesday? Was really
looking forward to this one (love meeting fans!), but
been summoned to another hush-hush meeting about
SecretProject#3. It's going to be a great day—give a talk,
judge a fancy dress compo, and have lunch with prize
winners from the local paper. Gutted not to be going—I
hate having to let down the children, seriously. They'll only
pay expenses, I'm afraid, but, if any of you are spare...?
Like · Comment · Share

Georgia Manse uploaded a photo **Cover of new
anthology**
2 hrs · 🌐
Like · Comment · Share
Vampantha likes this

Vampantha Looks LOVELY!!! Well done!!! Would have loved to been in this one, but having to turn down so many anthologies these days in order to concentrate on my film and TV work, when I'm not chained to my desk by Inspector Grangelove. Can you believe it's the third book already??? Anyway, best of luck with the anthology. Hawkword are a great little press doing some really interesting things, and I'd love to have taken part, seriously You know how much Vampantha hates saying No!!!!:):)
Just now · Like

Vampantha @VampanthaWrites · 8 Oct
wishes she was at @CrimeyCon seriously! Missing the #karaoke with @BrazWax12. Stupid #SecretProjects.

Vampantha @VampanthaWrites · 9 Oct
Quick 9km run in the rain (bracing!!!) and then 4,000 words before 10am #amwriting

Vampantha @VampanthaWrites · 10 Oct
Fans of the redoubtable #InspectorGrangelove will be pleased to hear he's got me under house-arrest. Seriously! #amwriting

Vampantha @VampanthaWrites · 11 Oct
So pleased for @BrazWax12 's new book deal. A talent who's finally found a place in the genre at last #KnewHimFirst

Vampantha @VampanthaWrites · 11 Oct
Nervous for the new #Grangelove book. Shippers will be in for a treat. Bit.ly/Grn8765

Vampantha @VampanthaWrites · 13 Oct
Have you read the new #Grangelove book? Dying to know what you think!!! Seriously. #FingersCrossed Bit.ly/Grn8765

Vampantha @VampanthaWrites · 14 Oct
Tempted by the raunchy new #Grangelove? Dive in to a
FREE chapter. Seriously. Please RT Bit.ly/Grn8765

Vampantha @VampanthaWrites · 14 Oct
ICYMI Tempted by the raunchy new #Grangelove? Dive in to
a FREE chapter. Please RT Bit.ly/Grn8765

Vampantha @VampanthaWrites · 15 Oct
For the morning crowd. Tempted by the raunchy new
#Grangelove? Dive in to a FREE chaper. Please RT Bit.ly/
Grn8765

Vampantha @VampanthaWrites · 2h
Male critics can STFU. I don't write for you. Never have.
Never will. #Bigots

Vampantha @VampanthaWrites · 1h
.@SarahDartford78 gone over to the boys club with that
review, I see? #StabbedInTheBack

LAST YEAR WAS an odd one for Vampantha. Her third Inspector
Grangelove ebook hadn't quite been the breakthrough success that
had confidently been predicted. Mostly by Vampantha herself:

> Stevedore—that's Grangelove's first name, by the way. I
> always call him Stevedore as he feels like an old friend to me.
> What's great about Stevedore is that he's kind of like a sexy
> superhero everyman. He's a crossover hero in so many ways,
> in that he solves crimes but he also has some fairly—shall we
> say—raunchy adventures. He's essentially a James Bond with
> sex. He's also got a really strong appeal among his female
> readers because he's written by a women and I think a lot
> of women recognise the authenticity of my voice. I'm writing
> from a female point-of-view.
>   Sometimes that's really hard. You know, it's difficult for a
> female writer to establish herself in the crime fiction genre.

There are so few really successful female crime authors. As a gendered-space it's quite male-dominated. I sometimes find it really frustrating. You know, I'll often be sat on a panel with the Same Old Men and I'll think, *You're lovely blokes but we've heard quite enough from you—where are the new women?* I'd love to see some raw female talent coming through. It can be quite lonely.

Erotic crime is easily dismissed by a lot of people. I don't know why. I really resent comparisons to *50 Shades*, you know. That feels really old hat. I was writing before that came along and I'll be writing long after EL is forgotten about. She's a lovely girl by all accounts, but what she's writing really isn't sex, or BDSM, or even erotic. People say it's been a great gateway for a lot of folks into reading, but if that's the case then I hope they read something better. No offence to EL. I've met her and she's a real sweetheart, but she does cast a bit of a shadow over us proper writers. And not just cos of the cakes.

Vampantha, interviewed on the "CrimeTea" Podcast

REVIEW: A Rubber Of Velvet:
An Inspector Grangelove Mystery
by Vampantha

This book is WEIRD. Actually, WEIRD doesn't do it justice. Neither does horrid, eyewatering, shoddy or grim.

The plot (oh there is one) is basically so old-fashioned it may as well be called *Confessions Of A Copper* or *Carry On Copper*. Someone has graphic sex. They get murdered. Inspector Stevedore Grangelove (hahahaha) is having sex when he's put on the case. He interviews suspects, has sex with them, gets leads, goes undercover (in a sex club), has sex with more suspects, finds out who the murderer is, has sex with them, and then hands them in, before going home to have some sex.

I'll talk a bit about Little Grangelove. His member is frequently described as 'purple,' 'throbbing' and 'angry.' I think 'bruised,' 'sore' and 'resentful' also make it in. The poor thing takes more of a pounding "than a hooker's behind" (this is a frequent simile). Apparently the PC's plodder is able to satisfy every conquest with a 'warm gush of love's fountain' but it has to do this so often I'm surprised it's not a dry cough.

I'm not sure what the story is supposed to be. There's a lengthy subplot involving possibly dyed pubic hair. There's whole chapters devoted to Grangelove's unique interrogation technique which features more use of the phrases 'paddle,' 'sling' and 'spreader bar' than you see in the police procedural manual. At every stage, you're made painfully aware of all of the tricks that Agatha Christie missed out on, such as putting arsenic in lubricant, or electrocution via butt plug.

You'll have gathered by now it's not really my cup of teabagging. Fair enough. Horses for courses (talking of which, I will never ride a pony again after that scene in the stables with Lady Vagenta). But you know, Vampantha is no EL James. Frankly, she's no Sid James.

The writing is execrable. Grangelove does everything 'wryly.' He drives wryly, he interrogates wryly, he has sex wryly. He probably drinks rye wryly. I counted 43 instances of the word 'gush,' 23 of 'pert' and 4 of 'cum guzzling slut whore.' The latter is, I guess, empowering. Go Women!

Every apartment is 'spartan,' but some are also 'cluttered' and 'homely' with 'earth tones' and yet also 'clinically white.' People can't pass a sunset without remarking on its 'glowing embers.' 'Red sky at night don't they say?' they say to each other three times at least. No-one ever pulls a gun on someone else without the detail being categorised in a way which, if it reminds you curiously of Wikipedia, is because every description is from Wikipedia.

If you can make it through all that, you're in for a treat. If you're a professional proofreader who loves unpaid homework. Otherwise, oh, my god, this is a cry for help. The standard of proofreading screams 'self-published ebook' more than the clip-art and the use of Arial on the cover. There may be a high body-count, but the biggest crime here is against the poor semicolon, which is often allowed to end a paragraph;

I'm not sure why that happens, but, oh, God it hurts me. The two chapter 47s are a treat as well. I kind of viewed it as like a choose-your-own-adventure flashback—if only *Warlock Of Firetop Mountain* had presented you with the choice of fighting or fisting an Orc. Ah well;

Avoid;

Reviewed on
"Crimes Against Language" Blog

THE THING ABOUT a bad review is to take it on the chin. I've seen friends get dumped on Facebook and fight back. It never ends well. The best thing to do is to walk away. I'm not sure if I could. (Mind you, I worry I'd just kill them. What have I become? When did murder become easier than solving a problem?)

Vampantha's book got a succession of really very bad reviews. And she replied to each and every one of them:

Hey there – I seriously don't have time to reply to this upsetting filth, but clearly you have LOTS OF TIME!!! Why don't you go and get a life? Sure the books got typo's, but its also got one thing that youlll never have and that's TRUTH. Buy a dictionary and seriously look it up why don't you?

Hi! Thanks for trashing my book without reading it properly. Wonder if any1's ever managed to finish any of your books? I seriously think not with you looking how you do.

A curious thing happened. If you were an author as well as a reviewer, and you'd reviewed *Rubber Of Velvet* badly, then the chances were that a series of one-star reviews would appear on your Amazon page. A typical sample would be:

★☆☆☆☆ **WASTE OF TIME!!!** 2 Nov 2014
By Vampantha
Avoid this book! Seriously, waste of time and money. Illiterete garbage. No suspense at all – obvious from the start that the detective's boyfriend did it! Lame.

Not all of these reviews appeared under Vampantha's name. She reacted to complaints about the ones that did with, 'CAN'T TAKE IT? THEN DONT DISH IT OUT. SERIOUSLY.' However, the reviews that weren't obviously written by Vampantha attracted more attention. As one blogger put it...

Declaration: I've only met Vampantha once at KetCrimeCon '12. She's not a friend, or even an acquaintance, really, but she was on a panel about Getting Started In Crime Writing, and I went up to her afterwards to ask her for advice. She looked me up and down and then pointed to her breasts (I am not kidding) and said, "Honey? If you want to get ahead, get a set like these. Seriously."

I thought that was a bit of an odd and sad thing to say. I'm a shy person and rarely manage to say anything clever on the spot, but I couldn't help muttering, "Is that how Dorothy L. Sayers did it?" To which Vampantha nodded, "Well, that's seriously how all the Americans get on."

She was on quite a lot of panels at the Con, and had no shortage of opinions. It was the last Con that Clayton Roberts ever did, and I was really looking forward to hearing him speak, but Vampantha was also on the panel, so, as it was clearly taking him time to draw breath, he didn't really get to say much. Vampantha did. She offered the following advice: "The thing is, I see Vampantha as a brand, and I've got to conform to my own standards. Always be polite, kind and damn witty. Seriously, I dress as the brand—I'm careful to ensure that I've a recognisable silhouette—always the dress and the corset so that, at a glance, people know that I'm Vampantha." There was a lot more in this vein.

Later on that night, I was chatting to a male publisher friend (someone who I knew so well I wouldn't dream of asking for help getting a book published. It'd mortify us both). We were chatting about the food at the hotel, when up came Vampantha. I kind of saw her approaching because, I swear, she was unzipping her jacket as she got nearer. You could hear it going *zizzzzzz*. And then she stood there and announced herself to my friend with, "Hey there.

Why you wasting time with that gal? Seriously, does she have THESE?"

That was Vampantha being polite, kind, and damn witty, right there. I'm no qualified feminist, but I am a woman, and I seriously just can't even. Especially, because there's a thing about these conventions that some of you may know—not all the men who go to them behave, perhaps, as the Complete Gentlemen they could be. I've 5 brothers, all of them sportsmen, and I must say, drunk Jocks have always treated me with more courtesy and charm than your average male convention-goer. I think, alongside a lot of female attendees, I've got used to smiling tightly as I remove unwanted hands from bits of my anatomy. To see Vampantha out there being so... Vampantha, well, I found it a little unpleasant. I don't want to say she's setting a bad example, as that makes it seem like I'm slut-shaming, but I will say that she came up to me the next day in the corridor and said, "Sorry about last night, honey. Seriously hope I didn't butt into your boy business. I didn't mean anything by it. I was just titnotizing him."

Titnotizing. Yeah.

I've kind of been aware of Vampantha ever since. You know, in a 'oh, right, her,' sort of a way. She's one of those figures on the Crime Lit Scene who you can be very aware of without ever having read one of her books. (Confession: I have read a couple, actually. She puts together some nice people you quite like and then kills them off in horrid ways. If that's your thing, then it's not bad.) Mostly I've heard of her anecdotally, or in one case having to try and counsel a friend after he left his wife for Vampantha only for her to say, "Oh, honey, that's seriously sweet, but no." (The best counselling I could offer was to punch him on the nose.)

Anyhoo, obviously I was aware of Rubber-of-Velvet-Gate. Or Rubber-of-Velvet-Gash as a friend called it. At the same time, I was having a bit of a personal voyage. Due to a deal falling through, I'd ended up self-publishing a project (*The Magpie Kiss*, if you're in the mood for a bit of post-war murder & melodrama).

One thing I've learned as a writer—we're hugely jealous of anyone else's success. Like there's a finite amount to go around. Like high school, only much more mental. If Sally got the captain of the football team, then fair enough. There was only one of those. But there are lots of publishers and lots of little triumphs—pretty much enough to go round.

So anyway, *The Magpie Kiss* came out and sold—well, pretty badly, but it actually sold. #12,354 in the category after a couple of weeks, meaning 30 copies. Ouch. Don't worry, I'll live.

Thing is, I spotted that *A Rubber Of Velvet* was at #12,355 in the category. In other words, I was outselling Vampantha. Result.

Only, it was waaaay more curious than that. Because Vampantha's book had some 1- and 2-star reviews (4 in total) and then 37 5-star raves. How, I wondered, could it have more reviews than copies sold? How? It's not like it was on NetGalley; I checked. Interestingly, a lot of the 'people' who'd handed Vampantha 5-stars are the same 'people' who handed her rivals 1-star reviews. And those are the only reviews they've ever written.

Sooo...

– an impossible number of reviews?

– by phantom reviewers?

– I'm titnotized.

Taken from
thesallyanneadventures.blogspot.com

VAMPANTHA DIDN'T COMMENT directly on the article. Her last tweet before she protected her account for a bit was, 'Some people don't get that I am a big thing. Seriously.'

VAMPANTHA ARRIVED AS an actual dossier. As in a proper wodge of print-outs in a manila folder pushed through my letterbox by hand. Because obviously the Killuminati knew where I lived.

I couldn't quite figure what they wanted me to do with her that she wasn't already doing to herself. Vampantha was basically committing career suicide.

Only then, she emerged in a Jackie Aspley profile. A photocopy turned up in the post:

THE HEARTBROKEN QUEEN OF CRIME

*One group you don't want to upset are crime writers. **Jackie Aspley** meets a Mistress of Crime who has upset the armchair murderers.*

Vampantha is a curious, some would say sad figure. She feels she owes the world an apology.

"I don't want to blame it on my brother's suicide," she begins, pouring me quite a nice glass of wine in the lobby of a very fashionable hotel. I'll say one thing about Vampantha, she does things in style.

"But yes, when he killed himself, it kind of took the joy out of my world and since then, seriously, there have been..."— she pauses, and rests a hand on mine—"issues. You know, sometimes, you're up seriously late, staring into the internet and you decided you're gonna fix it. Or rather, the wine inside you's going to have a serious go..."

Jackie Aspley, thedailypost.com

And on it went. There were two Post-it notes attached to it. One said, 'She's never had a brother.' The other said, 'Depression? Bollocks.' There was also a photocopy that gave away a few details about Vampantha's real name. She had recently married a Sodobus executive, which explained how she got by.

For some reason, Duster had her in their sights. And I was fine with that.

I 'REACHED OUT' to Vampantha.

Hello!

I hope you're well. I'm a publicist with over ten years' expertise at representing key brands and global clients in the corporate sector, but I'm now setting out on my own, looking to represent purely literary clients. I've read all your books (I hope you're not offended that they're my fave guilty pleasure!) and would love to represent you. As I'm looking to build up my portfolio, I'd initially be willing to represent you for three months for free, and then take it from there.

I look forward to hearing from you,

Brian McMullen

BRIAN MCMULLEN WAS a little shorter than me thanks to his terrible posture, but he was always very smartly turned out in a selection of bright shirts. His hair was swept over with gel, he had some quite natty glasses, and the softest of Morningside accents. Nothing threw Brian. I actually rather liked him, and sort of wished he was real so that I could turn to him for help.

Instead, Brian threw himself into helping Vampantha regenerate herself. As she lived in Milton Keynes, it was reasonably easy to assure her that most of my clients were London based. I'd even taken the precaution of approaching a couple of other authors who she knew, and had actually managed to organise a reasonably successful book launch by throwing the KillFund at it.

Vampantha wasn't as easy as my other clients. It was taking a lot of time but we weren't actually doing anything.

The peculiar thing about Vampantha was that she was always *on* whenever I was around. She'd invite me into her quite nice home, or to meet her at Costa in the shopping centre, and she'd be there in the nearly-ballgown-length dress and the Bristol suspension bridge corset.

It made relaxing in her house tricksy. Although she looked like she'd just come from dancing with the undead, her living room was full of piles of laundry and smelt a little of dog. Her sofas screamed 'DFS had a sale on.' They were a white sort-of leather and freezing cold. There were woodchip bookshelves clustered with copies of her books. The whole place had the chilly atmosphere of a nineteen-seventies film insert.

And there she'd be sat, all made up. Behind her on the mantelpiece were photos of her and a man. He seemed completely non-descript—a regional sales executive for Sodobus. He looked it in the photos. Next to him was Vampantha in her *off* mode. In sweatpants, or a dirty t-shirt, painting. She looked friendlier. Far friendlier and more real than the creature who sat opposite me, making earnest notes of everything I said in an oversized notebook with a studiedly genuine fountain pen. Purple ink, by the way.

We'd meet for long hours. She'd talk (in a studiedly vaguely transatlantic accent) about Vampantha the brand, Vampantha's personal appearances, Vampantha the victim, Vampantha the retribution. Curiously, she never talked about her work.

ONE DAY WE were sat drinking her god-awful tea. She looked tired. Her eyes flickered closed, and when they re-opened, they were just narrow slits.

"Do you like me, Brian?"

"Of course," I said. Had I spoken too quickly? Too slowly? Did I sound sincere?

Vampantha carried on looking at me. "It doesn't really matter. I don't give much of a shit. I just need to get some results. Raise profile, you know." It took me a while to realise. Her voice was different. A bit less Houston, a bit more Home Counties.

"I think I've done good work for you."

"Yeah," she said, dubiously.

"I've doubled your number of Twitter followers, I've got you press coverage, and at least three bookings at libraries."

"Libraries..." sighed Vampantha. "Bless 'em, they ain't Wembley."

Two weeks ago, she'd been really keen on library visits. And so I'd set them up. She'd done two so far, sat perched on a giant mushroom reading from the saucier bits of *A Rubber Of Velvet* to appalled pensioners, some snoring quietly.

She tapped me on the nose and I suddenly realised it was the first time she ever touched me. "In that head of yours, there's a great brain, isn't there? And it's not always doing what it's saying, is it? It's there, isn't it, drawing up vast calculating tables and spreadsheets. Every time I speak you're slotting little bits of me into boxes, aren't you?"

"You got me," I smiled weakly. "It's a habit. It's how I operate. I study people. It tells me how to target them."

"And what do you think of me?"

"That you're very bright," I said sincerely. "And that you use what you've got."

She laughed at that. "You've read about the titnotizing."

"Of course I have."

She shook her head. "Doesn't work on you, though. It began as a weapon, you know. First time I went to one of these crime things. I was shy, I was a fish totally out of water. I didn't think I'd know how to talk to any of the men there. Turned out, I didn't have to." She cupped her breasts. "These little ladies did all the talking. I could have strode around with a paper bag on my head. Would have made no difference. It's like I was trying to talk to men who'd never talked to a woman before. Or toddlers fixated on working out which teat to suckle on. At first I thought it was disgusting—I mean, it's like they don't know how adult men behave. And then I thought, *Hey girl, you can use that,* and so I did. It didn't make me popular with the"—elaborate air quotes—"'feminists,' but it made me very popular with everyone else. And, you know, by putting the goods on show in the shop window, it stopped people noseying around the store. If you know what I mean."

I didn't, but Vampantha explained, her smile sour. "It was like they were too distracted to bother pinching my arse in the lift. Like sheesh, are all male authors Jim Davidson? It's the twenty-first century, who even does that now? Still, they mostly kept their hands to themselves and that was nice."

I nodded. She nodded.

"Yeah, doesn't work on you. Are you a fag?"

I shook my head. "Just... it's not a technique that's to my taste."

Vampantha smiled. "Yeah," she said slowly again. "I figured you'd say that. You don't approve. But you know what? It works. Who'd have thought it was so easy to just use my puppies to get work out of the boys? It shouldn't be that simple, should it?"

"In an ideal world, no—" I began.

"I mean, chrissakes. Look at some of the other girls—just look at them. Ex-nuns playing at being librarians."

I hadn't seen it myself. I'd done some research of other authors Vampantha reckoned herself against. They all seemed, well, normal. Nice. People who owned clean kettles. But not to Vampantha. Odd how some women are the harshest judges of other women's appearance.

"Anyway, screw 'em. Century Twenty-One, seriously. If I wanna wear a basque everywhere, it's my business. It's hard enough—" She pointed at the dowdy plate of biscuits she'd brought out and not touched. "Jesus, it wouldn't do some of those cats any harm to learn what a diet's like. I'm so hungry."

Yes, I thought. Hungry summed up Vampantha so well.

ONE DAY I received a breathless phone-call. "Vampantha's got great news, Brian. She's been *nominated* for an award. Seriously."

More than nominated, actually short-listed.

"Congratulations!" I said, a bit startled.

"Hey, sorry, I'm just—" And she whooped. "So stoked. Have I caught you at a bad moment? You shopping?"

I was actually out chugging. About half a mile from her house, outside the shopping centre. If I moved a little to the left, I could see her through the windows of a restaurant. Sitting at a table with a man.

"Yeah. You celebrating?"

"Oh, my gosh, yes. I've seriously just been told. This moment. I had to call. Can you rush out a press release?"

I couldn't be arsed. But I'd learned how to say this in a publicist way. "Hmm. That seems over-eager. Let's go grass roots with this, Vampantha. Put up a tweet saying that you're humbled to be considered, namecheck some of the other people on the list. Let your fans retweet it. I'll take care of that." I ran two Twitter fan accounts for Vampantha. They occasionally had spats with each other. It amused me. A very little.

Her response was muted. "Sure. Okay. If you think it's seriously best."

"I do," I said. "I don't want you to seem over-eager. After all, you might not win."

"Nooo," she said, strangely, "I suppose that's possible."

* * *

HER TWEET:

> **Vampantha** @VampanthaWrites · 6s
> HELL YEAH. Best crime ebook? That's a nom I'll om-nom-nom. Seriously.

She posted it fifteen seconds later. As though it was already in her phone. I stood outside chugging away. I saw her leave the restaurant. She was off-duty. Accompanied by the man who looked like he was her accountant. That would be the dull husband. They walked right past me without even noticing.

I actually spoke to her. I knew I could get away with it. "Hey there! Do you have time for—"

Before I could even get to cancer/kitten/children, she put up a hand, "Nah," and walked away. There wasn't a trace of the Deep South in her accent. She and the dull man pottered off.

"I CAN'T BELIEVE she'll win," said Amber. I was having dinner with her and Guy and was amazed when Amber brought her name up in conversation. Turns out she'd found the blog about titnotizing on Twitter.

We had to explain The Vampantha Phenomenon to Guy, but he looked far more interested in his carbonara. "It's just chick-lit." He wasn't really listening. "Do they even have awards for that stuff?"

"Yes," snapped Amber, "because all books written by women are chick-lit."

"Yeah, anyway"—which was Guy's masterful attempt at pulling out of an argument—"it doesn't really matter, does it?"

He went back to his pasta. As far as he was concerned, the world had moved on.

I'LL SPARE TELLING you too much about the Kettering Crime Convention. The awards were hosted by Jarvis Chapman, the actor currently famous for playing outspoken TV detective Inspector 'Crass' Carmichael. It was kind of a big coup for

Kettering Crime Convention, and, forgetting that Vampantha was my supposed victim, wearing my publicist hat, I was really pleased at the notion that she'd be pictured on stage next to a very bankable TV star. #GoodForSales

Vampantha didn't see it like this. I woke up one morning to discover she'd gone *mental*.

> **Vampantha** @VampanthaWrites · 46m
> Wait. WAIT. They're letting CRASS CARMICHAEL present the @KetCrimeCon? Seriously? WHAT THE SHUDDERING HELL?

> **Vampantha** @VampanthaWrites · 43m
> Seriously, I've really enjoyed knowing that, were I to win a CrimeConAward, the host wouldn't call me fat. #SackCrass.

> **Vampantha** @VampanthaWrites · 41m
> The thought has seriously crossed my mind, What will Crass say about the dress I wear to the awards? #SackCrass #FatShamer.

> **Vampantha** @VampanthaWrites · 40m
> Thanks, @KetCrimeCon, for taking a safe space away from women #SackCrass.

Someone had responded, 'Er, you know he's just an actor, don't you?' To which she'd replied:

> **Vampantha** @VampanthaWrites · 38m
> Exactly! Not Someone who ACTUALLY UNDERSTOOD THE AWARD and WHY WE WERE THERE. #SackCrass.

She'd followed up with:

> **Vampantha** @VampanthaWrites · 35m
> Also, and this is no way sour grapes speaking, but: I HAVE VOLUNTEERED TO HOST THE @KetCrimeCon. I've done similar stuff. #SackCrass.

Vampantha @VampanthaWrites · 31m
'Hey, let's get Any White Male Bigot.' Like there was a shortage. Seriously. #SackCrass.

Vampantha @VampanthaWrites · 30m
So @KetCrimeCon don't even "oh, widening appeal" That is insulting and belittling your followers, seriously. #SackCrass

Vampantha @VampanthaWrites · 27m
Seriously scuppered my chances of winning with #FreeSpeech but I don't care. I'm standing for women. Someone has to. #SackCrass

Someone from KetCrimeCon tweeted: 'We very much appreciate the feedback we've received about our host. Just to make clear, no award decision will be influenced by feedback.'
To which Vampantha replied:

Vampantha @VampanthaWrites · 21m
Better Not Be.

Vampantha @VampanthaWrites · 19m
Confirm Or Deny: How much is he being paid?

Kettering Crime Convention
@KetCrimeCon · 15m
He's volunteering his services.

Vampantha @VampanthaWrites · 11m
So it's true, HE'S NOT GIVING HIS FEE TO CHARITY? #SackCrass

Kettering Crime Convention
@KetCrimeCon · 7m
How can he?

Vampantha @VampanthaWrites · 52s
Seriously? UNBELIEVABLE. I can't even answer you #SackCrass

My jaw was on the floor. I sent off a gentle email to Vampantha before my brain had even had a chance to go, 'Wait, she's doing you a favour by killing herself.' She shot back, 'As a white man, naturally you'd be on his side. You're fired, fuck off. Seriously.'

STUNNED, I LOOKED back at her stream of invective. Underneath all the madness, I suddenly saw her genius.

She'd manoeuvred the convention committee into basically announcing that her outburst wouldn't harm her chances of winning. Even more amazing, she'd effectively guaranteed a cry of foul if she didn't win. It was utterly brilliant.

I nearly emailed to tell her so, but then I got distracted by Twitter. Because #SackCrass was being taken up. People pointing out that the actor was different from the character he played ('Laurence Olivier not actually child-killing psycho despite playing Richard III') were swept aside. 'He took the part, so he got behind those views #SackCrass.'

'KetCrimeCon has worked so hard recently to distance itself from bigotry and hate and this is a MASSIVE step back #SackCrass.'

THEN IT GOT odder:

Barney the Dinosaur @BarneyDino · 3h
#SackCrass is just baffling. Jarvis Chapman = Actor.
Crass=Character.

Kevin @Kev00 · 3h
@BarneyDino @KetCrimeCon has worked to inclusion. This
is a NO. His perceived persona is a detractionist slur.

Barney the Dinosaur @BarneyDino · 3h
@Kev00 But...

Kevin @Kev00 · 2h
@BarneyDino Also, there are accusations of sexism and
bigotry by Chapman on set.

Barney the Dinosaur @BarneyDino · 2h
@Kev00 Really, do you have a link to them?

Kevin @Kev00 · 2h
@BarneyDino Transphobic remarks I believe, also incidents
with female guests stars.

Barney the Dinosaur @BarneyDino · 2h
@Kev00 Not aware of his transphobia. Will look it up.

Kevin @Kev00 · 2h
@BarneyDino Do so. Educate yourself. It's another blow for
the BoysClub of CrimeCon #SackCrass.

Poor BarneyDino. He went out for a run (Twitter told me so)
and a nice snack (Twitter told me this too). He came back in to
find #SackCrass still going.

Barney the Dinosaur @BarneyDino · 22m
I'm sure that, as host, whatever claims are made, Jarvis
Chapman isn't going to make fat or gay jokes.

Cisyphus @Cisyphus1 · 16m
.@BarneyDino How many times, Transpeople
ARE NOT GAY. TRANSPEOPLE ARE NOT GAY.
#MistakesWhiteCisMenMake.

Kevin @Kev00 · 13m
@BarneyDino hmmm does it matter whether he would have
done them at the con, if he HAS done them elsewhere?

Barney the Dinosaur @BarneyDino · 10m
@Cisyphus1 I wasn't talking about any trans remarks
specifically. I can only apologise.

Cisyphus @Cisyphus1 · 6m
@BarneyDino At least you have the balls to apologise. Unlike
some #SackCrass.

Barney the Dinosaur @BarneyDino · 4m
@Kev00 @Cisyphus1 BUT I've yet to find any links to these
remarks. Have you anything I can see?

Kevin @Kev00 · 2m
@BarneyDino you miss my point. If X says things elsewhere
does it matter that they won't say them to your face?

Barney the Dinosaur @BarneyDino · 11s
No, get your point @Kev00. I'm saying I haven't seen
evidence that he has said these things. Not disputing, just
want to see it. Links pls?

Of course, there was no answer from Kev00. This didn't stop
people repeating his accusations, and even adding to them.
That's not to say there wasn't evidence of a sort—previously
amusing gifs of some of Inspector 'Crass' Carmichael's more
famous catchphrases were pulled out and re-used against the
actor playing him, frequently '#unfortunate' because obviously
they *proved* that, among other allegations:

   —he was racist
   —anti-semitic
   —homophobic and transphobic
   —sexist
   —had fat-shamed an actress shortly after she'd given
   birth
   —regularly hit or punched crew
   —bullied those who worked with him
   —shagged teenage fans
   —hired prostitutes on a fairly regular basis
   —had had an affair with a co-star and then had her fired

Basically it was an endless list of accusations, and, because no
evidence existed to directly contradict any of it, *clearly all of it
was true.*

*   *   *

SUDDENLY JARVIS CHAPMAN went from being one of the nation's most beloved actors to a sinister, malodorous figure, one the cameras had clearly just caught on-set in a rare moment between prossie-shag and hate crime.

POOR JARVIS CHAPMAN. The good thing about Twitter is that, while those on it assume they're engaged in the most public flogging imaginable, a good ninety-seven percent of the population couldn't give a shrugging toss. The bad thing is that, of the three per cent, a lot of them sat on news desks.

BY THE NEXT morning, Twitter was feeling very pleased with itself, and sounding just a smidge like BoneyM's 'Rasputin,' 'WHY WON'T SOMEONE DO SOMETHING ABOUT THIS OUTRAGEOUS MAN?' was fairly common. Very few people stopped to think that maybe the answer could be that he hadn't done anything. But perhaps the establishment was colluding in the cover-up. '@MetPoliceUK Why persistent silence over #SackCrass? Chapman's victims once again denied a voice.'

The various police forces being @ed kept their peace. They'd realised that to even say that any allegations would be investigated would lead at least three papers to announce that the police had assembled a special task-force to investigate Jarvis Chapman.

EVERYONE INVOLVED WAS now stuck, like a Cold War summit. As soon as Vampantha kicked off, Jarvis had about half an hour in which to say, 'Well, I offered to do the awards as an unpaid favour. But fair enough, I won't.' There'd have been grumbling, but a lot of it would have gone in Vampantha's direction. But now it was too late. If he pulled out, it would look like an admission of guilt.

KetCrimeCon were also landed with a poison host who they'd previously assumed was a massive coup. A committee member had already posted an anonymous blog about how, despite their lone voice, there'd been much back-slapping and "this is putting Kettering on the map" from the committee "completely failing to investigate all the terrible allegations which have now come to light." It was as though the KetCrimeCon committee were simultaneously prophets and the *Sunday Times* Insight Team. If KetCrimeCon dumped Jarvis, they'd look like they were confirming the allegations against him. So now Jarvis and Kettering were locked together in a grudging forced marriage. One that would take place next weekend with rather more of the world's press in attendance than was normally expected at a small hotel in Kettering.

Well done, Vampantha.

THE HOTEL WASN'T even in Kettering, as it turned out. The building itself was a generic hotel, designed to give great views of the local landscape, but in this case unable to offer little more than a promising glimpse of the access road and a nearby industrial estate. A sign in reception displayed information about buses to catch to 'Downtown Kettering,' offering it up with all the seedy allure of nineteen-twenties Chicago.

Hotel carpet zig-zagged in a migraine-inducing pattern in every direction as people tugged wheelie-luggage around and made the long-suffering sigh that Sir Edmund Hillary must have given out when finally capping Everest. Reception staff stood there, greeting everyone with the same empty smiles they'd offered out for the previous weekend's Furry Convention.

The staff were the only people smiling. On Friday morning things had just been settling down. Thanks to the *Daily Mail* doing something *outrageous*, the twitchmob had moved on. But at lunchtime, in order to remind everyone of her existence, Vampantha had tweeted that she looked forward to extending a welcoming olive-branch to Jarvis when she met him, and a lot of people had retweeted saying how magnanimous she was, like it was the Good Friday Agreement and he was a reformed terrorist.

However, shortly after lunchtime, Jarvis's wife left Twitter. A professional wedding florist, she'd spent most of the last week keeping her head down. As Jarvis wasn't on Twitter, a fair amount of invective had come her way, but she'd ignored it. And then:

Maggie @Magzzz83 · 8m
.@BloominChaps A friend processing yr adoption
says they've turned you down cos you married a
WHOREBANGER #NoBaby4U lol.

Friday afternoon is when the offices of the world piss around on the internet. They're hungry for distraction to get them through the sleepy slog from two pm to half five. Anything will do—a quiz about 'Which Dead German Are You?' or a cat Tumblr, or the tupperware lid being lifted on a juicy bit of scandal.

Magzzz83's tweet was soon retweeted everywhere, sometimes prefixed with a 'HORRIFIED' disclaimer.

Jarvis Chapman's wife did the smart thing. She didn't reply, but deleted her account, phoned her lawyer, and then did a lot of crying while cutting the stalks of expensive flowers far too short. Jarvis Chapman took a phone call from her and left the set, his thunderous face caught by a pap as he got into a cab.

Meanwhile, every single tabloid newssite saw the tweet for the gold it was. From 'JARVIS: MY BABY AGONY' to 'Horrific privacy breach reveals child heartbreak of TV's Crass.' Have cake, eat cake, pen column about why cake shouldn't have been eaten, speculate about whether the cake is a lie, and then write an open letter to the cake.

MAGZZZ83'S TWEETS WENT private. The social services department in Hampstead announced they wouldn't comment while letting it be known that a member of staff was now under investigation.

Vampantha moved quickly to distance herself from Magzzz83 and express her horror. "Malicious attacks? Get the hell away from me. Seriously. I don't know you." She then went on to talk at some length about her own infertility woes and subsequent suicide attempts.

And the few members of the press who weren't already heading to Kettering hastily booked themselves tickets on the train.

Vampantha had played a blinder and she knew it. Standing on the flattened ziggurat of hotel carpet, she wore her triumph with the humble dignity of a funeral director.

I tried to get up to her, to tell her how well she'd played this, but of course she blanked me. There was a gaggle of people around her, and she was dressed like a Valkyrie. Regally, she treated the lobby as an antechamber to her inevitable coronation.

Of course she won. I'll hurry through the obvious stuff first. Jarvis Chapman turned up to present the awards, ashen and furious. He refused to answer any press questions on the way in and strode into the hall chewing bees and clearly wishing the whole hotel swallowed even further into hell than Kettering.

Naturally the event started late and everything went horridly wrong. First the committee stood on stage and gave short speeches that dragged unappealingly, margarine spread into every corner of the slice of bread. Then Jarvis was finally introduced. The president of KetCrimeCon tried to say something smooth and instead said, "After somewhat of a tough week for him and for us, we're delighted to welcome Jarvis on stage to present this year's awards. Phew."

You know, it was one of those sentences that meant well but ended up *there*.

Jarvis lurched on stage, and couldn't get through his dreadful ordeal fast enough. There was some polite applause. Mercifully no one booed. But naturally, the microphone didn't work. Then the backup microphone failed. And Jarvis stood there with a seasick grin. Instead of looking like a dashing leading man in his mid-forties, he just looked small, untidy, tired and in desperate need of a hug.

He'd carefully prepared his opening remarks to look spontaneous, but by the time he got to serve them up they were stale. His casualness looked forced, his guarded swipes at the press were blunted, and his thanks to everyone for his warm welcome looked chilly.

He pushed on through the awards, slogging away with the determination he'd used during a disastrous touring pantomime. His performance was actually pretty good—he'd clearly read all the winning entries and most of the nominations, and if anyone had really been listening, they'd have been impressed by how much he knew about crime fiction. But everyone was just waiting for him to put a foot wrong.

Anyway, finally the time came to crown Vampantha. A few weeks before she had been a punchline to every joke about self-published crazy people, but now she was a powerful voice whose time had come and who had exposed a villain.

Best eCrime wasn't the final award of the ceremony, but everyone knew it was the only one that mattered. Jarvis handled the announcement with wry sincerity. He wasn't even at all sarcastic when he said "It gives me great pleasure to announce that the winner is... Vampantha, for *A Rubber Of Velvet.*"

Of course there was lots of applause. Of course the cameras clicked, catching every moment, hoping there was a gesture where he looked ill-at-ease or sneering at her triumph. But Jarvis's face stayed rigidly composed, and he shook Vampantha's hands warmly. He didn't try and hug her, or do anything that would appear to be a misstep.

She leaned in to say something, and she was smiling warmly. A few cameras caught a slight frown on his face, but she was away and Jarvis was there alone, seemingly a little shaken, picking up the next envelope and moving on to a lifetime achievement award that no one cared about.

If the microphones missed it at the time, a deaf viewer caught a YouTube video of it and tweeted what she'd said. "Seriously hard dealing with a woman with brains, isn't it?"

That got a lot of retweets and applause. Someone stuck it on a t-shirt. Vampantha courteously denied she'd said anything of the sort. But still. T-shirt.

OUTSIDE IN THE vast migraine of a lobby, photographers demanded a picture of Jarvis with Vampantha, and reporters pressed for an interview. But, while Jarvis handed out the last couple of awards, Vampantha had already done a Queen of Sheba sweep, progressing up into a lift advertising the hotel's 'imaginative' breakfast buffet. Finally, Jarvis was on his way through and out, grim as a hangover. He wavered in front of the pack, wondering whether he should say something or not. The whole thing just struck him as so bizarre that perhaps he should just... and then a journalist pressed forward, her face harder than it needed to be at such a young age. "Is it true," she asked. "Is it true that your wife's just taken a load of kids' toys to Oxfam?"

Jarvis Chapman left KetCrimeCon without another word.

I WASN'T THE only person sticking around to witness this triumph. At the back of the lobby hung a downlit pencil drawing depicting a thatched cottage and water wheel, with a lonely miller making his weary way home to his dumpling wife, his footsteps weaving through scratching graphite chickens. Underneath the art was a sofa that no-one had ever put their feet up on to read the Sunday papers. Perched on the sofa—you could only really perch on it, not sit; it was pretty much a bus-stop bench clad in the minimum of blue leather—perched on the sofa was a little nothing of a man making a great play of checking his phone on the hotel's free-in-the-lobby wifi.

As I sauntered past he was looking at me. I nodded, and, for something to say, managed, "Funny day, isn't it?"

He gave that sort-of-grunt that people do when they don't want to talk, but don't want to seem exactly rude, and carried on checking his phone. Tap, tap, swipe. Tap, tap, swipe. But he was still watching me. I carried on walking, aware of his gaze not quite on me. Was he someone working for my mysterious Killuminati? Was that it?

Someone else busied past me, one of the tireless convention martyrs, jammed into an unflattering gilet printed with the convention name. She was all about the lanyard, flacking it about as though she was both Mulder and Scully. She plonked herself down on the sofa, which gave a little plastic fart, and tumbled speech at the man. "What a day I've never known a KetCrimeCon like this I've been picking up guests from the station since seven but mind you I didn't get to sleep till two but then I never do at CrimeCon you don't do you and the press so demanding so awful and they took my picture and asked me what I thought they won't use it of course but I hope I did the right thing I said the committee had worked hard and the awards would go to the winners and isn't Vampantha marvellous she is ever so marvellous isn't she?"

"Yes," said the man without looking up from tap, tap, swipe. "She is."

I wandered away, his eyes boring into me. It took me two minutes to discover he was the chair of the judging panel. And then I remembered him. I'd seen him in pictures on a mantlepiece. He was the man Vampantha had been having lunch with in Nando's. Her husband.

IN THE WHIRL of being a media darling, Vampantha hadn't got around to unfriending me on Facebook, so I was able to see that she was friends with Derek Ayres. At first glance Derek only shared his Facebook with friends, but there was still a surprising amount to see about Derek and Vampantha.

Up until a few years ago Derek had combined being regional sales executive for Sodobus with running a reasonably successful ebook imprint as a hobby. In 2012 that had all changed.

Vampantha had gone to Kettering CrimeCon in 2012 looking for a publisher, and ready to do anything to acquire one. During the debacle over the reviews of *A Rubber Of Velvet*, before Vampantha became a feminist hero, various blog-posts had made catty remarks along the lines of, 'It seems anyone can stuff themselves into a basque these days and call themselves an author. This book reads like the kind of thing written by someone who handed out backrubs and handjobs to get where they are.'

A notably owlish and monkishly asexual critic who also ran an imprint had popped up on quite a lively thread to announce, 'My dears, even I got one. And I'm rather gay. But you know, never one to turn down a freebie. Chin-chin.'

Derek Ayres had been Vampantha's 'mission accomplished.' He was the first one to offer her a publishing contract at his ebook imprint. Derek was also the head of KetCrimeCon's award committee.

VAMPANTHA WAS CLEARLY a genius at pulling things off. She'd rehabilitated her reputation, she'd engineered an award for herself, and she'd managed to do it in such a blaze of publicity that she'd completely cast into the shadows any question of how she'd managed to win the award. She was the justly-lauded authoress who had somehow been abused by the vile Jarvis Chapman.

And the whole thing was a hoax, one that had smeared Jarvis, and done real harm to his career and his family.

But I knew enough to smash it all wide open.

ONE THING I'D forgotten though. The quiet eyes of Derek Ayres watching me as I walked away.

VAMPANTHA HAD A final tug the next day. As Kettering CrimeCon hadn't booked any leading female crime authors that year, she'd been invited onto lots of panels in order to make sure they weren't all slightly wizardy men with beards. Vampantha didn't mind being the token woman on a panel. In fact, she thrived on it. Until her recent sainthood, many people muttered "oh, God, not HER again" while bemoaning that more established female crime authors ran a mile from being on a panel with Vampantha. As one put it in an interview, "You know, I've written a dozen bestsellers translated into a dozen languages and one was even made into a god-awful film in Japan. I think I'm doing quite well for myself. So it's a bit hard being lectured on How To Succeed As An Author by a pamphleteer" (after Vampantha's award, she had to apologise, and the two were later pictured having a particularly grim tea).

THE SUNDAY MORNING, Vampantha was on a panel about 'Murder International.' In the middle of it all, having mentioned her award a dozen times, Vampantha suddenly announced, "The secret of anyone's success is to have good publicity. A lot of people will say that, in order to do that, you need to have a publicist. Well, up until recently, I had one. And let me tell you. He did no good, seriously. His name is Brian McMullen, and let me tell you all to avoid him like the plague..."

This was only the start of the diatribe. It went on for eight minutes and thirty-four seconds, with frequent stops for applause. It was a masterful bit of character destruction that I wasn't even aware of (apart from wondering why I was getting a few odd looks in the lunch queue). But it neatly ensured how formidable Vampantha and Derek were. Had I suddenly rushed forward to expose them both, it would simply have appeared to be sour grapes by Brian McMullen, the recently sacked publicist who had told her, and I quote, "Girl authors should suck it up." There was also a t-shirt made of that. Christ, who makes these t-shirts?

I LEFT KETCRIMECON in a hurry after someone threw a glass of wine over me. At twelve quid for a glass of house red, they must really have hated me.

I WENT HOME, chalking up Vampantha as a failure. I'd met my match.

I couldn't expose her. It was too late to switch horses and try and bump her off—Brian McMullen was an obvious suspect and an investigation of him could lead back to me.

MY GOD LADY, I thought, you're worse than me, and I'm a murderer. But fine. Vampantha was utter poison, but that was okay. I'd bide my time and try again in a bit. After all, there was no shortage of awful people.

CHAPTER NINE
THREE LITTLE PIGS

THREE PEOPLE WALK into a room.

If they were interesting people, and this were a joke, then they would be an Englishman, an Irishman and a Scotsman. The Englishman would say something sensible, the Scotsman something mean, and the Irishman would say something stupid. If the joke were working at a slightly higher level, then the Irishman would still say something stupid, yet walk away the winner.

Or perhaps the three are a priest, a vicar and a rabbi walking into a bar. Oddly enough, it's never a priest, a rabbi and an imam, which implies rather unfairly that imams don't have a sense of humour or can't order a soda water.

Actually, one of the three walking into the room was a woman and another Jewish, but it honestly has nothing to do with the tale. By even mentioning it, I'm skewing how you perceive the tale, because it's not a joke, it's about money. And everyone knows that money is serious.

As I SAID, the three weren't that interesting. Annette Gough had a bird-like alertness, but, put together with the black dress, it was the alertness of a raven. Her face was settled into a small near-smile, one that you just knew was only waiting to be alone so that it could switch off completely.

Jamie Beaston looked like a cheap boiled ham served up with the string still tightly wrapped round it. At some point he'd been an athlete, but he'd now gone to seed, wearing an expensive suit that didn't look it, his face flushed as though the central heating was on too high. His nicely striped shirt didn't even try to hide his expansive waistline. He was a man who entered a room as though acknowledging delighted applause.

Wilson O'Reilly exuded the air of an unpopular headmaster who, following the mysterious death of a relative, had found himself enormously wealthy. He had a shifty alertness to him, as though already preparing an answer to exactly what had become of the skiing trip money.

The only thing the three of them had in common was something that none of them could hide. They were all enormously pleased with themselves.

Well, except when they noticed each other. Then the three's faces became hard and wary. Each suddenly adopted the expression they used when appearing on the news to say things like, "That's a good question, David, but..." "What you don't seem to understand here, Michael..." or, "If I may, the thing I've actually come here to talk about today, Samira, is..."

They all, as one, pocketed their smartphones and looked each other shiftily up and down. This wasn't what they were expecting. They nodded to each other, but said nothing more. None of them wanted to be drawn. Each was feeling a little disappointed, but wouldn't show it. Each had thought themselves the only person invited to this meeting, but, realising the other was there, was already accepting it. This was business. The invitation had seemed too good to be true, and, as they all knew, there's very little in life that is good or true.

They helped themselves to coffee, fingered the biscuit plate for chocolate ones, then settled down into a harrumphing silence which went on just long enough. Any longer and one of them would ask the other about holidays, family, the news, or the journey down. The one thing that they didn't talk about was business. Occasionally one would sneak a hopeful look at the door, expecting a fourth person to come in, but no-one did. Fingers tapped the formica desks, chairs rocked back, and the smartphones came out again. But annoyingly, there didn't seem to be a network.

Without any fanfare a projector sprung into life. For a moment it glowed blue and flashed 'NO SIGNAL' as it paged through its connections. Then it went to a PC desktop. A disembodied mouse pointed at a file on the desktop labelled 'Presentation. PPT.' It double-clicked.

The presentation started to load up. As it did so, some anti-virus software popped up to recommend an update, and then Java Updater joined, in along with Adobe. The mouse shifted across the screen and dismissed all three with a trace of annoyance.

Then the presentation began.

LEVERAGE:
A PROPOSAL
Monday July 13th

In attendance
Jamie Beaston, *MooLaLa*
Annette Gough, *BettyPoke*
Wilson O'Reilly, *Ubanker*

SLIDE TWO: AGENDA
- Thank you for coming.
- A brief introduction to
why I've called you here.
- An offer you can't refuse.
- Coffee.

SLIDE THREE: THANK YOU FOR COMING
- Firstly, apologies for not being here in person
- The reason for this will soon become clear
- Anyway, if I were here
- I'd simply be reading these
bullet points aloud to you
- And don't you just hate that?
- We could all read by the age of 8,
couldn't we?

- So why waste time? After all...
  - TIME IS MONEY.

SLIDE FOUR: MORE INTRODUCTION
- Forgive the slightly unusual nature of this presentation
- What I'm about to offer all of you is well worth your while
  - But I need your absolute discretion within this room
  - Instead of making you sign a blah blah blah NDA
  - I've blocked all mobile signals during the presentation
    - And locked the door.
- Don't worry about the last part!
- As soon as we're done it'll open.

SLIDE FIVE:
EVEN MORE INTRODUCTION
- So, there we go. That's the introduction over with.
- Apart from a health and safety note.
  - We're four floors up, so don't try jumping out the window.
    - Kidding.
- But seriously, four floors. Ouch.

SLIDE SIX:
CASE STUDY ONE—MOOLALA
1. CEO: Jamie Beaston (38)
2. Started in 2011
3. Offers payday loans
- Slogan: 'Slip a little moolala into your pocket.'
- Our little secret: Interest rate of 12,000%
  - The media say: 'Borrow a fiver. Pay a million two years later.'

SLIDE SEVEN:
CASE STUDY TWO—BETTY POKE

1. CEO: Annette Gough (47)
2. Started in 2007
3. Bingo, poker, online gambling
- Slogan: 'Feel lucky tonight.'

- Our little secret: Beginner's luck algorithm designed to lure people into betting more than they can afford
- The media say: 'I thought he was just playing games, but now I've lost the house.'

SLIDE EIGHT:
CASE STUDY THREE—UBANKER

1. CEO: Wilson O'Reilly (54)
2. Started in 2004
3. Online banking, investment and finance
- Slogan: 'Hassle-free banking.'

- Our little secret: Unsecured savings placed offshore, investment portfolio set to report a massive loss, 83% of accounts over-charged fees, donated £3million to the government. Paid average bonuses of 217% of salary to senior executives while making 200 call centre staff redundant.
- The media say: 'Guilt-free banking.'

SLIDE NINE:
ANY QUESTIONS?

There weren't any questions, but the three little pigs huffed and they puffed. But there was no-one in the room but each other. They sort-of looked each other in the eye and said things like "outrageous" or "nonsense," or affected to be bored.

Annette ran a hand through her piled-high hair and said, "We've heard all this before," with a weary chuckle. Wilson muttered, "This has been before a select committee, you know." Jamie looked around the room, thought about saying something, but kept his silence. He affected a knowing smile that said, 'well, I was expecting this.'

SLIDE TEN:
- Basically,
- You're all shits.

SLIDE ELEVEN:
- And what are we going
  to do with you?

At this point, Jamie Beaston stood up. "Hey guys, you got me," he spread out his hands and did a monstrously fake laugh. "All very funny, I'm sure. But I won't waste my time on this." He made for the door.

SLIDE TWELVE:
- Please don't touch the door.

At the time, no-one noticed that slide. Because they were too busy staring at Jamie screaming as he tried to tear his hand from the electrified doorknob. After a few seconds, the current cut out and he fell back, leaving a smell of cooking bacon in the air.

But that wasn't all.

"Jesus," he swore from the floor, "I've shat myself."

The other two stared at him in disgust.

He stared back at them from the nylon carpet tiles, defiant. "Oh, don't be such babies," he said. "It's not a full on jobbie, more of a wet fart. Jeez. I'm the one who got fried."

The other two continued to stare at him.

"Listen, I don't suppose either of you have a paper towel or..."

They both hastily shook their heads with the thoughtless haste of people being asked by a tramp if they had a spare cigarette.

"Fair enough," Jamie Beaston stood up, eyeing them warily. He sat back down. "Thanks. I should have known better than to ask a banker for a loan."

"Coming from you?" snapped Wilson.

"Yeah," said Jamie, the Yorkshire accent strong is his voice. "And go fuck yourself."

"Could you perhaps sit further down the table?" asked Annette.

"No."

A surly silence settled over the three.

SLIDE THIRTEEN:
• Shall we continue?

SLIDE FOURTEEN:
• I have a proposition for you.
• It's really easy.
• And accords with all of your institutions.

SLIDE FIFTEEN:
• 'Charity is at the heart of MooLala'
  – Jamie Beaston.
• 'BettyPoke likes to give back'
  – Annette Gough.
• 'We're an ethical reinvestor.
  That's at our core'
  – Wilson O'Reilly.

SLIDE SIXTEEN:
• Actually, what that last quote means,
  no-one really knows.
• But only 27% of Ubanker's
  money is invested in arms.
• Woo.

Annette had started nodding and now she stood up, smiling wearily. "This is all some childish attempt at blackmail, isn't it? Yes, that's right." She nodded to herself.

SLIDE SEVENTEEN
• No. Not Blackmail.
• Charitable giving.

One of the others started to speak, but Annette held up a hand and carried on talking. "To the charity of you, is that it? Well then. We've been stupid. We've walked into this. Call it a tax on our stupidity. How much do you want?"

SLIDE EIGHTEEN
• Ah.

The suggestion of rounding up some rotten bankers came from the Killuminati. I was kind of happy with it as an assignment. For one thing, these were the kind of people it was easy to hate. I wasn't going to end up having the same pangs as I did towards Harry Paperboy. Or even Todd.

Also, after Vampantha I needed an easy win.

The great thing about the three money makers I'd selected was that they were fairly easy pickings. They managed a great overlap.

- They were all publicly known about and loathed.
- They all had lots of money.
- Were clearly horridly corrupt.
- All high-profile 'Talk to me' business leaders.
- And yet thunderingly stupid.

On that basis it was fairly easy to hire a business suite anonymously, and invite them all to a meeting there, having sent them a set of proposals for an investment portfolio that just looked too rich to refuse. I was careful to make the investment opportunity satisfyingly, but not suspiciously, juicy.

I was making no mistakes. I had never at any point met any of them personally. Nor was I actually in the business suite at the same time they were. I'd kitted it out and specced it up, but had made sure that I'd done so in a disguise.

The big thing was making sure they couldn't summon help. This was actually pretty easy. The building had wifi, but needed a password. And, thanks to Google, I was able to build a fairly decent mobile phone signal jammer, just the sort of thing they use in cinemas and schools. I'd buried it under one of the floor tiles.

Not that there was anyone around. I'd picked a slightly miserable building on the edge of London's Silicon Roundabout. The kind of place that charged an outrageous price for a view of Wetherspoon's and a dual carriageway. This meant that the meeting room I'd booked was the only busy thing on the floor. And all I needed was to keep the three there for an hour.

The thing is, they were stupid, but they were cunning. I gave them a five minute break, watching on the webcam as Wilson paced back and forth, Jamie remained sat down, and Annette started jimmying away at the window latch. The locks were fairly tight, and I was pretty confident that they wouldn't be able to open one. But if they did, who would she call out to? This was London, after all. People tended to avoid paying attention to other people who shouted...

SLIDE NINETEEN
- We're going to start with three case studies.
- Each one a noble cause.
- Between you, choose which
one to donate to.

Jamie looked at this with a wry smile. "I know where this is going," he said.

"Oh, aye," Wilson paused in his pacing. "You're the man who knows where everything is going, don't you, laddie? Well, I never listened to my dad, so I don't see why I should take advice from someone sitting in his own shit right now."

Annette carried on doggedly working away at the window. She was now on her third meeting room pen, their shattered carcases mounting up like crashed rocketships.

"Fair enough," said Jamie, rubbing away at the burns on his hand. "Don't say I didn't try—"

"I'm firing my PA," announced Wilson. "She set this meeting up."

"Harsh," said Jamie. "You came. We all did. Our own look out."

Annette snapped another pen but carried on working. She nearly had leverage, but then bent back one of her fingernails and fell back with an anguished cry. She sucked at the damaged finger, her face flushed. For a few moments there was none of the glacial calm people associated with her. There was just rage. Rage in a tight black dress.

She reminded me a bit of a parent throwing a wobbly at their kid in a shop. Just a lot of screaming, and the others looking at her like frightened children.

"Wow," whistled Jamie. "Just wow."

Wilson nodded approvingly to himself. "Ach, seems I'm the only one not an infant."

"Jeez," said Jamie. "You're always scoring points, aren't you?"

"Getting ahead," intoned Wilson, "is all about staying ahead, laddie."

Jamie rolled his eyes.

Annette strolled back over to the table and sat down. She was rubbing her injured hand.

Jamie smiled conspiratorially at her. "Here's us two, looking like we've lost a wanking competition, and there's him over there"—he nodded at Wilson—"wanking with his mouth." Jamie let out a laugh. Annette made no effort to hide her disgust.

Wilson turned on Jamie with a snarl. "What? I'm not going to take a lecture on leadership skills from a man who needs a nappy."

Annette stood up, ever the peacemaker. "Come on now. We should at least try and be civil. And let's spare each other the business speak. That kind of thing's all very well when lecturing staff about little people problems. But not here. Not now. It's just us. We'll be human. Can you all do that?"

Wilson stared at her, baffled.

Jamie leaned across the desk to Annette and, in a stage whisper, said, "I don't think he can be human, do you?"

"Not very, perhaps," agreed Annette, sucking her injured finger.

Wilson brushed invisible dandruff from his jacket. "I think you'll find" – he looked sulkily at both of them for a bit, then toughed it out – "that there's nothing wrong with positive motivational speech. Personally I find it empowering and it's really moved my organisation forward."

"Get her," whispered Annette. Jamie giggled.

"Eh?" snapped Wilson.

Annette turned to face him. "Your bank," she said, "is going down the pan. You've just told us all you've flushed it there with all those nice speeches."

"It's a difficult market, but we're a nimble operator and fiscally it's crucial not to judge a single snapshot but instead drop more of a time-lapse lens over the operation."

Jamie whistled.

Wilson growled.

Annette nodded. "However you put it, Wilson my dear, you're still looking at one of those comedy graphs going downhill. If your business was a slope, I'm rather afraid I wouldn't fancy skiing down it."

Wilson was about to say something. I could tell. Instead he quietly sat down, his eyebrows thunderclouds.

SLIDE TWENTY
- Where were we?
- Ah, yes.
- Three case studies.

An embedded video played. It showed a really scummy room. It had once been one of those 'student pods' that developers were throwing up across the country, all pristine walls and shiny surfaces. And then a student had moved into it, and covered it with laundry, half-read books, mugs and crumbs. Most of the floor space was taken up by a laundry hanger, empty of all but a pair of trainers dangling like a muddy wind-chime.

A figure shuffled into view, wrapped in a stale hoody.

"Hi. My name's Rahim and I've utterly screwed up my life. Right. Okay, I'm a student, so I know that about half of youse watching this will hate me now. But you know, proper subject—biomechanical engineering So, like, not media studies or town planning or any shite. But a science, get in. This country needs scientists. That's what the government says. That's what this uni says in the brochure. That's what my careers adviser and my teachers told me.

"Problem is, that's all very well, but they've made it bloody hard to get a job. 'Cause, right, you have to go to university to learn proper science, and that's really fooking expensive. Like mentally expensive. Thing is, they say 'that's no bother as it's a growth sector' as though it means I'll be able to stroll out of here into a highly-paid job and pay off all my tuition fees. That's what they all tell you. But that's not how it works.

"This is how a growth-sector works (and yes, I'll get to my point). Okay. So, biomech is cool. It's a going-places field. So *everyone* wants to work in it. Which means that yeah, there are loads of jobs for graduates (yay!) but they're all really badly paid (boo!) because there's so much competition. And what with one thing and another, it's actually quite hard to make ends meet. I know what you're thinking, *Filthy skiver, go get a part-time job.* Well, guess what? All the part-time jobs are taken by all the people who graduated last year and haven't been able to get a proper job. Honestly, go down the pub and you'll get served your curry club special by an MA Geologist. How cool is that? Not very.

"So. I'm living off my student loan which gets spread very thin.

"But that's okay. Nae bother. Cos there's all these adverts in the student newspaper and around halls saying..."

And here he held up a flyer:

Need a bit of extra MooLaLa?

We all know that student loans are brilliant, and sometimes far cheaper than your standard personal loan. BUT... what if you end up borrowing more than you need? You could end up out of your depth in hot water, with a nasty debt that'll take you years to pay off! BUT... with a MooLala loan, yes, our interest rate is a little higher, but you only borrow from us for a little time and you pay it back to us on a date that suits you.

So, if the end of the week is looking a long way off—Why not treat yourself to Friday on a Wednesday? COOL!

"Now, the thing is, we all know this is bollocks. Dancing bollocks. But then you think, well no, someone sat down and wrote that advert, and they know what they're doing and they can't be targeting me with lies can they? 'Cause it's not lies, it's an advert. These things get checked. By grown-ups. I'm not a grown-up. Look at me. I'm nineteen. I put Fairy liquid in the washing machine last week. Anyway, I needed a hundred and fifty pounds for a festival. Sponsored by MooLaLa, oddly enough. I had a brilliant time, bee-tee-doubleyou. Not that I can remember it, but the Facebook pics look *amazing*.

"And then came trying to pay it back, and of course I couldn't.

Not all of it. So I figured I'd let it ride for a week. No one rang me up and bollocked me. So I let it go for another week. Still no phone-call.

"Now, do you want to know how a four-thousand-one-hundred-and-twenty-four-per-cent interest rate works? A month later and I owed them three hundred quid. They let it ride another month. Then they emailed me to ask for the five hundred I now owed them.

"Also, I'd been smart. Yes, I'd ticked the box that said they could just charge my card directly. But I'd been clever and given them the details of my credit card. Which I'd then told the bank I'd lost. But that's not good enough—'cause they've an agreement with the bank that lets them force through the transaction as technically it had been set up before the card was cancelled. So they went for my account. And it was empty.

"But the bank had been smart too. Fed up with workshy students like me scumming off their overdrafts, they had only let me set the account up if it was guaranteed by my mum. My mum who works fifty hours a week as a care assistant and then another twenty off the books in a care home. So, they emptied her account.

"She's a proper grown-up. She checks her account regularly. She rang me in tears. She didn't believe I'd just got a loan. She thought it was drugs. I told her what I'd done. She couldn't believe it had just been for a festival. 'At what I earn, that's like half a week's wages—for what? Dancing?' She sounded so tired, so sad. And so I paid it all back. Just like that. By getting out another loan, of course.

"I went to the uni bursar to ask about the hardship fund. You know, the safety net. As I started telling them, they rolled their eyes. 'Not them again.' The bursar, she was a nice enough lady, for a tight-arsed cow. She told me how often she'd heard the story, and they'd made a decision. 'So sorry, but we've had to draw a line in the sand. The hardship fund is for people who can't make ends meet. Not to pay for festivals. Or servicing interest on a loan.'

"I argued with her. In the way you do when you know they're not going to change their mind. I asked if I could lie and say it was 'cause I'd spent too much on food, and they said, well maybe, but I'd already told them what it was really for. I tried saying that hadn't they let the company put the posters up and sponsor the festival and so on...

"And she said, 'Oh, God, tell me about it. I'm getting ten people a week who've done just the same as you. Which is why we're now saying no.'

"I'm screwed. Like utterly screwed. The only person I know who is fine is Gay Chris down the hall. You know the thing about Jap businessmen who buy schoolgirl knickers? Well, turns out the gays are just like that. They'll *pay*, actually *pay*, for his used pants. I mean, I know Gay Chris. He's you know, pretty typical of a student. I can't think of anything I'd less rather shell out for than his pants. It's probably a hazmat crime to even post them. But that's how he got himself out of the mess. Wearing three pairs of boxers a day. He's got no pants now, but also no debt.

"Me? Well, not gay, and don't fancy posting out my pants. I just don't know what to do. 'Cause it's all very well saying 'live on beans for a month.' But I'm a student. Hello. I already live on beans. I live in this box. It's got heat and light and power and it's all paid for. But other than that, I've got nothing. You know. This laptop. And a heap load of books that I need for my course. And that's it. I've cash-converted all my CDs and films for pence. 'Cause everyone else had done that. And that's it. The end of the line.

"So there we go. I've totalled my life before I'm 20. It's not supposed to happen to me—I'm not a single mum on a housing estate in Salford."

JAMIE LOOKED AS though he was about to say something. He was starting on the carefully media-trained head shake and wry smile and launching into "We've heard all this before," but then the second video played.

THIS TIME IT was quite a nice cottage. The camera panned around with a bit of a wobble, and was then placed back down. The picture flared slightly, but then focused on a roaring fireplace and a sleeping dog. And then a woman in her mid-forties sat down. She was sensibly dressed with sensible hair. Underneath it all she looked tired, terribly tired. She held up a letter.

"This is a letter from my mortgage firm. It's good news. My mortgage is paid off. We now own the house."

She leaned back, dropping the letter.

"Which is a pity really, as now BettyPoke can take it from me. Well, take it from *us*. My husband doesn't know that yet—I hope he never sees this. He's the local vicar. This would ruin him. It's all my fault that it got this far, really. I tried to see a divorce lawyer a few months ago. Don't get me wrong—I love the Rev very deeply, but I wanted to get a divorce so that he'd get the house and everything, and also, so that everyone in the parish knew it was my fault. He'd keep the house and his career at least. The problem was the divorce lawyer—oh, she was ever so kind—but she said there was little they could do if the bank suspected that I was acting to try and save the house. The irony, of course, is that when the Reverend Dearly Beloved finds out now, he'll probably want to divorce me anyway. I know I would.

"It all started... well, about eight months ago. Yes. I'd entered the menopause, and started the HRT and all that, 'cause it was like my body was cooking in an oven. There was a tiny side-effect. Just a little bit. Insomnia. In the early days, I found it rather peaceful. You know, up and about when everyone else was asleep. It was magical. I read books, I listened to the dawn chorus. It felt like special time. Time to myself. I've been married nearly twenty years you know, and I'd forgotten how that felt.

"That was initially. And then, oh, I dunno... I think I was checking the telly and there it was, an advert—'Go on, have a flutter,' and I thought, well, what's the harm? I mean, they gave you a thirty-pound stake to start with. The worse that would happen, I figured, was that I'd lose their thirty pounds and learn my lesson. But maybe—just maybe, I could pay for the guttering.

"I lost most of that thirty-pound voucher. But not all of it. As it nearly went, a little bit came back, a tiny win. So I ended up with twenty-three pounds. I felt really good about that.

"I'd never gambled before—you know, I mean, not beyond a tombola or a raffle. But this was ever so clever. All the games on the site were so bright and so much fun, and you could even chat to other users. Some of them were great friends immediately, others were such mardy cows that you bet against them just to bring them down. But you know, it felt like I was joining a secret society of three-am gamblers. You know, *The Midnight Folk* or something.

"I kept coming back for the community. I kept topping up my initial stake out of my housekeeping—the odd ten pounds here or there. Just keeping that thirty pounds afloat. And I was doing so well, that I dipped into the holiday fund—thinking, you know, that when we took the cruise, perhaps this time I'd be able to get us a cabin above the water level with a great sea view and a balcony—wouldn't that be something?

"But I don't know what happened, I guess I wasn't looking, but I lost the lot. No cruise. Just gone, gone like that. I felt so sick. So sick and cross with myself. I'd not felt so bad since I was a little girl." The woman on screen paused and smiled sadly. "So you know what I did, don't you? The Christmas fund went next." She pushed her hands through her hair and the grey roots showed through the gold. "It all went," she said, her voice becoming empty. "I look back and I think, *My god, how mad.* But I was like someone on a ship trying to keep the engine going. You know, first I burnt the furniture, then the fittings, then the floorboards, the decks, the mast, until all there was was a raging hungry furnace and no boat, nothing to keep that fire afloat. It had all gone. Sinking in flames. I was just chucking anything in. I was borrowing from friends. I was stealing money—from my children, from the Church Benevolence Fund, from the Village Residents' Association. Last year we had three trips for the village, even getting as far as Bruges. Not any more. They'll be lucky if they can get to Whipsnade.

"It was amazing how far I could get before people even got suspicious. I mean, I'm the vicar's wife. I'm rather more trusted than God. When I say I'll do more than my fair share of the flower arranging, everyone smiles like I'm the answer to their prayers. It's a long time before someone mutters, 'Oh, that's quite a thin-looking spray,' and even then she's answered with, 'Well, flowers are very dear at the moment. And you know what Judy's like—she won't use cheap flowers from a supermarket. Not like some I could mention.'

"And all the while I'm doing bloody wonders with some tired things from the Asda bargain bucket and some tulips I've stolen from the garden. And... and the graves.

"Just to feed a ravenous, stupid hunger. Not to get rich. Not to do anything really except scrabble back to where I was. Just a few months before.

"The funny thing about money is that you assume that if you can just give it back to people that'll square everything up. Forgetting the hurt I've caused. The way I've betrayed everyone.

"And for what?"

Here she laughed, and it was the laugh of a carefree young girl. "Sounds so stupid doesn't it? To confess you've lost the house to bingo?"

"We have a helpline," Annette said, puckering her lips. Which was true. Calls to it cost 20p a minute and it operated between 9am and 5pm. It was of no use whatsoever at 2am when you were throwing the money for the council tax bill on Number 9.

Wilson was stood up, his school teacher air wrapped tightly around him. "I suppose it's now my turn to be lectured by some barrack-room lawyer with a sob story," he shrugged. "I hope they've chosen well. I don't know about you, but I'm praying for a little old lady with a wheelchair. They always play well."

Instead the screen now showed a video of a quiet, mousy-looking man, sort of like a young Wilson. He was sat in an office decorated with Ubanker logos.

"Hey, my name is Charlie, and I'm a manager at Ubanker. Probably won't be for very much longer, but hey-ho. I'd like to start by reading you a letter from Wilson O'Reilly. He sent it out last winter:

"'Dear Team Member,

"'When we set up Ubanker, we made it a new kind of bank. The bank doesn't own you, you own it. We all do. Every investor, every worker. And, at this time of year, as a valued worker and co-owner, you'd normally be expecting to receive a share of the bank's profits based on your share of our firm. But I'm afraid I have bad news. For the period January to June we made an operating loss, so we don't have a profit to distribute. I know that times are tough for all of us, and I know how disappointed you'll feel about this news. But the good thing is that the bank is strong. We're doing all we can. Stick with us.

"'Wilson.'"

The young man sneered and screwed up the letter. "Of course, what Wilson didn't tell us was that, even though the bank had performed really badly, some people were still being paid their dividends. It seemed there were two kinds of shareholder. The secret top tier were the people who'd overseen the nosediving investment division, the fraudulent tax deal with Sodobus, the insurance mis-selling, the failed attempt to open high street branches, the disastrous merger with a bank in Iceland, the attempt to rig the exchange rate, and some insider dealing. The people looking after all these cock-ups, yeah? They were getting rewarded. But not us—not the people who answered the phones to worried people, who took the flack after we'd obeyed instructions to sell insurance that people didn't need.

"Last year was the bank's worst year. We all got nothing. But Wilson O'Reilly got a million on top of his two-million salary."

The little man smiled. "I'm here to tell you why he's worth every penny. Because he's a very shrewd investor. I found this out through my girlfriend. Yes, I have one, thanks. We met at a party and it was a while before I realised what she did. She kept saying she was 'sort of' an estate agent. I just assumed she was a bit sheepish about it. No.

"Her firm identified areas that were up-and-coming. Specialising in rubbish bits of London and Manchester that were little more than slums. They were able to identify them as areas that 'had potential' in about five or ten years time. This was fed back to my bank, who then fed these postcodes into their mortgage-lending criteria.

"Basically, if you rang up the bank and wanted a mortgage in one of these areas, you got it. It didn't matter if you didn't have quite enough dough, or were a bad bet. In fact, it actually weighed in your favour. The bank was, if you'll forgive me, banking on you taking all the risks for them. It hoped that your area would indeed be up-and-coming, partly thanks to nice people like you moving into the area. It was hoped that you'd keep your head above water for a few years—right up until the interest rates soared. Then, yeah, your mortgage would get a little more pricey. With luck you'd default and the bank could then seize your property and sell it off. According to projections the property would have doubled or trebled in value. So the bank would be left with a tidy little return on their original outlay. Especially as Wilson had a relationship with a property speculation consortium.

"The bank was making a nice profit, the developers were making a nice profit, and the little people were taking all the risks.

"Super brilliant. But all of it hidden behind a lovely, friendly website and an advertising campaign featuring cartoon animals. But for all the laughing squirrels, every bit of data you clicked and checked was counting on your failing. On losing your house. On being in rented accommodation all your life, on not having a proper pension. Because, let me tell you something—if you've got a pension with us, it's doing really badly indeed.

"How do I know? Because I've a pension with Ubanker. I've a mortgage with this bank. I'm so screwed. I should have known the first time my girlfriend came over and said 'Oh? This is where you live.' I thought she was impressed because we were an up-and-coming area. But it was quite the reverse. She recognised the mortgage. She even asked me if I owned the flat, and I proudly told her that, as I worked for Ubanker, I had a three-year fixed rate mortgage. She stopped talking about that then. I just thought I was boring her. You know, it's an early date and you're talking about your mortgage.

"It's only now, now that the bank is tanking, now that they've announced that the chief executives are being paid 'top ups' to replace profit share bonuses because there is no profit, that we realise how screwed we are. There's not just no money to pay a few staff, they're getting rid of a thousand of us.

"So, yeah. There are rumours that they're looking at flogging off the bank to Sodobus. Not that it matters to the people who run it. Turns out they get massive pay-offs if that happens.

"Basically, like their mortgages, whatever happens, they won't lose."

The little man stood up, shaking his head. "That's why I'm speaking out. Because I'm going to lose anyway. That's the world we live in, isn't it? I wonder if that's why we're all so angry all the time. Because we've no power left. Never had. Never will have. But it's so obvious. So clear."

THE SLIDESHOW ENDED, and Wilson made a few dismissive clucks about "wee sour grapes" and "what they don't understand is that the pay is in line with similar institutions."

"Really?" scoffed Jamie. "Similar failing banks?"

Annette nodded at him approvingly.

IN TRUTH, IT hadn't been hard to source these three videos. I'd asked for submissions on YouTube. They'd come rolling in. There were quite a few more, but I'd chosen these three as reasonably representative.

SLIDE TWENTY-ONE
- There we are.
- All I want is for you to choose one of the three.
- And pay off their debts.
- Then you can go.

END OF PRESENTATION

Annette started to laugh. Rueful; a good-old fashioned word like that described her manner well. "It's a game," she smiled with that little Jack Frost smile of hers. "I'm good at games."

Jamie, more for want of something to do, joined in her bonhomie. When he laughed he looked like a schoolboy who'd never really grown up.

Wilson, who'd never been blessed with a sense of humour, found their behaviour remarkable. "Genuinely interested," he said, "but what do the two of you find so funny?"

Annette waved a hand around the table. "This!" she exclaimed, "Oh, dear me! All of this! We spend all of our time telling the press that these poor people only have themselves to blame and only got themselves into their mess... and then it happens to us! Oh, it's a hoot, really!" She rubbed her chin. "Really, solving this is fairly easy, isn't it? We just have to pick one of these three..." She paused, fishing for a word.

"Boobies," said Jamie because he'd always liked the word.

"Very well, then," Annette tried not to frown. "Three boobies. Which one should we bail out?"

"I'm not playing this game," snarled Wilson.

Annette tutted. "Oh, come on, surely it's simple enough."

"I really need a shower," pointed out Jamie.

"Fine," said Annette. "Then we'll decide between the two of us. I vote for the vicar's wife."

"You would," smiled Jamie, slyly. His smile didn't hide his quick calculation. "But that's because she's your client."

"Oh, more than that, she's my ideal demographic. If I rescue her, I'll be a hero to middle-aged ladies. It'll reassure them, give them a comfort blanket. I'm one of them, after all."

"On the same level," said Jamie, "I'd say let's bail out my client. He's just a kid. He could do with a break. I mean, he's a stupid idiot and deserves everything he gets, but, if we have to pick one of these idiots... Then he's going to come out of it the best."

"We'll have to agree to differ," sighed Annette. "Wilson?"

"Yes?" Wilson looked up grudgingly.

"We've hit a stalemate. I don't suppose you'd care to have a casting vote, would you?"

Wilson shot her back a pitying look. "I'm not playing."

"Oh, come on, I'm a gambler," said Annette, "And I know when something is a safe bet. Some crusader has brought us all here to teach us a lesson. But, like most do-gooders, he's not realised that the benefits could well outweigh the cost to us. If we rush out a press release, we can make it look like we're acting benevolently."

Wilson shook his head. "We'll get begging letters."

"What of it?" Annette smirked. "We don't have to answer them. We'll have a golden example to point to and we can say we prefer not to talk about the rest of our charitable giving..."

Jamie laughed. "And then do bugger all?"

"Precisely," Annette beamed.

Wilson stood up and crossed to the window, staring out at the traffic failing to crawl onto Old Street. "You know what," he drawled eventually, "let's say we do..."

"Oh, hello," sniggered Jamie, "He's going to suggest we bail out his bank manager."

Wilson held up a hand. "Not at all... not necessarily. Let's try and work out what the costs to us will be of each case."

"You mean just a total sum?" Annette pulled up a notepad and started totting up figures. Jamie moved over to help, but when Annette wrinkled her nose slightly, sat back down. "Hurry up," he growled. "I really need that shower."

"Quite," said Wilson. He had the air of command about him, dominating the room. "Of course, it's not just about the money—"

"Of course not," muttered Annette softly.

"—but it's simply one co-factor important in evaluating the best outcome."

"Uh-huh," Annette said, the pen carving across the pad.

"I mean obviously"—Wilson waved a hand loftily in the air—"we can discount the laddie from my firm. That's sheer sour grapes with no quantifiable harm done. Simple bad luck on his part and an inability to accept blame. So, as I said, we can discount that..."

Jamie looked up. "Really? This wouldn't have anything to do with the fact that if you settled his case, it could count as an admission of guilt in a billion-dollar fraud?"

To his credit, Wilson didn't flush or even blink, but simply stared ahead, holding to the line. "Simple sour grapes, that's all. Moving on, naturally, Annette, to your case, the poor woman in question..."

Annette looked at her calculations "I'm guessing in the region of thirty-to-fifty grand."

"I see," Wilson nodded gravely. "And the young student?"

Annette again glanced at her pad. "Jamie's client is down about three thousand."

Wilson nodded again. "So it's between those two, isn't it?"

All three nodded.

"The thing is," said Annette, "I'd happily pay them both back their money—"

"As would we all," agreed Wilson.

"It's just that, as the lady said, it's not so much the money as the feeling of betrayal. That can't be paid back. In many ways—"

"—we'd be rewarding her for her dishonesty?" suggested Jamie.

"Quite."

"Whereas your student—"

"Has his whole life ahead of him..."

"...a simple naïve error..."

"...too young to understand the consequences..."

"...impoverished background..."

"...so hard being young..."

"...if we are not to offer a helping hand..."

"...then who is?"

All three nodded.

"Anyone got the cash on them?" asked Annette.

Jamie patted down his pockets. "Not quite. And also..."

Wilson sniffed. "Indeed. Let's settle this by cheque. Our money's good."

"Is it a chequebook for your bank?" asked Annette, to which Wilson barked with rare laughter, "Of course not!"

All three produced chequebooks from a distinguished private bank and each wrote out a cheque for a thousand pounds.

SLIDE TWENTY-TWO:
- Thank you for your generosity.
- You may go.

"That was barely the cost of a heavy lunch," said Wilson. The other two nodded.

"Talk about getting off lightly," agreed Jamie.

They went to the door. Annette reached out a cautious hand. It sprung open. All three breathed sighs of relief. Annette paused on the threshold. "You know, I've got to thinking, there might be useful synergies arising from this."

"Indeed?" Wilson arched a brow.

"What say you all come for a drink at my club and we can see how we can turn a profit from this."

"Capital idea," Wilson suddenly shone with ebullience.

Jamie coughed. "I'll just pop to the office, shower and change."

"The G&T will be waiting for you on the table," Annette assured him. "Reward for a tough day."

"Indeed."

THEY WERE ALL about to vanish into a long a boozy afternoon, when a noise alerted them: the projector.

SLIDE TWENTY-THREE:
• One more thing...

SLIDE TWENTY-FOUR:
Every word of your conversation has been broadcast to
• your customers,
• the media,
• the police.

SLIDE TWENTY-FIVE:
• Enjoy your drinks.

CHAPTER TEN
SKULL AND CROSSBONES

REMEMBER GUY'S GIRLFRIEND Amber? You've probably forgotten her. But I hadn't. For some reason I spent ages following her on Facebook. You know what it's like. You actually, genuinely, literally mean to do the washing-up but suddenly half an hour has sailed by and you've been looking at someone's holiday in Thailand from 2008?

That. It kept happening with Amber.

Which was strange as I hadn't seen her for ages. I hadn't seen either her or Guy really. They'd got on with their lives and I'd been busy saving the world. But I'd kept up to date with her—liking photos of their weekend in Paris, or their long country walks (turns out they really were a couple who did that kind of thing). I felt bad that I wasn't really seeing as much of Guy as I used to, but I think things were awkward between us. It was like an unspoken argument. We'd kept on trying to rearrange lunch, and then he'd announced he was doing yet another fun run, and this time, I'd not put £20 forward for it. After that, arranging lunch had kind of petered out.

Meanwhile, Amber's life had been roaring ahead. Remember I told you she was Far Too Cool for Guy? Well, she was in a band. She sang and played guitar. I think Guy's highest musical achievement at school had been an uncertain 'Twinkle, Twinkle' on the recorder. But Amber was both absurdly hot and talented. I mean, I say that, but I've never really been one for music. But I can tell you objectively that Amber was good at music, because her band had been signed up by a proper label, the kind of people who definitely don't run their business from a garage.

Although, actually, the label's office *was* a converted ex-garage in Old Street, but it was achingly cool. And Amber's band were signed to them. High Visibility Kevin ('HiVizKev') were pottering along nicely. A fair bit of air play, a few festival bookings, support act at the Roundhouse for someone who'd come along from Sweden to scream about how miserable his life was.

The plan for HiVizKev was to spend the summer touring and then release an album in the Autumn off the back of the following they'd built up at festivals.

Amber was sharing this news enthusiastically. "A whole summer of camping! I'm double-washing my clothes now to get ahead! My family are so furious, aunts I've never heard of keep ringing me up in tears." And so on.

It was all going brilliantly well. She was posting daily updates from the studio and then getting ready to do a few gigs around London before hitting the festivals.

She looked so happy I risked a direct message: 'Looks like you're having an awesome time!'

She replied, 'x.' I guessed that was good.

To BE HONEST, I had other things on my mind, and it felt awkward that Guy and I weren't really speaking. It was a bit like we'd had a fight without ever having bothered having the fight. It felt like those rows at school that'd be solved by you both saying "whatever". Only it was never that easy online.

Eventually, I messaged Amber about it:

How is Guy?

You 2 still not speaking?

Not really :(

Shame. You're not expecting me to wade into this?

Nope!

Thank God. Listen, and this is awkward... but it's partly because of Danielle, you know.

Understandable

[that was an understatement]

Hey, I'm not exactly going to be on his side on that
one. But it's all the stuff that goes with that.

Yeah.

Come to the gig in a couple of weeks. He'll be there.
Plus it'll be AMAZING.

Sure it will!!

CU x

BUT A WEEK later was her Facebook Dresden. She posted
in quick succession, 'FUCK YOU ALL,' 'FUCK EM,' and
'U!N!B!E!L!I!E!V!A!B!L!E!!!' and then a lot of weird pictures
from the recording sessions.

There was a small spate of 'u ok hun?' and 'pay no attention to
h8rz' and that kind of thing, but no actual answer from Amber.
Until someone posted, 'Hey A, speaking as a friend, you might
just want to check your privilege on this one. I'm sure your life
can at times be tough, but you've got an amazing job, a hot
boyfriend and (fingers crossed) working ovaries. Stuff's good for
you, gal. So don't sit and stew in it. You're about to be famous.
HUGSxxx'

To which Amber replied, 'Fuck it all and fuck you. You KNOW
NOTHING!!!!'

I SENT HER a message to ask her what was going on. Which led to
us going for a drink at 1am in a little place down the road. She
turned up drunk, and had been crying so much her make-up had
done the Sad Clown Run.

"What's the problem?" I asked her.

She made a face. Even utterly miserable and pulling a face she
looked stunning.

"Seriously? Do you not check Twitter?"

"I'm, er, not one for online, really," I said.

She reached for an olive, squished it, and then squished a
couple more.

"HiVizKev are doing amazingly well on SoundCloud. Like several hundred thousand listens, along with a hundred thousand more on YouTube."

"That's amazing," I beamed, topping up her glass. Her face didn't move. "Isn't it amazing?"

She pushed a piece of paper across to me:

Dear HighVizibilityKevin,

It has been brought to my attention that an illegally pirated copy of the entire 'Double Yellow Stripes' album has been published online. While we have issued takedown proceedings against the relevant sites and torrents, we believe that the audience the pirated copies have reached far exceeds the predicted sales forecasts for a relatively niche album.

Regrettably, therefore we have taken the tough decision to cancel the official release of the album pending the results of an investigation into how the leak occurred.

I'm sorry not to have better news,

Regards,

I read it a couple of times. "What?"

She shrugged angrily. "You can read, can't you?"

"Yes, yes I can, but I can't work out what it means. Did you leak it?"

"No!" she shouted loud enough for someone else in the bar to glance over. "No!" she repeated in an emphatic hiss. "Of course not. We've been pushing for this for years. We wouldn't be so suicidal."

"Well, you know, you might... you, or someone else in the band, might have got so excited at the prospect that you... ah... you know... made a copy for a friend and then..."

Amber shook her head emphatically. "No, absolutely not. No. And you know why? *Because none of us had a copy of the album.* The label didn't trust us with one."

"So who did it—the label? In a weird conspiracy way...?"

Amber shook her head. "Maybe. Or maybe someone at the studio." She picked around on her phone and showed me a screenshot from a forum:

Hey guys—who are HiVizKev? I've been sent a copy of their
album to bounce down and tag for iTunes. Anyone want a
preview copy? S'okay.
   → Torrent plz. I'm they're number one fan!!!

Lots of people had replied asking them to seed a torrent. And
away it had gone.

"The irony, the ankle-biting irony is that we're a success. Such
a success that our label has dropped us."

Amber finished her glass of wine, slurping away at the dregs
like a kid with a milkshake.

"Basically, I shouldn't be talking to you about this, but I am so
screwed."

"Yeah," I agreed. "Someone needs to be—"

"Don't," said Amber sharply, and then softened. "You're
bloody useless."

I WENT HOME, feeling a bit weird. Column A gave me 'Odd
situation that needed fixing' and Column B supplied 'She kissed
me on the nose when she said goodbye.'

I stayed up playing with the cat and, thanks to bittorrent,
listening to the HiVizKev album. It was so bloody easy to
get hold of. Lots of people were sharing it on music forums,
with encouraging notes like, 'HiVizKev album drops! Give
it a spin' and 'Love those guys!!!' The SoundCloud posting
was similarly littered with 'awesome!!1!' and 'wooo.' It was...
anyway, the point is, not my cup of tea, but I'd never dare say
that to Amber.

It was just incredible hearing her voice. On a proper record.
Whenever I'd been to see them live, it had been a bit lost under
the speakers-made-out-of-washing-machines that most music
venues use.

Over the next few days, there was a lot of discussion. First
about the album.

Then when Digital Spy reported 'Label "cans" HiVizKev.' That
brought a lot of people out onto the forums.

Curiously (and many people admitted to pirating the album)

no one accepted that the label dumping the band because of piracy was their fault.

> Yawn! When are lables gonna catch up with C21? Piracy boosts sales. I bet that 000s of people have now heard of HiVizKev who wouldnt have otherwise and so if only 1% of them converts into buyers of the album thats still a massiv profit. Stupid lable. Boycott there stuff.

was the most highly rated comment.

AND HERE'S WHERE Amber weighed in on Facebook:

> A month ago, I was going to be in the lucky position
> I never dreamed I'd be in. Quitting my job in order to
> be able to work on my music full time. I wasn't going
> to be a millionaire, and maybe it wouldn't work out in
> the end—but for maybe a year, I and my best friends
> in the world were going to be High Visibility Kevin full-
> time. It was my dream to be in a band since I was 12.
> And I nearly had that dream come true.
> But now, I have to go and explain to my 12-year old
> self that dreams are never gonna happen. Because the
> album got pirated and the label invoked a clause in our
> contract. Simple as that. We're not happy about that.
> Neither are the label.
> So, listen, for all your arguments about how piracy is
> basically "free speech" and "good for sales" and other
> BS... please remember: I nearly got to be in a band for
> a living. Now I don't.
> BY PIRATING MY ALBUM YOU HAVE STOLEN FROM
> ME.
> Like · Comment · Share

Within about 5 minutes Digital Spy had made this 'HiVizKev Singer "Slams" Pirates.' And Amber was on the receiving end of a huge amount of criticism.

*   *   *

I CALLED HER to see if she was okay.

"Jeez," she said eventually. "It's like when I first dated Guy. Only more... hatey."

> Bitch didn't deserve a career. Goodbye.
> Don't understand music? Loser gets out of the game.
> Whore singer screams at fans. Nice.

I WON'T BORE you with any of the arguments about piracy. Hell knows, you're probably reading a pirated epub of this on your phone and thinking *Thank God I didn't waste my money on this* before passing this on to ten of your friends. Thanks. I hope your cock falls off. If you don't have a cock, I hope you grow one and then it falls off.

I've done my bit of charity—I've killed some arseholes. The least you can do is buy my manifesto (I guess that's what this is). Also, I'll tell you the other thing I hate—when people say "I hated it. Glad I didn't pay for it." Guess what? I don't think you're allowed to hate something you haven't bought. It doesn't work like that. Remember when you'd buy a book and you'd start reading it and then about thirty pages in you'd realise you'd rather tidy the kitchen? That. That's earned hatred. Picking up a pirated ebook and throwing it to one side? No. Doesn't count.

SAME WITH MUSIC, really. Like emails from an ex, the arguments about piracy are complicated and long and whiny. Basically, all you need to know is that I was on Amber's side. Probably because I fancied her rotten. But also because I thought she had a point.

WE MET FOR coffee one day.

"Guy's kind of glad it's all over," she said. "He's sort of glad they've stopped hating on me. A bit. But it's also a bit as if... well, my friend Michelle says maybe he didn't want me being in a band in the first place. You know. Maybe being a little bit famous. Is Guy the jealous type?"

I was stuck right there. True answer: "No." False answer that may make her like me: "Well, no... maybe a bit... I mean, I certainly wouldn't call him jealous."

I went for the latter, and she nodded at me gratefully. I realised that it had been a while since I'd seen her not crying. Like Britain in winter, I thought her beautiful even through the rain.

"The band were thinking... well, you know, do we split up now, or do we do one last fuck 'em gig?"

"Yes!" I laughed, "You should totally do that. And you should call it that."

And that was how The Fuck 'Em Gig was launched.

IT WOULD HAPPEN in a week. And it would be streamed live. Just to prove that HiVizKev actually had understood the internet after all.

THE DAY BEFORE, Amber was in despondent mood. "To be honest, I was expecting more of a fuss from the label." The ex-garage in Shoreditch had been approached to see if they'd have a problem. "They sort of muttered and shrugged," Amber said. "But they were basically waving us on like Nina Simone used to wave the white people into hell at her concerts. Apparently the label think what we're doing is 'interesting.' Someone even wrote 'paradigm' on a vintage chalkboard. As they did that I wondered whether we were better off without them."

She gave me a bleak smile.

"How's Guy been about it?" I asked.

Amber's smile didn't waver. "Oh, fine," she said. "He's going to try and come along." She squeezed my forearm in a gesture that either meant 'marry me' or 'I'm fairly absent-minded' and dreamily stared out of the steamed-up coffee shop window.

"You will come, won't you?" she asked. I guess this was exactly how Mary Queen of Scots went round when she was inviting people to her execution. "It'll be interesting."

"Oh yeah," I said, "I'll try."

Truth is, I had other plans that night.

EVEN THOUGH I wasn't there I can still describe the venue to you. You've probably been to the sort of place. A basement in a bit of London that's borderline fashionable. Currently it said 'performance space' but very soon it would say 'coffee shop.' Musty, damp-smelling curtains were draped over the concrete walls. A sharp whiff of mould and urine hung in the air and didn't vanish, not even when the club filled up with people spilling beer.

There were a lot of people there for 'High Visibility Kevin's Fuck 'Em Gig.' The poster on Facebook promised 'Breaking Up Live On Stage.'

Amber strode out along with her bandmates who I didn't fancy (although, turns out, I had kissed one of them drunkenly at a party a couple of years ago). They were faced by a pretty decent crowd. About half of them had heard of the band before, and the rest were a collection of music bloggers and social media rubberneckers.

"Good evening Wembley," drawled Amber with huge irony. "Let's have a car crash."

Then the music started.

THERE WERE A lot of people tuning into the webcast. I was one of them, nodding my head along to the music as it played tinnily in the background. While I got on with my work.

"THANKS," BREATHED AMBER. It was nearing the end of the gig. During the webcast, she'd mastered the pop star's on-stage demeanour that was stand-up/cool teacher/messiah. "Even though you're not here for the music, you'll admit that was pretty good. And now it's time for the band to disband. High Visibility Kevin will go back to selling shoes, filing and answering the phone. But first, we'd like to say goodbye with a few numbers that if you want to hear again—well, tune into a digital station at two am, or just steal the torrent. Everyone else has." She shrugged and the band launched into the opening notes.

And that was the last music they played that night.

The speakers gave a horrid squeal of feedback and then cut out dead.

A projector fired up in the venue, bathing the band and the backcloth briefly in 'NO SIGNAL' and then a masked figure in a pirate's costume stepped into the camera view.

THIS WAS MY moment.

"Avast there, me hearties," I said. Three years. Three years at drama school. I thank you. "Oi yam a poirate." I dropped the accent right there. That's a professional simplification. I tailed it off. "You may have wondered why I brought you all here today. Well, a crime has been committed here. I'm a pirate. You're a pirate. We're all pirates."

There was some noise at that. A bit of wooing. Some cheers. Some boos. And a pretty good amount of genuine confusion from the band. Amber managed "I'm not—I don't—" then realised her microphone had been cut, so stood back, shaking her head, prowling the stage.

"Don't worry. I'm not here to judge—"

"Good!" screamed someone. Hecklers are dull. They're like people who reply to a tweet with a lame pun. They've always existed. They've never contributed. Like wasps.

"I'm here because I love High Visibility Kevin!" (some screams) "As much as you do!" (more screams) "If not more!" (boos) "No, no. I am their real number-one fan, and I'm going to prove it."

There was interest from the music bloggers by this time. A few of them were filming the video on their phones. They knew enough about the industry to know that it was possible to capture the live stream at source and convert it to a video file and upload it... but that it also relied on asking a favour of someone in the office the next morning who already had their day planned out and would probably just about do it at lunch time. So they were better off slapping up the shaky-phone cam feed at once and then sorting it out properly later.

Doing things properly takes time, and the internet has taught us that none of us have time.

(Remember when you were young adverts said, 'Please allow 28 days for delivery?' Can you imagine if anyone tried that shit now?)

Anyway, I was about to offer everyone in the room something interesting.

"LET'S JUST CHECK, shall we—can all the numberone fans give a massive shout out?"

All the fans shouted out.

"Would you do anything for the band?"

Massive shrieks.

"Now then, who here pirated the album?"

Two people shouted. In the semi-defiant, semi-sheepish way that people do.

"Cool. Just two of you out of a hundred?"

There was muttering.

"I've a word for you naughty guys. Proxies. Good luck trying to find me, because I'm hiding behind seven of them. But what about you lot?"

Names started scrolling across the screen. People muttered. Some called out when they saw their names, or cried for the ticker to stop so that they could take a picture of their name.

"Okay. Cool. These are the names of people in this room who pirated the album. Who stole it."

Some of the people crying to see their names on screen again stopped.

"Yeah. Thought so."

There was muttering.

"Now, the thing about you all is that it was pretty easy to find you. I'll tell you how. This'll get boring, but here we go. You told Facebook you were going. I could use that list of names to find usernames on blogs and torrent sites. I could also use that list to find out where you lived on the electoral register. And, of course, I already knew that you'd be out tonight."

The camera panned back. And back. "It's been a bit of a rush job, I'll admit. Seven of you, well done on your home security arrangements. Two of you, brilliant news about your dog. The rest of you... well..."

By now the camera showed the pirate figure was standing in a floodlit supermarket car park. A pretty empty car park. Apart from a couple of sofas.

"You've had a car boot sale. Of the contents of your homes. Everything I could cram into a few trips in an easyVan."

There was muttering and shouts and howls.

Amber burst out laughing.

"You fans, you said you'd do what you could for the band. Well, we've made quite a lot of money. On behalf of High Visibility Kevin, I'd like to thank you. And with that, perhaps a round of applause for the band and an encore? Goodnight."

The projector snapped off, there was another howl of feedback.

But the band didn't play.

Instead a fight broke out. Some people were fighting to get to the stage. Other people were fighting to hold them back. I'd like to say something simple like, "The people who had had their stuff stolen were trying to get it back and the people who hadn't pirated the album wanted to stop them," but really it was a melee of screaming and shouting and spilled drinks and fists.

Up on stage, as a dozen camera phone flashes went off, High Visibility Kevin were trying to work out the right facial expressions for this occasion. I can tell you now that no one got it right. But that it didn't matter.

And, in the middle of the crowd, most of a pint on his jumper, stood Guy. And he didn't look pleased.

So, now, here's the aftermath.

Amber and the band had enough nous (thanks to the drummer having most of a law degree) to rush out a statement saying they had no idea about the burglaries and that they would not be accepting any of the money, and urging people who had got things from the car boot sale to return them. It wasn't a terribly successful campaign. I'd sold off quite a few PlayStations for two quid a pop.

The webcast was quite the hit. The camera phone replays and then the proper video clips went into a lot of places. Digital Spy, HuffPo, BuzzFeed. UsVsTh3m did a little game where you could supermarket sweep round a fan's house. It was only reasonably popular since it didn't feature any cats. There were a few arguments about what kind of crime had taken place.

Naturally, I'd screwed up. When you're carrying out so many burglaries in a frantic hurry dressed as a pirate, you're going to put a foot wrong. I'd emptied the wrong bedroom in a shared house, and naturally, there was a lot of noise about this is why vigilante justice is the wrong thing. Guiltily, I made sure the victim received an anonymous envelope of cash, but he curiously made no mention of this fact to anyone.

Actually, this worked out in my favour, as, when his housemate found the envelope, she then called the police, so the utterly innocent housemate was, for a while, held up as the possible suspect. It helped that he was about my height and build and had once gone to a party dressed as a pirate. Serves the cheeky sod right.

The really important outcome was High Visibility Kevin. Their record label rang to invite them to a meeting in their ex-garage and offered to pick up their contract. High Visibility Kevin told them to take a running jump, as they'd already received another offer. A lot of bits of paper were waved about. Turned out record-label-in-a-garage had lawyers who worked in a shiny glass office. But then, so too did HiVizKev's new label.

New label rushed out the album (now retitled *Heavily Torrented Album*). The physical CDs looked home-duplicated and someone from the band wrote the album name in a sharpie on each one. Well, at least that was true for the first thousand or so copies. The handwriting was quite nice on the first few, and then really a bit shaky by the end.

Heavily Torrented Album sold really well, especially on CD. Which then generated a further gale of blogs and comment pieces. Did this prove that piracy had no effect on sales after all? Was this a rebirth of the physical medium for music? Should we think it was all an elaborate publicity stunt? Where were the truths and where were the lies? Who were the winners and the losers?

*   *   *

THERE WAS ONE final outcome.

I got a black eye.

"WOW," I SAID. Actually, I didn't even say that. I wondered who was making the squealing noise for a bit, then realised it was me and slowly picked myself up off the lino in the hall. I was rubbing my eye.

"Don't rub your eye," said Amber, "it'll get bloodshot."

"You just punched me in the face," I pointed out. It really hurt.

"Yeah, yeah," she said. She was still standing on my doorstep. Through my one working eye I could see that she looked expectant.

"Come in?" I asked, hesitantly.

Amber leaned against the doorframe and breathed out, a really long, angry breath.

"Sure," she said.

WE WENT INTO the living room. She was shouting. I was trying to think straight. Truthfully, there was a lot of pain going on in my face. Like I'd stubbed my toe. But all over my face.

For a moment or two I wondered if the Killuminati had tipped her off. But from the amount of shouting she was doing, I guessed that no, that wasn't it at all. She'd managed to work it out for herself. Which was, in its own way, chilling. Would she be able to work out what else I'd done if she put her mind to it? Or would I, by some lucky chance, be okay?

I MEAN, OVERALL, it had been quite a successful stunt. No one had been killed. Amber had her career again. I'd even managed to make a few points that people had taken seriously. It was a good thing, really. Just about.

Only, of course, you could argue that it was my most successful crime yet. You could argue that it was my least successful crime yet, as it was the one where I'd got caught.

I stood there, rubbing my eye and trying to make sense of my brain and hoping that Amber would just shut up for a minute as my face really really hurt and the cat was whining for food or something and I tried to explain and—

—ANYWAY, WE WERE kissing. Which was utterly weird. You know when you kiss someone for the first time and your arms go down and slide around them? Well, when one arm is glued to your eye by the pain, that doesn't happen, so instead the other one over-compensates and it's all stupid and weird because this is the moment that you've really hoped for for a really really long time and there it is with you looking like you're miming ballroom dancing while watching a 3D movie and somewhere in-between all this nonsense is the reality that you're kissing the girl of your dreams and—

Actually rather brilliant. Well—

"WHAT THE HELL?"

Guy was standing in my flat. I didn't remember inviting him in. But then I didn't remember closing the front door.

"I knew something was going on. I just knew it. You're my oldest mate." Like a lot of what Guy says, there always seems to be about two words missing, but you get the point. To kind of emphasise it, he punched me in the other eye.

SO THERE WE all were in my living room.

There was Amber, standing there sort of slapping Guy.

There was Guy, kind of kicking me.

There was me, rolling around on the floor, hands cupped over my eyes, wishing I wasn't being kicked.

There was the cat, weaving around all of us in a 'hey gurl, this is interesting, also, hungry' way.

THIS WAS THE point that someone else walked into the living room.

"I hope you don't mind," they said, and I tried to identify the voice. It was familiar, but my hands really wouldn't move from my eyes. "The door was open, so I came in."

"You couldn't shut the door?" I whined.

"Sorry, man," said Guy. He sounded sincere, even though he was still, I noticed, kicking me.

"What the hell are you doing on the floor?" said the voice.

I opened my eyes and groaned.

It was Jackie Aspley.

CHAPTER ELEVEN
LOVE AND WAR

JACKIE HAD CHANGED. Gone was the look of a scarecrow trying to run a charity bookshop. She was wearing a tight-fitting dress, an expensive coat, and hair that had a personal trainer. Her make-up was impressive, in the same way that you might say a pickled sculpture by Damien Hirst or spray-painted concrete by Banksy was impressive.

"Woah," I said.

Jackie surveyed the scene. Which, let's face it, was mostly me rolling around whimpering.

"Is that bit undamaged?" she asked. Guy shrugged, and Jackie landed a sharp kick somewhere around my ribs. As I lay there bleating, she took in the room, then picked up my cat and made a fuss of it.

"You precious little fuzz baby, your daddy took some finding," she said. "But I managed it."

"Who is this?" asked Guy

"Yeah," said Amber. She didn't sound impressed.

BUGGER.

We've all heard of the prisoner's dilemma, even if it never makes any sense. But this is the coward's nightmare. There were three people in the room, none of whom I could tell the entire truth to. Or even a safe partial truth.

I couldn't tell Jackie and Guy I was in love with Amber, I couldn't tell Guy I murdered his old girlfriend, I couldn't tell Amber I'd once lived with Jackie under an assumed name. And I certainly couldn't tell *any* of them that I've been killing off the most annoying people on the internet with the support of a sinister faceless syndicate.

One of the great lessons in life is that everyone wants to say something and no-one really wants to know what you think. The number of times when you actually have to say anything is quite small. Even when you're being directly questioned, whatever you say will simply be taken as a confirmation of whatever it is the person talking at you has already decided.

Most of talk is noise. Angry noise. Hurt noise. And, very rarely, comforting noise. The actual words matter very little. Sorry, poets. It's tone we listen to. It's why you can always tell it's an episode of *EastEnders* on in the next room—because of the furious buzzing sound.

The nice thing about lying on the floor was that my own personal soap opera was taking place five and a half feet above my head. A confederacy of giants. While they rumbled on, I had time and a half to think. The only thing in the room at my level was the cat, and it was giving me a look of 'You are so on your own.'

I formed a strategy. The best thing was to explain and then isolate Jackie Aspley from the other two. As the most unusual thing in the room, she would divert attention. She must have come here wanting something, and whatever it was, whether sex or help or whatever, the simplest thing was to give it to her. With her out of the way (and hopefully me with her) then Amber and Guy could sort out their problems or make up their own lies or whatever allowed them to sleep at night. So long as they left my flat.

Excellent. First job, to stand up.

This wasn't as easy as you'd think. They say the human body can only feel pain in one place at a time. I really think they're wrong about that one.

"Jackie," I winced. "These are my friends Amber and Guy."

They muttered greetings to each other.

"I met Jackie on holiday," I temporised. Almost true enough, almost little enough detail. Don't over-elaborate. "How... however did you find me?"

Jackie held up my cat again, which was even now beginning to pedal the air uneasily. "Through this little tyke. The vet had scanned her microchip, so I persuaded him to give me your address off it. Then I came."

"Fancy dinner?" I asked.

Jackie looked around, her eyes flicking over the angriness of Guy, the confused hurt of Amber, and then back to me. Just for a moment I could see how bored she was by all of this, and then her smile snapped into place. "Of course," she said. "I've already booked the table."

"Now see—" began Guy. Or Amber. I really didn't know which. I didn't care.

"Doesn't matter," Jackie assured them both and we went out.

I glanced back, with a sheepish look that I hope conveyed 'ah well' and 'we'll talk later.' Basically, they were still standing in my flat. Maybe they'd still be there when I got back. I bloody hoped not.

THE RESTAURANT WAS very Jackie Aspley. What amazed me was that it had somehow been hiding within a short walk of my flat. The rich decorations were almost hidden by the tapering candle-light. The tables were covered with more types of folded cloth than a linen closet. A waiter served as a semi-permanent murmuring attachment to the back of your chair.

"How homely!" cooed Jackie. It was clearly anything but.

She picked up one of the three menus and immediately started hunting for things that weren't on it, and tutting with delighted disappointment. "No celeriac chips."

A waiter brought me an ice pack for my face.

I ordered the soup. If I could have had my way I'd have followed it with more soup, but instead I plumped for something simple-enough looking from the mains.

Jackie ordered almost everything and ate almost none of it.

"So," she said, "Apparently your name is Dave."

"Yes," I admitted miserably.

"Nice to meet you, Dave," she said icily. "Did I walk in on your little personal life?"

I found it quite hard deflecting her. She was, after all, a trained journalist. And I spent so much time ducking her enquiries as to whether or not Amber was my girlfriend that I completely forgot to mount any defence against her real query.

"So, why did you leave me?"

I gave her an answer. It was full of ums and ahs and tortured phrases. I spent so much trouble on trying to come up with something convincing that it left me completely exposed to what Jackie said next.

"Well, that's all right, then," she nodded, closing the subject firmly. "As I'm also very much in love. Which is why I want your help."

"YOUR HELP?" THE velvet walls of the restaurant had closed in a little.

Jackie nodded. I rubbed my hand through the breadcrumbs I'd scattered along the tablecloth. Little crumb, little crumb, big pebbly crumb, little crumb.

"Darling," Jackie leaned forward. "I'm occasionally very good at my job. I didn't just pester the vet. I also did a little bit of digging. You see, people are always sending me things. When I started writing about you, I got sent a lot of letters about you. I ignored all those, of course. But, after you left, I was sent a file. It was full of the most fascinating gossip. Like your real name."

I felt a chill pricked at the back of my neck colder than the waiter's breath. The only people who could have done that were the Killuminati. But why?

Jackie carried on smiling at me. She was suddenly all lipstick and teeth. "I did some digging. I used to be a really good journalist. Nowadays people just want my opinions, but I used to be really decent at research. Proper research. Going to a library. Looking at books. Ringing round. It seems you didn't quite tell me the entire truth about yourself. Instead of the bumbling artistic technophobe you told me you were, in fact it turns out you're quite the... is 'hacker' the word? Or should I go for 'failed actor'?" She shrugged. "I honestly can't think why you'd try and hurt me so much. I'm not sure it matters. I really do pick them. Anyway, discovering so much about you, well, it inspired me. I got online."

She beamed at me. The soup sat heavier in my stomach. "Initially, well, I tried to find out even more about you. But then I got distracted. I Googled myself and found out what everyone was saying about me. People are so cruel." Her lips thinned. I tried to work out if there was heartbreak there or not. "It's so strange. That lonely midnight feeling when you're staring at the internet. I read that pensioners say the thing gives them company, but I've never felt more alone than when reading the internet. What a lot of time people have. And how lonely and bitter they all are. After a while I despaired, I really did. And then I started, for the first time in my life, to feel properly good about myself. I'm quite a successful failure, really. And at least I don't have to go to work and pretend to be coping. But they all have to. And it eats away at them." Jackie beamed. "But I'll tell you what I did next. I signed up to a dating site and I fell in love."

As Jackie talked on I started to lift the cold vegetables from her plate. I wasn't really hungry, I just wanted to keep my mouth full so that I didn't have to say anything. I was starting to feel a creeping relief.

"Really, I was looking for love nearby. Perhaps in the next village. I did find a man in a village, but that village was in Kenya." Oh, God. "He seemed to find me ever so attractive— exotic, I guess, and he poured out his soul and I poured mine out. He has a tiny little job and so many degrees and is such an honest and true man." She pushed a print-out at me, a much folded inkjet photo of a smiling man in a polo shirt. "His name is Kenneth Kambata," she said proudly. "And he's ever so clever and he loves me. But the problem is that the real world just keeps getting in the way."

Even though I had a mouth full of cold potato, I had to speak. "You do know what he is, don't you?"

"Well, I do now," Jackie nodded, as though accepting that all men would let her down. "But you know, it was all so thrilling.

Like a motion picture. He wanted to come and see me almost at once. So I sent him the money for a ticket. He didn't turn up at the airport and my heart broke at Arrivals and again in the cab home. Then his auntie (such a nice lady) Skyped me to break the bad news to me, through her tears, that his car had had a crash on the way to catch the flight. He was terribly smashed up and they didn't have the money to pay for his treatment there much longer..."

I'd run out of breadcrumbs. There was a little vase of breadsticks on the table. I picked one up and snapped it until the table was scattered with bits, bits that I could roll my fingers across. The contrast between the tiny rocks of bread and the expensive softness of the tablecloth was once more reassuring.

"His aunty was terribly grateful for the money. The transfer went over so easily and she was sending me pictures of Kenneth in bed. Of course, sadly, they needed a little more money for medicine..."

I felt tired. My bruises were starting to throb. The restaurant was really dark and warm and the walls throbbed with crimson. It was less like being in the womb and more liked being rolled around in a giant mouth.

"And he was, well, naturally, he was dreadfully behind with his rent..."

I always wonder where they get the pictures for restaurant walls. Are there special galleries? Imagine the phone call—good news, we've sold all your art; bad news, it's to McDonalds.

"But he was soon well enough to travel, only there was a problem with his passport, and his uncle explained that he was too embarrassed to ask me himself as he was ever so grateful..."

There was no water in my glass any more. My throat felt dry and I wondered if I could somehow order some. I hate trying to order tap water in posh restaurants; they always pause before they nod and say "but of course."

"...so yes, anyway. I started to get really upset for him. The immigration difficulties he was experiencing sounded really appalling. Apparently, he was on a watch list after once protesting a Sodobus factory. But what's the harm in that? He was only coming to see me on a holiday—I mean, I know I've written a lot about foreigners trying to move here, but none of it's true." She waved a hand around dismissively, and I wondered what Jackie Aspley really did believe in. "Yet he was having so much trouble getting clearance and getting his paperwork in order. So I did the sensible thing. I decided to help him. He said there was no need. His uncle agreed, although he did suggest I perhaps send a little more money. Balls to that, I thought. I've a good journalistic brain. That's about my only skill. So I Googled 'Kenyan holiday immigration visas' and, you'll never guess what the first link was..."

I groaned. "A site about fake dating profiles?"

"Yes," Jackie nodded. "Apparently it's called a catfish, which seems unfair to cats and fish." The dopey smile had gone from her face. "Kenneth had me completely. I guess I've always trusted the wrong men." She looked at me sharply. "And anyway... since I lost my regular writing gig, I've basically been relying on my savings—*what* savings, hah!—and sending most of those over to him. Only now I realise he doesn't exist. Or, if he does, he's still sitting on a vast pile of my money. My first thought was to Skype his Aunty Sarah, but then I realised that, of course, she's in on it too, and then my world fell apart. Which is when I remembered you."

"What?"

"You're the computer whizz," she said in the tone people used to say 'information super-highway' in. "You can get me my money back," said Jackie. "I don't care about... about Ken." I wasn't convinced. "I just want my money."

"How?"

"I don't care about that either. I'm sure you'll think of something terribly clever," said Jackie simply. "Just do it, or I'll see if I can find an interesting way to use what I've found out about you. If my editor won't take it, I'm sure the police will."

Oh.

So. My life was falling apart. I could list the ways, but let's face it, the biggest problem I had was that I was being blackmailed. I had two days to get some money from someone I'd never met before in Kenya. Perhaps I could write to him and say that I'd just inherited a gold mine in Kidderminster?

LUCKILY JACKIE HAD brought her laptop with her and she was more than happy to leave the files with me. Or rather, just the laptop. Like a lot of people who claim to be 'stone broke,' she had an odd relationship with money. She'd helpfully bought a new MacBook just for her online dating escapades, and saw no reason for needing it.

This was actually very handy as she'd kept video copies of all of her Skype chats with Kenneth. Another curious thing about people—people who loudly claim to be "an utter luddite when it comes to technology" are amazingly skilled when it comes to porn. The Porn Principle drives the internet—if a technology can't be used for porn, then it's going to fail because no one will bother learning how to use it. It's also why Groupon is doomed but Bitcoin isn't. A few months ago, Jackie was very proudly assuring me she was "hopeless" about technology. Now she was screencapturing entire Skype chats simply because her handsome Kenyan was having quite an impressive fiddle with himself.

When I'd dated Jackie, she'd said she was more into cuddles. Clearly she'd become rather more liberated. Without going into detail, there was a lot of Kenneth to see on Jackie's laptop. Which was a goldmine. A real Kenyan goldmine.

First I needed to find out who Kenneth was. He obviously wasn't 'Kenneth Kambata,' but luckily there's a simple online tool that's only too eager to help out. I uploaded a few clear face shots of Kenneth to Facebook and showed no signs of tagging any of them. That really got Facebook's goat, and it couldn't resist popping up to ask 'Who is this?' and providing a few suggestions. Ones that were backed up by a Google reverse image search which turned up some visually similar results of that same man. Only with his clothes on.

Turns out 'Kenneth Kambata' did live in Kenya, but not in a rustic village idyll. Instead he lived in Lang'ata, which Wikipedia told me was a suburb of Nairobi. His name was Joshua Bomas, and, joy of joys, he was a pastor.

Google Maps told me that the Gospel Harvest Fellowship was in a splendid white stone building with neatly-tended lawns. Transcripts of his sermons were spiced with sulphur. I found quite a few photos of Pastor Joshua casting out hellfire with all the enthusiasm that I'd seen him scattering his seed.

This was all very helpful in constructing a fake identity for myself. First I needed an authentic sounding name. I picked 'Precious Ramotswe,' realised what I'd done and hastily changed it to 'Abuya' as this was the first name in a Kenyan Babynames chooser. It means 'born when the garden was overgrown,' by the way. My local evangelist church is always advertising on the back of buses, so I plucked a photo from their site of a reasonably stern-looking matriach and, lo, Abuya Ramotswe. The garden was overgrown and it was time to do a little weeding.

I sent Pastor Joshua a gushing message about his latest sermon and a friend request. It was speedily accepted. I was in. I joined the church's Facebook group.

Dawn was coming up in London, but it was nearly 9am in Kenya, and this was clearly Pastor Joshua's peak time. The Facebook group was flooding with photos of his last sermon, some wise thoughts, and praise from his flock. Everything he posted was getting a fair number of likes. Good, clearly the faithful were sitting up and paying attention.

I'll take a moment to tell you a bit more about my friend Jay. After university, he did a bit of porn (he's long since hung up his ankles), but in the early days of Facebook, people were always tagging him in pictures that showed that he was an unusually talented project manager. It was a nightmare for him and a chore for his friends as we had to see his sex face on a regular basis (it looked like he was doing hard sums with numbers he didn't much care for). How utterly embarrassing for him, I thought.

I subjected Pastor Joshua to similar treatment. First I posted a heavily cropped and seemingly innocuous shot of his face at his personal Hallelujah Chorus. 'Praise the lord!' A lot of his flock liked that. Forgive them, Pastor Joshua, they know not what they do.

Then I uploaded a second picture, zoomed out to show a little more of his very manly chest. This got some likes and a slightly puzzled, 'Pastor, have you joined a gym?!?!?'

And then I uploaded the full shot. The money shot. Pastor Joshua wanking away with all—and I mean *all*—his might.

Pastor Joshua moved swiftly and in a not very mysterious way. He immediately de-tagged himself from the pictures and they vanished from the feed. Then he sent me a message.

> Dear friend,
> May I ask why you do such unkindness to me
> with such egregious fakery? Please, I ask you in
> the name of myself and of the Gospel Harvest
> Fellowship to prayerfully desist in these actions. If
> you have listened to the slander of serpents, I tell
> you now to turn away your cheek from LIES and
> to follow once more the true path that leads to
> righteousness.
> To reiterate once more, these pictures are
> nothing but obvious fakes thrown in my way by
> the devil, and if you spread them further you are
> doing the work of the evil one. Fakes, remember
> that in prayer,
> Pastor J

> > Dear Pastor Joshua
> > I am most sorry to hear that these pictures are
> > fakes because I have so many of them. I have
> > personally found them most enlightening. Never
> > have I felt I've been shown the way to heaven
> > more clearly than when you shoved your finger
> > up your arse.
> > In faith,
> > Abuya Ramotswe (Mrs)
> >   ✔ Seen 16:42

I posted a relevant picture to his timeline. It was a corker. He detagged it at once. He was quite the dab hand at snap. He also swiftly detagged the one of him on all fours, made a short statement urging everyone 'Not to believe SATAN'S LIES AND FAKES!!!' and then defriended me. Smart move.

*   *   *

BUT I'D ALREADY made friends with some of the congregation on the Facebook group, and showed them my gratitude by messaging them a brief video clip. The sound was muffled but enthusiastic.

TWO MINUTES LATER Moses Gamba was saying, 'Friends, various seniors in the Gospel Harvest Fellowship have been sent a very worrying piece of media which, after some discussion, we have strongly agreed not to post until a full and honest investigation of it has been made with Pastor Joshua.'

A MINUTE LATER someone posted the video itself.

By now I had Pastor Joshua's email address. I sent him my Skype address and another video clip. Thirty seconds later I donned a balaclava and accepted the incoming call. He had barely started screaming at me when I held up my hand.

"Let me just stop you there. First mistake, Pastor. The background you're using is exactly the same as in your other videos."

Pastor Joshua looked over his shoulder and then went very quiet.

"If only you'd hung an eye-catching print over that wall, well then, you'd have been fine," I tutted.

He stared at me in pure hatred.

"You are ruining my life," he growled. "What do you want?"

"It's very simple. You have stolen some money from a friend of mine. If you return it, then I will publicly apologise for faking videos of you having sex. If you don't, then I've got lots more."

He shook his head. "Impossible," he said. "The money... The money alas is spent. I am afraid I used it for my church. We need a new roof." He spread his hands out in a simple gesture, as if to say 'what's a guy to do?'

I shook my head. "Sadly, no, pastor. According to the Gospel Harvest's excellent website, you had a new roof installed two years ago. I think you've still got the cash."

He paused, and then spoke in a voice of contrition and honey. "I misspoke. The truth, my good friend, is that these things take time. Even if I could, alas, it takes many days to raise a money transfer in this country. Almost a week, in fact. Perhaps we could talk again on Friday when I have made the arrangements?"

I tutted. Which, actually, looked a little silly on screen. A man in a balaclava tutting. "Now, see here, Joshua... you were paid by PayPal. So I'm sure you can return the favour. Immediately. As I'm sure she's not the only one, I've emailed you your victim's details and the amount. To jog your memory."

Now Joshua nodded and smiled ruefully. "It is all right. I know already. It is Jackie." He gave me a curious look, and a small smile.

"Will you make the payment?"

He hesitated. "Today almost definitely. Tomorrow certainly."

"No. Pay now. During this call." My voice was very firm. "You forget, I've also got footage of the conspirators you roped in to play your relatives. Who both appear to be deacons in the church. They're not as entertaining as the other videos, but they could certainly be diverting."

He glared at me with simple hatred. "You are unspeakable. I consider that what I have done is no more than... I provided company to a lonely woman. And, if I perhaps accepted some remuneration... it was no more than a fair fee."

I laughed at that. "Not quite."

"Oh, believe me, I think so," he chuckled. "These women know what they are getting into. And, if they do not, then it is not my lookout. Otherwise you are suggesting that I have given my time for free? Talking to her and, shall we say, providing other services? That is wrong, my friend."

"It's simply what every single person around the world does with their free time, Pastor. Are you married?"

He looked nervous. "I am engaged. I am awaiting the blessing of the bishop before I can take things further."

I nearly tutted again. "I'm sure his approval would depend on you having an upright moral standing. Something harmed by pictures of bits of your upright standing."

He frowned. "I do not understand."

"Pay up."

"It is not simple," he began again. "It is, as you must understand, my friend, very complicated." He was definitely wheedling, playing for time.

"Nope," I said. "Pay up now."

He glared at me. I glared back.

We kept up the silence for a whole minute, the clock ticking slowly past. The cat weaved curiously around my legs and I worried for a moment that it would leap up onto the desk and into shot, totally ruining my cyber-terrorist credentials.

The silence reached that uncomfortable point. When someone could have said something and didn't. I'll say this for Pastor Joshua, he did a good stare, mixing aggrieved and furious.

Finally, he blinked, and glanced away. Then he tapped a few keys.

"It is done," he said. "Can I trust you, in good faith, to do your part of the deal?"

I nodded. "The emails are already written," I said.

My phone pinged. It was a text from Jackie. It said, 'YESS!!!! Xx'

I sent the following message to Facebook:

Dear friends,
I humbly pray that you will forgive me. I have been misled by a serpent into trying to incriminate our good Pastor Joshua. I am a widow and I hoped to win his affections, but the Pastor nobly and politely rebuffed me, telling me that his life was with the church and urging me to follow that same road.
It was then that I decided to blacken and incriminate him, getting my son to doctor the pictures and other media that I have sent to you in order to blacken the name of one whose only crime was virtue.
As you will see from the attached original files, Pastor Joshua is not involved in any way. I humbly beg that you will forgive me.
Abuya Ramotswe (Mrs)

The faked 'originals' just about passed muster. It's actually reasonably easy to do an almost fake. I'd even changed the background. The thing is, if people really want to believe something, then that helps them along enormously.

PASTOR JOSHUA NODDED, a tiny smile tugging at his lips. "It will not work, not completely... but then, perhaps it is a punishment I deserve. No man should ever be regarded without suspicion." He looked at me. "As for you, my friend, vengeance shall call you to account some day."

"I hope not," I said and terminated the call.

MY PROXY SERVER pinged back at me. Someone had been trying to run a trace route to see who I was. Luckily, I was using Jackie's laptop.

JACKIE RANG ME a few minutes later.

"That was bloody amazing," she said.

"Have you got it all back?"

A tiny hesitation. "Yes." Well. "Almost all. He kept a very little back, but that doesn't matter. Not in the scheme of things. But honestly, an utter lifesaver. I was down to my last pennies."

"Where are you staying?" I asked.

She named a five-star hotel.

"Fine," I said evenly. "I'll hand your laptop in at reception."

"Thanks, darling," she cooed. "I owe you one."

"Then I'll ask a favour of you. Whatever you choose to write about in the future, stay away from Vampantha."

"Who?" Jackie looked puzzled. "Sounds familiar..."

"Oh, it doesn't matter," I assured her, warmly. "She's a best-selling novelist. You've interviewed her already. People say a lot of mean things about her, but I think she's an admirable modern feminist role model."

"I see," Jackie nodded, clearly clocking the name for future reference.

"Leave Vampantha alone from now on, that's all," I said and terminated the call.

Job done.

I HAD ONE more thing to do. It was all getting a bit too close to me. I was making mistakes. It was time to end my relationship with the Killuminati. I'd never find out who they were or why they were. Like everyone watching the final episode of *Lost*, I just didn't care anymore.

I logged into MySpace and messaged Duster. "It's over," I said.

There was no reply.

IT WAS TIME for bed. It had been a long night, and the doorbell had kept going intermittently. To start with, the noise had thrown me out of my concentration, flooding me with adrenaline. But I'd ignored the bell. I needed to solve one problem. And now I really needed bed. Really, really needed bed.

I made the necessary mistake of going down into the street and putting Jackie's laptop in a cab to her hotel, then I took sinking treacle steps back up to the flat. I was just threading my way through the cat towards that lovely inviting duvet and ready to sink into the pillow when the doorbell rang again.

Groaning, I opened it.

There was Amber. Looking furious.

SHE LOOKED AMAZING. I'd had no sleep (apart from ten minutes when my head had nodded off over a chicken cup-a-soup). She'd clearly had much more.

"So you're in," she said.

"Yes."

"Good morning," she said. "You're covered in bruises."

"You and Guy beat me up," I said.

"Well, yes. Where the hell have you been all night?"

"In here."

"I know. I could see from across the road."

"So it was you ringing the bell?"

"Yes. Why didn't you answer it?"

"Didn't fancy it."

"And now?"

"Still don't fancy it much."

We stood there for a moment. I wasn't going to invite her in. I'm not sure she wanted me to anyway. Refusal often offends.

"How's Guy?"

"Oh, fine."

"And you?"

"Fine."

"Good. I'm fine too."

"So I can see."

"Yeah. About last night..."

"What about last night?"

"Well, you know... oh, where to start?"

Amber narrowed her eyes. "Do go on," she said. Her tone was menacing.

"Okay, so, dashing off in the middle of a... discussion—can we have *discussion*?"

She considered. "Yes, we can have discussion."

"Dashing off in the middle of a discussion, then."

"Yes?"

"Well, I'm sorry about that. But she was..." I was careful to avoid Jackie's name.

"An ex?"

"A bit. Sort of. You okay with that?"

"Why would I not be?" Amber's voice was very flat indeed. A plane slowly went overhead, leaving behind two long white lines in the sky.

"Great, great," I said. "I mean, not that she's my girlfriend now. No. Because she's met someone else."

"She wants you back?"

"God, no," I said a little too quickly.

"Right."

"No, no, she's kind of moved on. She's very happy."

"Like Guy and me?"

That took some wind out of my sails. I rallied. "Yes," I said hesitantly. "Just like you and Guy."

Another silence settled over us.

"The police came round last night," said Amber.

"Really? Why?"

"The gig. I wish you hadn't done that."

Right. I had genuinely forgotten. Yes. Right. That was a problem. Yes. One large jumble sale.

"Oh."

"You idiot."

I smiled.

"What?" she said crossly.

"Sorry," I giggled uncontrollably. "It's just the way you say 'idiot.'"

"How?"

"Kind of fondly. It's nice."

"It's not meant fondly. Idiot." She smiled. Just a little.

"So, how was the police thing?"

She shrugged. "How do you think? Guy and I were in the middle of a Korea-sized row. The police turned up to ask a couple of tiny questions about some burglaries."

"Uh-huh. And of course you told them you were innocent."

"Of course I told them I was innocent."

"And you are."

"Only..." Amber looked down at the ground. "That's why I came round to see you last night."

She'd told the police about me. She'd betrayed me. It's rare that you get to feel betrayed by someone; almost exciting. I just felt rather dead about it. Curious. When you get a filling and tap a spoon or tinfoil along your teeth one at a time until you find it and all the nerves in your head explode? That. I was working through my brain, tapping my feelings. No explosion. Nothing. Numb.

"You told the police I organised the stunt?" Still nothing.

"No." Amber was annoyed by the question. "Look, there's something we need to talk about—"

"Who told the police?"

Amber sighed. "Guy did."

Bang. There we go. Explosion.

*   *   *

I'M NOT GOING to say, "All things considered, the police were quite nice about it." It's just that it could have been so much worse. I was kind of expecting my first visit to a police station to be about any one of a number of deaths (I'd even made a list—an unwritten list obviously—of which one was most likely to get me investigated). Instead, here I was being rather glumly investigated over a series of "internet related burglaries."

The room itself was so dull. Deliberately dull. It was an anti-room. I'd hired enough of this sort of space. Light came in from high windows, presumably so that passers-by couldn't gawp in, and so that people inside couldn't daydream of a world outside.

I think I was supposed to be frightened. Or nervously intimidated. I wondered about feigning the correct emotions. But I just felt really tired, and then there was the pisser that Guy had dobbed me in. I didn't expect he'd be that fond of me right now, but this felt really... unfair. I mean, yes, I had kind of fallen in love with his girlfriend, and yes, I had kissed her, but to hold that against me seemed mean.

The police seemed nice enough, and their questions were doing all the proper things. It was curiously like interviewing someone when you were out chugging. Lots of, "How do you feel about...?" and "Can you just talk me through...?" Over and over again.

Too tired to muster a proper defence or character I produced a lacklustre Hugh Grant. I heard the recording back recently. "I'm afraid you must think me dreadful..." "It comes across to me as a prank, if prank is the right word..." and even "gosh" and "these pirates—they seem pretty ghastly people though, don't they?"

You can also tell I'm tired. Dog tired.

They wander around the point of the conversation like lazy sharks, sauntering closer and closer to the real subject. There's the occasional diversion.

"Can we just ask—would you like to receive medical attention? You appear to have some small injuries to your face. We'd like to assess them, if that's okay with you. Have you been in a fight?"

I politicked how to answer that one. I figured that something like the truth would do no harm.

"Ah, well... My friend Guy and I were engaged in... perhaps 'horseplay' isn't quite the right word, is it? Anyway, we had an altercation, you could say." It's funny how when people talk to the police their diction jumps sideways, like they're emulating an officer giving an "I was proceeding in a westerly direction" statement from a 1940s film. As if anyone ever spoke like that.

We strolled back and forth and around that fight. They would sidle out a gently probing question, "What would you say the provocation for this altercation was?" See? Even they were doing it now. And I'd counter with something bashful, "Well, I'd say he was very cross with me."

Their eyes were clear. They both looked young and neat and just a little bored. This was clearly their routine. There was no chemistry or spark between them. Her name was Julia. His was Mike. They had that look of graduate trainees. Working steadily through an assignment.

You could jab away, just a little, at their carefully constructed personalities. For instance, if you said something like, "Well, you know, some people are asking for it aren't they?" they'd reply, "That's quite an aggressive thing to say, don't you think?" and you could then counter it with, "Well, he was very cross. I don't blame him for lamping me."

We were basically knitting between us. They were painting me into a corner over the thefts. I was constructing a picture for them of Guy as a violent, unpredictable man. Mostly for my own amusement. Because he'd dobbed me in to the police. 'Dobbed me in?' See? It's impossible to talk around the police properly. No matter what you do, where you try and move yourself, your inner ITV Drama voice comes out.

I was being quite careful about the actual thefts. I told them I didn't have an alibi, that I was watching the webcast. Both of these statements were true. They hadn't yet asked me directly if I did it. There was a lot of, "We're going to show you a piece of video. Would you agree that the person in this video could be you?"

"Well, of course, it could be. But then again, it could be anyone. You're going to just use the first bit of that, aren't you? Well, I mean, fair play to you if you do. I wouldn't blame you."

You can hear me on the tape. I'd punch me. I don't quite know what I was playing at.

THE MORE THEY talk about my situation, the more I realise how terribly alone I am. Oh, it's nothing they were doing. It's just that the penny gradually dropped. I'd been in here for a long time, and it had just been getting more and more boring. The last time I'd ever been in a police station was to report a stolen bicycle and they were far less thorough then. This was... forensic.

Oh. That was the word. The troubling word.

Thing is, we'd pretty much reached the end of the park. Or the centre of it. I was a bit confused about my metaphor. But basically, you know what I mean. I'd led them along a path, digging it as I went along. I'd thrown out my evening to them, my day, telling them that while I'd actually been hiring a van and breaking into people's homes I'd really been chugging. It was a reasonable lie. It was solid enough. I stepped back to have a look at my handiwork. It looked fine. All things considered. But I knew there was something wrong with it. What was it? Something glinting in the sun, exposed in the light.

"That all seems great," said Julia.

Mike nodded.

"I was wondering," she said. "Can we ask you something?"

"Sure, shoot—er, oh, I'm most dreadfully sorry, I can't remember your name."

"Inspector Franklin. Julia."

"Right, yes, right. Sorry. Anyway, ask away." That was right. She was Inspector Franklin and he was... Mike... I couldn't remember. I felt so tired and I was trying to remember their names. I've never been good at names, but this was worse than being at a party. I conjured up a mental image. A drawbridge? Oh right. His name was Keep. Couldn't even remember his rank. Let's call him Inspector Keep as well. Inspector Keep leaned forward. "We just wanted you to talk us through it all again."

This time Inspector Julia nodded.

"Okay," I said, glancing back down the path. Yeah. Seemed stable enough. I opened my mouth, ready to take the first step.

"Only," Inspector Franklin's interjection was sudden, "before you start that, I just thought I'd say that a few months ago, your friend's girlfriend died. There's been some talk about the coroner's verdict. Have you anything to say to that?"

The roof of my mouth went dry. "No." My voice on the tape recording is quite clear. Remarkably so.

"And shortly after that, a number of threats were issued to Ms Dass when she began a relationship with Mr Hammond. Coincidentally, some of the people issuing these threats were themselves victims of assaults. Have you anything to say about that?"

"No, no." My voice sounded absurd. Like I was disputing the likelihood of rain.

They both looked at me. They knew. They bloody knew.

"No? Interesting." Inspector Franklin said, her voice amazingly flat. How did she do that? "Anyway, could you walk us through that statement of yours?"

"What?"

"Your statement about the events of last night."

"Sure, I—" I swung my foot out onto the path. Only the path had vanished. I had no idea what to do next.

THERE WAS A rap on the door. Inspector Franklin looked annoyed. Keep got up and went out. There was whispering in the corridor.

She stared at me. I stared at her.

Julia. She'd not said at any point, "Call me Julia," but it was there. I knew her first name. We were sort-of friends. Perhaps if I told her, we could sort this out. No, that was lunacy. Unless I just told her about the burglaries. That was fine. Just a prank. Great. I was making a political statement. Or something. Julia smiled at me without smiling at all.

I think I looked like a goldfish. On the tape you can hear a pop-pop noise.

And then, absurdly, if you listen closely, you can hear me humming. Just very gently. It sounds as though it could be any tune. It could be. Absurd how you hum these things. But, if you knew the song, you'd know it was 'Love In The First Degree' by Bananarama.

Then Keep came in. He didn't address Julia. He didn't really address me. He was speaking to me, but looking at a drab grey patch of drab grey wall.

"Your solicitor's here," he announced.

My solicitor?

OKAY. HERE ARE the facts about my solicitor.

She looked exactly how you would expect a solicitor to look. Her name was Andrea and she just exuded that feeling of healthy country living. For all I knew she'd come straight here from walking the dogs and riding the horse. She was very smartly dressed, but wore her expensive clothes with the air of someone throwing on some old tweeds to do weeding. She looked constantly on the verge of laughter and greeted me as an old friend, and I had never met her before in my life.

We met in a tiny little room little different from the tiny little room I'd already been in. I have no idea why they bothered moving me.

She sat down and banged a file onto the desk. It was red, a vivid splash of colour in the muted space. "Paperwork," she announced with a laugh. "It always creates a good impression. I feel naked without it and absolutely no one takes you seriously unless you have a folder, but really, it's all on the iPad. This is mostly just print-outs of a couple of emails and directions from Google for finding the nick."

"But—"

She rambled on, looking around the room as though planning on moving in and working out where to fit the sofa. "They always make police stations so hard to find. Whenever they say on the news 'bailed to appear at' I always roll my eyes and try and imagine the god-awful rabbit warren they'll have hidden the poor sod in."

"Have I been on the news?"

She barked at that. "Get over yourself, sunshine. This case is one up from rag week."

I flooded with relief. I gushed with it. I suddenly realised that I did care very much about what was going on.

"Who—"

Andrea seemed not to have heard. "You know, I'm often tempted to bring in a scented candle to these places. I'm sure I'd be told off." She beamed. "Calendula, or blueberry, or just plain old chocolate. Something heady and sweet." She pushed the folder towards me. "Anyway, paperwork, including the confirmation that I've been engaged to act as your solicitor."

I opened the folder. There really was very little in it. One sheet of paper said the following:

> *This woman is your solicitor. You can trust her. By agreeing for her to represent you, you hereby agree to keep our relationship silent. She will get you out. In return, you must do one last thing for us.*

"Always read the small print," beamed Andrea implacably. "Small print's a bugger."

CHAPTER TWELVE
NEVER MEET YOUR HEROES

THE DOOR WAS opened.

"Come in," said the voice. It wasn't an invitation. It was an order. "I know who you are." A small, grating pause, as gum was chewed. "I mean, I know who you really are."

I stepped inside. The door closed.

THE SMELL HIT you first. Teenage bedroom and mildew. A persistent musty sense of dirt. The place was so dark that smell was about all you had to go on at first. Then, like stars slowly coming out in the night sky, details presented themselves.

The hallway was dark because it was wood-panelled, like a tiny baronial mansion. Dark red carpets soaked into the floor. Only one door was open off the hallway, and that was lit solely by the blue twinkle of a laptop screen. The heavy curtains were drawn. The thick air suggested they'd never been opened.

Standing in front of me was a man. He looked like all of his photos, but only in the sense that, in person, you could kind of see how he could look like he did in his photos. In photos he was commanding and dignified, a bulky suited figure dominating the room. A huge bear of a man. In the flesh, he was simply quite a lot of flesh, squeezed into running gear that had never gone faster than a trot.

So, I'd done smell and sight. Sound was also troubling. There was an odd wet clicky-clicky noise. I realised it was coming from his mouth. He was chewing gum constantly.

This was it. I was standing in front of an internet pioneer. The man who invented the slogan, 'All Knowledge Good.' The man who thumped the desk until it agreed with him. Henry Jarman.

And he knew who I was.

WE STOOD THERE, in the foetid hall. It felt like a blind date. Except that on a blind date the only things you know about each other are what you want each other to know. And they aren't true anyway. You've probably not bothered to update your favourite film for three years. You may say you 'love cake,' but what does that even mean? We're just trying to make ourselves sound interesting. And we're not.

But I'd read everything about Henry Jarman. I'd worshipped him for years. Even when he was wrong, he was interesting. And he was here. In front of me. Which was awkward.

And he was speaking, his lips were chewing, constant motion. And he was just staring at me. Every time he blinked, he chewed. It was like his eyelids were wet and sticky. It was a revolting sound.

"See," he breathed, "I have to be careful. It's not as though I let anyone in to see me. Especially not an interview request from someone who claims to be a journalist, with a made-up name, who has never written anything, from a blog that barely exists. So I did some digging. And some more digging. And the more I looked the more I found out. And yet—" He stopped talking. He even stopped chewing for a long time. And then it came. A blink and a chew. "Yeah... You could call me a fan. I've long been interested in meeting you. I really have. All Knowledge Good, you see. You hungry? I know a really excellent place."

THE WALK TO the restaurant was awkward. For a start, Jarman had wrapped himself up like the Invisible Man, his eyes darting above his scarf niqab. "Got to be careful," he murmured. "To be perceived is to be."

We trudged on, with the awkward and occasional small talk that happens between people who are uncertain of each other.

"Cigarette?" he offered. I declined. "Force of habit. I don't have any," he sighed, still chewing manfully away. "Gave up. Used to smoke on the doorstep, but then it turned out They could see me. The scum."

Uh-oh. There's nothing like a proper blast of paranoia when you've just met someone.

We came to a halt outside what seemed to be an unprepossesing Indian restaurant. A yellow plastic sign said, 'The TAJ.' The phone number used the old 01 London area code.

Jarman halted, a pilgrim in front of Xanadu. He slowly and theatrically unwound his scarf, sticking his neck out and sniffing the air appreciatively. As he did so, a muffled-up young woman, seemingly walking innocuously past, held up her phone with a flash-click, smiled and hurried on.

Jarman turned to me, smiling with grim satisfaction. "See?" he intoned. "They're everywhere." Vindicated, he threw open the door and paused on the threshold, allowing the bell's tinkle to fade away before announcing, "This is the finest food outside Delhi. Amazing. It will make you cry."

Then he led me in.

The restaurant was dark and empty. Red velvet paper clung valiantly to the walls. Distantly, someone sang over a zither. A sign said, 'Please wait to be seated.' There were no other diners. There were no staff.

Just us.

The singer sang on, her wail rising to a scream that echoed off the fur of the walls.

A kitchen door swung open and a waiter wandered past, carrying a half-empty bottle of Pepsi. He spotted us with some surprise and silently pointed us to a table.

"Ah, my old friend! Away from the window, if you please, Imran," boomed Jarman.

The waiter shrugged, and wordlessly pointed us to a table in the middle of the room and went away.

We sat down. There were no menus. Through force of habit, I hunted around for one. There was only an old piece of yellow rice stuck to the tablecloth.

"Don't bother," growled Jarman. "The food here is exquisite, and I know the menu like the back of my hand. I'll order for us both." There was to be no question about this.

We sat in more awkward silence until the waiter came back and then Jarman bellowed what sounded like the entire menu at him. I began to understand his size from his definition of lunch. He refused to "talk shop" until after food, so we had another wait to endure. Jarman finally found a topic, holding court on an interview with him in the *Metro* the previous week: "The girl turned up and she asked stupid questions, so of course she got stupid answers," he rumbled. "I don't know why I bother. Life's too short to think about people like that. I rang her editor and told him so personally."

I was sat in a restaurant with Henry Jarman waiting for lunch. This was my last assignment for the Killuminati. And I felt a terrible sinking feeling.

THE NINJA HAD been waiting for me when I'd got home from the police station. The cat was weaving around her legs.

"Right," I said. "Hello."

Actually, it didn't really come out like that. A fair bit of startled yelping went on. It's not every day you find a hot Ninja in your living room. Her arms were crossed. She looked patient. Like... well, you know when you're playing a video game and you can't quite think what to do? The world's exploding, dragons are attacking, and, lacking input, your central character just folds their arms and waits for instructions? The Ninja was doing that.

She wasn't quite tapping her feet. But she was curious.

"What are you doing here?" I asked.

This was it, I guessed. Now I was working for the Killuminati again. All part of the package.

"We've got to be careful from now on," she said. Again, that hopelessly cool Scots burr. "Subtle. Getting the police involved—that was a mistake. You've got careless."

"And sending a ninja, that's subtle?"

"Subtler than you."

"Look... I've never said this to a ninja before, but would you like a drink?"

"No."

"I don't know what to do. I mean, I could make tea. But you'd look silly. Sipping it through your mask. Wine... but that dulls the senses, doesn't it? Perhaps just a glass of water. Or milk."

"You're babbling."

"I've had a long and weird day. Couldn't my lawyer have handled this?"

"Andrea is for the nice things. I'm here to talk to you."

"Nicely?"

The Ninja shook her head.

I felt a little sick.

She stepped forward, striding around the flat, with the slow, authoritative prowl of a hunter sizing a space up. Recognising supremacy, the cat followed on behind, adoringly.

"You've done what you've been told so far..." she said.

"Yes." My mouth was drier than I'd have liked.

"And it's worked well. But when you've gone rogue—"

Gone rogue. Wow. She spoke like Andy McNab.

"—it's not been so clear. You've grown sloppy."

"It's fine," I said. "It's absolutely fine." I held up my hands. "It's really fine. Tonight's been a bit of a wake-up call. I can't believe I've got away with it for as long as I have."

"You're not done," said the Ninja. Underneath the mask, I sensed she was smiling. "You're done when we tell you you're done."

"What?"

"Small print'll get you every time," she said, echoing Andrea. Whereabouts in Scotland was she from, I wondered? Was she from Glasgow's East End, or from somewhere nice in Edinburgh, or somewhere grey like Aberdeen, or some remote Highland? I had an absurd image of her standing in the prow of a small boat as it drifted across a loch. God, dates with her must be kind of exciting. "So, I'm a digital experience strategy consultant—and what do you do?"

The Ninja slapped me in the face. The pain woke me up. The pain more than woke me up. I fell back, my eyes stinging.

Someone had hit me. In my own flat. This was getting to be a habit.

"You weren't listening." She didn't sound angry, just mildly annoyed. "And it's important that you listen to me."

"Okay," I said. There wasn't, when I thought back about it, that much of a whimper.

"Check your email. One more job. Follow the instructions."

"No," I said. "You can hit me again, but no."

"Oh, you'll do it." The Ninja sounded smug. Like she'd peeked into the future.

"Listen," I said to her, holding up my hands. Showing I wasn't a threat. "Listen—right... if they're employing you as well as me... well, why don't they use you instead of me? I mean, you're obviously better than me at everything. And way more..." I didn't say *sexy*. Never tell a ninja they're sexy. "Way cooler. You're what I'll never be."

The Ninja nodded. She took the compliment. "Think about it," she said. "Think it through and you'll realise."

The only solution I had was that I was disposable. I didn't say it out loud, but the Ninja nodded again. Like she could read my thoughts.

"Get out your phone," she said. "Get ready to film something."

"A confession?"

"No. Not really. Just something that will get a lot of views on YouTube."

I pulled my phone from my pocket and fumbled with it. My hands were shaking so I set it down on the counter, resting up against a cookery book. Filming most of the room.

The Ninja nodded. The she picked up the cat, stroking her. The cat purred, rubbing against the mask, pushing it up, teasing me with tiny glimpses of face. For an absurd moment I wondered if it was Amber. But it couldn't be. Instead of Amber's delicate Indian skin, the Ninja's skin was so pale. Almost transparent. The cat purred and nuzzled.

I normally have ever so much trouble fitting the cat into her box for trips to the vet. But she climbed into the microwave without protest. Just sat inside mewing gently.

I was screaming by this point.

"So," said the Ninja. "What do you think works? Defrost? Do you think a minute on defrost and she'll be fine? Or is it just 10 seconds on full? Which do you want to try? You choose."

I just stood there. Shouting.

The cat looked at me. And mewed again. She tapped the glass door curiously.

The Ninja dialled up some numbers. Beep. Beep. Beep. Her finger hovered over start.

I threw myself at her, but she blocked me with an arm. And then pressed start.

The microwave started up. The slow whirring grind. The table trying to spin. The cat scrabbling against the glass.

I howled.

The Ninja pressed 'stop,' with a cheerful 'bing.'

She stood back, looking at me.

The cat watched her curiously from inside the microwave.

"Okay," I said, crying. "You've made your point."

"Good," said the Ninja, and headed for the door. She paused. "At the end of the day, it really is all about the cats."

I never saw her again.

So, THAT WAS why I was sat in a restaurant with Henry Jarman waiting for lunch. And I felt a terrible sinking feeling.

Eventually the meal turned up, and it was horrible. Lumps of school-dinner meat stewing in either oil+cream or oil+tomato soup. I was worried that I'd have to politely pick away at it, but I didn't get a chance.

Jarman shovelled all of the food bar the oily residue onto his plate and devoured it, pausing to smear curry kisses across his cheeks with the tablecloth. He slung three pints of lager down his maw as well, filling the air with the smell of hops and chilli. Only as his feasting began to subside did I realise that he was still chewing Nicotine gum. My stomach turned. Dutifully I turned my attention to the quarter of naan bread I'd left on my side plate, but discovered that Jarman had already reached over and was rubbing the grease from a silver bowl with it.

He said only one thing, and that was rather curious. "The condemned man," he belched, "ate a hearty meal. Ha ha."

When he'd finally subsided, he summoned the waiter over.

"My compliments to the chef!" he announced. "Bring him to us. I wish him to meet my old friend." He turned to me. "Mahmood is a splendid chap. A real jewel. You'll love him. He's one of my oldest comrades-in-arms. For an army marches on its stomach, and he is my victualler. Bring me Mahmood!"

The waiter demurred. "I'm afraid, sir, that today the chef is rather busy."

I looked around at the empty restaurant and back at the waiter. His eyes were fixed on the tablecloth.

"Nonsense!" cried Jarman. "Fetch us Mahmood!" He thumped the table with his fist.

THIS WAS ALL unbelievably awkward. This was a man who had bullied governments, wooed and ruined *Guardian* journalists, campaigned on four different continents for free speech, been elected honorary Vice Chancellor of three different universities, been talked of for a Nobel Peace prize and turned down *I'm A Celebrity*. This was, I knew, my one chance to talk to him. And here he was, behaving like an irate child.

The waiter swallowed like Kermit the Frog and slumped off miserably towards the kitchen. The door swung behind him, disclosing a strong waft of frying onions.

Jarman turned back towards me. "Young man," he said, steepling his fingers, "we have much to talk of—once, of course, you've met Mahmood. The man is an inspiration, a genius *non pareil*. A philosopher chef."

The kitchen door opened a little too loudly and a face peeped through, then the door closed again.

Jarman pretended not to notice, his fingers dipping and licking among the leftover chutneys.

Finally, the Great Mahmood appeared. He was wearing an overcoat and carrying a Tesco Bag For Life. He gave every indication of having rapidly mugged up the part of 'Man In A Hurry To Be Elsewhere.'

Jarman threw himself to his feet and grabbed the man in an elaborate bear hug. "*Namaste,* Mahmood," he breathed into the man's ear. Mahmood nodded, and then turned to grimace weakly at me, Jarman clapped across his shoulder.

"This man," chuckled Henry, "This man has been my culinary Tzensing as we've climbed the summit of many a Curry Everest."

"Ah, indeed, sir," offered Mahmood uncertainly, transferring his shopping bag from one hand to the next and back.

"Do you remember that time when we entertained those backstabbing *Guardian* hacks? Oh, that *was* a meal, wasn't it?"

Mahmood nodded.

"What was it you served...? It was brilliant!"

Mahmood glanced helplessly at Henry. "A special dish, for certain."

"Yes. With almonds."

"Almonds, yes, certainly..."

I STOOD UP, and excused myself. I went to the bathroom, which smelt of liquid soap and fennel. I washed my hands three times, dried them thoroughly on a ragged pink towel, and then headed back.

Mahmood had departed. Jarman sat back, looking satisfied. He was clearing up a last scrap of sauce with a splinter of poppadom I'd left on my plate.

"Delicious," he proclaimed. "Unbeatable. That man is the Berners-Lee of biryanis."

He pushed the plates into a teetering pile in the centre of the table and fixed me with a gaze. "So then, shall we get to business?"

I glanced furtively around the room. A distant fish tank glowed. It was empty of fish, a fairy tale castle waiting in vain for anything to peep through it.

Jarman had assumed an air of jocular smugness. "Oh, we're quite safe here, you know. I'm very thorough." He let out a belch. "Not only is this restaurant of impeccable quality, it also has no CCTV. It's not Nando's, or some other capitalist sell-out. The walls of the building are thick enough that radio scanners can't pick us up, and the double yellows means that a suitably-equipped van can't park outside." I had no idea what he meant by a suitably-equipped van. And I doubted the intelligence services were scared of traffic wardens. "Of course, they've made approaches to Mahmood from time to time. But he's turned them all down." I wondered if they had. I wondered if he would.

Fundamentally, I realised I was at the beginning of a lecture. From a vast man wearing a shirt covered in rice and slowly drying scraps of curry.

"Of course, you were my idea. Yes, I dreamed you up," announced Henry, smirking. He jabbed a bitten-down fingernail at me. "I may not have picked you out, but I certainly have been foretelling your existence for a number of years. As soon as I became aware of what you were doing, I knew I'd invented you." He beamed. "You know what caused you? It's LOL I blame. That was the root of it all. When people started writing LOL to each other. Think about the number of times you've ever laughed out loud. It's not very often, is it? But suddenly we were LOLing all over the place, all the time.

"People have been sneering at LOL for years. But they've missed the point of it. It is an insidious little thing. Because it's so friendly. Suddenly people are LOLing all the time, but never actually doing it in real life. Not only that, but its ubiquity makes it meaningless. It's used to soften blows, to show that you're a nice, cheerful person." Henry threw up elaborate, tumeric-stained air quotes. "'We were never dating lol.' But the shift has begun—emotion expressed purely on line and not in real life. And, because it started with something as friendly as a laugh, it seemed like a good thing. But it started the online expression of emotions. Our laughs, our smiles, our winks and our tears—we steadily removed them from our faces and placed them into our words. We don't look at each other anymore—we're staring at our phones, and, anyway, if we did look each other in the face, there'd be nothing to see any more.

"We've placed all our emotions out there, in words and at the end of sentences. It took us a while to get to grips with expressing ourselves online. It was so easy to misconstrue what people said, to take offence. So we had to say when we were being funny, or serious. And this led to us starting to tell other people how to feel.

"Those stupid sites run by liberal toadies with their 'After fifty-four seconds your heart will break,' or 'your jaw will drop' or 'your mind will be blown.' It's all rail-roading emotional response. It demands an instant response and answer, one that it is becoming increasingly easy to give, 'Wow. I cried' is suddenly so easy to type. Because no one knows if you did. No one checks. And one day soon, no one will know what crying really looks like.

"Behind all this... all this emotional wallpaper, that's where the hate lurks. We put all of our open emotions online, and then the more hidden, dark ones soon followed. The anger and the hatred, stuff that we spend all our time bottling up, that came running along in the shadows.

"If it was suddenly okay to tell people that we cried, perhaps it was fine for us to say out loud that someone on television looks like a slut, or a Jew. Or that they needed killing. Because that's what we really felt. And the internet had told us that it was now okay to feel. Hadn't it? And, after all, if it looked a bit stark, we knew just how to soften the blow. 'He looks like a yid lol.'"

Jarman had got into his flow. He actually stood up, initially to start pacing around, but basically to stand in his TEDTalk posture.

"Two decades ago, the internet taught us that laughter was easy. Now it's taught us all to hate." He turned around and he pointed at me. "Oh yes. I foretold *you*. When I started up my All Knowledge Good movement, I did it for a reason... I did it because one day, I knew you would come."

"Me?" I said, a little unnerved. "What have I done?"

"Oh," Jarman flapped a belittling hand. "Very little, actually. Little more than a slug or a cockroach. But it's what you stand for. You're acting from a pure heart, from clean motives, and you're getting nowhere."

"I'm trying," I protested, feeling a little like Elliott when he found he was pedalling his bike through the night sky.

"And you're failing," nodded Jarman, tapping the side of his head. "But it's the simple fact that you are acting. That's what people will notice. People talk hatred online all the time. But you... you do it." He giggled, a snorty little laugh of derision, and then he stared at me, and his eyes were suddenly clear and blue. "That's what will change the conversation. Up until now, when people have issued death threats on Twitter, there's been that slight frisson of 'Ooh, I've received a death threat' while safe in the reassurance that there is no bomb waiting in your car. Because no-one is ever serious. But you've taken that away. Suddenly, all those Social Justice Warriors with their angry retweets, their whiny petitions and their boycotts – they're *nothing*. You've taught us all—you mean exactly what you say. When you say LOL, you are actually laughing."

I nearly bought it. I nearly got swept up in it all. But then, this was Henry Jarman. That's what he did. His Wikipedia entry was a comet-trail of grand statements, self-boosting, and start-ups that had never really got going.

"Actually, I've not got much of a sense of humour," I said.

Jarman didn't bat an eyelid, he just watched me, chewing away loudly. "Few people do," he told me. "But that doesn't stop them from pretending they have. We all say we have a Good Sense Of Humour. But what does that even mean? *So many feels*. Pah! Words, words, words. We soak the world in them. But nothing means anything anymore." He wheeled on me. "I bet you have a cat, don't you?"

I nodded, thinking of its furry face squeezed up inside the microwave. I shuddered, but Jarman beamed with satisfaction. "I knew it. People like cats because we can project onto them. They're so internet. But they're also like you—no matter what people, even me, say about you, at heart, you're just a selfish killing machine."

I BLINKED A little at this. I've never really thought of myself as a killing machine. I remember a classmate at school who'd got into trouble for carving 'I Am A Cum Machine' onto his desk. Even at the screwed-up age of fourteen, this had struck me as a bit of a reductive goal in life. It also posits that there's a need for such a device, when really, it's simply advertising a pretty unwanted surplus. On the same basis, my nan could describe herself as a 'Tea Wee Machine,' but I think she'd be mortified.

"Oh yes, you are a killing machine," Jarman nodded. "No one knows for certain that you exist. There's no proof. But you're an exciting conspiracy. There are theories and blog posts about you. You may think you operate *sub rosa*, but the dark net casts long shadows..." He went on for a long while in this vein, and I can't even contemplate trying to reproduce it. He mentioned an "eviscerating" post on one forum and a "truth-telling blog" somewhere else. He told me there was a "devastating exposé" in a podcast that he couldn't wholly put himself behind. He assured me he was merely confronting and challenging my preconceptions. All the time, he was gripping the headrest of his chair, leaning more and more of his weight on it.

"You have to ask yourself," Jarman leaned forward, his breath all spices and beer, "who are you working for?"

"Myself," I said, but even I could tell I didn't mean it.

Jarman took a hand off his chair, and jabbed his own chest with it. "For instance, you've come here to kill me today, haven't you?"

Well, I had. That bit was true.

"Interesting isn't it? That people still want me dead." Jarman seemed almost buoyant at the news. "The forces of Big Government still fear me." He nodded again. "That's what you're a pawn of. I don't need to tell you I've stoked up a few nests of wasps and vipers with my crusading against Surveillance States. They need to bring me down. Ah, yes, indeed they do."

JARMAN DRAGGED HIS chair around to my side of the table and sat next to me. Sat very close to me. He cracked open a fresh piece of nicotine gum from its blister and chewed away. He slung an arm around my shoulder. Up close, the smell of curry barely masked the mildewy odour which had followed us from his house. He leaned in, and I wished he hadn't.

"You know what we should do? You and I?" He shook his head and his jowls wobbled. "We should unite. We should go public. We should really show them—I've got friends, I've got contacts. Together we should really show everyone. A bold move and then a joint statement. A manifesto." He gleamed as he said it.

"What are you proposing?"

"Simplicity itself," said Jarman. "We'll control-alt-del the world." He leaned even closer, even more confiding. "We will do the ultimate. We will give the world back its conscience. How? Simple." He paused for effect. Of course he did. "We will turn off Twitter for a day."

I blinked. Jarman didn't. He simply stared at me with the fervour of a prophet. One talking absolute nonsense. I'd come to see the Wizard of Oz and the great man wasn't in, but the curtain had some daft ideas of its own.

A day without Twitter wouldn't reset the world's soul. It'd simply be a day of whingeing on Facebook and "Is Twitter working for anyone? Or should I restart my phone?" The world wouldn't change. It would just be a tiny bit annoyed for a bit.

But Jarman didn't seem to notice my reaction. He didn't even care. He was on about Them again. Everyone, he was explaining, who had ever betrayed him, had done so only because they were working with Them.

ACTUALLY, THIS HAD given me pause for thought. The thing about Henry Jarman is that I can tell you I'd really admired him for years, but I'd pause before mentioning this down the pub. Henry Jarman's was a name that frequently made people wince. You just had to mention it, like a budget airline or a tax, and people would flinch a little. Henry Jarman was seen as necessary, but not popular.

His methods had seen him top a poll of terrible bosses. His feuds with people who were trying to help him were legendary. The claims that he'd stolen work and credit were legion.

Then there was PantsGate. The thing is, we've all posted things online at stupid o'clock. That's why they call it stupid o'clock. But Henry Jarman popped up on the forum of a site he'd founded—'a free interspace'—to announce, "It'd be really nice if you posted pictures of yourself in pants."

There were a couple of baffled responses, and someone wondered if he was joking or asking for charity.

"No, I am deadly serious. I've created this forum, I've saved the internet. The least you can do is post some pictures of yourself in pants. (White cotton. Boxers not briefs.)"

It had happened a few years ago, before Twitter was really a thing. But even then, there had been a flurry of amused responses to it. There was the .jpg of Superman, only wearing white pants, with the caption 'Saving the internet. BRB.'

There were pictures of famous statues with white pants photoshopped onto them.

Even though the post was deleted the next day and he'd never directly commented about it, PantsGate still hung around Jarman. Some newspapers had dug into his background, and finally found a female intern who had obliged with a tell-all about her time at one of his start-ups. There hadn't actually been that much to tell-all about, but she'd tried her best. Apparently he'd hugged her at her leaving do. She thought it had been a little bit of a long hug. Henry Jarman's magisterial response appeared in the comments section. He posted a YouTube clip of his appearance on Jonathan Ross where he'd hugged the host for twenty seconds: 'Now that's what I call a long hug. Ross hasn't sued me yet. PS: Before you ask, he was wearing Donald Duck pants.' It almost won people round.

If the press had hoped that a slightly dull tell-all would flush out some juicier gossip, they were disappointed, but that marked the turning point in Henry Jarman's fortunes. He wasn't a sex maniac, but it now seemed officially all right to dislike him a bit. He went from being typically referred to as 'outspoken' to 'hectoring' and then 'bullying.' BuzzFeed ran a 'What kind of boss are you?' quiz, with losers told, 'You are Henry Jarman, the ultimate tighty-whitey.'

The targets he picked also seemed increasingly safe. Saying you didn't like shadowy government suppliers like Sodobus was now so trendy it was boring. Gone were the days when he'd exposed previously beloved institutions. He just wanted low-hanging fruit and any kind of attention.

Yet I still admired him. When the Killuminati asked me to go after him, I actually got a bit of a thrill. Not just from hero worship, or from the conflict of knowing that I'd have to kill him, but from realising that this meant that, yes, Jarman was still relevant. He had to be if someone wanted to kill him.

I BECAME AWARE that Jarman was stood there in the restaurant, waiting for my reaction. He'd obviously finished speaking, and I'd not even noticed. He was just a man shouting hot air in an empty restaurant.

Jarman stood, looking at me. The only sound was the chew-chew-chew of his Nicotine gum. It popped out between his teeth, stained yellow with turmeric. Jarman sucked it back in, and carried on regarding me.

There was almost a twinkle in his eye.

"I'm not going to kill you," I told him.

Jarman wrinkled his forehead. "No?" Was that disappointment?

"I just..." I sighed. I'd be kind. "You're right. I'm being manipulated by an outside order. They're not... they're weird. There's a proper assassin working with me. I keep pulling back. I know when to stop. But she doesn't. She goes one step further."

"Does she now?" Jarman chewed, interested.

"But I'm not going to dance to their tune. Not this time." Not because you're a sad old hasbeen, but because I'm nice. "I've always admired you. I just wanted to see you face to face." I went to shake him by the hand, and he grabbed me in a hug, which, truth to tell, did go on for quite a while. "Don't mention it," said Jarman.

We stood there, looking at each other for another moment, each of us assessing the other.

Then I turned to go, and the waiter was stood by me. Holding the bill. Jarman waved in my direction. "Most kind, most kind," he boomed. Without thinking I handed over my debit card, and then froze, trying to grab it back, hurriedly replacing it with cash. The waiter stared at me. I shrugged.

"There wasn't the money in the account," I said, stuffing the card back into my pocket as though it was going to try and break away. "Sorry,"

"Of course," the waiter bowed his head and vanished.

Jarman observed the pantomime, smiling.

"There's a war coming," he announced to the waiter's retreating back. "I don't know if it's a religious war, or a class war, but there will be a war. And it will start on Twitter and then spread. And you're the first soldier in that battle."

"I certainly am not!" I snapped at him.

"It's irrelevant what you think." He favoured me with a patronising smile. "From here on in it's about what people think that you think. I can see it all, you know. And... I've planned ahead. For the future."

"Oh, yes," I was using the tone when Mum starts going on about foreigners.

"There are over two hundred pre-written blogs, and several thousand tweets all set to publish at various times. My team know my wishes and my style. My great work will carry on."

"I'm sorry," I was baffled. "I thought you'd heard. I'm not going to kill you."

"It doesn't matter." Jarman shrugged, waving this away like an inconsequential detail. "I have heart disease. I've really not got very long left. But I wanted to go out in a special way. And you have made today very special. You've treated me to some wonderful company and some impeccable food. Thank you."

"Okay." My voice was uncertain. My eyes kept darting to the exit. *Get out get out get out.*

"And you have allowed me to do a final service for humanity. Or rather, two final services. You have shown me attention and made me relevant again. And you have allowed me to unmask you as the internet serial killer."

"What?" I jabbered. "But... I'm not. I mean, I'm not going to kill you."

"You already have," rumbled Jarman. "I wondered if you'd be up to it. One should always prepare for an important lunch. While you were in the little boys' room, I took the precaution of placing a lethal dose of digitalin in my leftover sauce. Fairly soon I shall slip away. In fact, if you don't mind, I shall just sit down now." He sank into his chair, and I noticed the sheen across his forehead.

"What?" I think I said that a few times. Panic had grabbed hold of my chest and was giving it a squeeze.

"I've already explained," rumbled Jarman, his eyelids half-closed. "As you wouldn't kill me, I've done it for you."

"But—"

"Oh, it doesn't matter." Jarman's eyelids closed and then bounced open a little. "This way I get to go out with a bang, rather than be found dead in bed."

"I'll go now. I'll leave the restaurant." I could hear I was gibbering. "No one will know."

"There's Mahmood and the waiter, they're both witnesses. And also, there's that photo."

I remembered as we'd walked in. The flash. I'd assumed it was someone taking a picture of Jarman.

"My assistant—the ever-so capable Michelle Fischer—took it. It's a picture of us both together, my boy. The assassin leading me to my last meal." Jarman chuckled, his eyelids fluttering. "I'm so tired," he said, his breath coming in snores. His jaw went slack, and his gum rolled out onto the thick carpet. "It's all been worth it..."

I stood there, slapping him, screaming at someone in the restaurant to call an ambulance. But there was no rousing Henry Jarman. I brought the phone out of my pocket to call 999. And then I stopped. What if they could trace me, trace my voice? The same thing would happen with a landline. Crap. I considered picking up the landline using a paper napkin and speaking into it, muffling my voice, making the call, wondering if the operator would believe me. But no, they'd expect me to stay with the body. And I couldn't. I just couldn't.

Henry Jarman's head drooped onto his chest. He seemed to be smiling.

The bastard was dying knowing that he'd won.

*   *   *

I WENT TO the kitchens. There was no sign of the chef, or the waiter, just a vast pile of chopped onions. I went out through the fire escape and then I started to run.

VAMPANTHA'S SERIOUSLY DARK SECRET

Jackie Aspley *has a surprise for the erotic novelist*

My friends swear by Vampantha. "She is SUCH a guilty pleasure," they tell me.

That's the problem about living in the countryside. No one has any fun or even knows how to have it. So they buy ridiculous pot-boilers that describe ludicrous sex acts so that they don't have to bother with them and can carry on spending all their spare time on jam-making and jigsaws.

Vampantha is quite the rave in the village at the moment. Everyone's reading her. "My dear," they confide in me in the village shop, "it's so wonderful. I can read her on my Kindle and no-one knows!"

Trust me, everyone does. Because you can't shut up about it. "She's so racy and so rich. You should write one."

I'd rather work in an abattoir. I've interviewed Vampantha before. Back when she wasn't famous and I was. Stupid of me to brag about these things, but she was grateful to meet me. Now it is she who is doing me the favour.

She's late. You can tell when someone's made it. They think it's cool to be late. She's not quite at the stage of granting interviews in hotel suites. She meets me at a posh London club. It's artfully chic and used by people in suits to bray at each other over their iPad presentations. It's utterly hell and the only person who looks extraordinary is Vampatha.

She's calmed down the undead chic, but she still looks like an abandoned upholstery project. There's a lot of velvet and lace. But it's no longer trying quite so hard to be noticed.

She gets some glances. The men-in-suits stare at her cleavage. The dieting women in pencil-skirts gawp at her fleshiness. Her bulk is commendable.

She's allowed success to settle on her. Both on her manner and her hips. She's the voluptuous side of fat. She's commanding. She progresses around the room. She's seen me already, but she wants to make the most of looking for me. Little Bo Beep looking for a vampire sheep.

"Vampantha," she says, holding my hand firmly. "Seriously charmed."

"Me too," I tell her. I talk to her about her books. There were some thumbed copies of the paperback editions at a White Elephant stall. I figured if I just read the pages with turned down corners, I'd get a fair flavour. But I got rather more than that.

"What does your husband think of all this?" I asked.

Her answer is rehearsed and prepared and ever so careful. Her tones are warm and honeyed and I won't bother reproducing her answer. You've read it a dozen times before. I'll spare you the time.

I work through all the other touchstones, as bored as she is. The abuse, the accusations about her early career, and then her emergence as a thoroughly controversial feminist icon.

"I seriously adore the controversy," she pats my hand. "It's just divine, isn't it? Whatever I do, they'll tell me I'm wrong, so I may as well do what the hell I please."

"I've a confession to make," I tell her. "I've not read all of your books."

"Oh, no?" she looks a little disappointed. "Journalists are so lazy these days."

"But what I have read..." I smiled. "Impressed me."

She nodded, taking the compliment.

"Some of the writing is really, really good."

She nodded again.

"I wonder if you could sign an autograph for me?"

"Seriously delighted."

I start rifling in my handbag, among the mints and the tissues and the sheer crumpled hell. As I do so, I talk. "I learned to be a journalist when we still did research. It's so time-consuming and expensive. I've only just got the internet at home, and I can see how it makes it all so easy. So simple to just pull in what everyone else is doing. Talking of which... Yes, this is the book I'd love you to sign."

I push the book across the table. She pales. Underneath her pale make-up, she pales.

"I first read *Under The Milk Dark Moon* when I was twelve," I told her. "It was on my grandfather's bookshelf. It's completely forgotten now. Have you ever read it?"

"No... not that I can recall,"

"Interesting," I said. "Well, when I say completely forgotten now, I mean by clearly everyone except you and me. Granddad never knew what to talk to me about, so we always chatted about that book. He'd liked it a lot. The odd thing is... well, it's completely forgotten, and yet, curiously, whenever a copy comes up for sale, it's almost always bought up by the same person. Your husband. I wonder why that is. Maybe he really likes it..."

"I don't know," she begins. Her hands are twitching, like she wants to grab the book from me. "Seriously I don't."

"We're about the same age," I tell her. "Underneath all the make-up. Perhaps we both read it when we were children. Maybe you still have your childhood copy. I say 'maybe.' I know full well you do."

"I seriously don't know what you're talking about."

I yawned. "Research took a while. The thing is, I've got good at the internet. This book's theoretically out-of-copyright. There's a lovely site that offers up these things for free. Sadly, *Under The Milk Dark Moon*'s not made it there. So I scanned the text in and uploaded it. That's what's so lovely about ebooks. You can search the text instantly. For similarities... in fact"—I smiled again—"anyone can. Now I've uploaded *Under The Milk Dark Moon* to Project Gutenberg. Enter in any sentence from that book, and it'll pop up on Google. As will, of course..."—I fished out a paperback with a toffee stuck to it—"quite a lot of *A Rubber Of Velvet*."

"I really don't... I'm sure it's accidental..."

"I'm sure it's accidental too. That someone took a forgotten old crime potboiler and stuck a lot of frisky sex into it. So cleverly done. Must have taken hours."

"Seriously..." begins Vampantha. But it doesn't matter. No-one will ever take her seriously again.

Jackie Aspley, The Daily Post

I WAS ON the run. I was hiding out in the last place anyone would look for me. A resort hotel. People construct elaborate attempts to go on the run. Really, I'd just laid my plans down carefully. The fake passport didn't even get glanced at, and the Killuminati would have been delighted to know that I'd got a really decent rate.

The hotel itself was a lot of empty luxury in the middle of nowhere. I was going mad, but it was completely anonymous. It was an all-inclusive deal, which meant that the bars and the restaurants were crammed from dawn till midnight with a glut of humanity, heaping their bowls high and making it a double. People came and went. Some of them wore identical orange tour jumpsuits, like fat convicts. Some were large families, having a blow-out. There was a phalanx of grumbling pensioners, sitting in a corner, tutting at everything. Some of us were French, some German, some Russian, and some English. All we were interested in doing was stuffing ourselves. Constantly.

I've never felt more anonymous in my life. No one talked to me, no one looked at me. No-one cared.

The hotel was in a small town nowhere near anywhere. There were trips to interesting places, which I didn't go on. There were quiz nights which I didn't go to. I simply ate and sat in my room and read. Occasionally I walked into the small town, and sat at a restaurant where I ordered my food and enjoyed the wait for it.

It passed the time.

Occasionally I'd check the news. Just to see if I was on it. But I wasn't, really. The murder of Henry Jarman had all seemed so baffling to everyone. Everyone thought the CIA had done it. Apart from the CIA. Who were blaming Russia.

I'd not used the internet for a while. I didn't dare log into Facebook. But I did check Twitter from a terminal in the lobby. I'd cracked. I immediately wished I hadn't. There was something I had to go back for.

* * *

AMBER AND GUY had a Lego-themed wedding. Oh, God, I know. The whole thing was so lamely two-thousands, or what people who aren't quirky think is quirky.

The wedding invite was made out of Lego: 'You are cordially invited to the wedding of Guy Hammond and Amber Dass,' photographed in little coloured bricks.

The wedding cake was made out of marzipan Lego bricks. There were little Lego figures on each place-setting. A Lego train laden down with brick-encrusted cupcakes wound around a table. As it was the evening do, some people had come in Lego costumes.

Everyone was wearing the same tired-at-the-edges smile that Lego people wear. *I am always happy because I live in a land where the firemen never have to put out a fire and people always come out of hospital with good news and where there's no such thing as a Lego cemetery. Or maybe my frantic smile is because I'm bursting to go to the loo and there's no such thing as toilets in Legoland?*

Of course, I was going to despise the wedding, ridiculous theme or not. The woman I loved had got married to my best friend. And I'd not been invited.

To be fair, though, I had been on the run, so maybe the invite hadn't reached me. Yes, that was definitely it. Not that they didn't want me around. So I went anyway. It was reasonably easy to sneak into the reception. I dressed in a 'could be waiter, could be guest' dinner suit.. Amber's band played at the wedding, even though they were a big thing by now. They were all (hilariously) dressed as Lego pirates. Quite a few of Amber's aunts were there, splendidly failing to mask their disapproval.

Everyone was dancing. Children were taking the table ornaments apart. Aunts aside, it seemed a happy place.

Amber was, of course, everywhere. It's odd that people obsess about having a wedding so much. It seems like electing yourself to be a crisis-laden CEO on an away-day where all your staff are drunk. People kept on coming up to her, patting her, taking pictures with her, and laughing. Just standing there and laughing.

Which seemed odd, but people are really odd at weddings. The ultimate prize is getting me-time with the bride. Which, let's face it, if she really is your BFF, then it's something you get to do pretty much every week.

I'd only come here to see Amber. I had no reason to see Guy, and wanted to make sure he didn't see me. He'd defriended me on Facebook. If we met he'd only go and do something Alpha Male. I'd run through scenarios in my head, and all the possible outcomes ended either in "Listen, mate..." or a threat of violence.

Anyway, it was Amber I wanted to see.

Amber who I couldn't get to.

I hung back against the wall and waited. I'd done it enough in bars and clubs. I was good at being a wallflower. It taught you a lot of decent skills.

For example, and I say this trying my best not to sound like a stalker, it teaches you that everyone needs to go to the bathroom eventually. It's the one point when they can pretty much be relied upon to break out of their social groups.

Turns out, it's not quite true of a bride at a wedding. When Amber eventually headed for the Ladies, there was a small trail who followed her, buzzing and laughing like a royal escort. Amber's big smile tugged a little at the edges. She'd reached the point where she just needed a break. And then she saw me.

I'll give her credit. That smile didn't quite go.

To give her even more credit, she didn't say any of the things that soaps tell us people are supposed to say, like, "What the hell are you doing here?" or "You have a nerve!" She just stopped, looked me up and down, and then turned back to her gaggle.

"Hey, Michelle," she said, "I just need to go and talk with this guy."

"But—" said the pinkest of the bridesmaids, looking alarmed.

"It's cool," insisted Amber.

And suddenly we were in a lift, and away. Just for a moment she relaxed, a little huff of air coming out of her. "They are exhausting," she said, more to herself than to me. Then she turned.

"Hello."

"Hello," I said.

* * *

ODD GOING INTO the bridal suite with the girl you really fancy on the day of her wedding to not you.

A little tingle of trespass went up and down my spine, stepping into a room I had simultaneously no reason and every reason for being in.

"This is nice," I said.

"Yeah." Amber didn't even look around at the room. She marched over to the desk, sweeping a lot of rose petals and heart-shaped chocolates off of it. She perched on it. "Damn dress means I can't sit down properly." She paused. Clearly it was my turn.

"Happy Weddingsday," I said.

"Yeah," she said. "It is, thanks."

"Good."

Another pause.

"Where the hell did you clear off to?" she said. It would have been nice if she was shouting it. Or crying. She just seemed mildly annoyed.

"Oh... well, you know... travelling."

"Yeah, right. Seems like one minute you were kissing me, the next you'd run away."

I was going to try out a lot of truth here. "You seemed happy with Guy. And actually, it's a little more complex."

"Are you going to tell me you've been having a tough time recently for personal reasons? 'Cause I love hearing that one."

"No..." I coughed. "It's a bit more than that."

"Oh, do go on," Amber yawned, leaning back against the elaborate mirror. "I've got all the time in the world. It's only my wedding day." Casually her hand dipped into a silver bucket at her side, and then, as though surprised, pulled out a bottle of champagne. "Bubbles?" she said. "Personally I'm so full of them, but, you know, hospitality."

"No, it's fine—"

"I insist," she said, uncorking the bottle. She poured us two glasses. "Here's to Happy Ever After," she said.

"You really are a cow," I said.

We clinked glasses.

*   *   *

CONSIDERING SHE'D DECLARED herself full of champagne already, Amber sank two of them remarkably quickly. "I worry all the booze is trapped in my cleavage by the corset," she sighed. "And when I take this bloody thing off I'm just going to die."

"This is nice. You seem really relaxed," I said.

She shrugged. "Just cold. It's so easy to let life's little disappointments screw you up. So when it pisses me off, I let it really piss me off. Then freeze it." She smirked, a little tipsily. "Frozen piss. That's not quite what I meant. But anyway. Not mad at you. Just cold." She flapped a hand vaguely in my direction. She did, all of a sudden, seem a little drunk.

"Right."

"Yeah," she narrowed her eyes in a cartoon squint. "So spill. What made you run away?"

"Er..."

"Come on."

"Well, it's like this. I was framed. It's really hard to explain, but basically I'm a suspect in a suspicious death because... well, and you won't believe this, but I was set up by a vast international conspiracy."

"A *vast international conspiracy*?" Amber did air quotes while holding her champagne glass. She was laughing openly at me.

"Yes." I finished lamely. "I know how that sounds."

"You're sure about this?"

"Yes, they sent me messages on MySpace, they provided me with cash to carry out missions..."

"Missions?" Her eyes were wide.

"Erm... well, yes. Er. Nothing bad. Not really. I mean, Jackie, you remember from that night—"

"Jackie Aspley?"

"Yes. She was one of them. I had to make her happy."

"Uh-huh."

"That sort of thing."

"You were being paid by a secret cabal to make people happy?"

Amber kept on looking at me. Distantly I could hear, of all things, 'Agadoo' playing.

You know how, sometimes, you think about something, you agonise about it, and you examine it, and then when someone talks about it, you realise it's a bit odd?

"Yes."

"Yes?"

"Yes."

AMBER SLID TO the floor, kicking off her shoes as she went. "There's something I need to show you," she said, padding over to her luggage. It seemed to be mostly underwear. She pulled from it a folder and handed it to me.

"I need to show you this and then I need you to really politely get out of my life," she said. "I brought it along. Just in case."

I opened the folder and the world took a little tip. The pineapple was pushed and the tree was shaken.

I stared at the top sheet of the folder. And then back at Amber.

"A vast international cabal," I repeated.

"Hi," said Amber. And waved.

I STARED AT the folder in horror.

"You knew all along?"

Amber nodded. "From that evening in the bar. I saw what you did. And... well, I knew Danielle. I'd always thought Guy could do better." She smiled and the room filled with the silent sound of my heart breaking. "So, you see, when I saw what you were doing, I really couldn't blame you. I thought about phoning an ambulance, but I was drunk. So I just pocketed her phone and then went home."

"You went home drunk and set up a vast international conspiracy?"

Amber laughed a lot then, shaking her head. "Well, along with my friend Michelle. She was in the bar with me. It was quite easy, really."

"I don't believe you," I told her. My voice was broken. Shaking. So many questions.

"You were Duster?"

Amber nodded. "Always figured there'd be a use for MySpace. You were such a sucker—turns out, if you tell someone you're watching them all the time, they pretty soon believe it."

"But... I..." I was blushing. Odd reaction, but there it was. Utterly humiliated and I could feel my cheeks blooming like I'd wet myself at a childhood birthday party.

Amber laughed, and it wasn't a very nice laugh. "Don't say you loved me. You don't really know me at all!" Well, that was certainly true. "Come on, Dave! I know every bit of your life for the past few months. You're so screwed-up it's untrue. First there was that boy in the bag, then there was Jackie Aspley..."

"It was you! You told her my real name!"

"Guilty," nodded Amber. "I was feeling jealous-slash-pissed-off. No, I'm not consistent, but people aren't. Surely you've learned how petty we are?"

A big question appeared. One that was much easier to talk about than feelings.

"Where did you get the money from?"

"Crowdfunding," said Amber.

"What?"

"I crowdfunded the whole thing. On Kickstarter—well, not Kickstarter, but something with a few less, you know, morals. Turns out there are loads of people out there who want to get annoying idiots bumped off. So, we sorted out your assignments based on who really pissed people off..."

"What the hell? I mean..."

Amber sorted through the print-outs. "It's all here," she said. "Seriously."

"But no-one talked about it?"

She laughed. "We talked about it all the time. To each other. There are even t-shirts. The thing is... well, we're not what people were looking for, were we?"

I sat down on the edge of the bed. It all seemed so thoroughly, poisonously unlikely. I'd been wrong. Henry Jarman had been wrong. There was no giant power moving the pieces across the board. At the best I was working for a charity. At worst I was working for a lot of drunk students, hipsters and bored web designers. No-one had even noticed.

"You're a meme," said Amber. She sounded both proud and sad.

It suddenly meant nothing. None of it did. None of it ever had. The only things *I'd* done, the only things that had ever had any meaning... like saving Amber's band, or not killing Henry Jarman... I'd cocked up.

I was a failure. I was a t-shirt.

Then I had an idea.

"But what... what about the Ninja?" I said.

Amber looked at me. Startled. I knew it. I *knew* it. She was a catspaw. I tried telling her this.

Which was when Guy walked in.

I THINK, IN hindsight, there was something absurd about being beaten up by a man in a morning suit while a woman in a wedding dress tries to break things up by throwing bags of sugared almonds.

No one came to help. Of course no one did. Hotels are used to hearing loud noises coming from bridal suites.

In the end, Guy ran out of energy. I'd tired out his fists.

He just slumped at the side of the bed, panting.

"You're an idiot," he said.

"Yes, yes I am," I agreed.

THAT WAS THE last time I saw him. I picked up my folder, smiled brokenly at Amber, and left.

Sat on a nightbus going who knows where, I didn't even care about showing up on the CCTV. It didn't matter anymore. Nothing did. I glanced through the paperwork.

Then I checked my phone. The Ninja. That was it. That was the last hope.

I watched the clip. The clip of the Ninja threatening my cat. I had to find her. Somehow I had to find her. The impossibly cool, glamorous woman like a video game heroine.

You've worked it out, haven't you?

The video clip just showed me, picking up my cat. And placing her in the microwave. Talking to myself.

That was what the Ninja had been all along. How I'd wanted to appear. The person I could blame when I just went too far.

A non-existent assassin working for a non-existent conspiracy.

It was all utterly meaningless. There was no big war room full of sinister people controlling my every move. If you'd gathered them together, they'd be a bunch of people in amusing t-shirts drinking green tea and lattes.

The whole thing was a lie.

I SAT BACK, going through Amber's paperwork. And then I spotted something.

All Knowledge Good.

CHAPTER THIRTEEN
THE HEART OF THE INTERNET

IT WAS A lazy, sunny morning and I was nervous. It shouldn't be this way, of course; I'd done this before. But a heaviness had settled between my stomach and my bowels, in the nasty little spot reserved for that first day at a new job, for swimming lessons, first dates and driving tests. I was nervous because I had come to find my last victim.

I looked around, convinced everyone was looking at me, talking about me, thinking about me. "Was this him?" they were wondering as they pointed at me, took photos of me, tweeted about me.

But really, they weren't. They didn't notice me at all. I was just a loser in a tabard with a fake smile, chugging away. I was nobody.

People were milling around the square in an almost exact replica of the Photoshop mockup from the architect's original plan.

Long ago, this had been a square of elegant mansions in a distant London suburb, with plenty of space for carriages and communal gardens. Then, after a mixture of the Blitz and development, it had become a surly mixture of flat-conversions, council block and a utilitarian office building. Very East London.

Now, after the latest surge in property prices, the whole area had been cityscaped and reclaimed. The communal gardens had been replaced with an 'urban hangout' plaza, a mixture of raised flowerbeds, wavy benches and coffee carts. The last few remaining houses were gone, their fronts retained, with an effect rather like substituting a lifesize standee of Han Solo for Harrison Ford. It didn't matter. What dominated the plaza was the sculpted glass carapace that had devoured the once-ugly concrete office. The tinted glass relentlessly reflected the surrounding skyline. Even though it wasn't really worth reflecting.

I stood there, waving my clipboard, trying not to show my fear. I couldn't stop looking at the building. The way it was both simultaneously imposing and also self-deprecating. "Look at me," it said. "I'm not really here." The office block was a giant mirror, studiously reflecting all the square back at itself. If I looked really closely, I could see myself. Ignored by everyone. The building that wasn't really there told me that neither was I.

The office was the headquarters of Sodobus. Or rather, it wasn't. True, a lot of people worked here. And, if you'd asked them, they'd have told you they worked for Sodobus. A few of them would have cannily added 'Sodobus [UK],' leaving unspoken its relationship to 'Sodobus S.à r.l.' of Luxembourg. If called before a Commons Select Committee (as executives frequently were) they would have explained with the patience of dentists that, although they were a vital part of Sodobus's UK operation, they in no way contributed to the profitability of the parent company, which went a long way towards explaining why Sodobus, despite employing several thousand people in the UK, paid really very little tax there indeed.

The company regularly pointed out that it did pay the legal amount of tax in the relevant territories, but no one was quite sure where these were. In fact, no one was exactly sure what Sodobus did (or didn't) do. Like a badly-cut jewel, if you looked at it through one prism, it provided school meals; from another angle, it ran hospitals and prisons. Take a step back and it oversaw government data systems delivery contracts. Squint and it provided broadband infrastructure, mobile phone masts, and, curiously, wind farms. Glance over your shoulder and you'd perceive that it also provided health screening, credit reference checks, and disability benefits tests. Plus there was a controlling interest in a home-delivery network and a dating website.

There's a famous story about a member of parliament. He was a fairly insignificant back bencher, but he was diligent and helpful. Short of cash, he offered to fill in the tiresome expenses claims of other members for a small fee. As he was 'one of their own,' colleagues gladly took him up on the offer. A few months later and he earned himself a small promotion by gently letting slip some titbits he'd gleaned from doing a member of the opposition's paperwork. A job as a government whip followed, allowing him to ruthlessly exploit the various trifles he'd helped his honourable friends claim for. Soon he had a seat in cabinet. And all because he'd become expert in looking after the little things that no one cared about.

What I'm saying, the reason why I'm telling you this, is that on the one hand, Sodobus did a reasonable job of mundane tasks. But on the other hand, Sodobus ran the country.

Sodobus was everywhere. When we talk about Skynet in *Terminator*, we talk about an omniscient, cunning cyber presence. But really, Sodobus wasn't particularly clever. It just knew all the dull things about you. If you bought some daffodil bulbs from them, they'd have your name, number and postcode. They'd know from trying to deliver if you were likely to be in during the day time, which would match with whether or not you were receiving disability or unemployment benefit or were simply unable to find a job because you'd just come out of prison or hospital, all of which would count against you the next time you tried to renew your credit card, get health insurance, change broadband provider, or apply for a job which went through one of their screening systems.

Sodobus had spent years snapping up unconsidered trifles to make itself a king of shreds and patches. That's a high-faluting way of saying it owned you. The thing is, you could try very hard to sidestep Sodobus, but they'd still get you. They didn't run a bank, but they did run a network that processed contactless payments for a range of supermarkets and chemists. Which meant that they knew exactly how much you drank before you lied about it to your GP.

As you'll have guessed by now, my last victim wasn't a person. It was a company. And there was a good reason for it.

- At the risk of sounding like a nutter on the Tube, Sodobus were behind everything. Even me. At first glance, I was a lone crackpot, driven on by Amber and her friends. It was as simple as that.
- Only... Hold up the prism, turn it a little, squint, look at it another way. There was a different story to be told. Imagine you were one of those smart data-driven news sites that cover current affairs through pie charts and Venn diagrams and infographics. If you checked my career in killing for coincidences and overlaps, then another picture emerged. Little dots of information were joined up to spell out a name. Sodobus.

At first I thought I was clutching at straws. When I ran away from Amber's wedding, I felt like I'd just been dumped by the world. "I think we should see other people," humanity had said, trying to be kind but also eager to finish its drink and get along home.

So ANYWAY, THERE I was, running out into the night with nothing. Literally nothing. Even my cat was staying with neighbours. And I couldn't very well turn up and reclaim it. I may not be being watched by a global conspiracy, but surely by now the police would have worked out what was going on. They didn't deal with a world of fantasy. They dealt with evidence. That's how you caught stupid people.

That night I was staying in a bland hotel. There wasn't even anyone on reception to lie to. I went up to my bleak little room and flailed around it in despair. Then I went down to the grim corner-shop opposite and bought a hideously expensive bottle of bad scotch. I didn't even really like scotch. I just figured it's what you drink when you're having a breakdown.

I sat sipping it from the already-cracked plastic tooth mug and I went through the file Amber had given me. At first I just denied it all. I'm not sure any fact has ever changed its mind simply because it's been shouted at. But that's what I tried first.

Then I went through the paperwork again. And that's when I spotted it. At first I pushed it to one side. Because I was aware of how mad I now was, I just didn't trust any thought I had. After all, it may have been put there by a ninja. Or the tooth fairy.

But I carried on going over the paperwork. I put the exciting glimmering notion to one side and just worked through the paperwork—what amounted to Amber's confession. She was, it had to be said, pretty thorough. It was all carefully ordered and scrupulously filed. She'd even kept accounts. No wonder she'd been so freaked out when I'd gatecrashed her band's gig. She'd never even considered she might be caught, so she'd taken no steps to hide the evidence.

The thing is, the more I went through that evidence, the more a name emerged. Sodobus. Eventually, I allowed the penny to drop, to listen to how it sounded. And it sounded good. What if there really was a conspiracy after all?

What if Sodobus had been controlling me? Not since the start, but pretty much, nudging Amber's scheme along, gaming the results. They'd not directed every hit. But more than you'd think. Fast Eddy, for example, had been the whistleblower on one of Sodobus's dodgy database contracts. Jackie Aspley had written up a bad profile of their CEO. Vampantha's husband was one of their regional sales executives. And Henry Jarman had warned everyone about them. The stupid fool had been right all along. I still didn't know how, and I didn't know why. But they were involved.

I drank some more scotch and I swiftly emptied the KillFund. I was on my own now. I knew what I'd had to do. I'd found my last victim.

I WAS NERVOUS. But that didn't matter. The only thing that mattered was that it was a nice, lazy sunny morning in the plaza. People pottered in a self-important way between shiny offices and expensive coffee shops, occasionally loitering to make phone calls while puffing away on electronic cigarettes.

Everyone was ignoring the chugger. Especially when the drone turned up.

As a marketing campaign, the small remote-controlled helicopter was a bit of a failure. It flew above the square with a banner that said '#SodobusOwnAllOfUs.' Some people noticed it. Most of them worked for Sodobus. A few people wondered if marketing had really got their head around the hashtag as a concept. No one actually used it. A spate of people tried to scan the QR code, after a PA had pointed out that no one ever used QR codes, and that she'd once won a holiday purely on the basis that no-one else had bothered entering the competition. Those that scanned the QR code found that nothing happened—but then, it was quite small on a moving object a bit away, so it wasn't really surprising.

One person noticed the helicopter and groaned. It had made a bad day that little bit worse. His name was Ray, and I'm going to tell you all about him.

RAY RICHARDSON LIKED to tell his colleagues that he was the only person from around here. It was stretching it a bit—the estate he'd grown up on was about half a mile away—but it had been pretty much the same. "I remember when this was all burning cars," he was fond of saying. He'd always thought the area was a dump. It didn't seem much better now. The idea that people were fighting to pay half a million to live in one of the same grim boxes his family had grown up in appalled him as much as it made his mother laugh. He marvelled that people would want to live somewhere like here, where, for all the coffee shops and sandwich bars, the streets were still full of drunks with dogs. Only their flats were now worth a fortune, because they were 'just half an hour from Liverpool Street.'

ONCE HE'D EARNED enough, Ray had run in the opposite direction, to a charming village that had made an earnest point of how accepting it was of a gruff-voiced black man and his endlessly smiling "yes, yes I am white" wife.

Ray Richardson was the head of Marketing & Communications at Sodobus [UK]. He was the man I'd come here to meet. I tried stopping him as he crossed the plaza. "Good morning! How are you today?" I beamed at him.

"Well, you can sod off," said Ray and went in to work.

"Have a good day!" I said. I knew he wouldn't. He'd be back.

RAY WAS MY new best friend. I'd got to know Ray very well without ever meeting him. It was actually really easy. Amanda was now at that stage of pregnancy where she felt too bloated to go to work and too miserable to stay at home, so she spent most mornings in the village cafe, swiping her iPad and cursing the sluggish wifi. She was in the mood for a distraction, and that was me. I found her through an article in *PR Week* on Ray's appointment.

A year ago Ray had quite a nice job in technology journalism. Then Amanda had got pregnant and Ray had realised the time had come to use his contacts and get a better-paid job in PR. After casting around quite hard, he'd been approached by Sodobus. He'd wrinkled his nose slightly, but nothing better had come along. At one of several interviews he'd asked, "But why do you want me, exactly?" It was the most tactful way he could think of saying, "Is it because of the colour of my skin?" Certainly, for a supposedly global company, the people he'd seen so far looked not just white, but pale.

The crisply Swiss woman interviewing him had assured him it was for his contacts. Really? Surely a vast multinational like Sodobus needed someone more experienced? There was a shrug. Of course, he was told, Sodobus itself was a vast international conglomerate, but the UK branch was little more than a cottage industry. "Practically a jam factory," the Swiss woman had told him, with a laugh that afterwards had struck Ray as peculiar. Journalistic instincts firing, he'd asked, "Is there anything bad I should know? Anything brewing?" The Swiss woman had shaken her head.

One month after his appointment, the tax scandal had broken. All of the problems of the world suddenly landed on Ray's desk. There was an 'unwitting' double-charging fraud in a hospital contract. And then the revelations of the 'completely accidental' leak of data between two legally unlinkable databases which resulted in thousands of people being denied home insurance because of things they'd declared on a dating website. On the long train journeys home to Amanda, Ray would switch his phone off mid-ring and leaned back exhausted in his seat. He was hopelessly out of his depth.

"He's been set up," Amanda told me. We were sitting in the village cafe. I'd got to know her by mending the wifi on her iPad. "Are you good with these things?" she'd asked me. I'd done my best. All part of my helpful personality. I'd created the air of someone "taking time out," renting a mobile home on a nearby farm. Maybe I'd had a breakdown. Maybe I was writing a book of country walks. Maybe I was a reclusive millionaire.

I liked Amanda. She was fun. She was comfortable being comfortably in her late thirties. She was pushing a cake around her plate. "Being pregnant is great," she enthused. "Everyone goes on and on about the eating, but there are so many other advantages. There's not bothering to dye my hair"—she pointed to the fetching flecks of grey—"and then there's the farting. It's blissful. I'm like a whoopee cushion, and no-one every suspects it's me because I'm a pregnant woman. We're like saints."

As I said, I liked her. I even told her my real name. After all, it didn't matter anymore.

We'd bump into each other, for a gossip and a natter. She didn't find me threatening. "Frankly, if you were wanting to have an affair with me when I look like I've swallowed the Hindenburg, well, good luck to you." And I think she was also a bit bored. "Being this pregnant—well, I'm waiting for a really important, painful kettle to boil."

Fairly soon we were talking about Ray's problems. "Basically," said Amanda, "They hired Ray because they were looking for someone to blame. They knew all this was going to come out. Sodobus will let him try and deal with it. Then they'll say the problem is with the job he's done of it, not with whatever they've been up to. Then they'll fire him very nicely. If we can just cling on till we get a juicy settlement out of them, it'll probably be okay, but I'm applying for jobs that start about a week after I've squeezed this one out." She patted her bump and then slurped at her decaf coffee.

Amanda's suspicions had been proved grimly correct. Within a fortnight of joining, Ray had noticed the few competent members of his team were 'rotated' out to other tendrils of the Sodobus spider, replaced with gawky interns or the kind of PR women who set feminism back about four hundred years. On the other side of the fence, he'd always laughed at posh, dim blondes running events. Now he had an office full of them. Was there a collective noun for them—An Activia? A Pimms? There was one dismal product launch where the entire gaggle had all worn the same t-shirt and Ray had been confronted by half a dozen identical blondes with the same hair, height and make-up, all drinking the sparkling water meant for the journalists while talking excitedly about their next skiing holiday. Ray had never been on a skiing holiday and felt a bitter resentment that people who worked for him could somehow afford them while his idea of luxury was to get the Jamie Oliver meal deal at Boots.

SUCH WAS THE personal misery of Ray Richardson the morning I turned up chugging outside his office. I was fine with him ignoring me. I'd see him again later. That was all part of the plan. Ray was a good man. It had taken a while to find one. And I wasn't going to let him go.

SHALL I TELL you what Ray did that morning? He endured a lot of pointless meetings, he wondered about the drone buzzing past his window, and he blamed it on the blonde petting zoo they'd replaced his marketing department with.

He flung open the glass door to his glass office. "Who did that?" he said, waving behind him at the helicopter. Of course, it had now gone, so his bemused team looked up to see Captain Angry pointing at the empty sky.

* * *

WHEN RAY RICHARDSON left the building at lunchtime the helicopter was still circling. "Sod you," he snarled to it. He looked again at the text on the banner, and tried futilely zapping the QR code as it zipped close to him. His cameraphone clicked and then connected to the wifi zone at the nearby coffee shop in order to bring up a web page. Eventually the browser admitted defeat, 'Page not found.'

"Stuff your granny and your dad," growled Ray. Trust his team to launch an awful social media campaign and then not bother to build the website to go with it. He stalked off to Boots to get his meal deal, and the helicopter drowsed past him as Ray neatly sidestepped a chugger. Ray hated chuggers.

"Have a great day," I said, smiling to myself.

AT SOME POINT that night, while Ray was asleep, he received an email. It moved swiftly from his unread to his read items and he knew nothing about it until two days later when he was going through his post.

THE NEXT DAY the helicopter was back and so was I, chugging away. Mostly I was watching the electronic billboard dominating the plaza. Ray's predecessor had launched it as an exercise in 'Profile Raising Through Living Social Media.' It rotated various Sodobus adverts and occasionally fed through some tweets (the tweets were carefully screened after it had first gone live and been swiftly spammed by people delighted at the idea of putting swearwords up on a digital display). Today the screen appeared to be slowly playing through a series of extraordinarily bland mission statements that someone in Internal Comms had fed through to it.

'Sodobus: Together is better' went alongside a picture of a tiny child smiling at a well somewhere in Africa. Ray found this objectionable for quite a few reasons. Sodobus's only interest in Africa was in 'Law Enforcement Protective Equipment Upsales.'

Also, the photo of the child at the well had nothing to do with Sodobus. It was from an online photography site. It still had the watermark slapped through the centre of it.

I watched the billboard, and I imagined Ray, up in his office, opening his post. It was 11am. From what I'd learned of his routine, he'd be getting to it about now.

HE'D OPEN THE envelope. A set of black and white photographs would slide out, along with an eBay invoice. The top picture was a reasonably innocuous black and white photograph nearly a century old. It was of three pretty girls, perhaps about twelve, dancing around their smiling mother in sailor outfits.

The next few photographs saw the dancing continue, but with less clothes. After a while the dancing stopped, but the activity didn't. And all the while the mother continued to smile. And then she helped out. He would stare at the pictures with a horrified fascination. From lettering in the background, he could guess the studio was in Germany, and the clothing scattered everywhere suggested the 1930s. As did the swastika. Historically, the prints were probably fascinating... if you liked collecting vintage child pornography.

Perhaps someone would come in to ask him an inane question, probably about the building being on fire or something. He would hastily slap the photos face-down on his glass desk, praying they weren't reflected somehow.

When they'd gone, he'd examine the eBay delivery slip, and then stumblingly check the Gmail on his phone. He'd find the original email showing that he'd ordered the photos and then notice with horror that it had been read. The original listing seemed innocent enough, but if you read it knowing what it really contained, then the wording was laden: 'A series of intimate family portraits... revealing childhood passions... experimental studio prints... will arouse more than academic interest... a peep into Weimar home life...'

Ray would sit back in his chair and work out if there was a way he could possibly claim that he'd bought Nazi child porn by accident. And then he'd realise that no one would believe him. Especially not his wife.

He could send a furious email to the eBay seller, but that would involve engaging with them. Perhaps he could complain to eBay. But that would be bolting the stable door after the horse was on fire. He'd been set up and he was in a corner.

I knew exactly what he'd do. He'd curse ("Granny's tits"), he'd stuff the photos into a cross-shredder, maybe post them abroad, and then he'd go outside for a proper cup of coffee and a think. I checked my watch. 11.20am. He'd be due out about now. I hoped.

'SODOBUS: A FRIENDLY EYE' said the billboard against a picture of a young woman walking alone down a rainy street at night. There was no sign of Ray. I felt a moment's worry that it had all gone wrong—but no. There he was. He stalked past me, his face screwed up with fury.

"Excuse me, sir, do you have a moment—" He ducked aside from my over-eager chugging, but somehow failed to avoid having a flyer pressed into his hand.

I watched him go. He wandered into the coffee shop. The queue was long, long enough for him to calm down a bit, long enough for him to glance idly at the flyer he'd been handed, and then to run pelting back from the shop.

WHICH WAS WHEN Ray Richardson met me properly.

He was waving a picture of a teenage Nazi's vagina in my face. "*What the sodding granny fuck?*" he was screaming at me. And waving around his arms. It was a risk I'd been prepared to take. Despite the fact that I was a chugger, people were stopping to almost notice the scene. After all, it's cheering to see a charity mugger being threatened with violence by anyone. And the thing about Ray Richardson was that, even after a few months in PR, he was still a solidly-built piece of engineering.

"Is this man bothering you?" a few people asked.

"Lay off him, mugger," said someone else.

Ray bristled even more at this. Because, obviously a black man punching a white man only happens for one reason.

His expensive suit was because drugs or crime or something, obviously.

"It's fine," I said loudly. "The guy really doesn't fancy giving money to cats, that's all." I laughed, breaking the tension. A few people scowled, but the tension went out of the scene. Ray realised that overt aggression wasn't winning him prizes and instead stood there, concentrating his simmering rage into a look that boiled the piss in my kidneys.

When the small sort-of crowd had got back to ignoring me and wandered away, Ray leaned forward, forcing a pleasant smile onto his face. "Who the hell are you?"

"I'm your new best friend," I told him. "First of all, I'm not blackmailing you. Not really. Actually, I kind of work for you."

"Your granny you do," said Rick.

I produced a flask from my tabard. "Fancy a coffee? This is really good."

IN THE CENTRE of the plaza, two people drank coffee on a bench carefully designed to be comfortable to sit on for only ten minutes and absolute agony to try and sleep on. A small remote-controlled helicopter weaved overhead. A billboard flickered. 'Sodobus: Every Child Taken Care Of,' against a stock photo of a teddy bear abandoned in a puddle.

"WHAT DO YOU want?" Ray's opening gambit was defused by the coffee. It really was very good.

"I want to know if I can trust you," I said to him. "I've recently discovered that I'm employed by your company, at arm's length. As... well, I guess you could say a cleaning contractor. And I need to be absolutely certain you know nothing about me."

"Sunshine, I can assure you I know sod all about you and what goes on here." His face narrowed in suspicion. "Why are you doing this to me? What do you do for me? Is this another plot to trip me up?"

"I kill people."

"Bugger my Uncle Ted." Ray had had enough. He gave me a look of disgust and stood up. "I don't believe you," he said firmly. His expression told me he probably did. "You expect me to believe any of this?" he restated, just to make sure I knew he didn't believe me. "I mean," he went on, "let me assure you, this isn't Ghana, and we're not an oil company. We don't go around bumping off people. I mean, why would we? There are so many easier and more effective ways. I don't believe you."

I listed a few of the people I'd disposed of. "But they don't matter. This is about something else. Something bigger. The cat in the room."

Ray finished his coffee, laughing. "This is like a mumbled YouTube conspiracy. You seriously expect me to believe that Sodobus paid you to assassinate Henry Jarman?"

I smiled. "Well, sort of. I wasn't actually going to kill him— thing is, he was so mental he actually committed suicide to prove he was relevant. And so that his followers would start releasing the Jarman Manifesto."

By now the Jarman Manifesto had become quite famous. It had been published for months, tweet by tweet and blog by blog, each one spreading out. Some of it was bonkers, some of it had been turned into cat .gifs, but a lot of it made sense.

A lot of Jarman's more recent posts had been about how governments couldn't help taking control of the internet, and that perhaps, rather than fighting this, a middle ground had to be found whereby each country's internet access was effectively placed under the notional control of a charitable trust. An unassailable organisation that existed purely to protect the freedom of access to that information, and would guarantee that the pipes couldn't be hacked into, spied upon, censored or filtered. The late Henry Jarman made much of the fact that students at Chinese Universities had the fastest internet access in the world, yet had no idea what a 1989 photograph of a boy standing in front of a tank had to do with them.

The late Henry Jarman wanted these charities to operate outside governments, to be unassailable forces for internet good. To be 'vast cuddly Stephen Frys.' On our side and talking to each other. Organisations that were, like the internet, hard to filter, block or divert.

It was a good idea. It was contentious, but what had made it immediately popular was that the government had immediately denounced it as nonsense. If Henry Jarman had been alive, people would have called it the bonkers ramblings of someone who no longer got invited onto *Question Time*. But, because he was dead, he was suddenly accorded a lot more respect and sympathy. The leader of the opposition said it "certainly raised interesting questions." Several bodies had stepped forward to offer to model this foundation. Which would, naturally, be called The Jarman Freedom Foundation.

CURIOUSLY, THERE WAS no proof that Henry Jarman had actually written his manifesto. It was all being handled by his previously unpaid media advisor. A young woman called Michelle Fischer. She'd not been with Jarman long before he died—this wasn't suspicious, as his staff churned like his temper tantrums. What was interesting was that she'd previously been an intern at Sodobus. Sodobus who were also, very quietly, and at huge arm's length, becoming involved in setting up the Jarman Freedom Foundation.

I FINISHED TALKING. I felt like a proper spy, pulling from my 'Save The Earth' satchel various supporting documents and photographs. I was also about five per cent aware that I looked like an utter nutter.

BUT RAY RICHARDSON had stopped laughing. He took another sip of coffee. He moved awkwardly from side to side, as the bench was getting uncomfortable.

It was easy to dismiss all of this, but I could see that one tiny bit of it had struck home. Michelle Fischer. He'd actually encountered her during her internship. He remembered her because she wasn't blonde and seemed quite competent. He'd even caught her rolling

her eyes during an interminable presentation. He'd offered her a
job in his team, but she'd declined. He suddenly wondered why.

"Look," said Ray, "what do you want?"

I'd shrugged. "These benches are agony and I'm freezing my
bum off. Can I come and meet you in the office later?"

"Dressed like that?" he said.

I smiled. "No, I'll be even more disguised in plain clothes. I'll
come in as everyone's going. Just stay late and it'll be fine. I'll
find you."

RAY WENT BACK to his desk and got on with his work. He looked
around the office, drowning in sudden paranoia. Even the
ludicrous billboard and the laughable helicopter fed his irrational
panic. I may not have changed the world, but I'd shaken him a
little. What if Sodobus was actually secretly a lethal organisation
that was just pretending to be hapless? Lulling the world into a
false sense of security through its vague incompetence? After all,
despite all its many failings, it was still making huge amounts of
money. Ray looked out into his office bowl of blonde clownfish.
What if his Marketing and Communications team were all skilled
assassins working very hard at overthrowing governments while
also carefully inserting spelling mistakes into press releases?
When he was a child, he'd been ashamed of his dad's job at a
builder's merchants. That was until one day when he'd realised
that his dad was secretly a spy. That had made it all okay.

Even when he was being taunted at school, it had given him
the strength to continue. Because he knew, he knew that deep
down, the colour of his skin or the cheapness of his clothes or the
nastiness of their flat didn't matter. Because his dad was a spy. He
had to be. It was all that made sense.

THE OFFICE EMPTIED at 5pm. Actually, the office emptied by about
quarter to. By half four there had already been two childcare
emergencies and someone else had sloped off wordlessly. One
man had gone to get changed into sports gear and sat at his desk
in lycra, swigging a protein shake.

Ray normally tried not to notice this, but he couldn't make his mind stick on anything.

Soon he was alone with just his fevered thoughts and his endless email. He heard the contract cleaner pottering around.

He went through to the kitchen, figuring he may as well risk a cup of machine coffee. He entered his PIN and pressed a button. And then waited while it went through its pantomime.

At first taste, Sodobus coffee was remarkably like coffee. The machines went to elaborate lengths to convince you that this was freshly ground. A dome of coffee beans jiggled with a reassuring grinding noise whenever you entered your PIN and pressed the 'Americano' button. But the level of the beans never went down. They were as ornamental as a snowglobe. Whatever happened inside the coffee machine was carefully hidden away and contained no contamination from real coffee beans.

"I wouldn't drink that if I were you," I said. I was standing next to him, wearing a cleaner's outfit. I hadn't been lying when I said I worked as a cleaner for Sodobus.

Ray smiled at me. "Very clever," he said approvingly. "Now, what's this about the coffee? I wouldn't drink it either. It's vile, but still..."

I shook my head and gestured to it. "Why does it have a keypad?"

"Oh..." Ray wasn't sure. "The photocopiers and printers have them. It's something to do with cost codes."

"And your PIN code is..."

"The department's or something I guess," Ray shrugged. "Why?"

"What about if your PIN number was unique? What would that then mean?"

"Only that they'd know I liked strong black coffee and... and... how many cups of it I had a day, and when, and..."

Ray Richardson stopped talking and stared at the machine in horror.

"So that's why it tastes different as the day goes on..."

I nodded at him, and handed him a print-out from the caterer. It showed details of the slightly different blends of coffee handed out:

Good Morning—the perfect pick-me-up cup
caffeine derivative
Meeting Blend—the grab for those on the go
caffeinated beverage
Slow Roast—a mellow savour for the dedicated fan
of caffeinated products

"My granny," whistled Ray. "What the hell are they putting in it?"

"Well, caffeine's a drug," I said. "They just add a few things as well. All perfectly legal herbal extracts and so on. Slow Roast is actually a decaffeinated blend with valerian extract. Of course, if you don't like it, you can go out to the posh coffee shop opposite. That Sodobus also owns."

Ray boggled. "They're controlling our moods, selecting coffee for us based on algorithms? But what... what if my PA gets in twelve coffees for a meeting?"

I shrugged. "The algorithm gets screwed."

Ray tapped the print-out against his cheek. I could tell that this little detail had swung him. He turned to me. "So, how did you get this?"

"The helicopter," I explained. "It's a relatively simply drone. It's been hacking into everyone's phones."

HACKING INTO A phone this way is reasonably easy. What we don't realise is that our phones are constantly making noise even when they're silent. If you've got your wifi enabled, then it's constantly checking to see if any of its approved networks are within reach. Fly a drone past an office space and it'll encounter a building full of phones chirruping to see if they can connect to the free wifi they're signed up to at the nearest coffee shop. It's fairly easy to use the drone to capture that data.

It's easy enough to pop into the coffee shop, find the details of their wifi network and set your drone up to mimic it. When the drone wanders back within range, those phones will automatically try to connect it, thinking it's the coffee shop. Actually, it's acting as a relay to the coffee shop, which will allow you to scrape the data that's filtered through it. It's not a perfect technique, but you should soon gain an idea of who owns the phone, what their passwords are, and even their credit card details. If you were able to zap the QR code it just took your phone's browser to a seemingly empty page that actually gave me even more access to your phone. Thank you.

Corporations spend a fortune making sure that their own IT is securely nestled behind firewalls and Virtual Private Networks and so on. The problem with this is that it's fiddly. And everyone who walks into and out of the building has a phone on them. The phones are far less secure because their IT security isn't looked after by a paranoid man with a ragged ponytail and careful training. The phone's owner is in charge of its security—and is in a hurry, is busy, or just doesn't care. The drone even offered unsecured free wifi. Quite a few chumps took advantage of it. Thank you more.

One thing we've all learned from the last few years is that corporate email is stored, internet usage is logged and blocked. The great thing about your own phone is that it isn't. If you want to gossip or backstab, you can send bitchy Gmails without your boss knowing. Maybe the government, but not your boss. Your phone will let you look at Facebook and porn without getting you fired. One thing that your phone also excels at is making your nice safe corporate internet insecure. Got a long dull meeting? Not a problem, set up your phone so that you can access your work emails throughout. Brilliant.

And all so very, very handy for me. In addition to several gigabytes of personal email data, I also had the usernames and passwords to several people's company email accounts. And as I was here on an overnight cleaning shift, I had plenty of time to log on and use them. And was even being paid to wipe my fingerprints off afterwards.

*   *   *

RAY LAUGHED WHEN I finished my explanation. It was a nice laugh, and he should have done it more often.

"So, what do you want?" he asked.

"Revenge," I told him.

Ray looked at me carefully, considering his options. "Let me show you something," he said.

RAY SHOWED ME his inbox. Recently, he'd noticed it was being clogged with documents. So many emails were being sent to him that IT had written to him to warn him about excessive bandwidth usage and then sent him on a compulsory all-day training session about 'Inbox Zero.' On the day he'd been away, the volume of emails he'd been sent had exactly doubled. Nearly all of the emails contained a big attachment, frequently in French, German or Italian, and occasionally he'd spot something jaw-dropping hidden away on slide 37 of a PowerPoint deck.

"What's it all for?" he asked me. "I go home every night wondering how many things I've missed. Thousands of unread PowerPoints, .pdfs and spreadsheets. How many things I've unwittingly signed off on. Are you in there somewhere?"

I squinted at the hundreds of unread messages, all of them red-flagged as urgent. I shrugged.

"I think you're being set up," I told him.

"Really?" said Ray. "That's what my wife thinks."

I nodded. "Funny that."

RAY RICHARDSON CAUGHT a late train home that night. He'd followed my instructions and gone to a high street store and bought a cheap notebook, plugging in the USB stick that I'd given him. He sat scrolling through the data I'd mined from the drone. Most of it was junk, but every now and then he'd spot something and move it across. It turned out Ray was a natural at this. Trying to keep up with his Sodobus inbox had taught him invaluable data-sifting skills. He sent me a text using the pay-as-you-go phone I'd given him. "I think I've found something," he said. "They wanted inbox zero? I'll give them inbox zero. Sod 'em all."

He walked through the door late and his wife looked up, surprised.

"You're smiling," Amanda said.

"Yup," said Ray and kissed her.

"I'll open a bottle of wine," she said. "Non-alcoholic wine that tastes of sweat and strawberries."

IN ORDER TO bring down an evil company, you had to find the one good man who worked for it. Because you could bet that he really hated his boss.

I CAN DESCRIBE the head of Sodobus [UK] pretty well, because I'd spent much of the last couple of weeks cleaning her office. That lets you really get to know someone. The things they throw away, the things they try and hide, the things they ostentatiously display.

Elise Olsen was a mother of twins. This was about the only fact of any interest anyone knew about her. On her desk was a photo of two Aryan teenagers grinning mid bungee-jump. It was angled so that she could see it, but also so that everyone who sat opposite her knew that she was human really, that she had emotions, that she had children, that she hadn't simply been recently unwrapped from cellophane.

Everything else about her was carefully Edam-bland. She belonged to a family of Swiss bankers adept at handling the accounts of Nazis and Russian oligarchs with cold discretion.

If anyone knew what was really going on at Sodobus, it was Elise Olsen. But she'd spent her whole life giving nothing away. The only thing you'd remember from a meeting with her was that picture of those two golden children, forever falling, never hitting the ground.

*　　*　　*

CATWALKING!

NotGayTwins
Subscribe

333+ views
(actually 1,899,375)

TRANSCRIPT

[On screen are two young, sandy haired ideals of youth. They are laughing as they put on t-shirts. The camera has just started rolling, missing them being fully topless but still providing a tantalising hint of flesh.]

CAESAR: Hey, amazing! Allow your hating, we're here!
BRUTUS: Yes. We're here, we're here, and we're not legally allowed to drink beer.
CAESAR: But where are we, bro?
BRUTUS: Well, bro, can you believe it?
CAESAR: I cannot.
BRUTUS: We are at an actual fashion shoot. With models. And pretty people.
CAESAR: And us.
BRUTUS: Speak for yourself, fatty.
CAESAR: Speak for yourself, spotty.

[They playfight, laughing. They do this knowing that their fight will be screencapped, giffed and pored over by their fans #somanyfeels #icanteven #brusar #caesus]

BRUTUS: Today, we've been asked to do a catwalk show. AMAZE.
CAESAR: Exactly. We'll be draped out in the sickest fashions and learn to sashay and twirl with some upcoming hotwalking catwalking talent.
BRUTUS: Brother, sick is like not a thing anymore. It's shaming. All we have to do is promote the HEDZUP clothing brand.
CAESAR: But that's not a problem as we just love these clothes.

BRUTUS: Love love love them!
CAESAR: Stop that bro, you sound a bit gay.
BRUTUS: Not that there's anything wrong with that.

[They hug for the camera, knowing full well it'll be turned into moah gifs #bromance]

[Rapid montage, at first to a Lady Gaga track of the boys (frequently in pants) changing into various HEDZUP outfits. We repeatedly cut to the same Lady Gaga track, only being played by Brutus and Caesar on ukuleles. In their pants. #somanygifts]

[Now Brutus and Caesar are wandering backstage at the HEDZUP show. Brutus is wearing a red wig, Caesar is wearing a blue one]

BRUTUS: Here we are.
CAESAR: Backstage at the fashion show.
BRUTUS: How real?
CAESAR: Much real.
BRUTUS: Number of times we've been arrested?
CAESAR: Actually literally zero.

[Jump cut. On stage at the fashion show. Brutus playing the ukulele while Caesar sings "Yellow Submarine." Models stride around them, seemingly without noticing.]

[Brutus and Caesar are now interviewing one of the models. Katrin]

BRUTUS: Believe this.
CAESAR: I do not.
BRUTUS: We are standing in our pants.
CAESAR: Interviewing a model.
KATRIN: In her pants. Hi internet!
BRUTUS: Yeah. Hi, everyone. This! Is! Katrin!
KATRIN: Hello.
CAESAR: Have you been a model long?

KATRIN: Well—
BRUTUS: He means "Do you know who we are?"
KATRIN: Sure.
CAESAR: Cos you're now mega famous on YouTube.
BRUTUS: The haterz are so gonna hate you.

[They already do. Should you check Katrin's Twitter feed it is suddenly clogged with people calling her an unworthy whore.]

KATRIN: But why would they hate me?
CAESAR: Because I think you're amazing.
KATRIN: Really?
BRUTUS: Dude, allow your libido.
CAESAR: It's fine bro. These pants are really tight.
BRUTUS: Totes. It's like rush hour on the Victoria Line down there.
CAESAR: Hashtag London Joke.
BRUTUS: So, Katrin, tell us what you're doing later?
KATRIN: Being a model. What about you?
CAESAR: Playing the ukulele.
BRUTUS: Man, our life sucks.

TRANSCRIPT

HELENA LLEWELLYN [producer *My Mum Is Gonna Kill Me*]:
   The thing we're really doing with our show is trying to push back the boundaries, reach out to the streets and, in a platform-agnostic sense, grab hold of our demographic by really moving television beyond the fourth wall.
JOSHUA PACKARD [aka 'Jpac,' star of YouTube and producer of Caesar & Brutus]:
   Even saying "moving beyond The Fourth Wall" is so old. Generation YouTube has only one wall. That's our bedroom wall. That's what you traditional television makers don't understand.
HELENA LLEWELLYN:
   [is about to say something. Stops. And sighs] You know

what? Actually, I'm really tired of being told how do make television by ageing teenagers who can't even afford a proper microphone.

The Future of Television,
Radio Four

LET'S TALK ABOUT Thursday. It began with Amanda's morning sickness taking a turn for the worse. She cancelled meeting me later in the village cafe.

"I'm worried about Ray," Amanda texted me. "He was up half the night. I think it's work. Also, I'm the size of a jelly house."

That was fine. I had other plans.

ELISE OLSEN SAT at her desk, watching her sons' latest video. She felt a moment's pride that she didn't mind if anyone saw. She was really proud of them. Today was going to be a good day.

AS A RESULT of the twins' video, the HEDZUP website crashed. This was a good thing. There was no such label as HEDZUP. I'd simply mocked up a site, then bought some stuff from Primark and poster painted slogans onto it. It really was awful. But the thing was, Caesar and Brutus liked it. I'd paid them to say so.

I SPENT THE day standing outside in the rain. I sold absolutely no subscriptions to kittens, kids or cancer. This was kind of handy as I'd actually made today's charity up. There's no such charity as Kittens With Cancer. And if there was, its logo certainly wouldn't be a kitten with its tail turning into an IV drip. I'd been a bit bored.

I kept the helicopter drone circling the building, gathering information.

It wasn't hard to spot Ray Richardson when he strode out of the office. For all its claims, Sodobus really wasn't the most ethnically diverse company going. A good-looking black man in an expensive suit really stood out. Even if he did look dog-tired.

I passed him a leaflet. He passed me a USB stick.

"Inbox zero," he whispered.

From: Ray Richardson
To: Elise Olsen
Subject: URGENT

Dear Elise,

I'm afraid I won't be in for the rest of the week. Amanda's been taken into hospital. Looks like the baby's coming early. Sorry if I'm not making much sense, been up all night. Appreciate this leaves you in the lurch, and apologies for that. Obviously, wouldn't do this if we had any major product launches, and I've managed to clear my emails. The great thing about my team is that I know that you can rely on them. I'm obviously available to discuss this.

Regards,

Ray

Sent from my iPhone

FRIDAY WAS A lazy sunny day in the plaza. There was no sign of the helicopter in the sky. But there were two people chugging. No one really noticed them, even though one of them was black. After all, there's nothing that unusual about a black man in a tabard, is there?

The Sodobus screen was working exceptionally well that morning. Elise Olsen was startled, and then delighted to see it was playing the video of her sons at the fashion show. It was a bit off-brand, but then again, someone on Ray's team was probably doing it to suck up to her. And, despite having no sense of humour, Elise had an enormous sense of pride. So she smiled anyway.

*   *   *

WITH A LAST twang of the ukulele, the video of the two blonde teenagers at the fashion show stopped.

ANOTHER VIDEO PLAYED. At first glance it seemed to be part of the same thing. It was the boys' dressing room at the fashion studio, but filmed from a high angle. You could see the red and blue wigs on the floor. Along with the underpants. And there on the couch were the two brothers being vigorously naked with Katrin.

"You are utterly amazing at *that*," brayed Caesar.

Katrin shrugged. "I'm French. We start young. Not bad for a fourteen-year-old, no?"

"No," breathed Brutus delightedly. "Best blowjob from a fourteen-year-old I've ever had."

"And he's quite the virgin surgeon," chuckled Caear. "Now, behold this. What would you call this? Masculine or feminine?"

"Oh," laughed Katrin. "Decidedly masculine."

The brothers laughed and then nothing much was actually said for a couple of minutes.

"Hey," said Katrin. "You know what would be cool? If you two kissed."

Caesar shrugged. "Sure," he said. "Why not? We do it all the time."

"And more," smiled Brutus.

And then, the moment that over a million fans on YouTube had secretly prayed for finally happened but in a way that no-one wanted. Caesar and Brutus kissed.

NOW, JUST TO put myself on the right side of this, Katrin was actually eighteen, not a model, and from Stoke Newington. She was an actress friend of mine. Throwing all caution to the wind, I'd approached her directly and paid her a lot of money. She promised me she actually had "a huge crush" on Caesar and Brutus, "even though they were so annoying. Rich Tory jailbait." So, please don't worry about her. She's fine. Although her boyfriend was kind of furious.

*　　*　　*

ELISE OLSEN STOOD at her window watching the video of her children. She'd stopped smiling. She turned away, and, as she left her office, she made a small noise. It was the tiny single sob she'd first made when the twins were babies and had both caught measles. Elise Olsen was going home. She was going to look after them.

ELISE OLSEN STRODE through the square in a hurry, her silver hair catching the sunlight. She was looking anywhere but at the screen. Her eyes fell on me, at first not really seeing me at all, and then focusing sharply. And that's when I recognised her. The figure I'd seen that first night, outside McDonalds in Leicester Square. Then, as now, she'd locked eyes with me briefly and hurried away. And I wondered...

THE VIDEO PLAYED another time. If Sodobus was broadcasting child pornography, we may as well make absolutely sure people saw it. Thing is, I felt a little sorry for Brutus and Caesar. They were just posh white boys with a nice camera and fair deal of privilege. They were fairly harmless— that's why people get to be YouTube stars. Not because they're weird, or different, or have anything interesting to say. But because a lot of teenage girls and gay men quite like to see reasonably posh, quite pretty white boys talk about their problems and their hair.

They really weren't the most deserving targets. It's just that I really needed their mother out of the way.

A CROWD HAD gathered in the square. This is when the video screen really came into its own. It was controlled through an app. I knew already that Ray's team were trying to log into it to turn it off, but I'd already found out the password and changed it. Even now they were raising it as an urgent call with IT, so I had about ten minutes before someone ran out to unplug it by hand.

What could happen in ten minutes?

I filled four of those minutes with a stream of emails gleaned from Sodobus employees over the last few days. Some of it was pure office trivia—affairs and petty theft and constructive dismissal and sex selfies and so on. But it worked. Start with the lurid gossip and you get everyone's attention.

Then I flicked through a few of the PowerPoint slides the firm wouldn't want you to see. The slide that showed how they skewed job applications against people whose supposedly private medical records showed they'd had more than ten days of sickness in the last year. How they planned introducing pay-as-you-go televisions into prisons. How their recruitment staff had deliberately made nurses at a hospital redundant in order to hire in temporary staff from an agency run by Sodobus. How they ran a uniform dating website in order to keep tabs on the personal lives of contractors working in their hospitals, prisons and security forces.

The list went on and pleasingly on, finishing with a flowchart that someone had helpfully produced to explain exactly how Sodobus cheated its tax bill, and an email from the head of HMRC personally approving the scheme.

This left me with two minutes. And I betted that, by now, if I worked in IT for Sodobus, I wouldn't be running from the building. I'd be strolling. Especially after we'd put up the slide about the plan to relocate the IT Helpdesk to Puerto Rico.

So up *I* popped on the screen, in a recorded message. Filmed, curiously enough, in Sodobus's offices the previous night.

"HELLO, I'M DAVE. I kill people. I've spent the last year doing it. I thought I was doing it in order to make the world a better place, wiping out people who annoyed me on the internet. Actually, I was doing it for Sodobus. I didn't even know I was working for them, acting on their orders. But everything I did was for them. I was even ordered to kill Henry Jarman. They've been making me get rid of people for two reasons. Firstly, it was a cheap way of wiping out those who were in the way. Secondly, they wanted to convince normal people—that's you, hello—that the internet was something to be afraid of. That it's causing the end of the world as we know it, and needs to be controlled. That was their plan. They were going to take over the internet.

"For our own good. You may genuinely think that the internet is evil, that it's making people full of hatred. Perhaps it is. Or perhaps we never were very nice and it's just giving us a chance to be honest about it. Whatever happens, please don't use me as an example. Not everyone who gets cross is going to start killing people. I know I'm the worst person in the world to offer you advice about how to behave online. But one thing I do know is that the internet loves a good quotation above anything else. So, my mother once said to me:

"'If you can't say anything nice, then don't say anything at all.'"

YOU CAN KIND of guess the rest. With my remaining time, I pulled up the emails onto the screen. Amber's crowdfunded Killuminati project, the proof of the transfers to it from Sodobus, the links to Michelle Fischer, the paper trail that fizzled out somewhere near (but still deniably far from) Elise Olsen's office.

Who was Michelle Fischer? If you looked her up on Facebook, you'd have discovered we had a one mutual friend. Amber. They'd been having drinks together, that first night. The night I'd killed Danielle. They'd been to university together. Amber was the fun one with all the cool friends. Michelle was the serious one who everyone knew would go get a proper job, who would ruthlessly trample over people to get ahead. I'd even passed Michelle in the street, muffled-up to take a photograph of me and Henry Jarman together.

Inasmuch as there was anything to be behind, she'd been behind it all. But had she really done it all by herself?

That was the annoying thing. There was actually no proof that Elise Olsen had directly come up with the plan, or instructed Michelle to carry it out. No one could be directly blamed. The funds had come from a marketing budget, just before it vanished at the end of a financial year. Elise notionally had control of it, but various people had sign off on it. I knew that in the ensuing court case, she would look older and tireder, but still maintain that she'd known nothing about it. Nothing about it at all.

In fact, as far as the courts could determine, no one at all had known anything.

It was almost as though Sodobus had *accidentally* paid me to put its enemies out of the way.

I've said before there's nothing at the heart of the internet. Not even a giant cat. But perhaps I was wrong.

RAY RICHARDSON HAD heard my theories. He still thought I was a nutter. But today, on that lovely lazy day, he looked around him at the chaos we'd created together.

"Sod you all," said Ray Richardson, smiling. He took a photograph of the crowded plaza and texted it to his wife. She laughed and then went into labour.

THAT ABOUT WRAPS it up, really. Jackie Aspley started getting work again. Partly because of her articles about *I Dated the Internet Serial Killer*. And partly through the story of her remarkable marriage to Pastor John.

I'D PREPARED TWO versions of my presentation. One which left Amber out of it. One which dropped her right in it. In the end I used the second one. And I'm completely happy about that. After all, she had used me and broken my heart. She and Guy have split up now. Well, no, they haven't. That's my last lie. He's sticking by her through the court case, and says he'll wait for her, until she gets out—if she gets convicted. Some people are just puppies, aren't they? Of course, I don't know the latest details. We're no longer Facebook friends.

RAY RICHARDSON CAME back from paternity leave early, as they'd placed him in charge of Sodobus [UK]. It was really the chance to be boss of a poison chalice, but he couldn't pass it up. Amanda made that quite clear. Ray came out of both the internal enquiry and then the rather more thorough police enquiry with flying colours and smelling of roses. It could be shown that staff had been directed to not tell him anything about anything that mattered, and that there had been a deliberate policy to try and hang various scandals on him, all of which he'd spotted and flagged up.

The police inquiry, without saying so bluntly, found that Ray Richardson had been hired as a scapegoat. Sodobus needed to be absolved of their sins before they became involved in running the internet. They'd brought him in to eventually take the fall for their tax problems, and kept him in a silo and flung mud at him. It all looked rather shoddy and racist.

The least they could do now was keep him on. It would make them look good (if anything could). And he was the only executive they had who looked anything like clean. His wife negotiated a pretty amazing pay deal for him, ensuring that, even if Ray's job only lasted six months, Baby Tintin would never go hungry.

Ray promptly made a lot of announcements about corporate honesty. He then fired the entire Marketing and Communications team. People assumed this was a brave example of clearing out the stables, but he did it simply because they annoyed him. Marching out of the office with their possessions in boxes, they looked like a lot of suddenly-unemployed shop dummies.

After that, he did very little else, really. He made a lot of good noises, but he was basically having a grand time running a fire sale.

HE DID DO one final thing, though.

Years ago, Sodobus had bought a small island off the Scottish Highlands. The original idea had been to farm organic vegetables, but they'd not flourished in the soil. It had become a science and weather monitoring station, issuing daily reports that it was, indeed, still raining. The reports are made by the one man who lives on the island, alone apart from a cat that enjoys frightening the seagulls. It was the last place in the world you'd think of looking for anyone.

The man was hired for the post by Ray personally.

The man makes his daily reports by radio. The island does not have internet access.

He's very happy.

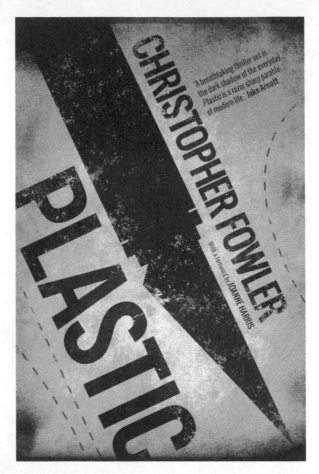

'A breathtaking thriller set in the dark shadow of the everyday... Plastic is a razor sharp parable of modern life.' Jake Arnott

CHRISTOPHER FOWLER

With a foreword by JOANNE HARRIS

PLASTIC

June Cryer is a shopaholic suburban housewife trapped in a lousy marriage. After discovering her husband's infidelity with the flight attendant next door, she loses her home, her husband and her credit rating. But there's a solution: a friend needs a caretaker for a spectacular London high-rise apartment. It's just for the weekend, and there'll be money to spend in a city with every temptation on offer.

Seizing the opportunity to escape, June moves in only to find that there's no electricity and no phone. She must flat-sit until the security system comes back on. When a terrified girl breaks into the flat and June makes the mistake of asking the neighbours for help, she finds herself embroiled in an escalating nightmare, trying to prove that a murderer exists. For the next 24 hours she must survive on the streets without friends or money and solve an impossible crime.

 WWW.SOLARISBOOKS.COM

Follow us on Twitter! www.twitter.com/solarisbooks

In Hollywood, where last year's stars are this year's busboys, Fictionals are everywhere. Niles Golan's therapist is a Fictional. So is his best friend. So (maybe) is the woman in the bar he can't stop staring at. Fictionals – characters 'translated' into living beings for movies and TV using cloning technology – are a part of daily life in LA now. Sometimes the problem is knowing who's real and who's not.

Divorced, alcoholic and hanging on by a thread, Niles – author of The Saladin Imperative: A Kurt Power Novel and many others – has been hired to write a big-budget reboot of a classic movie. If he does this right, the studio might bring one of Niles' own characters to life. But somewhere beneath the movie – beneath the TV show it was inspired by, the children's book behind that and the story behind that – is the kernel of something important. If he can just hold it together long enough to figure it out...

IVO STOURTON THE
HAPPIER DEAD

WHAT WOULD YOU DO FOR THE CHANCE TO LIVE FOREVER?

'Stourton is a name to watch' *Publisher's Weekly*

The Great Spa sits on the edge of London, a structure visible from space. The power of Britain on the world stage rests in its monopoly on "The Treatment," a medical procedure which transforms the richest and most powerful into a state of permanent physical youth. The Great Spa is the place where the newly young immortals go to revitalise their aged souls.

In this most secure of facilities, a murder of one of the guests threatens to destabilise the new order, and DCI Oates of the Metropolitan police is called in to investigate. In a single day, Oates must unravel the secrets behind the Treatment and the long-ago disappearance of its creator, passing through a London riven with disorder and corruption. As a night of widespread rioting takes hold of the city, he moves towards a climax which could lead to the destruction of the Great Spa, his own ruin, and the loss of everything he holds most dear.

 WWW.SOLARISBOOKS.COM

Follow us on Twitter! www.twitter.com/solarisbooks